Most *Beloved* Enemy

Enjoy!

Margaret Worth

A NOVEL BY MARGARET WORTH

◆ FriesenPress

Suite 300 - 990 Fort St
Victoria, BC, v8v 3K2
Canada

www.friesenpress.com

The digital image modified and used on the cover is courtesy of the Getty's Open
Content Program:
Julia Margaret Cameron (British, born India, 1815–1879)
[Alethea], 1872, Albumen silver print
The J. Paul Getty Museum, Los Angeles

ISBN
978-1-5255-0057-2 (Hardcover)
978-1-5255-0058-9 (Paperback)
978-1-5255-0059-6 (eBook)

1. FICTION, COMING OF AGE

Distributed to the trade by The Ingram Book Company

*To my Beloved Family, who taught me the meaning
of unconditional love!*

And to Dear Peter, who made this book happen.

England 1884

The scream hung urgent in the summer air, diminished into an aching sob then hurtled upward, clawing at the edges of my mind before fading into silence.

I was fifteen on that June afternoon, the day my sister Edie was born, the day my mother died.

CHAPTER 1

It was in the early winter, before little Edie was born, that I first learned something of the events that would change our lives forever. I had walked alone down by the river one chilly November afternoon. My sister Nell was meant to accompany me, but she chose instead to bury her head in one of her precious books. So I went alone, reveling in the cold wind that blew gusts of rain into my face, and the damp ground underfoot that left my boots muddied and my skirts wet.

The grey afternoon was darkening into an early dusk when I slipped back indoors, shivering as I pulled off my bonnet and cloak before sinking onto the wooden bench in the vestibule to remove my wet boots. The gas lights were not yet lit for my father did not approve of waste. I had pulled off one boot and was just about to remove the other when I realized that I was not alone. My parents were standing on the other side of the door that opened into the hallway, and it was something in my mother's tone that made me shrink silently against the row of damp cloaks.

Mama's voice was filled with pleading and she sounded as if she had been weeping. I could picture her clearly, one hand on my father's arm looking up at him, her eyes filled with unshed tears.

"Robert. I can't do this again," she said. "I've lost three since the twins' I don't think I'm strong enough, not this time. . . ." Her voice trailed away as my father broke in, his voice edged with impatience.

"Eleanor, all I want is a son, and that is not too much for any man to ask."

I heard a small gasp from my mother and the swish of her skirts as she turned and walked quickly away. I stayed motionless, hardly daring to breathe until I heard my father's footsteps retreating, and the slam of the study door. Even then, I stayed where I was, too frightened to move until my father's manservant, Drake, came to light the lamps.

But I was a young girl of fourteen then, and soon put the incident from my mind, and busied myself instead with the familiar joys of family life and the bustle of preparations leading up to Christmas.

One day in early February, Mama had the carriage brought round, and she and I, wrapped warmly in blankets and furs against the chill English winter, set off towards town. Nell was invited to accompany us but refused; she was thirteen that year and very busy with her own pursuits.

As we approached the market town of Wimborne, nestled in the Dorset hills, I leaned forward, searching eagerly for the tall spire of the minster. We were not allowed inside the church for we were Methodists, but I loved to ride past its ornate wooden doors and peer at the gravestones half buried in the mossy grass of the graveyard.

My mother stopped first at the chemist shop where she and the old chemist whispered together while I peered curiously into the great glass jars filled with coloured water that adorned his window. Next, we visited the haberdasher's, where Mama bought stockings for Nell and me, and bright ribbons for my twin sisters, Lily and Iris. Then, linking her arm through mine, Mama smiled with a hint of mischief.

"Come along Ada my dear it's time for us to visit Mrs. Seaton and Angela," she said cheerfully.

I beamed happily as we hurried down the street towards my favourite shop.

Mrs. Seaton owned a small milliner's on the high street. Mama liked to go there to gossip and try on hats, but I went to spend time with my dear friend Angela. She and I were much of an age and loved to giggle and gossip together. We were fast friends in those days.

As soon as Mama was seated on one of the little gilt chairs in front of the mirror and Mrs. Seaton was reaching for the very latest design in hats, I hurried to the back of the store where, hidden behind a heavy curtain, I found Angela. She was sewing silk pansies onto a large purple hat but the moment she saw me, she threw the hat aside and springing to her feet gave me a fierce hug. We were soon sitting cozily together, ready to exchange news.

My friend was usually impatient to hear the latest adventures of my family, but today Angela had something else on her mind. As soon as we were seated, she leaned towards me, her blue eyes shining with excitement.

"Ada," she breathed. "It's so exciting. Do you know when your Mama's new baby will arrive? My Mama thinks it will be in July but. . ." She broke off in alarm as I jumped to my feet.

"Why would you say such a thing?" I demanded. "It's not true, Mama is much too old and we have the twins." But even as I spoke, my voice faltered as I recalled what I'd heard all those months before as I sat cowering in the vestibule. I looked pleadingly at my friend.

"It can't be true," I whispered.

Angela didn't answer. Instead, she pulled me to my feet and led me over to the curtain that divided the workroom from the shop.

"Look," she said, softly.

Mama was still perched on the chair in front of the mirror while Mrs. Seaton, who was simply an older version of Angela herself, hovered quietly behind her. I looked critically at my beloved mother in the mirror. Her small oval face was framed by thick brown hair that held auburn lights in the sunshine. It was swept up into curls at the top of her head and perched on top of the curls was a ridiculously small hat, a cluster of ribbons, feathers, and crushed green velvet. It was very becoming, but I knew that we wouldn't be taking it home in one of Mrs. Seaton's striped hat boxes. Papa would not approve of that hat.

Mama's large hazel eyes sparkled as she laughed at her reflection in the mirror and she looked very pretty. The thought that Angela spoke the truth and that my mother was indeed to have another child filled me with fear, as I remembered the number of times Mama had been ill since the seven-year-old twins were born, and the three little wooden crosses in our family burial plot that no one ever spoke of.

"See!" whispered Angela. "See how full her figure has become?"

I leaned forward, the better to see my mother. Mama was small and slender and she looked no different to me, though it was hard to tell, for on this cold winter morning she had come wrapped in a warm cloak that she had pushed partway off her shoulders in order to try on hats.

"I see no difference."

My friend was watching me closely, her blue eyes wide with concern. Then she let the curtain drop and pulled me back into the room.

"Ada, listen," she said, seating herself once more and pulling me down beside her. "I'll tell you how it happens." She leaned back against the cushions watching me closely. I bent my head and didn't respond.

Angela took a deep breath. "First, your Papa asked your Mama if she would do him the honour of bearing him another child. When she agreed, together they begged the angels to bless them."

Angela closed her eyes before continuing. "When they knew their prayers had been answered, your Mama began to prepare herself." Her eyes flew open. "That's why she is becoming plump. She stores all the milk for the baby in her belly!" Leaning forward, she searched my face. "Did you know that, Ada?" I shook my head doubtfully and looked away, wishing that Angela would stop talking.

I didn't know if what she said was true, but I did know that after my twin sisters were born, two wet nurses had been engaged from the local village to feed and look after them and they had stayed almost two years until the twins were weaned. I had no recollection of Mama feeding the babies, nor could I imagine her doing such a thing.

Angela didn't wait for my answer but continued busily, "and when the time comes, your Mama will retire to bed." My friend paused for a moment and looked at me solemnly, "which must be strewn with rose petals, Ada: pink for a girl and. . ." She paused a moment. "White for a boy! Yes, they must be white. The rose petals are very important; please don't forget them."

Then, returning to her usual rather breathless tones, my friend continued. "After that, the doctor will come with his black bag that holds a darling child. He will present this child to your Mama, who will lean down and gently breathe into its tiny mouth and the miracle of life will begin!" Angela sat up quickly, her blonde hair fluffing about her head, her eyes bright with unshed tears.

"There!" she said, clutching my hand. "Isn't that romantic? You're so lucky, Ada."

I squeezed her fingers, but kept to myself the uncomfortable memory of my mother's pleading tones on that cold autumn afternoon.

After that day in Wimborne, I began to watch my mother more closely, and as the months went by, I noticed her body thickening and her movements slowing. She wrapped herself in large shawls and no longer hurried about the house leaving a trail of perfume and laughter behind her. We no longer walked into the village and almost every afternoon, Mama retired to the small sitting room that led off her bedroom.

One day when I was bored and lonely, I asked my mother if we could go into town, but she shook her head.

"No, Ada," she said, irritably. "I have no wish to go anywhere." I almost asked her about the baby then, but my courage failed me.

As winter passed and the days warmed into spring, Mama no longer accompanied us to chapel on Sundays. When the twins asked why, they were hushed by their governess who was fearful that Papa would overhear and become angry. He didn't hear though, because he always strode briskly ahead of us, waiting at the chapel door while we hurried to catch up to him.

April came, snowdrops and crocuses gave way to beds of daffodils, and the surrounding woods were carpeted with bluebells. One day, some men arrived with ladders, brushes, and pots of paint. Mrs. Carter our housekeeper showed them briskly to the top floor of the house, shooing Nell and me away when we asked what was happening. This floor housed the servants' quarters at the back of the house and the nurseries at the front. There was a heavy cream door that separated the two wings and, as children, we were never allowed through that door.

The nurseries consisted of five rooms. On one side, there was a large bedroom for the twins, with a smaller room beyond it, where the governess slept. In the middle, there was the schoolroom, a big bright room furnished with tables and chairs, an old piano, and two faded leather armchairs set by the fireplace. It was in this room that Nell and I had learned all our lessons. Nell was truly musical and played the piano well, and although I could not match my sister, my voice was clear and true, and we had spent happy hours together learning old songs and performing them at occasional dinner parties given by our parents.

My sister enjoyed every moment of all her lessons, but I was heartily glad when Mama told me, shortly after my fifteenth birthday, that I need no longer attend these lessons.

On the other side of the schoolroom was another smaller room, and off that, a tiny box of a room with just one narrow window. It was these two rooms that were to be painted.

"It'll be cream for the walls and brown for the skirting boards," I overheard Mrs. Carter tell Cook one day as they sipped their mid-morning tea. I had been on the point of entering the kitchen when I overheard them talking, but I stopped abruptly outside the door, unashamedly eavesdropping.

"I hope it's a boy this time, Cookie," Mrs. Carter continued, blowing noisily across the top of her cup. "Due in the middle of July, all being well," she added, comfortably.

I didn't wait to hear Cook's reply, but turned and slipped quietly up the back stairs, my errand quite forgotten. It was true then. I was to have a baby brother in July.

One warm summer morning in late June, Mama joined us as usual for breakfast, though I noticed that she ate nothing. She retired upstairs shortly afterwards and as I was leaving the dining room I saw my mother's maid, Jennings, run quickly down the stairs and knock on the door of Papa's study.

There was much scurrying to and fro after that, and Mrs. Carter dismissed us sharply when Nell asked her what was happening. So my sister flounced off to her lessons and I spent the morning pretending to work on the sampler that I was sewing, though my ears were tuned to every sound in the house.

I heard when Papa cancelled his trip to London and instead sent his manservant, Drake, with some important papers and strict instructions that they were to be delivered immediately. Papa did not join us at lunch, but I heard him pacing back and forth as I passed the heavy study door.

My sister and I ate a silent meal, then Nell disappeared again, and after a while I walked upstairs and stood outside my mother's bedroom door. I could hear the murmur of voices through the wood, first my mother's low, clear tones and then the sharper voice of Jennings.

Jennings had been with Mama since she was a little girl and sometimes spoke to her as if she was still a child and not the mother of four children—but my mother never seemed to mind.

As I listened, my ear pressed to the door, I heard the maid's footsteps approaching. "We'll send for the doctor right away, my Lovey, don't you fret," she said, and even through the thick wood I could hear the anxiety in her voice. As she came closer I turned, intending to slip quietly along the corridor to my own room, but I was too late. Jennings had already opened the door.

She was a small, thin woman and, as she stood in the open doorway, I could see past her. I had a fleeting glimpse of my mother standing by the window. Her face was pale and drawn, as she clutched at the drapes and her breath was coming in quick, painful gasps.

Jennings glared at me before stepping out of the room and closing the door behind her.

"What are you doing here, Miss Ada?" she asked sharply. Not waiting for an answer, she grabbed hold of my arm. I squirmed under her bony fingers but she held me tight. "You can make yourself useful now. Run quick and tell Ned to fetch the doctor, fast as possible, the baby's coming," she hissed. "Do you understand?" I nodded dumbly and turning ran quickly down the stairs.

Mrs. Carter was in the kitchen, dozing in the rocking chair, but the moment I stumbled into the room she was on her feet, eyes wide with fright.

"Jennings says Ned's to fetch the doctor as fast as he can," I gasped. Before I could finish, Mrs. Carter was on her feet and in a flash was out of the back door and into the vegetable garden where Ned, our handyman, was working. Moments later he was gone, riding hard towards Wimborne to fetch Dr. Wainwright.

I stood helplessly in the empty kitchen. I wanted to do something for my mother; I had seen the pain on her face and, in my mind's eye, I could still see her slim fingers clutching at the edge of the curtain. I racked my brain for some way that I could help Mama. Suddenly I knew.

Hastily, I made my way to the front hall and into the vestibule. Reaching up to the high shelf that was above the wooden bench, my fingers closed quickly on the slender knife that Mama used for cutting flowers. Then reaching for a basket I hurried outside.

Flowers were blooming everywhere; there were geraniums and sweet Williams and tall hollyhocks and wallflowers that dropped their velvety amber petals onto the newly cut grass.

Ignoring all of them, I turned and hurried along the front of the house and rounded the corner. This side of the building faced south, and it was here that Mama had her rose garden.

I was determined to fill the basket with white rose petals, as Angela had told me. Mama would be so happy to see them she might even allow me to sit next to her and watch, as she breathed life into my new baby brother.

Red, pink, and yellow roses grew in abundance along both sides of the path, but I did not see any white blooms. I searched from one end of the rose garden to the other, but nowhere could I find a single white rose.

At last, fighting back tears of disappointment, I retraced my steps towards the front door; I knew that I simply had to greet this new baby with rose petals.

Beside the steps were two standard rose bushes. The flowers hung heavy, their perfume sweet in the soft afternoon air. On a sudden impulse, I stopped, dragging at the heads of the huge blooms and tipping the petals into my basket. Then I turned and hurried into the house. Red rose petals would just have to do.

The hall was empty as I ran lightly up the curved staircase, and I was thankful there was no one there to see me. I didn't want to have to explain the contents of my basket to anyone. At the top of the stairs, I paused and took a deep breath. Then basket in hand, I approached the closed bedroom door. I was excited by the thought that I should be the one to strew the fragrant rose petals on my mother's bed, but

I had to be there before the doctor arrived, for then I knew it would be too late.

I knocked timidly on the door and waited. There was no answer. After a while, I knocked again more loudly, and listened as hurried footsteps approached. I held the basket in front of me like an offering, but as the door opened a crack, I saw that once again it was Jennings who peered anxiously out. Catching sight of me, she opened the door a little wider and glared at me as I held out the basket.

"I've brought these for my mother and the baby," I said as firmly as I could.

Jennings did not even glance down. "Go away, Miss Ada," she snapped. "This is no place for you!" And with that, she closed the door in my face.

I looked down at the basket, tears welling in my eyes. I was sure that if my mother knew I was here she would let me in. I stood for a few moments more in front of the closed door, but in the end I was too afraid to knock again.

Sadly I turned and walked to a chair that was next to the half-open window. From here, I could see the rose garden, the croquet court, and the lawn that sloped gently down to the river. I placed the basket of rose petals on my lap and waited.

After a while, I heard carriage wheels on the driveway, and the sound of the front door opening. Then there was the rumble of my father's voice followed by Dr. Wainwright's lighter, brisker tones, asking a question as he turned and ran quickly up the stairs carrying his black bag.

Holding the basket in one hand, I rose and took a small step forward, waiting for the doctor to notice and greet me as he always did, but he didn't even turn his head. He just knocked lightly on the bedroom door before entering and closing it quickly behind him.

Soon after that, Mrs. Carter and Annie, our housemaid, came puffing up the stairs carrying jugs of hot water. Jennings met them at the door but did not allow them to enter. No one noticed me.

The afternoon dragged on. I could hear the tick of the grandfather clock in the hall below. It struck the hours of two, three, then, four o'clock. The shadows were starting to lengthen, but still the bedroom door remained closed. I pressed my back against the hard wood of the chair and watched a single sunbeam play along the edge of the carpet. The smell of roses drifted through the half-open window and I could hear Iris and Lily's excited shrieks, and the distant thud of a croquet ball. I supposed sleepily that the governess Miss Jackson was with them, but she was not good at controlling my mischievous little sisters. I wondered where Nell was. I had not seen her throughout this long afternoon and guessed that she was reading in some hidden corner, away from the events of this difficult day.

Lulled by the drowsy heat, my head drooped forward, my eyes closed, and, for a few blessed minutes I slept. Then the silence was broken: shattered by that cry of pain so terrible, so piercing, that I stumbled off my chair and ran towards my mother's bedroom door, scattering rose petals over the carpet as I went.

Blindly, I flung open the door. A blast of hot, stale air hit me. The blinds were drawn and the room was dimly lit. This was not what Angela had promised! There were no angels, there was no wonderful feeling of peace, and my mother was not lying propped gracefully beneath the covers, as I had imagined.

The creature on the bed did not even look like my mother. Her face was white and covered with sweat, her hair a tangled mass, her eyes sunk deep into her head. Her mouth was open, the scream still hanging in the air.

I looked at her ravaged face then unwillingly my eyes were drawn down to her raised knees, naked in the half-light, her rumpled nightgown drawn high above her waist and, it seemed to me, covered in blood. There was blood everywhere, on the white sheets, on the towels draped over the end of the bed, on the doctor's arms and the silver instrument he held in his hands as he bent over my mother. It was even splashed over his carefully rolled shirt sleeves. I remembered those sleeves long afterward; they were blue with white pinstripes.

Jennings was standing at my mother's head, a towel in her hand, and I was sure that even that was drenched in blood.

As I watched, horror-stricken in the doorway, I saw the doctor straighten and lift something from between my mother's legs. It was smeared with slime and blood and he bent over it and turned away. I, too, turned. I turned to flee from this dreadful room and from the hollow-eyed stranger who was my mother. As I ran, I tripped over the fallen basket and saw the spilled rose petals that were strewn all over the floor.

Desperate to escape, I ran as fast as I could to the quiet safety of my own room and flung myself down on my bed, hugging my rag doll Edith, closely to me. I tried to shut out the events of the previous few minutes. I tried not to remember the sound of my mother's screams, and the sight of all that blood. Red, like the rose petals scattered on the carpet—petals red as blood. Of course! This was my fault!

Surprisingly, I slept. I awoke sometime in the night, stiff and chilled. Outside, I could hear summer rain falling. I reached blindly for the chamber pot under my bed, relieved myself and fumbled out of my shoes. Then, still fully dressed, I crawled back onto my bed and pulled the quilt up over me.

CHAPTER 2

When I opened my eyes, early morning light was creeping through my windows. For a blessed moment, I did not remember why I was sleeping fully clothed and then memory came flooding back. I saw again the haggard stranger who was my mother and the thing in the doctor's arms who was the new baby.

Lifting my head from the pillow, I listened. There were none of the usual early morning sounds. I looked at the clock ticking cheerfully on the mantle. It said twenty minutes past seven.

By this time, Annie should be about the place, sweeping the corridors or wielding her feather duster. There should be sounds of activity from the kitchen as Cook prepared breakfast. I listened again. An eerie silence lay like a pall over the house.

Rising quickly, I pulled a brush through my hair, retied it hastily with a ribbon, and smoothed the worst of the creases out of my dress and smock. Then I walked over to my door and opened it. After a moment, I heard the sound of muffled weeping, so I stepped into the corridor and walked to my sister's bedroom door and opened it wide. Nell was lying face down on her bed, and sitting on a chair beside her was Mrs. Carter.

As I stood frozen in the open doorway, Mrs. Carter turned to look at me, her face swollen with tears, her hands twisting a large white handkerchief.

"Oh, Miss Ada," she said, reproachfully. "I don't know as how you could sleep so sound with your poor Mama lying dead in her bed," and she burst anew into noisy tears and turned to stroke Nell's hair. My sister did not make a sound, but the bed shook with her silent sobs.

The horror of Mrs. Carter's words filled my mind as I stared at the two of them, then, dropping my hand from the doorknob, I turned and fled. I ran down the dark corridor past the door where my mother lay dead, with blood everywhere, past the overturned basket with its rose petals scattered forlornly over the carpet and headlong down the stairs to the front door, desperate to escape.

The door was still bolted, and I struggled frantically with it for a moment. Then, giving up, I ran down the hall and into the kitchen. Cook was sitting in the rocking chair, her apron over her head, weeping noisily, while Ned sat at the table biting his nails. I paused for a moment to take in this scene before continuing my headlong flight through the scullery and out of the back door.

I didn't stop running until I reached the orchard. In amongst the old apple trees, I stumbled to a halt, sobbing as I tried to catch my breath. Eventually, I made my slow way to the old stone bench that was a favourite spot of mine and sank gratefully onto its cold surface. I sat there for a long time, trying to understand what had happened. Tears ran down my face, but I did not try to stop them. I just could not imagine a life without Mama.

I must have dozed after that, for when I raised my head again I saw that the sun had risen higher in the sky and now shone hot on my bare head. As memory returned, I felt a flood of guilt that I could sleep after yesterday's terrible events.

Reluctantly, I left the shadowed safety of the orchard and made my way back towards the house. As I approached, I saw Mr. Huxley's black, crepe-decked carriage in the driveway. He was the local undertaker and I knew that he was here for Mama. I blinked back hot tears and looked past the carriage and saw that all the blinds in the house were drawn and a great black bow decorated the front door. The nightmare was real; truly, my mother was dead.

Drawn up behind the undertaker's carriage was a small wooden cart. It belonged to Bert Baker, who did odd jobs around the village. He was lounging at the front of the cart and, as I watched, a woman emerged from behind it. It was hard to tell from this distance, but she appeared to be young, and she was carrying two bundles.

As I approached I saw that one of the bundles was wriggling furiously, and as I came closer, it proved to be a large red-faced infant of about a year. His mother, for such she obviously was, hitched him firmly onto her hip and turned to face me.

She looked dubiously at my rumpled clothes and tear-stained face, but then smiled cheerfully. "I'm Bessie," she said stoutly, "and this here is my Sam." She gestured proudly with her head towards the squalling child. "I got caught with 'im by one of them sailors, but I wouldn't be without."

I stared back at her blankly. "I'm the wet nurse," she said. "Here for the baby girl as was born yesterday. Sorry to hear about the Missus," she added, as a hasty afterthought.

Blindly, I gestured towards the back of the house. She nodded briefly, then bidding Bert to follow with her box she walked stolidly up the back path towards the kitchen door.

I followed slowly, thinking about what she had said. That thing in the doctor's hands had been alive then, and was my new baby sister. Sadly, I wondered why the baby had lived and my mother had died.

Sometimes, memory is kind in that it does not allow us to remember clearly those things that are truly painful. My memories of the next few days are mercifully unclear. I did not see my mother again, though Nell and the twins went to say their farewells. I kept to my room as much as possible and was glad when, five days later, we laid Mama to rest, lowering her into the rich Dorset earth in a simple pine coffin. Papa did not believe in displays of grief, and there were no flowers left on the dark mound as we walked away. Few people outside the household attended the funeral, but Angela and Mrs. Seaton were both there, Angela pale-faced and stricken. She took a step towards me but as our eyes met, I turned and walked away.

While the rest of the household mourned, upstairs in the nursery, Bessie sat suckling the lusty Sam on one breast and the tiny nameless girl child on the other.

After Mama's funeral, my father shut himself away in his study. Mealtimes came and went and I saw an anxious Mrs. Carter take trays of untouched food away from the study door. Once or twice late at night during that first week, I heard the creak of the stairs and the sound of Papa's dressing room door opening and closing. I was fiercely glad that he did not go into the room where Mama had breathed her last. Then, just two weeks after Mama's death, Papa resumed his usual routines of business, and carried on as if nothing had happened.

It was in the third week of July that Papa made his announcement to me. We were alone at the breakfast table. Iris and Lily still took most of their meals upstairs with their governess and Nell was, as usual, absent from the breakfast table. I knew she would stumble out of bed and up to the schoolroom at the last possible moment.

So it was just the two of us that morning when Papa folded his newspaper meticulously and pushing his chair away from the table, cleared his throat.

"I shall be away for two days," he said, glancing first at the end of the table as if expecting Mama to be sitting in her customary place, before turning his gaze quickly to me. "When I return, Ada, I will be accompanied by your Aunt Abigail. Mrs. Carter will make the necessary household arrangements."

A few minutes later, I heard the crunch of gravel on the driveway as Ned brought the carriage round to take Papa to the station. I wished that Nell had been with me then, so we could discuss this alarming news together. I remembered little about Aunt Abigail, but what I did recall was not heartening.

Papa was the youngest of three children. His parents had died when he was young, so his two older sisters, Abigail and Charity, had raised him. The sisters had never married, but lived together in the family home in Sussex. They did not usually venture far from home and on the one occasion that they had visited us, it was the Christmas when I was almost ten.

Nell and I were not allowed to bring holly into the house that year for my aunts thought it a pagan custom. Mama had laughed and insisted that we were just welcoming the Christ Child with evergreen, but in the end it was Cook who took the greenery down to her family in the village, the red holly berries bright against her dark cloak.

Now as I sat alone at the breakfast table, I wondered why Aunt Abigail had chosen to visit us at this time, when we were mourning the loss of our dear Mama. I went to look for Mrs. Carter, but she was unwilling to answer my questions. She just shook her head and told me to fetch Annie from the kitchen garden because the best spare bedroom had to be dusted and the mattress aired out before the master returned.

That night, I couldn't sleep. The air was hot and still and I tossed restlessly in my bed, aware of a dull ache in my stomach. Finally, I rose and went to sit on the window seat. I watched the moon glide slowly from behind the clouds, hanging like a silver ball in the midnight sky, and I wondered where Mama was. I hoped that she was looking down from heaven and that she could see me and would understand about the rose petals.

Then, unbidden came thoughts of the baby lying upstairs. The child I had not yet seen. She was the cause of Mama's death; maybe it wasn't my fault at all, in spite of the blood-red rose petals. I wished with all my heart that the baby had died and that Mama was still with us.

At last, I brushed away the tears that had been running unheeded down my face and, rubbing my still painful belly, I returned to bed. I did not sleep well.

In the morning, I awoke with a headache. Getting wearily out of bed, I walked over to the washstand and poured cool water into the basin to wash myself. As I pulled my nightgown over my head, I noticed a deep red stain on the back of it. I looked quickly over to the bed. There were stains there, too. Terrified, I clutched my nightgown to me as memories of my mother lying in blood-soaked sheets came flooding back. Sweat trickled down between my shoulder blades and, for a moment, I could scarcely breathe. Was it happening to me, too? Was I bleeding to death?

I sat unsteadily on the edge of the bed. After a few minutes, my breathing eased as I began to remember something that Mama had told me over a year before, just after my fourteenth birthday. She had taken me into her bedroom one morning and opened a drawer in her dressing table to show me a pile of soft cotton strips and some long pink ribbons. She had explained how I should use these strips when the time came, and how I should tuck the ends into the ribbon and tie it around my waist.

She had told me that I would soon bleed every month for a few days and called it "the flux." She said that all women did this. I was skeptical at first, and then a little frightened, but Mama had laughed and hugged me and promised me that I would be glad, because it meant that I was becoming a woman, and would one day be able to have babies of my own. I hadn't really understood, but she made it sound as if it was something wonderful that we would share.

Now I felt very alone. Mama wasn't here to help me and I had no idea what to do. The thought of going into her room to see if the cloths were still there filled me with horror; besides, I knew that all of Mama's personal things were gone, put away by a silent, red-eyed Jennings before she had packed her own bags and gone to stay with her sister in Gloucester.

In spite of the warmth of the day, I shivered. Finally, I got up and walked gingerly to the door and peered out. Annie was a little way down the corridor. I could smell the pungent fumes of vinegar as she cleaned a mirror. She turned her head as she heard the door open and her eyes took in my rumpled appearance and the stained nightgown in my hands, covering my nakedness.

"Oh, Miss Ada," she said. "Will you be wanting some cloths then?" She nodded towards the nightgown in my hand. "I'll fetch them for you Miss," she added before hurrying away.

Nodding dumbly at her retreating back, I closed my bedroom door and leaned against it until I heard a gentle knock from the other side.

Annie slipped quietly into the room. "Here you are, Miss," she said, proffering a bundle of folded cloths. On top was a length of pink ribbon. In her other hand, she held a small cloth bag.

"Where shall I put this, Miss Ada?" she asked. I looked at her, not understanding. "It's for the soiled ones, Miss. I'll be taking them every morning for the laundry. Miss Nell hangs hers on the end of her bed like this." She looped the cord of the sturdy bag over the low post at the end of my bed and smiled shyly, then bent her head as usual to hide the crookedness of her mouth.

Annie had been born with a harelip, and abandoned by her parents for her disfigurement. Mama had taken her in when she was quite young, and she had been our housemaid ever since.

"She's needed the cloths for six months or more," Annie continued. "She gets dreadful headaches, just like the Missus used to." Annie glanced quickly up at my face then looked away, uncomfortably. "There are more clean cloths in the linen closet, second shelf down, on the right-hand side, Miss, if you need them," she finished. And, with a quick curtsey, she left, closing the door behind her.

I stared after Annie, scarcely able to believe my ears. Nell was my younger sister and barely fourteen. I didn't understand how she could have done this first. I imagined Mama, her eyes bright with unshed tears, hugging Nell to her, stroking her hair and kissing her cheek.

It was certainly true that Nell had been complaining of headaches of late, but I had put that down to her excessive love of reading, something I felt sure was detrimental to her health. I had not noticed anything else different about my sister, but we had not been very close for some months.

Now, my eyes filled with tears, and anger swept through me. How dared Nell do this first, and how could my mother be cruel enough to die and leave me all alone? Filled with rage, I grabbed Edith, my beloved rag doll, the one that Mama had made for me when I was a little girl. I ripped at her woolen hair, pulled at her arms, and finally flung her across the room, where she landed with a dull thud against the wall. Her hair was sticking up on one side and one arm was almost ripped off. Sobbing, I flung myself onto the stained sheets and wept.

Much later, face washed and hair brushed, I sat at my dressing table and looked at myself in the mirror. I was a young woman now, and must face up to the new responsibilities of my life, I told myself, solemnly. I would start by doing the thing that I found most difficult; I would go to see my new sister.

Leaving my room, I walked along the corridor and up the back stairs. On the top floor of the house all seemed quiet and deserted. The schoolroom was dimly lit, the blinds were down and there was no sign of Miss Jackson or the twins. I crossed the room and pushed open the door leading to the nursery. Sunlight streamed into the room, but it, too, appeared empty. Bessie must be in the inner room with both of the babies. Then a slight movement caught my eye and I looked across to where a cradle was set beneath the window. Slowly, I walked towards it and found myself looking down at my new baby sister. She was beautiful. Her eyes were closed, her long, dark lashes lying softly on her tiny heart-shaped face, and her head was covered with a fuzz of dark brown hair. Her perfect little lips were pursed and one small hand had escaped the swaddling and lay rosily on the blanket. As I watched, she squirmed and stretched, and her lips parted for a moment as I'm sure, she smiled a drowsy, milk-filled smile.

Bewildered thoughts whirled through my head. The child looked like an angel, but I could not forget that this was the thing that the doctor had been holding in his hands as he stood at the foot of my mother's bed. I stretched out a tentative finger, not quite daring to touch the perfect little creature, this small enemy whom I was supposed to love.

"Isn't she beautiful?" said a voice behind me. I whirled around; Nell was standing by the door watching me. She had come in silently without my knowing.

I looked first at Nell then back at the baby. Then I ran, pushing past Nell as I went. My mind was in turmoil. I was so angry at my sister for being the first to become a woman, and could not forgive that beautiful baby for being alive while my mother was dead in her grave. As I tried to make sense of this I thought of running to the orchard again and letting the trees bring me comfort and peace, but I knew that I could no longer do that. It was time to face up to some of my new responsibilities.

For all that, I spent the rest of the day hunched miserably in my room thinking of the baby lying upstairs; the beautiful baby who had killed my beloved mother; I hated my little sister with all my heart.

I bestirred myself a little when Cook sent up poached fish and bread-berry pudding on a tray for dinner. Silent sympathy for what she and Mrs. Carter referred to as "the curse." Annie must have shared my news with them.

Much later that night, just as I was drifting off to sleep, I heard the sound of carriage wheels on the gravel outside. My father had returned.

CHAPTER 3

Early next morning, Annie came to wake me. "The Master's back and you're to come down as quick as you can, Miss," she told me, anxiously. I needed no second bidding; my father did not like to be kept waiting. I dressed quickly, not bothering to re-braid my hair.

As I ran down the stairs, I could hear the twins chattering excitedly to each other in the hall outside the drawing room. Their faces shone brightly, their hair was pulled into identical braids, their pink dresses and white smocks were freshly ironed and their black boots shone. Miss Jackson stood behind them, confident that her charges would not disgrace her.

In my own haste to dress that morning I had paid little attention to my appearance and had pulled my old brown print dress and plain smock from the wardrobe. I had to struggle into my dress, for these days everything seemed to be too tight for me.

We had all worn black for Mama's funeral. The local dressmaker, Mrs. Pettigrew, had been summoned hastily to the house the day after Mama died, and three days later, several large packages had arrived containing black dresses and bonnets for all four of us. After the funeral, Mrs. Carter had gathered up these clothes to be set in moth balls, and we wore them only on Sundays for chapel.

I looked around for Nell as I reached the bottom step of the stairs but there was no sign of her. Papa would be very displeased. I felt a glimmer of pleasure for I was still angry with my sister. As I waited next to the twins, the drawing room door opened and Mrs. Carter emerged. Her face was set in tight angry lines and she did not look at us as she flounced towards the back of the house.

As we filed obediently into the drawing room, I heard Nell's boots skidding across the polished floor of the hall, and she slipped into the room just before Miss Jackson closed the door.

My father was standing by the fireplace. He looked pale and tired. His fingers were drumming lightly on the white marble mantle, a sure sign that he was angry or uncomfortable. By the window was a small figure, completely swathed in black. Her back was towards us, but as the door closed, she turned around.

"Abigail," began my father, "I would like to present my daughters." With an impatient gesture, Aunt Abigail silenced him. "Let them speak for themselves," she said, turning coldly piercing eyes upon each of us in turn. "In chronological order, tell me your names and ages," she snapped. We all gaped at her in silence.

Nell was the first to recover. She had sidled up to me while Aunt Abigail was speaking. "You first, then me," she muttered.

I took a step forward "I'm Ada," I said, and stopped uncertainly.

"What is your age? I asked for your age, girl!" Aunt Abigail was glaring at me. Although she came barely to my chin, she was a daunting figure. Her eyes were so dark as to appear black and her mouth closed into a thin line. Her hair under her black day cap appeared to be dark like Papa's, but it was heavily streaked with grey. It was drawn back severely from her face and, in all the time I knew her, I never saw a single strand escape, not even in the stormiest weather. Her hands were small and, although it was full summer, she wore black fingerless mittens.

"I'm fifteen," I managed to gasp at last.

Aunt Abigail continued to stare at me. "Have you no manners, girl?" she demanded. "Kindly address me by name and don't stammer. It's most unseemly."

I ducked my head in embarrassment. "Yes, Aunt Abigail," I mumbled.

Then it was Nell's turn. She didn't hesitate but gave her name and age clearly, adding "Aunt Abigail," at the end. My aunt looked coldly at Nell.

As usual my sister was very untidy. Her thick black hair had defied her hasty attempts to capture it and was escaping in straggling tendrils around her face. Her dress was partly unbuttoned at the back and she was not wearing her smock. Her spectacles were firmly on her face but I could see that they were broken on one side and had been clumsily mended with gardening twine that she had most likely coaxed from Ned. Her boots were unbuttoned.

Aunt Abigail took a deep breath and I expected that she would scold Nell for her appearance, but she did not. "Nell?" she said. "What kind of childish name is that? What is your full name?"

Nell blushed scarlet. "It's Eleanor, for my mother, but . . ." her voice trailed off and she looked towards my father in a silent plea for help.

"She has always been Nell," my father said quietly. "I would prefer that to continue if you please, Abigail."

"As you wish, Robert!" My aunt pursed her lips in obvious disapproval, continuing to look thoughtfully at Nell before turning to the twins who were by now regarding her in wide-eyed fear.

"Well?" said Aunt Abigail. Lily, who was the bolder of the twins, managed to say her name, but Iris burst into tears and hid her face in Miss Jackson's grey skirts. Embarrassed, Miss Jackson curtsied deeply and started forward to introduce herself. My aunt stared at her for a moment then very deliberately turned towards my father, completely ignoring the governess.

"Where is the other child?" she demanded, "and what have you named her?"

There was absolute silence in the room. My father's face, already drawn with tiredness, paled as he looked down, his eyes not meeting his sister's sharply inquiring gaze. As far as I knew, not once since the dreadful day when Mama had died had my father spoken of, or acknowledged the existence of, the new baby.

The silence in the drawing room lengthened. Aunt Abigail tapped her foot impatiently.

"Edith," I blurted out. "We call her Edith." Edith was my rag doll that, even now, was lying torn and broken on the chest at the foot of my bed, where Annie had placed her with care after I had thrown her so angrily from me.

My father glanced fleetingly at me with what might have been gratitude. "Yes," he said. "Her name is Edith. She is upstairs with her nurse." Aunt Abigail pursed her lips, but did not respond.

Then she turned again to look disapprovingly at the four of us. "Why are these girls not in mourning clothes?" she asked sourly.

"I thought there was no need when they are around the house," my father's voice was subdued.

I glanced quickly at Papa. Could he be afraid of his oldest sister? Certainly he looked more uncomfortable and unsure of himself than I had ever seen him.

Aunt Abigail made a noise that in anyone else I would have called a snort. "What nonsense," she said briskly, turning back to where we were still waiting. Looking sourly first at Nell and then at me, she snapped, "You girls will go upstairs immediately and dress more suitably." Then she turned back to my father. "If the governess can sufficiently control her charges, they too should be more appropriately dressed. Really, Robert," she continued as if they were alone in the room, "to date, I find things here to be most unsatisfactory." Then she turned her back to look once more out of the window.

Papa glanced tiredly at us as we stood waiting, before dismissing us with a wave of his hand. As we left the room, Aunt Abigail's voice followed us. "You will all be at the breakfast table in precisely ten minutes." We were.

Aunt Abigail believed in prayer, she also believed in discipline, but most of all, my aunt believed that the devil would find work for idle hands. Our lives changed very much from the day she came into the house.

On that first July morning, breakfast was a painful meal. The twins, recovered from their initial panic, fidgeted and giggled as we stood behind our chairs, heads bent and hands clasped while Aunt Abigail prayed. When the prayer came to an end, Aunt Abigail—tiny though she was—moved with amazing speed to where the twins were standing, an embarrassed Miss Jackson next to them. Before they knew what was happening, Aunt Abigail slapped each child smartly across the face before she turned to glare at Miss Jackson. "Spare the rod and spoil the child," she snapped. "I will not tolerate this behaviour."

I looked at my father, expecting him to admonish Aunt Abigail for striking my sisters, but Papa had seated himself as if nothing had happened and we were all forced to followed suit. Lily and Iris, shocked by this turn of events, sat sobbing until Aunt Abigail told them sharply to stop.

Later that morning when Papa summoned me to his study, I wondered what else could possibly go wrong. Nell joined me at the top of the stairs and I could tell that she had been crying. "She's an old witch," she whispered. "Do you know why she's here?" I shook my head reluctantly.

"Well, I think she's here to adopt us and take us to her evil castle in Yorkshire or somewhere."

"Don't be silly, Nell," I replied as we walked slowly down the stairs. "For one thing, she and Aunt Charity live in Sussex, and for another, Papa would never let her do that." I broke off, for in reality I didn't know why my aunt had come. We looked at each other fearfully for a moment, then Nell knocked on the study door and we waited for the command to enter.

Papa was seated as usual behind the mahogany desk that dominated the room. Papers were stacked neatly on one side of it, and on the other I noticed a pile of maps. Papa's cut-glass inkwell was where it had always been beside the tray of neatly aligned pens. I used to play with those pens when I was a little girl, sitting on Mama's lap as she and Papa talked.

My father looked up as we entered, and gestured for us to be seated. He did not speak for a few moments, and when he did, his voice was quiet, and as I listened, my heart sank.

"I have to go away," he said, "and I will be abroad for some time." He fidgeted absently with a pen before continuing. "While I'm gone, your Aunt Abigail has agreed to stay and look after you."

"Papa," Nell said, leaning forward, "you can't, you can't leave us with her. She hates us! Please don't go!"

My father turned to Nell, his face darkening. "Hold your tongue Nell" he said sternly. "You will not speak of your aunt in that manner." Then Papa placed his pen on the desk in front of him and rubbed his hands wearily over his face.

"This trip was planned a long time ago," he said. "Your mother and I were preparing," he broke off. "No matter!" He shook his head as if to banish my mother's ghost, and after a moment, continued more briskly. "The arrangements are made. Drake will stay and will take care of supervising the servants while I'm away, and your Aunt Abigail will be the ultimate authority in my absence." He cast a keen glance at both of us. "I do not expect any problems."

Then looking down at the pile of papers in front of him, he waved us away. "You may go now," he said. "I have a great deal to do before I leave. I embark from Liverpool in mid-August and I will be gone for six months."

As the study door closed behind us, Nell grabbed my hand and dragged me across the hall. "Come on," she said urgently, "we need to talk."

At first, I didn't know where she was leading me then, as she slipped into the vestibule and opened the door that led to the conservatory, I remembered. When we were little, we had a favourite hiding place, where we would play for hours and hide from a governess we heartily disliked. At the very end of the conservatory, next to the door that led outside to the garden, was the little room that had been our refuge.

Originally, it had been used to store watering cans and old garden furniture, but it hadn't been in use for years, not since the addition to the conservatory, with its more modern tiled floor and fountains. I couldn't remember the last time I had stepped inside its dusty walls.

Nell pushed aside some carefully stacked flower pots that were in front of the door and lifted the latch; it opened silently, on well-oiled hinges. I looked around expecting to see dirt and cobwebs but it was very clean. There was an old bamboo chair in the corner with a rumpled pillow on the seat and several books piled on an upturned pail next to it. The wooden floor was swept bare, except for a few crumbs of food that might have been supper for some small creature.

I glanced at my sister. "This is where you hide, isn't it?" I said, looking at the pile of books. "You come here all the time, I know you do."

Nell shrugged. "What if I do? We're not here to talk about that." She stopped for a moment clutching at my black-clad arm. "You won't tell though, will you?" I shook my head and pulled my arm away. Who would I tell?

Nell gestured for me to sit down in the old chair and I seated myself gladly; my back was aching and I felt close to tears.

"Tell me something, Ada," she said, leaning against the wall. "Why did you tell Aunt Abigail that the baby's name was Edith? You had no right to do that. And why did you run away the other day when I found you in the nursery?"

"I'm sorry, Nell," I said. "Edith was the first name that came into my head, and Papa didn't seem to mind, and I ran away because I was upset. When Mama died, I saw her, there was blood everywhere, and then two days ago, I started, you know," I hesitated, "the monthly curse thing. And Annie told me that you'd had it for ages and I was really mad at you."

Nell shook her head in bewilderment and scooted down next to me so her face was close to mine. "Mama told me not to tell. She said that you'd be upset because you're the oldest, and you should have been first, but it was me, and anyway, I think it's disgusting." She stopped for breath. "And what do you mean, you saw Mama?"

I shrugged. "It was nothing, I didn't mean anything." I knew then that I would never tell Nell what I had seen that day when little Edith came into the world.

My sister sounded impatient as she sat back on her heels.

"Look, we need to talk about what's happening right now. Aunt Abigail sent for me after breakfast. She told me that I was a disgrace to the family and that if I ever again appear looking like a street urchin she will personally whip me."

I stared at Nell in horror. "Did you speak to Papa?"

My sister looked at me pityingly. "No, why would I? You saw what she did to Lily and Iris. Papa was there and he didn't do anything. She's in charge now and we just have to put up with it." She shuddered. "Do you think you could help me to get out of bed in the mornings, Ada? You know how I am, and that old witch has already told Mrs. Carter that Annie can't come to rouse us anymore. Mrs. Carter was furious." She leaned back to see my face more clearly. "Oh, and can you imagine how angry she and Cook must be about Drake being in charge of them?"

We looked at each other wide-eyed, our own troubles forgotten for a moment, and started to giggle. My laughter faded quickly though as a thought occurred to me. "You don't think Mrs. Carter will leave, do you?"

Nell shook her head quickly, still smiling. "No, I heard her tell Cook that she has to stay," she mimicked one of Mrs. Carter's more tragic tones, "to look after those poor motherless children." Then Nell's hand flew to her mouth. "Oh, Ada, that's right! That's what we are now, we're poor motherless children."

Feeling suddenly very grown up, I stretched out a hand to smooth a stray curl from my sister's face, but she pushed me angrily away.

CHAPTER 4

I left Nell to her books and started walking slowly back through the conservatory. After a moment, I stopped and looked about, remembering all the times I had seen my mother here.

She had spent much of her time here during the winter months, when the cold winds blew and she could no longer tend to her beloved roses. Then Mama retreated into the warmth of the conservatory and I remembered watching as her slender fingers gentled the earth around some foreign plant that demanded heat and moisture to survive. It was here that she kept her orchids.

I have never been fond of those exotic flowers. Their odd shapes and fleshy petals repulse me slightly, but my mother had adored them. My father had brought back a single plant for her when he returned from a trip when I was still quite little, and he had continued to add to her collection from time to time. It was because of the orchids that the conservatory had been enlarged.

Now as I looked across to the long shelves that housed these plants, I saw that they had been recently watered. They looked healthy and strong and I wondered who was caring for them.

At this time of year, the rest of the conservatory was almost empty. The sun shone brightly through the glass roof and I became aware of my own discomfort. The dark fabric of my dress was sticking uncomfortably to my back as I headed for the door and slipped gratefully back into the cool shadows of the vestibule.

Closing the conservatory door behind me, I peered through the stained glass window of the front door. Through the distorted panes,

I could see the trees that edged the driveway, swaying in the summer breeze. I thought I would walk down by the river to enjoy the cooler air. I needed to be by myself to think about what Papa's departure would mean for all of us. But as I reached for my bonnet, I became aware that I was being watched, and, turning my head, I looked through the hall door that Nell and I had carelessly left open. Aunt Abigail was standing at the bottom of the stairs.

"What were you doing in the conservatory?" Her voice was cold.

I felt my colour rising but I would never betray Nell's hiding place to Aunt Abigail. "I was looking at Mama's orchids," I said, truthfully.

"Looking at flowers is not a suitable occupation for a young girl," my aunt replied tartly. "I have useful tasks for you to perform."

Within a week of her arrival, Aunt Abigail had made many changes to the running of the household and I came to realize that Mama had been a gentle mistress, who took little interest in the day-to-day running of the house, though certainly she would make her wishes known from time to time. On the odd occasion that my parents had dinner guests, Mama would call for Cook and request a particular menu. This would throw Cook into a frenzy of activity and there would follow a great deal of banging and crashing of pots and pans in the kitchen, together with furious mutterings and threats of notice being given. The end result was always excellent, however, and Cook was certainly not above coming into the dining room upon request, to be congratulated on some particularly fine dish. Then after much blushing and bobbing of anxious curtsies, she would retire to the kitchen for what she described as "a small glass of tonic."

Under my aunt's rule, it quickly became clear that, henceforth, all household decisions would be made by Aunt Abigail. She demanded to see Mrs. Carter's housekeeping accounts, noting omissions, questioning purchases, and making changes to the manner of entries. An outraged Mrs. Carter seethed in silence. Then Aunt Abigail turned her attentions to Cook. There followed stormy scenes during which Cook reached new levels of histrionics and which culminated in a large china mixing bowl landing very close to where Aunt Abigail was standing. I believe that it took all of my father's diplomacy to smooth ruffled feathers on both sides, but this close to his departure he could afford to lose neither a trusted servant nor an angry relative, and from that time on, an uneasy truce existed between the two women. For my part, I missed my mother terribly.

A few days before Papa was due to leave, our dressmaker Mrs. Pettigrew again visited us at the house. We were measured for more clothes, which in Aunt Abigail's opinion were suitable for children still in mourning. After the dressmaker had finished with us, I noticed her in discussion with Aunt Abigail. My aunt looked displeased, but two weeks later when everything arrived, I found to my delight that my new clothes proved to be two long dark skirts with matching bodices. It was a relief to be dressed in clothes more appropriate to my age and which fitted me with much greater comfort. I sent a silent thank you to Mrs. Pettigrew for noticing my changing shape. Nell continued to be dressed as a child. She seemed not to notice, or if she did, not to care.

During this time, the house was bustling with preparations for Papa's departure, and on a bright August morning, my father left us. His trunk and valises were piled in the hall as I went down to breakfast, and shortly thereafter we lined up by the front door to say our farewells. The twins were not much affected by Papa's departure and their goodbyes were merely dutiful.

It was more difficult for Nell and me. My sister stood next to me, furiously scrubbing at her newly mended spectacles. Her nose was suspiciously red at the tip and I hoped that she wouldn't start to cry. Papa had never liked displays of emotion.

When it was my turn, I stepped forward and kissed him stiffly on the cheek. To my surprise, my father pulled me close, and gave me a small, fierce hug.

"Be strong, Ada," he said softly in my ear, and I watched his farewell to Aunt Abigail through a mist of unexpected tears.

I continued to watch as my father entered the carriage then as the door was closed by an attentive Drake, I turned and walked back towards the kitchen where I knew Aunt Abigail would already be waiting to start her morning instructions.

CHAPTER 5

The humid days of summer dragged on. During most after-noons, thunder growled and rumbled in the distance and I longed for the weather to break. When it finally did, it was with uncommon fury. For three days, great purple clouds swept across the skies lit by jagged flashes of lightning, and huge thunder claps shook the earth. The rain fell in torrential sheets, but did nothing to alleviate the brooding heat, and by the third day, everyone was irri-table and on edge. After lunch, I waited in my accustomed spot in the drawing room, ready for afternoon lessons with my aunt, but the room remained empty. Eventually, I went in search of Mrs. Carter and found her alone in the kitchen, sitting in the rocking chair nodding in the afternoon heat. She told me that Aunt Abigail had retired to her room directly after lunch.

"Seems she has a bad headache, so I reckon she won't be seeing you, not today." The housekeeper's lips twitched in a fleeting smile as she leaned back in the chair, rocking it lightly, before closing her eyes. "Must be the weather," she said, before adding under her breath, "'tis an ill wind."

Thanking her, I made my escape and went looking for Nell, but there was no sign of her and I was in no mood to persuade her out of her secret hidey-hole. This was the first time in almost a month that I'd had the opportunity to walk out alone.

Putting a light shawl over my shoulders, I tied my black bonnet under my chin and slipped out of the front door. I walked briskly down the driveway, and when I reached the road, I turned left. I had no real goal in mind, just a need to escape for a while.

After a few minutes, I came upon one or two scattered cottages by the roadside and realized that I was approaching the little hamlet that we had always referred to as the village. This was really only a scattering of ten or twelve cottages loosely grouped around a small central green. There was a tree in the middle of the green and the blacksmith's shop was close by.

Most of the cottages appeared deserted as I passed them, but from time to time, I spied faces peering out of open doorways, watching me with frank curiosity. I felt a little foolish and wished that I had thought to bring a basket with me, so that I could pretend to be on some urgent errand.

Then my eyes lighted on the smithy and I walked purposefully towards it. I would visit the blacksmith and ask if he had come up to the house lately to check on our horses. They needed to be shod regularly, and with all the upheaval of this summer, I told myself, it was reasonable to think that this task might have been overlooked.

As I picked my way along the rutted path that passed for a road, I rehearsed what I would say. But when I reached the smithy it too appeared deserted, with a large piece of leather hanging over the entrance. I stood uncomfortably in front of the entrance for a few moments then turned to go. As I did so, there was a sudden movement from within, and the smith's head appeared around the leather flap.

He looked surprised to see me. "D 'you be wantin' somethin' then, little Missy?" he asked.

I felt myself blushing. "I was out walking and wondered if the horses up at the house had been shod this summer since . . . since my mother's passing," I said, uncertainly.

The smith was looking at me kindly. "Don't you be frettin', my dear," he said. "They do be well looked after, same as always." Then he waited in comfortable silence.

"Thank you!" I said abruptly and, as I turned away, I was acutely aware of his amused gaze following me.

"Best hurry back, Miss," he called. "It be goin' to storm again."

I kept my head down as I hastened past the scattered cottages and hurried along the road towards home. I didn't stay on the road for long though because a glance at the sky told me that the blacksmith had been right. Thunderheads were gathering again, and a fierce, hot wind had sprung up, so I cut across the grass and up over the hill and was glad to see the red tiles of our rooftop beyond the trees. Slipping under the fence, I started across our bottom field where the horses were usually grazing at this time of year, but today it was empty. Ned must have taken the animals into the stable against the approaching weather.

I was halfway across the field when the storm hit. There was a sudden gust of wind and rain that almost blew me off my feet. Thunder crashed overhead and a flash of lightning hit one of the small oak trees at the edge of the road. Terrified, I struggled against the wind and rain and, hampered by my skirts, staggered at last into the lee of the stable building. This was a separate building, part of a much older house, long since destroyed. Our own house had been built some sixty years before, on higher ground, further away from the river and less likely to flood in spring.

As I rounded the corner, I paused for a moment, glad to be out of the wind, but the rain was falling in earnest now and I was soaking wet. I ran the last few yards to the stable door and pulled it open. Inside it was blessedly dry, and the noise of the storm was much reduced. I could still hear the crash of thunder, but as my eyes and ears adjusted, I could see the outline of the stalls and hear the soft shifting of the horses as they sensed my presence.

I was about to go forward and stroke old Dobbin's soft muzzle when I heard a sound that made me stop. It was a low, throaty laugh; a woman's laugh. I froze, wondering anxiously if a gypsy had found shelter here. They were often in the neighbourhood during the summer months, but Papa would not tolerate them close to the house. They frightened me with their dark skin and eyes and their strange way of talking. I had caught Cook giving them food on more than one occasion and she had warned me to be good to the gypsies lest they lay a curse on the house.

I shivered, suddenly unsure of what to do. Outside, the rain beat down more heavily than ever. Then I heard another voice, deeper this time, and with a note of pleading in it. I thought of going to look for

Ned, but the wind was buffeting the rain through the half-open door and I was already soaked through and thoroughly chilled. I waited in breathless silence for a few moments but I heard no more voices.

After a little while, curiosity overcame me and I began to creep towards the back of the stable to see if I could find out who was sheltering there. Any small sounds that I made were masked by the storm, and I stopped just short of the last stall. It was used to store fresh straw and feed for the animals. My eyes were accustomed to the gloom by now and I spied two figures lying amongst the soft bales of hay. One of them was Ned and the other was Bessie, Edith's nurse.

I opened my mouth to speak, but stopped and watched in dawning horror as Bessie lay back on a heap of straw with Ned poised above her. Her bodice was open, revealing two huge breasts; Ned was stroking and kneading them and, even as I watched she gave a little moan, and with a slack-mouthed smile lifted her skirts, dragging them up to her waist, and let her legs fall open. There was a flash of movement as Ned came down heavily on top of her. He had pulled down his breeches and his pink buttocks began to move up and down in quick thrusting movements while Bessie emitted small squeals that sounded just like the piglets that were for sale on Market Day in Wimborne. Ned punctuated his thrusts with deep throated grunts. I stared in horror for a few moments more then turned and ran. I'm sure they didn't hear me go.

It was still raining outside but I didn't stop until I was inside the house. I ran up to my room and pulled off my wet clothes. Wrapping myself in a blanket, I curled up on my bed, trying to make sense of what I had seen. I had seen animals mating before. Our neighbour Mr. Bradshaw regularly had his cows serviced by a bull from over Wimborne way. But Bessie had been lying on her back and that was not the way a cow was serviced. I stared sightlessly into the room. In my heart, I knew just what they had been doing and shuddered suddenly at my new knowledge. Then, curling myself into a tighter ball of misery, I tried to think of nothing at all, and in the end, I drifted off to sleep.

I never told anyone what I had seen in the stables, though one day when the leaves were starting to drop from the trees and I saw Bessie pushing the great double perambulator that had been used for the twins, I wondered who had been minding the two babies, her own Sam and our little Edith, on that wet August afternoon in the storm.

September came, the air cooled, and autumn vegetables graced our table. I missed my solitary walks down by the river and minded greatly that Aunt Abigail would not allow us to go down to the orchard to help with the apple picking.

Now our days were filled with other tasks. The twins and Nell were better governed during this time. Miss Jackson had been an early victim of Aunt Abigail's changes. Even before Papa had left, Aunt Abigail had insisted that the governess be replaced by someone more capable. So the poor creature had departed one hot morning, her grey skirts trailing sadly in the summer dust, her portmanteau weighing heavily in her hand. She had stubbornly refused a lift to the station, gathering the remaining shreds of her pride about her like a tattered shawl and walking straight-backed down the driveway and out of sight.

The twins had sulked for a few days but soon settled into the routines set by Miss Lucy Blackly, the new governess. She was a sensible woman in her early twenties who was engaged to be married to an army officer, presently serving in India. She was cheerful and practical, and Aunt Abigail did not frighten her at all. Lily and Iris quickly came to adore her and even Nell seemed to like her. She was the daughter of a local Anglican vicar, and took Sundays off so that she might attend her father's church services. Aunt Abigail disapproved of Miss Blackly's religious beliefs for she looked upon Anglicans with deep suspicion for being much too close to Papists. I found Miss Blackly kind and generous though, and on more than one occasion, I saw her returning with parcels of books for Nell to read.

Apart from our sewing lessons in the afternoons with Aunt Abigail, I saw very little of my sister. She seemed to spend much of her time up in the schoolroom, or off by herself reading.

My weekday mornings were spent learning how to keep simple accounts and I was instructed in the art of supervising the household routines. Careless work or tasks left undone were punished by a sharp smack across my knuckles with a small bamboo cane that Aunt Abigail liked to carry with her.

To my dismay, my aunt quickly discovered that my reading and writing skills were quite poor. I hoped that she might send me upstairs to learn with Miss Blackly, but she took these tasks upon herself and, in time, my handwriting did improve, though my knuckles were often made painfully sore in the process.

Reading became part of our afternoon activities. Initially, Aunt Abigail had read from the bible, but soon insisted that I be the one to read from the good book. At first, she had also required Nell to read, but realizing that my sister truly excelled in this activity, had instead set her to practice her needlework, a task at which Nell was quite hopeless. My sister preferred to use her left hand to sew, but Aunt Abigail forced her to use her right, and did not spare the cane on Nell's knuckles. I believe that it was on those golden afternoons, when the sun slanted through the changing leaves of the trees and the earth was rich and damp with the smells of autumn, that Nell truly came to hate Aunt Abigail.

Music was no longer a part of our daily lives. Every Sunday, Aunt Abigail joined in the hymn singing in chapel in a strong, clear voice, but considered all other music to be the work of the devil. Mama's piano, that Nell had so loved to play, was locked and Aunt Abigail kept the key.

As the days shortened and chill winds blew around the house, I became aware of a change in the way the servants treated me. Annie no longer lingered in the upstairs hall to ask if I needed anything, and Mrs. Carter was tight-lipped and resentful when I was sent to check on some of her household duties. She would stand watching me scornfully, arms folded across her chest, as I counted bed sheets and pillowcases. One day, when I told her that several sheets were missing, she swept past me, and with a withering glance over her shoulder, suggested that I check with the laundress who came to collect our dirty linens every Friday, and returned them clean and ironed the following Wednesday. She was of course quite correct. She and Drake continued to bicker, but without their old rancor. Mutual discontent around the managing of the household seemed to ease their relationship a little.

Cook still ruled the kitchen, but even she was constantly bad-tempered with me. As a child I had loved to sit and watch her as she moved quickly around the kitchen. Her fingers were light on the pastry board, deftly cutting and shaping huge pies or forming delicately fluted cream horns. I had once watched in fascination as she boned a dozen fresh herrings in swift, easy movements, when Ned had brought them back fresh from Poole.

Spending winter mornings in the kitchen with Cook, while cold rain beat against the windows and the wind caught gustily at the back door, had always been a magical time for me.

Now when I entered the kitchen I was greeted with a curtsey and a wary glance. If I lingered, Cook would stop what she was doing and inquire politely if there was anything in particular that I required. My heart ached, but I didn't know how to change things. Aunt Abigail kept a watchful eye on me and made it clear that I was not to behave with familiarity towards the servants.

As for Ned and Bessie, I did my best to avoid them. Since we no longer took regular trips into Wimborne, I had little need to speak with Ned, unless it was to discuss some aspect of the kitchen garden, and I did not often visit the schoolroom on the top floor next to the nursery, so my encounters with Bessie were few. I still had no interest in the welfare of my little sister.

CHAPTER 6

Late in October a letter arrived from Papa. I saw it one morning as I descended the stairs for breakfast. It was lying in clear view on the hall table and, with a happy cry, I pounced on it for it was addressed to me, 'Miss A. Baldwin,' and it bore the foreign postmark of Buenos Aires. As I clutched the big envelope, Aunt Abigail opened the dining room door. She looked at the letter I was holding and held out one black-gloved hand.

"It's from Papa," I said, breathlessly, "and it's addressed to me, Aunt Abigail!" I was amazed at my own daring. I didn't usually have the courage to speak so boldly to my aunt, but I was excited to be holding a letter from my father.

Her hand remained outstretched. "Give the letter to me," she said, coolly. "The salutation reads 'Miss A. Baldwin.' Kindly remember that while I am in this house, I am Miss Baldwin; you are just Ada."

She took the envelope from my stiff fingers, and turned back into the dining room. As I followed her, tears burning behind my eyes, I was certain that my aunt had already seen the letter when she came down to breakfast. The envelope was large and white and Papa's bold black writing would have been impossible to miss. I knew that she had left it on the table for me to see and had judged correctly what I would do.

After morning prayers were over, Aunt Abigail set the letter on the table in front of her. Nell started to say something, but I kicked her foot hard under the table; Aunt Abigail glared, and Nell subsided. The twins were too busy eating their porridge to notice, and Miss Blackly seemed to have problems of her own that day, for she frowned fiercely when she saw the envelope and kept her head bent for the remainder of the meal.

When breakfast was over, I looked across at Aunt Abigail. The pale fingertips emerging from her black-mittened hands were caressing the letter. She tapped it once or twice giving me a thin smile as she watched me with lidded eyes, then she rose slowly from her chair and, tucking the unopened letter into her skirt pocket, left the room without a word. Later that morning, I met Nell as she was crossing the hall headed towards the stairs. In a hurried whisper, I told her what had happened.

"I told you, she's a witch," she said over her shoulder as she ascended the stairs.

All that day and the next, I waited. I was sure that Aunt Abigail would give us news of my father. I longed to ask her, but I knew that to do so would be foolish and would merely give my aunt another opportunity to deliver a lecture on patience and humility.

Finally, it was Nell who broached the subject two afternoons later. I was struggling through a particularly difficult passage from the bible when Nell interrupted.

She looked up from the mess of stitching that she was undoing for perhaps the fifth time. "Aunt Abigail," she said sweetly, "I wondered if you could share news of Papa with us, since you have received his letter. We miss him very much, especially as Mama has been taken from us, and we long to hear that he is safe and well."

I flashed Nell a grateful smile, for it was prettily said, and it must have cost her dearly to speak so humbly to our aunt.

Aunt Abigail lifted her eyes from her sewing and looked directly at her niece. Nell gazed steadily back through her glasses, dark eyes to dark eyes. In that moment, my sister Nell and my Aunt Abigail looked remarkably alike.

Then Aunt Abigail turned to me. "Kindly continue reading, Ada," she said, as if Nell hadn't spoken.

I bent my head to the tiny print and struggled on, but as I turned the page, I noticed that Nell's fingers trembled as she continued to rip out stitches. A tear splashed onto the fabric and I knew that it was rage, not sorrow that made my sister weep.

Aunt Abigail never did share the contents of that letter with us, but we did get news of Papa, and from a most surprising source.

One cold night in early November as I was readying myself for bed, there was a soft knock on the door. I opened it, thinking that it was Nell, coming to talk to me. Since the incident of the letter, her misery had become obvious, but she had avoided any attempt on my part to discuss our situation. However, it was Annie who stood in the doorway. She looked nervously over her shoulder in the direction of my aunt's bedroom before slipping into the room and closing the door behind her.

"Please, Miss," she said softly. "Mrs. Carter says if you would come up to her room, Miss, it would be to your advantage. We're all there," she added as if that made the request more reasonable.

"What are you talking about, Annie?" I asked, irritably. "Why should I go creeping up to the servants' quarters at this time of night?"

Annie glanced quickly over her shoulder again. "Miss Nell's already there and, if you want to come, Miss, you'll have to be quick. Mr. Drake's waiting."

"Why is Nell there?" I demanded. "What's going on?"

"Please, Miss, it's Mr. Drake, he got a letter from the Master. We thought you'd want news, Miss, but I'll tell them no." She turned to leave, but I grabbed at her arm.

"No, wait. I'm coming!" Quickly, I took a shawl from the hope chest at the end of my bed, wrapped it around my shoulders, and followed Annie out of the room and along the corridor. We tip-toed past Aunt Abigail's bedroom and I sighed with relief when Annie pushed open the door at the end of the corridor that led to the back stairs.

We climbed the stairs, one behind the other. We had no candle with us and it was very dark. At the top of the stairs to the left, I could see a small flame flickering; a lighted candle in a pot of water in the schoolroom, perhaps to chase away the nightmares that I supposed still haunted young Iris from time to time.

We did not go into the nursery, though, but turned right instead, and through the heavy cream door that led to the servants' quarters. I had never been there before; there had been no reason for me to do so.

As the door swung behind us, I saw a corridor similar to the one that housed bedrooms on the floor below. There were several closed doors leading off the corridor, but one door at the very end was open and a warm light spilled from it onto the polished wooden floor.

Annie hurried along ahead of me. "Here she is then," she called breathlessly as she turned into the room. I paused for a moment in the doorway to let my eyes adjust to the light. The room was large and very cozy on this chilly night. In front of me was a fireplace with a coal fire burning brightly in the grate. Two deep armchairs were placed, one on either side of the hearth that had a rag rug spread in front of it and a big black kettle simmering on the hob.

In one corner to my right was a bed, partly curtained off, and I glimpsed a washstand to one side of it. On the other side of the room were two small windows snugly covered with brocade curtains that I recognized from our dining room from long ago.

Mrs. Carter was sitting in one of the chairs by the fire and Cook was in the other. Drake had pulled up a wooden chair, to be near the fire and Annie, after closing the door, walked to a small hassock and sat down close to Mrs. Carter.

At first, I didn't see Nell, but then I turned my head and she was there. She was curled in a large wicker chair close to the windows, wrapped in a deep pink eiderdown that I realized with a small shock used to be on Mama's bed.

Drake made as if to rise to give me his chair, but I shook my head and went over to where Nell was sitting. She smiled up at me rather wearily and made room in the chair, and I tucked myself beside her under the eiderdown and waited. I was glad that neither Ned nor Bessie was there, but wondered why Miss Blackly hadn't been included.

I asked Nell about it later and she gave me a slightly superior look over the top of her glasses.

"It's because they aren't regular household servants, Ada! For goodness' sake, don't you know anything about protocol in the servants' hall?"

As I settled back, I saw that Drake was busy fussing with several sheets of paper that were covered in writing that I recognized as my father's. As he did so, I looked at the other people in the room, all waiting eagerly to hear what he had to say.

Mrs. Carter was dressed in a deep brown dressing-gown that was buttoned down the front. Her feet were encased in matching slippers, and her hair was not covered, but caught in a soft bun at the nape of her neck.

Across from her, Cook was swathed in a red woolen bed-gown of enormous proportions. Her grey hair was in a night plait and her feet were plunged deeply into what looked like knitted boots. I caught a glimpse of a purple veined ankle beneath the bed-gown as she bent down to rub an aching knee.

Annie was still fully dressed, though she had shed her cap and apron and placed them neatly across her lap. It was Drake who was the biggest surprise. He had removed his jacket and shirt collar and his stomach bulged over his trouser tops. On his feet, he too wore slippers; they were a remarkable shade of emerald green leather and were backless with raised heels.

Drake cleared his throat importantly. "Ladies," he said, bowing first to where Nell and I were huddled together, and then to each of the others. "We are here to share news of the Master." Then he turned again to Nell and me. "It's against my better judgment to have you young ladies here," he said softly. "No good comes of us trying to hobnob with our betters, but Cookie here, and Mrs. C," he nodded towards the two women, "seem to think different, what with that one and all" he pointed his finger significantly at the floor, to where somewhere below our feet, Aunt Abigail slept.

I glanced gratefully at Cook and Mrs. Carter

"Well, then," muttered Cook, "Miss Nell there, she told me as how you girls was 'aving such a bad time, what with the new lessons and that letter and all."

Next to me, Nell shifted in the chair. "Thanks, Cookie," her voice was soft and she smiled at Cook, who winked broadly back by way of a reply.

"Do get on, Albert," Mrs. Carter broke in impatiently. "We all need our sleep; we have to be up and about in a few hours."

Drake cleared his throat again before picking up the letter that he had been balancing on his knee. Holding it at arm's length to better see it, he began to read.

"Mr. Baldwin says he arrived safely in Buenos Aires after a fair crossing. He is presently staying at the home of very good Christian friends who treat him like he was one of their own."

He broke off to look around with an expression of satisfaction on his round face. Cook and Mrs. Carter murmured their approval and Drake continued. "He says he took a bit of a fever on the journey, but is quite recovered and is going about his daily business and," Drake glanced up and gave both Cook and Mrs. Carter meaningful looks, "his plans are going ahead as expected."

At this, Mrs. Carter turned her head and looked sadly into the fire and Cook gave a stifled sob.

I nudged Nell in the ribs. "What's wrong with that?" I whispered. Nell just shrugged and continued to watch Drake.

"Mr. Baldwin says" continued Drake, "that good servants are hard to come by and so . . ."

"Albert!" Mrs. Carter interrupted sharply.

Drake stopped abruptly and looked uncomfortable as he glanced back down at the letter. "This part is mostly just household business for the likes of us," he finished, lamely.

Then, triumphantly he held up the last page. "Ah, here it is. Mr. Baldwin says that he hopes that the children are all well, and that Miss Ada received his letter safely."

At that, Cook gave a great snort. "Well, Mr. Drake," she said leaning forward in a swirl of red wool, "you'd best write back to the Master and tell 'im next time to address the envelope to Miss *Ada* Baldwin with a big circle round it so other folk don't take it for their selves." Cook leaned back against the chair, her double chins quivering with indignation.

As I watched her, I thought that she was upset by more than the letter Aunt Abigail had refused to share with us, but I had no idea what it was.

Drake had quite recovered himself by then. Ignoring Cook's outburst, he turned to us. "Now then," he said, solemnly, "I hope that you young ladies feel a bit better about things and I'll let you know if I hear news from the Master again."

As he folded the letter, preparing to put it away in his trouser pocket, Nell slipped from under the eiderdown and walked to where Drake was sitting.

She held out her hand. "Could we please read that for ourselves, Drake?" she asked, politely. But Drake snatched the letter out of reach and rose swiftly to his feet. He picked up his jacket and, slipping it on, became once more the familiar figure I knew.

"I'm sorry, Miss Nell," he said, stiffly. "There's other things in this letter that was meant just for me, and I'm not at liberty to share it with you."

Then he stepped away from Nell and, replacing the chair neatly beside Mrs. Carter's bed, bowed stiffly, wished us all a good night, and left the room, green leather slippers slapping on the wooden floor with each step.

Mrs. Carter reached for the kettle. "I think a nice cup of cocoa for everyone, don't you? Then our Annie, you can help these young ladies back to bed, and, mind, not one word to be said in the morning or any other time."

She cast a long, steady look in our direction and we both nodded our heads in agreement, but I had the feeling that Nell was not satisfied with what Drake had told us.

I hardly remember drinking the strong, sweet cocoa, or slipping with Nell and Annie back down the stairs and into bed. In the morning, I wondered if it had been a dream, but as I climbed out of bed in the grey dawn light, my foot touched a small feather attached to a pink thread from an eiderdown that certainly didn't belong to me.

Later that morning, I managed to give Aunt Abigail the slip and hurried once again up the back stairs. This time, I turned into the schoolroom where Miss Blackly was teaching the twins their multiplication tables and Nell was working on her own at a small side table. Quickly, I asked Miss Blackly for a private word. She paled a little and clasped her hands together.

"Do you have bad news?" she asked as I walked with her to the far side of the room so the others could not hear me.

I shook my head, startled by her question. "No, but I do have a favor to ask of you, Miss Blackly, I need to learn everything I can about Buenos Aires."

She smiled then, looking relieved at my request and gestured to where Nell was sitting. "Why don't you talk to your sister? She's been studying Argentina since your father left."

I looked at her blankly. "Argentina? No, I want to learn about Buenos Aires."

"Buenos Aires is a city in Argentina, which is part of South America," she explained, gently.

I felt foolish and knew that colour had risen in my cheeks. "Well, I need to know all of that, too," I said, defensively.

Miss Blackly continued to look thoughtfully to where Nell was sitting. "I would be glad to teach you what I can," she said, kindly, "but I thought your time was taken with other things."

"Oh, it is!" I agreed quickly, "every minute of the day. I'm sure that Aunt Abigail is looking for me right now, and that's my difficulty. I don't know how to find the time, but it's really important to me."

Miss Blackly tapped her mouth with a slender finger then, after a moment, she smiled. "If you are serious about this, Ada, why don't you come to see me after lights out tonight? I'm something of a night bird and I think that perhaps you are, too." She looked at me quizzically for a moment, and I remembered the flickering candle in the schoolroom the previous night. Perhaps the light had not been left for Iris, after all.

"Just be sure that nobody sees you," she added. "Your aunt might not approve of this, and I need to continue as governess here, at least for now." She looked down at the pretty engagement ring on her finger. "I've not heard from Mr. Atkins, my fiancé, for almost six months," she added in a sudden rush of confidence. "If I don't hear from him soon, I don't know what I shall do." Then she gave a weak smile. "Forgive me, I shouldn't burden you with my problems, Ada, my dear, and I'm sure the Lord will provide." But from the look on her face, I thought that she was more worried than she said.

As the short winter days passed, I continued my daily instructions with Aunt Abigail, but each evening I waited impatiently for the grandfather clock to strike the half hour after eight. As the chimes died away, Aunt Abigail would close her bible or fold away her needle-work and ring the bell to summon the servants for nightly prayers.

Prayers finished promptly at nine o'clock then everyone retired for the night. I waited in my room until I was sure that Aunt Abigail was in bed before slipping up the back stairs to the schoolroom to meet Miss Blackly and learn about the country that seemed to be so impor-tant to both my father and my sister.

Sometimes, as I reached the top of the stairs and crept past the door that led to the servants' quarters, I wondered if Cook and Mrs. Carter were gossiping late in the cozy sitting room at the end of the corridor with Annie drowsing beside them. But I was never invited back, and if Nell was, she didn't say.

CHAPTER 7

Christmas was fast approaching but I was sure that Aunt Abigail would not allow us to keep the season as we had in previous years; indeed, I could not imagine it. How could we celebrate with Mama gone from us and our father in some foreign land that I was still struggling to learn about?

I was correct in my surmise, for my aunt soon made it clear that Christmas was a religious holiday, and that we would be celebrating it as such, no more, no less. The part of me that mourned my absent parents agreed with her, but then I thought of my young sisters and how disappointed they would be not to receive even the small gifts that we had customarily exchanged at this time of year. Finally, I came up with a plan.

One morning when Aunt Abigail was safely in the kitchen having one of her silent battles with Cook, I crept up the back stairs to the schoolroom to talk to Nell. She did not welcome my presence there and at first refused to listen to what I had to say. It was only when Miss Blackly frowned sternly in our direction that I could get Nell to listen to me. "We'll just make small gifts," I explained. "I'll talk to Mrs. Carter. I'm sure she'll help. We can't let Christmas go by without doing something."

Nell glared fiercely at me, hitching her glasses more firmly onto her nose. "I can't do that stuff," she hissed. "You know what my stitching is like, and I can't knit to save my life. What do you want, a long string of crochet? That's about all I can do."

I patted her shoulder. "I'll think of something," I said. "I promise."

Nell gave me a sudden lopsided grin. "Right, you find something and I'll help. Just don't let Aunt Abigail know; she'll never let us do anything."

I rolled my eyes in mock horror. "Don't worry. She'll be the last to know."

Starting two afternoons later when our lessons with Aunt Abigail were over and my aunt had retired for a short rest, my sister and I slipped away to Mama's old sewing room and began to fashion gifts for our sisters.

When Christmas day finally dawned, it fell to Nell and me to dress the twins, for Miss Blackly was not with us. She had been granted reluctant permission to stay with her family for an extra two days so that she might celebrate the Christmas season with them. So Nell and I dressed Iris and Lily that morning with help from Annie, who proved to be adept at buttoning boots onto wriggling feet and plaiting curly blonde hair into neat braids. Nell was always impatient with the twins, and she left as soon as they were dressed, leaving me to look after them. They were eight years old that Christmas, and became very silly when they were away from the firm, calm discipline meted out by Miss Blackly. Since I had become better acquainted with her during our late-night lessons, I had come to admire our governess a great deal.

We walked to chapel that day and I exulted in the bright, clear morning air. There was frost on the puddles, but we did not often look for snow at Christmas in this part of the country.

The Minister kept the traditional Christmas service short, welcoming the birth of the Christ Child in simple language and reading to us from the Gospel of Saint Luke. As the familiar story unfolded, I thought of our own little family, so broken in one short year, and longed with a heart that ached for the feel of my mother's loving hand or the sound of my father's voice.

Family tradition had it that Christmas dinner was served at one o'clock in the afternoon, and even on this difficult day with Papa away and Aunt Abigail in charge, Cook had managed to do us proud. As usual, we started with soup—a rich broth made from goose giblets with delicately browned rings of onion and thinly sliced carrots floating in its fragrant depths. Then Drake entered carrying the great goose itself, lying golden-brown on a huge oval platter surrounded by small roasted turnips and parsnips.

Behind him came Mrs. Carter and Annie bearing tureens of steaming vegetables. The goose, fragrant with sage and onion seasoning, was filled with delicious sausage meat and goose liver stuffing, and the gravy was thick and rich. Cook brought up the rear with a huge jug of blackcurrant cordial made from her own special recipe.

As the delicious fare was set down on the table before us, I saw Aunt Abigail's mouth go thin with disapproval. "Let us not commit the sin of gluttony," she said, sharply. "There are many who go hungry today; it is well to remember them."

I looked glumly at my plate and tried not to remember other Christmases, when the room had been filled with laughter and the food was meant to be enjoyed to the fullest. As usual, Aunt Abigail seemed unaware of the pall she had placed upon the day. She ate sparingly herself, and admonished Lily when she asked for more goose.

The pudding that followed was a traditional Christmas pudding, dark and moist and filled with all manner of dried fruits along with some mysterious ingredients that Cook kept strictly to herself, pressing her lips firmly together and shaking her head when questioned as to its secrets.

In past years, at Mama's insistence, the whole thing had been doused with brandy and set alight, to the squealing delight of all of us children. This year, however, Aunt Abigail had forbidden the use of brandy, so the pudding was served with a lemon sauce. But I found myself wondering, as I bit happily into a steaming mouthful of pudding, exactly what had been in the tall, dark bottle that Cook had taken so secretly from its hiding place at the back of the pantry in September, when she was making both the Christmas pudding and the white iced Christmas cake with its thick layer of marzipan.

Traditionally, after the pudding was finished, the table would be cleared and re-set with bowls of nuts and sweetmeats. Often in the past, there had been wonderful delicacies that Papa had brought home from his travels: sweet dates that came in long thin boxes with each sticky fruit still attached to its stalk; or figs, fat and brown and filled with a thousand tiny seeds that stuck in the teeth and crunched deliciously long after the fruit itself was gone. This year, when Drake set out bowls, they contained only nuts. Aunt Abigail did not allow children to eat sweets.

It was at this time too, that the family had always exchanged gifts. Accordingly, Nell and I asked to be excused from the table and Aunt Abigail, after a brief disapproving pause, nodded, reluctantly. Quickly, we retrieved the small parcels that we had placed in the drawing room before dinner and returned with them.

The twins were squirming in their seats with excitement as Nell and I distributed the gifts we had worked so hard to make, but Aunt Abigail showed no sign of interest or pleasure.

When we had reseated ourselves, my aunt placed one thin hand on the small pile of presents before her. "Thank you for these," she said, "but I would remind you that gifts are to be given freely with no expectation of return. I do not give Christmas gifts, for the Lord gives us many blessings throughout the year. Now kindly stand, while we praise the Lord for his bounty."

In silence, we all rose to pray, and when we were finished, Aunt Abigail left the room, her gifts held loosely in her hands: an embroidered sampler from me and bookmarks from the twins. I do not know if Nell gave my aunt anything. At the door, she turned. "Since today is Christmas Day, you may spend one hour in quiet contemplation. I will expect all of you in the drawing room at precisely three o'clock for our usual bible reading."

Her eyes swept the room, taking us all in, Nell, looking mutinous; the twins, hot, tired and rather bewildered; and, finally, Aunt Abigail looked at me. As I gazed back at her, for a brief moment I felt a sense of overwhelming pity. Sadly, I turned my head away and Aunt Abigail closed the door silently behind her.

The twins were delighted with the stuffed dolls that Nell and I had made between us. They were fashioned from a pair of white stockings and were not the prettiest of things. They had buttons for eyes and Nell's strands of crocheted wool for hair. Mrs. Carter had kindly provided fabric to make clothes for each doll, and Cook had given us feathers to stuff them with. Given Nell's difficulty with sewing, I felt that stuffing the dolls was the safest task for her. Even so, I suspect that Mrs. Carter had a hand in the correct distribution of feathers into heads, bodies, and limbs.

The twins had made bookmarks for us, and my sister and I also exchanged small gifts, made in the secrecy of our own rooms. Before she left, Miss Blackly had given gifts to both Nell and me. For Nell, a book by a woman author who, the governess confessed, was one of her favourites. Nell had bent her head and fumbled with her glasses when she received this gift, a sure sign that she was fighting back tears. Then she, in turn, had handed over a somewhat smudged sheet of paper.

Miss Blackly looked at it curiously then her face lit up in a broad smile. "Well done, Nell," she said proudly. "This is a wonderful gift. Your first Spanish translation! I will check it carefully for errors," she added teasingly, giving Nell a quick hug.

Then she turned to me with a package in her hand. "Ada," she said, "this is for you." I held back, crimson with shame. I had not even thought to give dear Miss Blackly a gift.

Seeing my discomfort, she smiled. "My dear girl, the times you have spent up here learning and expanding your mind when you could have been sleeping, are all the gifts I will ever need from you." At that moment, I loved her dearly.

Nell, who did not know of my nightly excursions to the school-room, looked at me quizzically, but I ignored her.

Miss Blackly thrust the package into my hands. "Here," she said. "Use it well."

Reluctantly, I opened the small parcel. It contained a book, beauti-fully bound in leather. I opened it carefully. "English/Spanish Diction-ary" was engraved in gold on the cover.

"It belonged to my brother," she said. "He died overseas. I thought that he would have liked you to have it." I thanked her profusely, but wondered to myself at her choice of Spanish rather than French. She knew that I had no knowledge at all of Spanish, and that my French could most certainly use improvement.

I remember now with some distress that I did not think of little Edith that Christmas Day, nor had it occurred to me to make her a gift.

Later that Christmas night as I lay in bed, I wondered about the coming day. Papa had been insistent about the traditions of Boxing Day. It was the one day in the year that we fended almost entirely for ourselves. Early in the morning, my parents would present each of the servants with a Boxing Day gift, usually in the form of money. The rest of the day was theirs to do with as they liked. I doubted that Aunt Abigail would carry on this tradition, but I had not counted on my father's forethought in this matter.

On December 26, Aunt Abigail summoned us to the drawing room after breakfast. Everyone was included: Miss Blackly, who had returned late the night before; Bessie, with little Edith in one arm and a reluctant Sam lagging behind; Ned, who came shuffling in, looking uncomfortable in stocking feet, for he was not allowed to wear his boots in the house, and then the rest of the servants. They all filed in together with a terrified kitchen maid tagging along at the end.

Aunt Abigail stood by the mantle as my father used to do, waiting until everyone was standing uncomfortably before her. She was holding a small pile of envelopes in her gloved hands.

"I have here your Boxing Day gifts from the Master," she said, her tone level. "He also instructed me to allow you to have the remainder of the day off to use as you please. I trust you will use it wisely."

Then, straight-backed, she walked down the line, starting with Miss Blackly and ending at the kitchen maid who looked more and more like a scared rabbit as Aunt Abigail approached. She handed each person a stiff white envelope. As she returned to her place before the mantle, she made a small dismissive gesture with her hand. "You will return to your duties as usual by tomorrow morning," she said, coldly.

As all the servants were filing silently out, Aunt Abigail stopped Bessie. "Give the child to me," she said, reaching for Edith, who had been chewing contentedly on an escaped strand of Bessie's curly red hair. But as my aunt attempted to remove her, Edith screwed up her small face and emitted a cry that rapidly escalated into a howling scream. Bessie stood her ground, holding firmly onto the screaming child.

"If you please, Missus," she said, "she's still on the breast, and needs to be fed shortly, so I reckon as how I have to keep her with me." There was a cheeky assurance about Bessie that acted as a red flag to Aunt Abigail and, for the first time since I had met her, my aunt appeared to lose her temper.

A small patch of colour appeared on each of her cheeks as she let go of Edith and stepped back. Her eyes narrowed, and she spoke softly. "The child is now six months old, and it is early days, but you will see to it that you start weaning her. I will personally supervise this from now on. You may go."

Bessie gave a smirk and hitched Edith into her arms more securely. With Sam clutching at her skirts, she dropped a small, somehow insolent curtsey and turned to go.

As she reached the door, Aunt Abigail spoke again. "Bessie since you are still so essential to my niece's well-being, you may not have the rest of the day off. You will remain as usual in the nursery."

Turning her head, Bessie gave my aunt a glance of pure hatred before closing the door behind her.

Aunt Abigail turned to us. We had grouped ourselves by the window during this uncomfortable ceremony with the servants, and while I watched, I found myself remembering other years, when we had all run laughing with Mama into the kitchen, and demanded that everyone stop what they were doing and come with us to the drawing room; and how all the servants had pretended great surprise at this request, and followed us obediently to where Papa was waiting.

And then came the distribution of envelopes and small gifts, amidst much laughter and good cheer. The servants would then troop off to their own celebration and it was a strict rule that we should not, under any circumstances, disturb them.

For all that, large trays of cold goose, fresh bread, cheese, and fruit still appeared as if by magic in the dining room at our usual mealtimes. I hoped that would still happen today.

As the door closed behind Bessie, Aunt Abigail moved to the large sideboard that graced one end of the drawing room. She opened a drawer and removed four small packages. "Your father left instructions for you to be given these," she said coldly, as she handed each of us a package.

A voice from the shadows by the door startled me. I had not realized that Miss Blackly was still in the room. Now she stepped forward. "Excuse me, Miss Baldwin," she said, "but since I have already celebrated Christmas with my family, I'm sure that you wish me to carry out my usual duties today."

Aunt Abigail smiled thinly. "Yes, indeed, Miss Blackly, kindly take Iris and Lily to the schoolroom and since we are without the benefit of the other servants today, you may join us for lunch at one o'clock. We will then spend the afternoon outside, walking together." My aunt included Nell and me in her glance as she continued. "You will all employ yourselves usefully by reading the good book for the remainder of the morning; I will question you on it as we walk. Chapter nineteen, Book of Kings."

Miss Blackly and the twins were waiting for us at the bottom of the stairs. "I thought that you might like to come up to the schoolroom," Miss Blackly said with a smile. "Annie set a fire in there earlier, and it might be pleasant to open the gifts from your father together."

Gladly, we followed Miss Blackly to the schoolroom and were soon seated in front of the fire with cups of hot cocoa that Miss Blackly had poured from a large covered jug.

When we had finished our drinks, Nell gave me an impatient poke with her elbow. "Go on, Ada," she said. "Open your present first. You're the oldest."

I looked at the package on my lap. It was wrapped in blue paper and tied with a narrow white ribbon. Carefully I untied the ribbon and pulled aside the paper to reveal a velvet box. With the utmost care I opened it and, inside, nestled on a cushion of cream satin, was a necklace. It was beautiful; each large, silvery blue bead was enclosed at either end with metal filigree, with small matching beads linking them. The whole thing was strung together to form an exquisitely delicate necklace. The last time I had seen it, it was clasped around my mother's slender throat.

Tucked under the clasp was a piece of folded paper. Tears sprang to my eyes as I opened the note and read the message written in my father's hand.

"*My Dearest Ada,*" he wrote. "*Mama would have wanted you to have this. Treasure it always.*"

Memories of my mother flooded into my mind, and for a moment, I was quite overwhelmed with the pain of missing her. I wondered miserably if it would ever stop hurting.

When I had recovered my composure a little, I looked up to see Nell inspecting a thick silver bracelet engraved with flowers. I had often seen my mother wearing it. On the inside of the bracelet, I knew, was a small inscription that read, *"To E.B. with everlasting love."* It was not dated. The bracelet had come in a small, deep-red velvet bag with a black silk drawstring. Nell clasped the bracelet around her thin wrist and hugged the velvet bag close.

The twins were not forgotten. There was an ivory brooch for each of them made in the form of their namesake flower.

Later when we had cleared away the wrapping paper and further admired our gifts, Miss Blackly read us the required chapter from the bible. As I listened to her voice, I thought that she reminded me a little of Mama, or maybe it was just a trick of the firelight playing on her face and the way she read the ancient words, as if they were fresh and new and had deep meaning for her.

After lunch, which Cook had indeed provided for us, we set out upon our walk. The afternoon started out well enough. The twins ran laughing ahead of us and even Aunt Abigail relented somewhat and did not ask many questions, once she knew that we had studied the scriptures as she had directed.

When we were some distance from the house, an icy wind sprang up, and thick clouds obliterated the thin winter sun. Within minutes, sleet was lashing at our faces and we were forced to return home as quickly as we could. By the time we reached the shelter of the house, we were all soaked through, and I was thoroughly chilled.

I felt most unwell that evening. My throat was sore and it was painful to swallow. I longed to ask Cook for her hot lemon and honey drink, but I could not disturb her today.

As the evening progressed, I developed a headache that steadily worsened, and by the time evening prayers were over, prayers that had not included the servants, I was very glad to climb the stairs to my room. Here, a surprise awaited me. As I entered my bedroom, I saw several packages lying on my bed. There was a warm knitted muffler from Cook, some beautifully hand-stitched slippers in a rich blue from

Mrs. Carter, and a length of pale yellow ribbon from Annie. Touched by their kindness, I blew my reddened nose vigorously and decided to go at once to thank all these dear people and perhaps get something to help my headache. I think that my head was already addled with fever, for I had quite forgotten what day it was. It was Boxing Day, the one day in the year that belonged to the servants. So I ran unheeding down the stairs and burst into the kitchen.

As I entered the room I stopped, shocked by the sight that met my eyes. Cook was sitting with her feet up on the fender, her skirts hitched almost to her knees, displaying a great deal of plump ankle. She was clapping her hands enthusiastically, her face rosy and smiling, as she watched Mrs. Carter and Drake, splendid in his emerald green slippers, clutched together and dancing a spirited jig. Drake giggled happily as they twirled around the table which was piled high with the remnants of what looked to have been a very fine meal indeed. There were several bottles and jugs on the table and even I knew that they contained something much stronger than Cook's blackcurrant cordial.

Annie was seated next to a young man I had never seen before. He was playing a lively dance tune on a fiddle, and there were other people in the room that I did not recognize, including a large woman in a plaid shawl with a thin child perched on her knee and, in a corner sitting on another stranger's lap, Bessie, in a state of some disarray. Of Sam and my baby sister there was no sign. As I watched, Bessie wound her arms about the man's neck and kissed him greedily. As she did so, memories of the scene in the stable flooded into my mind.

Mrs. Carter was the first to notice me standing silently in the doorway, and she dragged the still giggling Drake to a stumbling halt. He hiccupped a little and swayed where he stood. The others gradually became aware that something was wrong and, as the music trailed to a stop, all eyes eventually turned to me

By this time, I was shaking with anger as I pointed an accusing finger at Bessie. "Where is my sister?" I demanded. "Where have you left her you Hussy?" The word came unbidden to my lips, a term I had once heard Cook use in regard to a kitchen maid who had found herself in trouble.

At my words, Bessie scrambled off the man's lap, not even bothering to adjust the laces of her bodice, her face flushed with indignation. "Don't you be calling me names, young Miss," she cried angrily. "I ain't done nothin' wrong. If that old auntie of yours 'adn't stopped all me fun, I could've had me supper down 'ere with the others. But, no, I 'as to wait upstairs 'til Miss Lucy Blackly comes back, then beg on me knees just about, so she'll look after little' un for a bit. And as for my Sam, well that's none of your bloody business, Miss Busy Body now, is it!?"

I took a painful breath, ready to pour more scorn on Bessie's defiant head, when Mrs. Carter intervened. "That's enough, Bessie!" she said sternly, before turning to me.

"Miss Ada," her tone was one I had not heard since I was quite little. "I'm sorry you came in here tonight. It's just the one day in the year we have to ourselves, and sometimes people take a drop too much. Now, is there something I can do for you?"

I shook my head miserably, completely forgetting my reason for being there. Silently, I turned and went slowly back up to my room wondering how I could face any of the servants again. The pain in my head had worsened and my breath was ragged as I stumbled into bed and gratefully closed my eyes.

When I awoke after a fretful night, I was burning up with fever and had great difficulty breathing. It was quite some time before I saw Bessie or Cook, or indeed any of the servants besides Annie and Mrs. Carter, again.

CHAPTER 8

I remember little of my illness, though I do recall late one night struggling out of a restless sleep to find Aunt Abigail, dressed in her nightgown, with a white nightcap on her head, all wrapped about with a blanket, reading beside my bed.

As I opened my eyes, she nodded and smiled a small, tight smile. "I see you are coming back to us," she said, glancing down at the bible in her lap. "I have prayed for you, child; I would not have my brother lose another loved one."

I tried to smile back, but my eyelids were heavy and I must have slept again, because when I awoke, it was morning and Annie was lighting the fire in the grate, and I thought that I could perhaps manage a bowl of warm bread and milk.

One day early in my convalescence, Mrs. Carter and Annie helped me out of bed and into a high-backed chair, tucking soft blankets about me and placing a warm stone water bottle at my feet. As I lay back against the pillows and closed my eyes, ready to enjoy the weak January sunshine that crept into my bedroom in the afternoons, I heard a soft knock at the door and opened my eyes to see Nell peering hopefully at me.

"Do you feel strong enough for a visitor?" she asked. "Please say yes! Aunt Abigail said that I might visit you for a short while instead of practicing my stem stitch. Please, Ada!"

I smiled a welcome at my sister, glad of company that was not intent on curing me. Nell came into the room on light feet and, curling herself onto one of the cushions in the window seat, beamed owlishly at me through her glasses.

"You gave us all quite a scare," she said. "Dr. Wainwright thought you had bronchitis and pneumonia! Aunt Abigail looked all grim and said that you are too much like Mama for your own good." She leaned forward, inspecting my face. "Are you really feeling better?"

I nodded and stretched. "Truthfully, Nell, I'm bored," I admitted. "Tell me what's happening in the house."

Nell settled back against the curtains. "You do know that Aunt Abigail and Cook had a most fearful row, don't you?" she asked casually.

My eyes widened in surprise. "No! Whatever happened?" I leaned forward in my eagerness to hear the story.

My sister smiled happily. She was blessed with a gift for mimicry and she now entered with great enthusiasm into all the roles required to tell the story in full and glorious detail. She soon had me giggling helplessly at her antics, tears running down my cheeks and my handkerchief stuffed into my mouth to stifle the sound. We both knew that sounds of laughter coming from my room would be thoroughly disapproved of by any passing adult. She had to stop once, because I was taken with a fit of coughing that left me pale and shaken and Nell remorsefully on her knees beside me, patting my hand and shushing me with anxious fingers against my cheek.

I marked the real beginning of my recovery from that afternoon with Nell. Each day I felt stronger, though it still took little to leave me breathless and exhausted. I sat by the fire in the drawing room in the afternoons as Aunt Abigail read to me from the bible. She read from the New Testament and I enjoyed the familiar stories from the gospel of John, though I confess that I often let my mind wander.

As I watched the rain falling drearily on the black branches of the trees that lined the edge of the driveway, I would sometimes think of the lonely grave on the hillside where my mother lay and wonder if anyone ever tended it. I was saddened to think that not once since my mother's death had I visited her grave, and I vowed to do so as soon as I could.

Sometimes at night, when I lay sleepless, I would listen to the wind gusting about the house, rattling at the shutters and poking into corners as if its bony fingers were seeking entry, and I would wonder if ghosts really walked the earth, and if my poor Mama was one of them.

One morning when I was alone with Mrs. Carter, I tried to apologize for my behaviour on Boxing Day, but she shushed me and fluffed my pillows for the third time. I wore the blue slippers she had given me and asked a delighted Annie to tie back my hair with the pale yellow ribbon that had been her gift.

The end of February was approaching, and with it, my sixteenth birthday. Nell had celebrated her birthday in September, but the day had been marked with nothing more than a cake that Cook had baked especially. Aunt Abigail had disapproved of even this and had lectured us on the sins of greed and avarice.

When the morning of February 22 dawned, I was not expecting anything unusual. I was now able to make my way downstairs in the mornings, though I still needed a little help to dress and braid my hair. Annie had come quietly into the room at dawn to light the fire that Aunt Abigail still allowed me to have. Unknown to my aunt, Nell often crept into my room to enjoy its warmth on these cold winter mornings, holding her petticoats to the flames until they steamed with dampness.

As I lay in bed enjoying the last few moments of comfort, there was a knock on the door and Mrs. Carter, Miss Blackly, the twins, and a triumphantly grinning Nell all crowded into my room.

"Happy birthday, Ada," chorused the twins, holding out tiny bunches of snowdrops still damp from the garden.

"Yes, happy birthday, indeed, my dear girl," echoed Miss Blackly, dropping a quick kiss on my head.

"Come along, then," said Mrs. Carter briskly to the twins, "back upstairs with you. I'll have them down in good time for breakfast, Miss, don't you fret," she added over her shoulder to Miss Blackly, as she bustled the twins out of the door.

Nell turned to me, pulling at my blankets. "Come on, Ada," she said impatiently. "Get up! It's your birthday!"

As I climbed a little unsteadily out of bed, Miss Blackly smiled. "We'll give you a few minutes to wash and then we'll be back," she promised. Then she and Nell exchanged conspiratorial grins and left.

I had barely finished my ablutions and was just pulling on my petticoat when Nell put her head round the door.

"Ready?" she asked, and not waiting for an answer, marched in. Behind her came Miss Blackly carrying a bundle of clothes.

As I watched, she shook out folds of midnight blue fabric. It was, I saw, a skirt in a style much like the one she wore herself, with a small gathering of extra fabric at the back that trailed most elegantly when she walked. With it was a matching bodice with a high neck and long sleeves.

"It's not new, Ada," said Miss Blackly. "It was my sister's, but Suzanne is married now, and living in London, and she has no need of it. I thought it might fit you, and it would certainly look very well with your chestnut hair."

I smiled as I thanked her, pleased with her description. I had always thought my hair a very dull brown next to Nell's thick black tresses and the twin's pretty blonde curls.

Excitedly, I reached for the skirt and pulled it on and then, with help from Miss Blackly, struggled into the bodice. They were both a little big for me, but after some careful pinning, they fit well enough.

Nell had watched this whole performance critically from the window seat, but now she jumped up. "I'm going down," she announced. "For once, I'll be early. I wouldn't miss your big entrance for the world, Ada." She grinned mischievously as she slipped out of the door.

"Now for your hair," said Miss Blackly, calmly ignoring Nell. From her pocket, she produced a box containing hairpins. Then, seating me in front of my dressing table, she twisted my hair into two becoming rolls, pinning them up securely on either side of my face.

I stared at myself in the mirror. I was still thin from my illness, and my eyes were a little shadowed, but I could see that the face that looked back at me in the mirror had changed, and with a small shock of realization, I knew that I looked remarkably like my dead mother.

I was nervous walking into the dining room where Aunt Abigail was waiting for us to join her for breakfast. Miss Blackly squeezed my arm just before we entered. "Raise your chin dear, and keep your back straight," she murmured.

I heard Aunt Abigail's sharp intake of breath as I entered the room, and saw the moment of shock reflected in her dark eyes. She drew her lips into a thin line. "What is the meaning of this, Ada?" she asked sharply.

Miss Blackly came to stand beside me. "Why, Miss Baldwin," she said calmly, "today is Ada's sixteenth birthday, so we have put her hair up and, since she has been so sick, I gave her a little assistance today. I also felt sure that you would not object to her wearing the gown I gave her. It is not new, but was a gift from my sister, whose husband, as you undoubtedly know, is a close friend of Mr. Baldwin. I'm sure that when Mr. Baldwin returns, he will be delighted with the excellent changes that he sees in Ada."

Aunt Abigail looked at Miss Blackly in silence for a few moments then bowed slightly, as if conceding defeat, before clasping her hands in readiness to pray. But after breakfast when Miss Blackly had gone, taking the twins with her, my aunt stayed me with her hand.

"You may remain in your birthday finery for today, Ada," she said thinly," but you will still carry out those household duties I have assigned to you."

In spite of Aunt Abigail, my sixteenth birthday continued to be a day full of surprises, most of them good. Shortly after breakfast, a package was delivered from Wimborne. Inside was an exquisitely fashioned muff made from soft grey rabbit fur, and a matching hat that would sit perfectly on my newly raised hair. I knew in an instant just who had sent it, and felt very guilty, for I had not written so much as a note to my friend Angela, though she had sent several letters to me over the last few months. I vowed to thank her and to send her a long letter very soon.

The final gift I got that day was quite unexpected and all the better for being so. A letter arrived with the midday post. It was addressed to "Miss Ada Baldwin," and it was postmarked Buenos Aires. This time, there was no mistaking for whom it was meant.

I snatched the big white envelope from the hall table and hurried to my room with it, just as the gong sounded for lunch. Pink with frustration but not daring to be late, I tucked the letter under my pillow and made my way downstairs. During the meal, I was in a fever of impatience to read Papa's letter, and, as a consequence, ate almost nothing.

When the meal was over, Aunt Abigail looked at me sharply and told me that I was to spend the afternoon resting, as it was evident that I was not yet recovered from my illness.

Barely concealing my delight, I returned to my room and retrieved the letter from its hiding place. Hurrying over to the window seat, I settled myself on the cushions and, as I did so, there was a tap on the door.

It was Nell, looking rather pale and anxious. "Come in," I said, "come and read this with me. It's a letter from Papa."

Instantly she was at my side, almost tripping over a stool in her haste as I opened the long white envelope and pulled out the single sheet of paper. My eyes filled with tears at the sight of my father's handwriting and, feeling suddenly weak and shaky, I thrust the letter at Nell. "Will you read it to me?" I asked, leaning back against the pillows.

Nell grabbed the paper eagerly from my fingers and began to read in her clear voice:

"Buenos Aires
January 14, 1885

My Dearest Ada:

Your Aunt Abigail writes to me that you are all well, and I trust that this letter finds you in continuing good health. I hope that you celebrated Christmas in a joyful manner and that you remember to thank the Lord, who in His mercy has given you so many blessings.

I am well, and my business here is progressing according to my plans. I pray that you stay obedient to your dear aunt, and that you remain a good example to your younger sisters. I trust, furthermore, that you are giving to your sister Edith the love and affection that she would otherwise have gained from your dear mother, who rests now in the bosom of the Lord.

I remain your loving father.
Robert Baldwin."

Nell looked at the letter in her hand for a long time before placing it carefully beside me. "He has sent me nothing," she said at last. "I have written two letters, and Drake assured me that both of them were sent with the other correspondence. I can't believe that Papa included nothing for me!"

Then my sister rose to her feet and looked down at me. "How lucky you are Ada that Papa writes to you. But perhaps you should spend more time in the nursery. You wouldn't want him to be disappointed in you!" With that, she turned on her heel and made for the door.

I stared after my sister for a few seconds then I picked up the letter and read it through slowly. It was just good fortune that it had arrived on my birthday, but I understood why Nell had felt so slighted. I held the letter close for a moment, reveling in the knowledge that Papa had written this just for me.

I was tempted to stay where I was and rest for a while, but my conscience had been stirred by Papa's words, so instead I made my reluctant way to the nursery. Nell was right. I should spend time with my little sister. Papa would certainly not be pleased to come home and find that the child did not even know me.

I had not been to the top of the house since Boxing Day, and I was apprehensive as I climbed the back stairs. When I entered the school-room, I was relieved to see that it was empty; Miss Blackly and the twins were probably taking their daily walk.

The door leading to the nursery was closed, so I crossed the school-room, opened the door, and stepped inside. Bessie was sitting on the floor with her back to me. On one side of her, Sam was lying on his tummy, playing a fierce game of tin soldiers, and in front of her lying on a woolen blanket was little Edith. My sister was completely naked, and as she lay there, she kicked her legs in the air and gurgled happily.

"Didn't think you was coming today, Miss; thought old auntie got you again," said Bessie, not looking up, but continuing to dangle a ball of brightly coloured wool just out of Edith's reach.

Something of my stillness must have communicated itself to Bessie, for after a moment, she looked round. In an instant, her face changed from smiling welcome to horrified discomfort. She scrambled hastily to her feet, and I remembered that I was wearing my new gown and that my hair was no longer dressed in a childish braid. Then I moved into the room, and in that instant, she knew me.

Colour washed up over her freckled skin and she bobbed a reluctant curtsey. "Pardon me, Miss," she said. "I thought as you was Miss Nell. She often comes in to see little Edie here."

I gazed in horror at my small sister lying naked on a blanket like some peasant brat and drew myself up, ready to remonstrate with Bessie, but as I did so, Lily and Iris burst into the schoolroom.

"Ada, you shouldn't be here," screamed Lily, jumping up and down with excitement. "Cook says your cake isn't coming 'til teatime and it's a big surprise." She broke off, glancing quickly at Bessie and me, eyes suddenly big. Iris moved forward silently and took her sister's hand. Miss Blackly followed them into the schoolroom, her cheeks glowing from the cold air, and her hair escaping in curly tendrils. She took in the scene at a glance, and moved swiftly to where I was standing.

She, too, looked down at the blanket where Edith was still kicking happily. "Goodness, Bessie, you'd better put some clothes on little Edie before she catches cold with this door wide open," she said cheerfully.

Then she took my arm. "Come Ada my dear, come sit with me for a few minutes while Bessie dresses Edith," and as the nursery door closed behind me, I allowed myself to be drawn towards the fire.

"Miss Blackly," I started, ready to protest Edith's nakedness, but the governess gave me a quick smile.

"Please call me Lucy," she said. You're a young lady now, and I'm really not so much older than you!"

Indignation momentarily forgotten, I felt myself blush with pleasure. "Thank you, I stammered. "But..." I gestured towards the closed nursery door. "Did you see? Edith had no clothes on!"

Lucy—how quickly I got used to calling her that—put a comforting hand on my arm. "My dear girl, Bessie is just allowing Edith to stretch her little limbs and grow strong. My sister in London tells me that some of the very best physicians in town now advocate this for the healthy development of babies. The odd thing," she continued, "is that Bessie seems to think it is the most natural thing in the world." She leaned forward and spoke just above a whisper, very much in the way of one adult sharing with another. "I sometimes think that the lower classes know better than we do in some matters! There now," she added with a bright smile, leaning back in her chair, "Let's see if Edie is ready for you, and later, as I'm sure Lily has already told you, Cook will be up with your surprise birthday cake." She winked solemnly and I found myself smiling back, and feeling very grown up indeed.

That was the first day I ever heard my sister called Edie, and it was also the start of my daily visits to see her, though Bessie and I were never comfortable with each other.

CHAPTER 9

I t was the middle of March before I went outdoors, and even then, I didn't venture far. But as the weather warmed, I dared to walk a little longer each day, inspecting the kitchen garden and even looking at my mother's rose bushes that already showed small green shoots at their roots.

One fine day at the end of the month, Aunt Abigail announced at lunch that she had ordered the carriage and would take a trip into Wimborne. This was most unusual and Nell, always more daring than I, ventured a question.

"Could we accompany you, Aunt Abigail?" she asked boldly.

My aunt smiled thinly. "Yes, Nell, you may come. I will have some packages for you to carry. But not Ada," she added looking across at me. "You are not yet sufficiently recovered."

I was very disappointed but I knew enough of my aunt's temperament not to argue, so I retired to my room after lunch and watched wistfully as the carriage set off down the driveway at a brisk pace, with Ned at the reins. As I watched from behind my curtains, I saw an arm come through the side window of the carriage and wave mockingly. Sometimes, I really hated Nell.

A little later, I saw Bessie pushing the big perambulator that held both Edie and Sam. The twins and Lucy were accompanying them and I watched as they set off in the direction of the village. Feeling very alone, I walked quietly down the stairs, thinking that perhaps I could spend a little time with Cook or Mrs. Carter, though I knew quite well that this was the time of day when they were often about their own business.

As I reached the bottom of the stairs, I noticed that in her haste to leave, Nell had left the door to the vestibule open. And as I approached it, an idea began to form in my mind. This would be a perfect time for me to investigate the conservatory. I would see if the young vegetables were growing as they ought to be. They would be ready for planting out soon if Ned had done his job well.

Stepping into the chilly vestibule, I turned and opened the door leading to the conservatory. Instantly, a wall of damp hot air hit me. I stopped for a few moments, allowing myself to get accustomed to the sudden heat. The big room was quiet and warm as I closed the door behind me, and the soft hiss of the coal stove in one corner made a comforting sound. The fountains kept the air constantly moist and, as I walked slowly down one side of the room, I saw rows of young spring seedlings already growing in their trays. In the centre were the huge palms that I remembered from last year. They had wintered well and their fronds swayed languorously in a breeze that wafted from somewhere far overhead. I reached the end of the conservatory and passed the battered door that led to Nell's old hiding place, but it had not been disturbed for a while. There was a dusty spider web that stretched from the doorknob to one of the flowerpots and all around was an air of neglect.

As I turned to go down the other side of the conservatory, I gave an involuntary gasp. On these shelves, plants grew in riotous abundance. There were orchids of all shapes and sizes, flowers of deepest purple with strange green markings, and pale yellow blooms with splashes of scarlet deep inside looking for all-the-world like blood. Walking slowly towards them, I bent to inspect a particularly beautiful bloom, when I became aware that I was being watched. I spun around and saw Ned leaning against the wall of the conservatory. He had a gardening fork in one hand and there was mud on his boots, so he must have come in through the outside door, and the hiss of the stove and the sound of water from the fountains had covered the sound of his entrance.

"Well now, Miss," he said as I turned. "I never seen you in 'ere before. Is Miss Nell sickly then? You tell 'er I'll take care of them blooms if she is."

I shook my head. "No," I blurted out. "She's quite well. I'm just looking." I was discomfited by his presence and wished that he would leave, but Ned nodded his head sagely.

"'Tis a fine crop this year. I reckon as Miss Nell got the Missus' green thumb." He leaned casually on his fork, watching me. I smiled nervously and then with a final glance at the orchids, turned and hurried away, conscious of his eyes following me.

That my sister had been caring for my mother's orchids throughout the winter months should not have surprised me, and as I walked upstairs to my room I thought about Nell. I loved my sister dearly, but she was an enigma to me. She seemed to do so many things effortlessly. She was clever and funny and it was not out of character for her to be tending Mama's flowers. But on the other hand, Nell was untidy, disorganized, and lazy. She would do almost anything to get out of chores that she disliked and she never paid the slightest attention to her appearance. Aunt Abigail had punished her more than once for this. Her hair seemed always in disarray, her boots were often left undone, and she frequently left smudges on her face as she pushed at her spectacles with ink-stained fingers. For all that I knew that she had a soft heart carefully hidden under a prickly exterior.

Once in my room, I stood before the mirror and took a long look at my own reflection. I saw with satisfaction that I really was quite pretty. Since I had put my hair up, I looked very grown up and my waist was satisfyingly slim. I was not yet wearing a corset, though dear Lucy had told me that I should certainly consider doing so very soon. I sighed as I turned from the mirror and flopped onto my bed. Being grown up was much more complicated than I had expected, and I wasn't at all sure that I really liked it.

Aunt Abigail and Nell arrived some time later that afternoon, with several packages containing bibles, purchased by Aunt Abigail for the people in the village, whom she suspected of being less than God-fearing.

I was kept busy for the next little while as Aunt Abigail seemed filled with a desire to spring clean the whole house. Surprisingly, Mrs. Carter and Annie did not complain.

"Same as every year, Miss," said Annie one morning. "We all does it, even the birds. Look at them, building nests and all." She waved her feather duster in the general direction of the window, making me sneeze. I didn't answer, but continued to remove piles of summer bedding from the upstairs linen closet, readying them for airing on the clothes lines. I was thoroughly cross and out of sorts by the time I was finished.

Much as I enjoyed wearing my hair up, no matter how hard I tried, by the middle of the day, small wisps were straggling about my face and I didn't dare to face Aunt Abigail in such a state. I decided that tomorrow I would have to seek out more hairpins from Lucy.

The next day very early, I climbed the back stairs to the upper floor with my hair still down about my shoulders. As I entered the school-room, I could hear the twins' squealing protests as they were readied for the day. Lucy was standing quite still, and she looked flushed and a little angry. She turned as I came in and, for once, did not greet me with a smile.

"Good morning, Ada," she said grimly and gestured to the twins. "As you can see, these young ladies are choosing to be difficult this morning. There will be no afternoon walk for them today."

Instantly, the twins were at her side, raising pleading faces and pulling at her arms. "No, girls, I'm sorry," she said firmly. "You have made such a fuss that your sister has come up to see what was causing so much noise. I hope that your Aunt Abigail is not also on her way up." She looked at me meaningfully.

I shook my head. "No, not yet," I answered, careful to keep my voice grave. "I thought I should come up here before she did."

The twins immediately looked terrified, and Lily allowed Lucy to start brushing and braiding her hair without further protest, while Iris stood anxiously next to her, stroking Lucy's skirt with a hand that trembled a little.

While Lucy worked, I explained the dilemma of my own hair and she smiled at me briefly. "Of course, my dear," she said. "I have been meaning to give you some combs I no longer use, I'll get them presently." With a final twist of the ribbon at the end of Lily's braid, she gave the child a little push.

"Now," she said sternly, pointing to the large padded bench that was situated by the door. "You are both to sit there and wait for my return." Then she turned and walked into her room and closed the door; she did not invite me to join her.

The twins sat quietly, gazing owlishly at me until I found myself fidgeting uncomfortably. Finally, when I could stand it no longer, I turned away and looked into the schoolroom. It was still in shadow and the nursery door on the other side of the room was closed.

Ignoring the twins' stares, I walked briskly across the schoolroom and opened the door, determined to say good morning to little Edie. She was ten months old now and had managed to capture my heart in a way that I had never thought possible. I especially loved to watch her at bath time, though of late when I arrived for the evening ritual, Bessie would give a sly smile. "Not tonight, Miss. I bathed the little mite this morning," she would say. Now I would catch Bessie unawares, and spend a few moments watching Edie splashing and playing in her bathtub.

As I stood in the doorway of the nursery I saw Edie sitting up in her cot; her hair was sticking damply to her forehead and, when she saw me, she opened her mouth and uttered a furious scream. She was very wet and the room reeked of stale urine. I glanced over at Sam. He had removed most of his clothes and was sitting happily playing with a large stuffed dog. There was no sign of Bessie.

In three steps, I reached Edie and tried to soothe her by stroking her back, but to no avail. Frustrated by her screams, I attempted to lift her from her cot but her soaked nightgown clung to my hands. With fumbling fingers, I freed the strings at her neck and pulled the nightgown over her head, then pushed her onto her back and undid the pins that held her cloth nappy together and dropped it gingerly onto the floor. Looking around, I spied a towel lying on a nearby table next to Edie's bathtub. In a moment I had picked it up, wrapped my baby sister firmly in its clean folds, and lifted her into my arms.

Edie stayed still and quiet for a few moments, but quickly began to wriggle and cry again. Not knowing what else to do, I stepped forward and knocked tentatively on Bessie's door.

"Wait a minute, you stupid cow, I told you, I'll be ol'right in a minute!" came from the other side of the door, followed by sounds of retching.

Cautiously, I turned the handle and opened the door. Bessie was sitting on the edge of her bed, her bright hair in a tangled mass about her shoulders. She was wearing a soiled nightgown that was hitched to her knees and between her legs she held a white enamel pail.

Without looking up, she said, "Oh for Chris' sakes, Annie, get me a cuppa tea or summat. God, I was never this sick wiv Sam." She passed a hand wearily over her tangled hair and looked up.

We stared at each other for a moment then Bessie started to laugh, great gasps of laughter that ended in another bout of retching.

I stood in the doorway with Edie still in my arms, unable to take my eyes away from the figure on the bed. Bessie was obviously not ill in the conventional way, and she still had tears of mirth running down her cheeks.

At last, the retching stopped and she looked up at me. "Off you go, Miss Prissy, go tell the old witch downstairs that bad Bessie got 'erself in the family way again. Reckon I'll be out of 'ere afore breakfast."

Then putting the pail aside and giving a half-hearted pull at her nightgown, she rose a little unsteadily to her feet. Placing her hands on her hips and planting her feet more firmly, she faced me. "Well, what're you waitin' for, the bloody H'archangel Gabriel or summat?" she demanded.

Speechlessly, I turned and fled.

Lucy was coming out of the twins' bedroom with some combs and hairpins in her hand as I hurried across the schoolroom. She looked startled at the sight of me carrying Edie.

"What are you doing, Ada?" she asked, a trifle crossly. "We'll be late down if we don't hurry. Give Edie back to Bessie and I'll do your hair."

I shook my head. "Bessie's sick, or something. She swore at me and I simply can't give Edie back to her." I clutched the now squirming child close to me. Lucy gave me a sharp look, then with a small huff of annoyance, walked briskly past me and into the nursery. Uncertain of what to do next I let Edie slide to the floor. She was still wrapped in the towel, but quickly wriggled free of it and lay on the floor happily sucking her toes. Lily and Iris, who had followed Lucy into the schoolroom, began to giggle and whisper at the sight of their naked sister lying on the carpet.

I turned on them angrily. "Stop that at once or I'll smack both of you," I said, fiercely.

Iris bit her lip and seemed close to tears, but Lily faced me boldly. "You can't tell us what to do," she said, cheekily.

Before I could reply, Lucy returned and, bending, scooped Edie into her arms and returned her to the nursery. Moments later, she was back and kicking the damp blanket out of the way with one neatly shod foot, she pushed me onto one of the schoolroom chairs and began pinning up my hair. When it was done, she stepped back. "There!" she said. "Now will you please take the twins down to breakfast? Tell your aunt that I am indisposed this morning and have asked if you might take care of the twins." She looked at Iris and Lily who were now waiting impatiently at the door.

"Girls, I have a headache, and Bessie is a little unwell. We will look after the babies between us. You will do exactly as Ada tells you this morning. I will be back with you this afternoon. Now, go!" She gave me a little push. "And for goodness' sake, Ada, don't say anything more than I have told you," she added, so that only I could hear.

I walked my two sisters down the stairs in silence, my head whirling from the events of the past half hour.

Aunt Abigail and Nell were already in the dining room. My Aunt looked pointedly at the clock on the mantle, but as I took a breath to speak, Lily forestalled me.

"Aunt Abigail, Bessie was sick all over and now Miss Blackly has a bad head and Ada has to mind us." Lily looked smugly up at me as Aunt Abigail raised her eyebrows questioningly in my direction.

"Yes, Aunt Abigail," I said, trying to keep my voice level, "Bessie is indisposed and Miss Blackly has a headache, but she has kindly offered to mind Edith for the morning, if you will allow Nell and me to take care of Lily and Iris." I added Nell's name, as I thought it only fair that she should share in this unexpected task.

Beside me, Lily took a deep breath, ready to impart more information, but I took hold of her arm, pinching it a little as I looked down at her. "I know that you're excited, Lily," I said sweetly, "but Nell and I will make sure that you do your usual lessons just as Miss Blackly instructed." Lily gave me an angry stare, but wisely kept silent as she took her place at the table.

Aunt Abigail was watching me thoughtfully. "Very well, Ada," she said. "I'm glad to see you taking some responsibility for once. I trust that whatever ails Bessie is not of an infectious nature?"

"No," I said. "It's just something that disagreed with her." While this was not, strictly speaking, the whole truth, neither was it an outright lie. By now, I'd had time to think about what Bessie had said in her angry outburst, and knew that she was going to have another child and I didn't think that it was something that pleased her.

After breakfast, Nell, the twins, and I made our way up to the schoolroom. Halfway up the stairs, Nell paused and although she spoke softly, her tone was irritable.

"What's going on Ada? Why do I have to help with these two? With Miss Blackly indisposed, I have other plans for this morning."

"I really can't tell you right now," I whispered back.

Nell looked annoyed. "Why not?" She demanded, in a louder voice. I shrugged my shoulders and gave a warning glance towards the twins who had stopped a few stairs ahead of us and were watching us curiously.

Nell put her hands on her hips. "Fine then," she snapped. "If you won't tell me, you can look after these two on your own. I have better things to do." And she pushed past Lily and Iris and stomped to the top of the stairs.

As she turned to go to her own room, I called after her, careless now of who heard me.

"I don't need your help. Why don't you go and water those weird old orchids or something?" Nell stopped dead and stared down at me, but I lowered my head and continued up the stairs, not looking at her.

To my surprise, as we turned the corner and drew level with her, Nell started to walk beside me until we reached her bedroom door, then she paused, her hand on the doorknob. "I might go and look at the orchids, Ada, or maybe I shall write another letter to Papa in

Spanish," she said, softly. "He likes it very much when I do that." Then she opened her door and slipped inside, closing it in my face.

The twins were watching me now with open curiosity. "What are you staring at?" I snapped, and pushed them along the corridor in front of me. I mounted the back stairs, with the twins in tow, wondering if Nell had by now received her own letter from Papa and had not told me; it would be very like her to say nothing.

When we reached the upper level, the schoolroom was empty and the nursery door was open. I put my head inside; the room was clean and tidy and, through the open doorway, I could see into Bessie's room. The bed was neatly made with the faded cotton cover folded at the corners. Her hairbrush was on the small dresser and a spare blouse peeked from behind the curtain that served as a wardrobe. Bessie was still here then, but of her, Lucy Blackly, and the two babies, there was absolutely no sign.

I soon set Lily and Iris to work. Though Lily was inclined to be sulky, Iris was always eager to please. In the end, they both worked so well that I promised to ask Miss Blackly to reconsider her decision and allow them to go for a walk in the afternoon.

At 12:30, Annie came in with lunch for us. She had a separate covered dish for Miss Blackly. "She'll be along soon, I shouldn't wonder," was all she would say, folding her mouth, as far as she was able, into an approximation of Mrs. Carter when she was unwilling to impart information. I wasn't hungry and didn't eat much of my lunch. The twins greedily finished my blancmange pudding between them, fighting over the last scraping of the bowl.

The schoolroom clock had just struck two when Lucy returned, and no sooner was she in the room than the twins demanded that they should go for a walk as I had promised.

Lucy looked annoyed at first, but then she sighed. "Yes, in all probability, that will do you some good," she said. Then she turned to me. "Thank you, Ada, I am quite recovered now, and I do appreciate you looking after the girls this morning." I waited expectantly, thinking that she would ask me to join them on their walk. "I have just spoken to your aunt," she continued. "She is waiting for you to join her in the drawing room for your afternoon instruction."

Disappointed and a little resentful, I went downstairs and spent the afternoon reading very poorly from the Gospel of Saint Mark, and sewing a hem that had to be ripped out twice by the time tea was served. Nell was with us that afternoon, but we avoided looking at each other. Aunt Abigail did not seem to notice anything amiss.

That night, after Aunt Abigail had retired and the house was quiet, I decided to go upstairs and confront Lucy Blackly and find out exactly what was going on.

I had not been upstairs at night since Christmas. After my illness, I had lost interest in Argentina. Tonight, though, I wrapped my warm woolen shawl about my shoulders, removed my shoes, and tiptoed along the corridor towards the door that led to the back stairs. As I drew level with Aunt Abigail's bedroom, the door opened silently; it was almost as if my aunt had been waiting for me.

I froze where I was, as she stood framed in the doorway, candle in hand, clad in her nightgown with her nightcap tied with ribbons under her chin.

"Where are you going, Ada?" she asked.

Hot colour flooded my face and I said the first thing that came into my head. "I couldn't sleep, Aunt Abigail. I was worried about Edith, in case Bessie's sickness was catching." My voice trailed off into silence.

Aunt Abigail looked pointedly at my dress and the shoes that I held clutched in my hand. "I have checked on the child myself and she appears quite healthy," she said, thinly. "You, however, may find that you sleep more easily if you attire yourself in your nightgown first. Good night, Ada." She stood watching as I returned to my room and closed the door.

CHAPTER 10

The next morning after breakfast, Lucy waited for me in the hallway. "I looked for you last night. I thought you might want to talk things over," she said, looking a little disappointed.

"I tried," I answered ungraciously, "but Aunt Abigail caught me."

"Oh, dear," her smile was sympathetic. "Nell was luckier than you then!"

I stared after Lucy as she turned and went up the stairs. I wondered how Nell had managed to sneak up to the schoolroom last night without getting caught. Perhaps Aunt Abigail had heard her in the corridor and had come to investigate just as I was passing. Giving a sigh of exasperation, I headed for the kitchen, determined to find out what Cook might know. At least Aunt Abigail never questioned my being there.

Cook was by herself, rolling the pastry for several pie dishes that were lined up on the table. I slid onto the old wooden stool that I had been sitting on since I was so little that Cook had to lift me onto it.

"I know that something's going on, Cook," I said in my most persuasive manner. "Please tell me what it is."

"I don't know what you mean, I'm sure, Miss Ada," said Cook primly, continuing to roll the rich dough under her hands.

I leaned forward. "Cook, I found Bessie being sick in a pail yesterday. She swore at me and told me that she was leaving because she was in, you know, a condition."

Cook held up a large red hand. "All right, Miss Ada. I suppose you do 'ave a right to know, though it's a bad world we've come to when innocent girlies like you and Miss Nell has to know stuff like this."

"It's nothing to do with Nell," I snapped. "She just stuck her nose in as usual. She didn't even help with the twins!"

"Now, now, Miss, I don't like to hear you talking so about your own sister! She's had it 'ard these months since your Ma passed over."

I stared at Cook in amazement. "So have I!" I burst out angrily, "but no one seems to care one bit about me, and I saw Mama. I was in the room when she was lying on the bed with blood all over her and the baby not breathing and the doctor all covered in blood, too, and, and . . ." Then I put my head in my hands and burst into tears

Cook left what she was doing and held me to her large floury bosom, rocking me back and forth, making small soothing noises as if I was a little child again. After a while, she handed me a square of clean linen and I blew my nose loudly.

"There, there, my ducky," she said, kindly. "You shouldn't 'ave been holdin' that inside all this time. Her soft Dorset accent was as comforting as a warm blanket. "I'll put the kettle on an' we'll 'ave a nice cup of tea an' I'll tell you what there is to know about our Bessie and 'er troubles."

A few minutes later while I sipped at the hot, sweet tea, Cook went back to her pastry, and started to explain the events of the previous day.

Bessie was indeed pregnant and was what Cook described as "pretty far gone" before she realized it.

"Trouble is, my dear, it's not the first time, is it? Most folks 'as sympathy for one mistake but two . . .? Well that's another matter! Of course by the time the silly hussy realized what's goin' on, it's way too late to do summat."

Cook stopped in mid-flight, patting absently at her second pie, as if suddenly aware that she wasn't chatting to one of her village cronies.

"Anyway, my dear, long an' short of it is, Miss Blackly there, she persuaded Bessie to go see your Auntie an' give in 'er notice, yesterday mornin'. "Our Annie took liddle ones out in that great perambulator, and nearly knocked 'erself over tryin' to get it back up the hill." Cook chuckled richly. "She's a good girl, our Annie."

"So what happened with Aunt Abigail?" I asked impatiently, look-ing over my shoulder towards the kitchen door, afraid that my aunt would appear at any moment.

"Well, now," Cook continued placidly, ignoring my interruption. "Your auntie was real upset like. She asks Bessie outright why she was leavin' an' Bessie says bold as you please, or so Mrs. Carter says, an' she was there. Bessie says, 'I've took a place with a new baby, seein' as 'ow you made me stop feeding liddle Edie. I'm losin' me milk wiv only Sam to feed an' that's me livelihood.' Well, your auntie goes all frosty like an' tells her that Mr. Baldwin had plans to keep her on as Miss Edith's nurse. Then said she was to leave in two weeks."

Cook leaned on the table for a moment and shook her head. "An' that Bessie, bold as brass, says, 'if it's all the same to you, Missus, I'll just take the one week.' Then out she goes. I tell you, that Bessie, she's a rare one!" The big woman shook her head reflectively before lifting both pies, one in each hand, and heading towards the oven.

I slid reluctantly off my stool. "Thanks for telling me, Cook," I said. "But," I hesitated, "who do you think the baby's father is?"

Cook looked at me sharply. "Well now, Miss, that's none of my business, nor yours neither, I reckon," and she turned away, busying herself with the oven.

I left the kitchen and walked upstairs to check the newly laundered contents of the linen cupboard, a job I should have done an hour before. As I went, I thought about all the information I had gained. I felt sure I knew who was to blame for Bessie's condition and I was certain that Cook did, too. But Ned was her nephew, and I knew she would never say anything against him.

I wished again that I had been able to go upstairs and talk to Lucy the previous night, and as I checked the stacks of sweet-smelling sheets, I found myself wondering if somehow Nell had alerted Aunt Abigail to my night time jaunt.

I felt a familiar prickle of anger at Nell, but I couldn't prove any-thing and, besides, now I knew as much as she did. I paused for a moment. Maybe I didn't know everything. Where had Lucy Blackly been all morning? If Annie had the babies and Mrs. Carter was with Bessie and Aunt Abigail, what was our dear Miss Blackly doing? I determined to ask her at the earliest opportunity—but as it turned out, I didn't get the chance.

CHAPTER 11

That afternoon, Aunt Abigail announced to the household that Papa was expected home within the week. The house was in an immediate uproar and Drake, who seemed to have spent most of the winter skulking in his little butler's pantry, was suddenly galvanized into action. I watched him a few days later, puffing his way importantly up the main staircase with a feather duster in his hand, headed no doubt for my father's room. I felt quite sure that we would all be happier with Papa safely back home.

On Thursday of that week, there was another incident that left us in a state of confusion. Nell, Aunt Abigail, and I were, as usual, in the drawing room after lunch when we heard the sound of wheels on the driveway. Not waiting for permission, Nell jumped to her feet and ran to the window. She pulled aside the curtain and watched for a moment.

"Oh, it's only Bert Baker with his cart," she said, letting the curtain drop and returning to her seat. At Nell's words, Aunt Abigail rose hastily and left the room. Nell and I gaped after her before following eagerly.

Bessie was standing at the bottom of the stairs. She was holding Sam by one hand and had a bundle in the other. As we reached the doorway, I saw Bert disappearing out of the front door carrying a small wooden trunk. Standing next to Bessie was a highly discomfited Drake holding Edie, who whose small face was still rosy with sleep.

Aunt Abigail was addressing Bessie angrily as we entered the hall. "Where are you going?" she demanded. "And how dare you presume to use the front door of this house!"

Bessie tossed her head. "Looks like I'm leavin' and I'll use whatever door I please," she responded cheekily. Then she marched to the open door leading to the outside. As she passed me, she gave a broad wink and a sly smile. "Thanks for not lettin' on, Miss," she whispered.

Fortunately, Aunt Abigail was too busy attempting to remove a now sobbing Edie from Drake's paralyzed grip to hear her. In the end, I was the one who took Edie in my arms and comforted her.

When Bessie had given her notice five days earlier, Mrs. Carter had immediately set about finding a new nurse for Edie, and had hired a young woman from a local farm who was to start with us on Saturday. She reasoned that this would give the girl one day with Bessie, to become accustomed to Edie's routine, but not long enough for Bessie to impart too much gossip or hard feelings. Mrs. Carter herself planned to spend much of Saturday with them. We had all presumed that Bessie would pack her things and take herself off on Saturday night in order to get a full week's pay. We were wrong.

Now, at Aunt Abigail's command, Nell and I returned to the drawing room where our aunt seated herself in her accustomed chair and, eyeing the still sobbing Edie with some disfavour, rang for Mrs. Carter and Drake.

The two servants entered the room together, Drake with obvious reluctance. His short encounter with a screaming child seemed to have unnerved him, and even Mrs. Carter looked flushed and a little apprehensive.

Aunt Abigail folded her hands in her lap. It was a gesture I had come to know well. "Were either one of you aware that Bessie was planning to leave today?" she asked sharply. Both shook their heads vehemently.

My aunt blew air audibly down her nose. "I understand that the new nursemaid is arriving on Saturday; what is her name?"

Mrs. Carter started forward anxiously. "It's Mabel, Miss Baldwin, Mabel Crossley from Jack Crossley's farm. She's the second youngest and . . ."

Aunt Abigail cut across Mrs. Carter's nervous flow with a wave of her hand. "Today is Thursday," she said. "Kindly send to the Crossley farm for Mabel to come at once."

"Oh no, she can't!" gasped Mrs. Carter. "She's gone to her sister's lying in, over in Weymouth, and said most particular that she'd be coming straight from there early on Saturday morning. I had a hard time persuading her to be here that early, Miss Baldwin, and that's the truth!"

There was silence in the room. I knew quite well that all the servants were desperately busy preparing the house for my father's return. Lucy had her hands more than full with the twins and, besides, I didn't quite see her fitting into the role of nursemaid.

Edie had subsided onto my lap, her head leaning heavily against me. Her cheeks were still stained with tears, but she had placed one small pink thumb in her mouth and was sucking it contentedly. I could smell the warm, clean smell of her and, as I bent my own head, a soft chestnut curl tickled my cheek.

"I'll look after her until Saturday, Aunt Abigail," I said, impulsively. They all stared at me as if I had lost my mind, but suddenly this seemed like the most important thing in the world for me to do.

"I can do it," I pleaded. "And it's only for a day or so. Please, Aunt Abigail!"

My aunt gave me one of her long, level looks and I held my breath. "Very well, Ada, it will solve our immediate problem. However, you are to keep to her routine. You must move up to the nursery to be with her." She turned and picked up her bible.

"You may go," she said sharply, dismissing us. Nell rose to leave with us, but Aunt Abigail's claw-like fingers closed firmly on her arm. "You are not finished your needlework, Nell. You are not dismissed."

As I left carrying the now sleeping Edie, I looked over my shoulder at Nell. She was chewing furiously on her finger and glaring after me. The idea of spending the rest of the afternoon alone with Aunt Abigail obviously did not please my sister. I was smiling as I crossed the hall and prepared to mount the stairs.

Closing the drawing room door quietly behind her, Mrs. Carter hurried after me, looking anxious. "Miss Ada, are you sure you can do this?" she asked. "It's not the easiest thing, looking after a little one, you know."

"Don't worry, Mrs. Carter," I answered airily. "I know what I'm doing".

Once upstairs, I entered the nursery, and set my still sleeping sister gently in her cot. Bessie had left the place scrupulously clean; Sam's little truckle bed was gone and, through the open door, I could see that Bessie's bed was bare. Wiping my damp hands on my skirt, I tried to think what I should do next.

Lucy and the twins were out for the day. I had heard Lily and Iris chattering excitedly on their way out in the morning. Miss Blackly was taking them to see some newborn lambs at a nearby farm, where they had been invited to stay for lunch. Lucy had also promised to bring the girls home by way of the village so that they could visit the blacksmith and see him working at his trade.

I had visited Edie in the nursery many times before, but the room seemed different now. I remembered vaguely when the twins were here, and I knew that both Nell and I had started out our days in this small room. I was pleased to see my old rocking horse still in the corner. It looked a little the worse for wear after all these years, and I thought that Sam had probably given it some exercise in the last few months.

I seated myself in the big rocking chair by the empty fireplace. Up to now, I had watched other people taking care of my younger sisters and they had made it seem easy and natural. Now I felt a flutter of panic; I really had no idea what to do, and began to regret my impulsive offer. Then, taking a deep breath, I straightened my shoulders. No matter what happened, I could not go down and tell Aunt Abigail that I had changed my mind!

I don't know how long I had been staring miserably at the empty grate when I heard a cheerful voice behind me. "Well, Miss, aren't you ever so kind!" And there was Annie, beaming breathlessly at me over a pile of blankets and pillows. I jumped gladly to my feet.

"Thank you, Annie!" I said, reaching to take the pillows from her. "I wasn't sure what to do about the bed, and of course I don't know exactly when Edie eats her supper, and do you think I should bathe her tonight?" My words tumbled out much too fast, but I didn't seem able to stop them.

Annie bustled into the tiny bedroom next to the nursery and, with an expert heave, flipped the single mattress over on the narrow bed.

"Well now, Miss," she said as she busied herself spreading a thick under-pad, then crisp white cotton sheets onto the bed. "If I was you, I wouldn't worry about bathing Miss Edie tonight, not unless you want to, of course. I brought up the water meself this morning so I do know that Bessie washed both the little ones afore breakfast." She spread two warm blankets on top of the sheets, tucking them neatly at the corners.

"As to Miss Edie's supper, well, Cook an' me was just sayin', beggin' your pardon, Miss, but we wasn't sure that you could manage alone. So if you want, Cook says you could bring the little one down later on. She could have supper and her bottle with us. Bessie used to do that sometimes when she wanted a bit of a night out." Annie paused for a moment as she realized what she had said, before continuing to busy herself spreading a bright counterpane on the bed.

"That won't be necessary," I answered, coolly. "I am quite capable of looking after my own sister."

Annie finished what she was doing then straightened up. As usual, she kept her head bent, but she continued, as if I hadn't interrupted. "Truth is, Miss, we all helps out a bit round here to make life a bit more bearable since the Missus passed.

"Your auntie never even thinks that we should have a bit of a day off. If it hadn't been for Cook, Bessie would've worked every day since she come here." She blushed suddenly. "Pardon me, Miss if I've spoken out of turn."

With quick, deft movements, she slipped the pillowcases on two fat pillows and tucked them under the counterpane. "There Miss, I'll bring up your tea when Miss Blackly gets back with Miss Lily and Miss Iris."

As she hurried away, I called after her. "Thank you, Annie. I really can manage." But she gave no sign that she had heard me.

I returned to my chair and sat for a while, thoughtfully rocking. It was true that I had never thought about Bessie, and the life she led up here at the top of the house, with two little ones to look after.

Lucy Blackly went off to her family every Sunday, and the twins spent the day with us. Lucy always returned in time to put them to bed. As for the other servants, I supposed that they still had one half-day off a week, following a schedule scrupulously set out by Drake. But no one seemed to have given a thought to Bessie! I shook my head, surprised that I was able to feel sorry for her.

I must have dozed, lulled by the quiet peace of the nursery, because I was jerked back to myself by the sound of the twins making their usual noisy entrance. Annie in her haste to leave had left the door into the schoolroom open, and now the two girls stood staring at me, open-mouthed.

"What are you doing here?" demanded Lily in her saucy way. "And where is Bessie and Sam?"

"Where *are* Bessie and Sam?" Lucy corrected, coming in behind the girls. "Remember, I told you earlier that they had already gone." Lucy stopped abruptly when she saw me.

"Why, Ada, my dear, I thought Annie would be looking after Edie until the new nursemaid arrives." Her tone was surprised.

"No," I said. "Annie is too busy and, besides, I want to take care of Edie."

"Well, goodness, that's wonderful of you, dear. I'm sure you'll manage very well." Lucy looked down at the twins, who were still watching me with deep curiosity. "Annie will be on her way up with tea, girls, so please change your shoes, she said pleasantly, before turning to me with a smile. "Don't let us interrupt you, Ada, but know that I am close by if you need anything." And with that, she followed the twins out of the room, closing the door behind her.

Feeling somehow as if I had been dismissed, I got up and fidgeted around the nursery. Edie was still sleeping, her cheeks flushed and her thumb in her mouth. I removed it gently and the little girl stirred, turning her head towards me before settling back to sleep. I sank once more into the rocking chair and peered out of the small window, as the spring light began to fade.

I could hear the twins in the other room laughing at something Lucy had said. There was an old clock on the wall above Edie's cot and, as I listened to its soft familiar tick, I thought over the events of the afternoon, of Bessie's bold exit and poor Drake looking so uncomfortable. Of my own impulse to look after Edie and everyone's concern that I wouldn't be able to manage.

Then as I watched the steady sweep of the second hand, I remembered Lucy's words when she came in, and wondered how she had known that Bessie had already gone when she and the twins had been out since early morning.

A slight sound from the corner made me turn my head. Edie was awake, lying on her tummy, peering at me through the bars of her cot.

"Come on, Edie, it's almost time for your tea," I said, cheerily. Edie watched my approach warily then looked past me, seeking for Bessie, or even Sam's familiar face.

After a moment, her own small face crumpled and she started to cry. I leaned down, ready to take her in my arms, but she screamed and wriggled desperately away from me.

"Hush now, pet," I crooned, just as I had heard Bessie do, but Edie screamed all the louder. That was only the beginning. Edie screamed when I changed her wet bottom and she screamed and pushed my hand angrily away when I tried to feed her, though Cook had sent up her favourite custard pudding and stewed apples.

She had quieted for a few blissful moments when Annie came in with our tea and to light the lamp, but as soon as the door closed behind her, Edie opened her mouth again and began to cry even louder than before.

She continued to scream even when I decided, rather desperately, that I would bathe her, and rang for Annie to bring warm water. Nothing worked. Finally, totally exhausted, I pocketed my pride and, lifting the sobbing child in my arms I dragged a blanket from the cot and hurried down the back stairs to the kitchen.

Darkness was falling and Cook was alone, sitting in her chair, warming her feet at the stove. A shaded lamp flickered on the table next to her. Her tasks were mostly finished for the day, and she was obviously enjoying this quiet moment, but she heaved herself to her feet when I stumbled into the room.

"Well then, my lambs, I thought as you might just be comin' down," she said, comfortably. She moved a pan of milk that had been heating gently on the hob, and poured it into the large, boat-shaped feeding bottle.

"There we go, then," she said holding out the bottle for me to take. I shook my head. "Please, Cook, can you give it to her?" I begged. "She won't do anything for me, and I'm at my wits' end."

Cook looked thoughtfully at me for a moment. "Well, maybe just this once," she said, as she took the baby from me.

A minute later, Edie was wrapped snugly in her blanket, hands grasping at the air as she sucked hungrily at the bottle of warm milk. I slumped down on a chair opposite Cook and watched wearily. Expertly, Cook patted Edie's small back until she gave a sleepy burp then settled back to finish what was left of the milk.

"Cook," I said, watching her with new interest, "how do you know what to do?

"You mean seein' as how I've never had a liddle one of me own?" she asked with a half-smile. I nodded uncomfortably, not wanting to hurt her feelings.

"Oh, well, there's some things as just come natural and I've had some practice at raising me sisters' babes, and all of you lot, too, come to that Miss Ada." I nodded silently, wondering if I would ever be able to handle a baby with such skill. It was very quiet in the warm kitchen. I heard the coals shift a little in the stove and watched Cook's comfortable outline as she rocked Edie in her strong arms.

"Do you think things will get better tomorrow?" I asked. Cook made a shushing noise and didn't answer. I couldn't see her face in the dim light, so I leaned forward. "The new girl is coming on Saturday morning, isn't she?" I continued insistently.

Cook sighed before she answered. "Yes and very kind of 'er it is too." Her tone was reproachful, but then she seemed to relent.

"She was plannin' on staying in Weymouth to look after her sister as had a baby boy last Monday gone. She's married to young Jimmy Miller." But I was no longer listening. Like Edie, my eyelids were closing, and my head dropped gently onto my breast.

Sometime later, I felt Cook's hand on my shoulder. "Come on, my beauty," she said, quietly. "You an' Miss Edie should both be tucked in your beds by the looks of you." I stumbled to my feet and, taking the peacefully sleeping Edie from Cook, I whispered my thanks and carried my sister upstairs and laid her in her cot.

As I straightened up, stretching my aching back, I looked around the room in dismay. It was a dreadful mess; the clothes I had pulled off Edie earlier were still lying in a heap on the floor, and two soiled nappies were draped over the edge of the pail where I had tossed them, filling the air with the acrid smell of stale urine.

Annie had removed the tray of almost untouched supper, but some spilled custard had run down the leg of the high chair and pooled in a sticky puddle on the wooden floor, and an early fly was buzzing around the stewed apple that had also spilled. I swatted ineffectually at the fly and started to clean up the mess. This was not the kind of work I was accustomed to and by the time everything was finished, I was hot, sticky, and no longer in the least bit sleepy.

It felt very late, I thought close to midnight, but when I glanced up at the clock over Edie's cot, the hands stood at one minute to eight o'clock. That couldn't be right! I peered through the partly open door into the schoolroom, where I could just see the big clock on the wall. I could not make out what time it was, so I stepped through the door in order to see better, just as the big hand jumped forward and the chimes sounded eight strokes. The evening was not yet over.

I turned to go back into the nursery but, as I did so, I heard someone running up the stairs and Nell burst into the room.

"Aunt Abigail expects you downstairs for prayers in half an hour!" she said, importantly, as she skidded to a halt and looked around. The door leading to the twins' room was closed and everything appeared very peaceful.

"Lucky you," she said, giving me a sidelong glance. "I should have offered to look after Edie; instead, I got stuck doing extra work."

I looked at my sister for a second, trying to decide if I should tell her about the awful time I'd had with Edie, but then I shook my head tiredly and spoke in a carefully neutral voice.

"Please tell Aunt Abigail that I will not attend prayers tonight as Edie is very fretful and restive."

My sister looked at me, disbelief clear on her face, then she tried to push past me into the nursery to see for herself, but I stopped her with my arm across the doorway.

"Don't you dare Nell!" My voice was a furious whisper. "I've just got her to sleep and I don't need you to waken her. Just go and tell Aunt Abigail what I said."

Nell retreated huffily, glaring at me as she turned to go.

Moments later, her voice floated up as she descended the back stairs. "Don't blame me if she comes up to check on you later. She probably won't believe me."

After Nell had gone, I sat once again in the rocking chair and wondered how Bessie had passed her evenings. My eyes wandered idly around the room and alighted on an open wicker basket piled high with clean linen; on top of it was a small wrapped bundle. Intrigued, I got up and walked over to the basket and picked up the bundle and opened it. Inside were sewing needles and spools of thread. There were also two thimbles and a small pair of silver scissors shaped like a stork.

I picked up the top article from the basket. It was a pillowcase, the lace trim hanging loose. With a shrug, I dropped it carelessly back into the basket. However Bessie had spent her evening hours, I had no intention of spending mine mending bed linen. Still restless, I wandered into the little bedroom next door and sat on the edge of the bed.

I could see my untidy reflection in the mirror, but didn't have the energy to do anything about it. I was still gazing reflectively at it a few minutes later when there was a light knock at the door. I sprang guiltily to my feet thinking that Aunt Abigail had indeed come to check on me, but when I answered, it was Lucy's smiling face that greeted me.

Stepping inside the nursery, she put her finger to her lips. "I've just got the twins down," she said. "I thought they'd be tired after our long day out, but tonight they found it hard to settle." She smiled at me again. "I see Edie is sleeping." I nodded, unwilling to admit that I'd had to resort to Cook for help.

"Well done, Ada. You'll make a wonderful mother one day." Lucy reached out to put a hand on my shoulder but I took a quick step back.

"No, I won't," I snapped. "I never want to do that. I don't intend to marry or have a child!"

Lucy looked at me in amazement. "My goodness, Ada, I really hope you change your mind. Ending up a spinster, looking after other people's children, is a very thankless way to spend your life." As she spoke, colour rose in her cheeks. "Not that I have minded my position here, of course. I've enjoyed it very much. It's just that I haven't heard anything from my dear Frederick for such a long time and I do fret so. I'm sure I'm worrying for nothing. I'm such a silly goose sometimes!"

We had been standing whispering in the nursery, but now Lucy stepped into the schoolroom and pointed towards the two old armchairs beside the fire. "Would you like to sit and talk for a while, or would you prefer to join your aunt downstairs for prayers?" Lucy headed over to the nearest chair and sank into it. "I could listen out for Edie for you."

"No! No thank you, I couldn't allow you to do that." I hurried towards the second chair and almost missed the twinkle in Lucy's eyes. I sank down gratefully and leaned my head back, closing my eyes for a moment. The chair smelt of leather and polish and something rather old and dusty. It smelt of my childhood. I opened my eyes and saw Lucy watching me.

"Have you eaten anything tonight?" she asked.

I shook my head. "I had such a hard time making Edie stop crying, I don't think I've eaten since lunch." I felt a huge sense of relief at my own admission and realized that I was very hungry. Lucy got up from her chair, but I stopped her with a gesture. "Please don't ring; the servants are all at prayers."

She smiled. "Yes, I know, and that is often the very best time to go down." With that she slipped quickly out of the room. I lay back in the chair again, looking at the small fire burning in the grate. Lucy must have lit it before she came to find me. The warmth crept across the worn rug and into my bones, and I gave a small shiver of pleasure.

In a very short time, Lucy was back carrying a tray loaded with food. There were slices of thick homemade meat pie, some pickled beetroot, and an assortment of cold vegetables, obviously left over from supper.

"Cook never minds my doing this when I miss dinner," Lucy explained as I looked doubtfully at the tray. "There's plum pie with clotted cream for pudding if you want, and I thought we might have cocoa afterwards to finish up." She pulled plates, cutlery, and napkins from the sideboard that housed the dishes for the twins, put a small saucepan of milk to heat by the fire and settled in the chair opposite me. I ate ravenously. Later, sipping the warm cocoa, I finally remembered to ask Lucy about her role in Bessie's leaving.

She paused for a moment before answering me. "After what happened the other morning," she said, "I knew that Bessie would have to leave soon. To be honest, I'd suspected her condition for a while, and didn't want to see the poor soul turned out with nowhere to go. So I told her to give two weeks' notice. I thought she would be happy to do that and perhaps even get a letter of recommendation into the bargain, but I hadn't reckoned on Bessie's temper." She smiled ruefully. "When I left, she was with Mrs. Carter, ready to speak with your aunt and I went to see friends of my family, Jack and Millie Crossly, they own a sheep farm."

"Yes, I know," I interrupted. "That's where the new nursemaid is from, isn't it?" I thought for a moment, "Mabel . . . is she their daughter?"

Lucy smiled and nodded. "Yes, Mabel loves babies, and she's been looking for work, so this seemed like a perfect opportunity. I've known the family for ages and I was sure that I could persuade them to take Bessie and little Sam in for a while, at least until she's had the baby and is back on her feet. They're very good people, even if they are Anglicans," she added with a smile.

"I took the twins over to see their lambs this morning and arrange the final details. I caught sight of Bert's cart with Sam sitting on top of it just as we were leaving the farm."

"So that's how you knew Bessie had already left!" I looked at her admiringly. "You are truly amazing, Lucy," I said, adding fervently, "whatever would we do without you?"

"You'll manage quite well," she said briskly, rising to her feet. "Now off to bed with you. You look worn out."

I stretched and yawned, nodding in silent agreement. Lucy stood surveying me for a moment. "Before you go, we have to do something about your clothes for tomorrow," she said. "You simply cannot wear those again!" I glanced down at myself and saw that my skirt was badly stained with custard that Edie had splashed on me, the front of my bodice was stained, too, and as I moved my head, I became aware of the smell of sour milk somewhere in the vicinity of my right shoulder.

"My other bodice and skirt will do for tomorrow," I said, carelessly rising to my feet.

"Yes, and a fine mess they'll be in by the time young Edie has finished with them! I believe that we are much of a size now, and I'm sure I can find something more comfortable for you." Lucy disappeared into her room, returning a few minutes later with a plain dark green skirt and a simple cream blouse.

"Here you are, these should do. You can roll the sleeves up when you are washing Edie, and I'll bring up one of Annie's big aprons for you."

While I was busy inspecting the clothes, Lucy gathered our dirty dishes and took them down to the kitchen, returning almost immediately with a crisply starched apron. "This will be perfect," she said, before helping me out of my heavy black skirt and top.

At Aunt Abigail's insistence, we were still in mourning for Mama, and it felt very strange to push my arms into the soft fabric of Lucy's blouse and step into a skirt that was not an unforgiving black. Lucy showed me how to button the blouse at the back, reaching a little for the top two buttons. The skirt was a little tight around my waist.

"This is meant for a corset," she said, as I sucked in my breath. "When your Papa gets home, you will have to persuade him to allow you to buy some more appropriate clothes. There! Now put on the apron. No not like that. It crosses over at the back." Lucy twirled me around and tied the apron in a firm bow, then she spun me around to face her again and stepped back to admire her handiwork.

"Perfect! And you would be wise to twist your hair into a bun at the top of your head. It will give Eddie fewer pins to grab!" I nodded wearily. Then Lucy stepped forward and gave me a quick hug. "Now, off to bed with you, Ada. Edie will be awake at first light."

I passed an uncomfortable night. I had thought that, tired as I was, that I would sleep deeply, but I had not reckoned on the horsehair mattress on the narrow bed, nor the fact that, in part, I was listening out for Edie. As I tossed and turned, I heard her every rustle and cough. I kept the door between the two rooms ajar so that I could hear her, and eventually fell into an uneasy sleep, only to be awakened at first light when, just as Lucy had predicted, Edie sat up, crowing happily at the sound of birds singing outside her window.

CHAPTER 12

I would like to say the second day was better, but it wasn't. Edie screamed when I changed her, threw her food at me, and wriggled away whenever I tried to pick her up.

At mid-morning, I took her downstairs, bundled in a blanket. Then pulling an old cloak and bonnet off the hook in the back porch and dumping Edie unceremoniously in her perambulator, set off on a walk. I remembered that Annie had been praised for doing this very thing, and was determined to be successful with something in regard to my little sister. Mrs. Carter called after me, warning me to stay on the path, but I ignored her and headed towards the river.

The perambulator had originally been used for the twins and then Bessie had made use of it for both Edie and Sam. It was very big, and by the end of the first half hour, I was regretting my decision. The carriage slid and slipped and thwarted all my efforts to push it up over the small curb onto the sloping back lawn.

In the end, by dint of digging my heels into the soft grass and dragging the perambulator backward, I managed to pull its unwieldy bulk onto the grass and set off. I had a mind to take the river path and perhaps show Edie the orchard, but I did not get far.

In the end, I admitted that I had no choice but to return back the way I had come, creating even more damage to the usually manicured lawn. I arrived back at the kitchen door hot, breathless, and thoroughly out of temper. Edie had closed her eyes the moment the wheels of the carriage started to move, and slept blissfully through all of my futile endeavours.

Panting from the effort of pushing the perambulator back into its accustomed spot, I looked up and saw Cook, waiting for me at the door.

"You just leave her to sleep, my dear," she said with a twinkle in her eye. "We can 'ear if she wakes. You set yourself down and 'ave a liddle something."

Although it was a little too early for lunch, I found that I was ravenously hungry. Cook set a bowl of thick chicken stew before me, adding a hunk of freshly baked bread, still warm from the oven and dripping with butter. I had never tasted better.

While I ate, Cook had been eyeing my clothes. Now she gave a sigh of satisfaction. "Well, now, I do like the way you looks this morning, Miss. Like a proper liddle nursemaid and no mistake. Right pretty, I reckon!"

I looked down at my stained and crumpled apron. "I hope Annie doesn't mind that I borrowed her apron," I said. "Miss Blackly lent me the rest; she thought it more practical than my black."

I allowed Cook to feed Edie her lunch, which she ate without a single tear, smiling and giggling every time Cook called her "Liddle Lambkin," and opening her mouth obligingly for each spoonful. I watched silently, shaking my head at Cook's skill.

Later, I carried my little sister upstairs and she was content to play for a while, laughing happily and chattering nonsense to her floppy-eared rabbit before dropping instantly asleep when I put her down for her nap. I was delighted with this turn of events and, as the afternoon stretched on, I dozed quietly in the rocking chair thinking that finally Edie was starting to accept me.

My confidence was short-lived, however, for as soon as Annie appeared with Edie's tea, the whole process began again. Once more, I was the target, as a scarlet-faced Edie flung her boiled egg with surprising accuracy in my direction. When I changed her, she scratched at me with her fingernails and my face was red with anger and pain as she dragged at handfuls of my hair.

Finally, I put her in her cot and, closing the door on her angry screams, ran downstairs to beg some salve from Mrs. Carter.

I walked into the kitchen to a scene of absolute chaos.

Everyone seemed to be running at once. Cook, even rosier than usual, was heaving a large piece of trussed lamb out of the oven. Drake was counting out knives as if his life depended on it, and Annie was up to her elbows in hot, soapy water, washing the best china plates that hadn't been used for months.

Mrs. Carter was nowhere to be seen. As I stared about me in amazement, salve quite forgotten, I realized that there was only one explanation for all this much turmoil. My father had returned home!

I crossed the kitchen swiftly and pushed through the swing door that led to the rest of the house. As I ran down the corridor towards the main hall, I could hear male voices and I skidded abruptly to a halt. Then I saw them. Papa was standing by the dining room door talking to a beaming Mrs. Carter. Next to him was another man, a handsome stranger with a very dark complexion who looked uncomfortable and out of place. For now though, all my thoughts were on my father. As I hurried across the hall towards him, he turned and, seeing me, broke off his conversation with the housekeeper.

"Girl," he called, impatiently, "Tell Drake I need to see him at once." I stared at my father for a moment in confusion. His face was leaner than I remembered and deeply tanned and he was looking at me in mild irritation, wondering why I did not curtsey dutifully and obey his order. Then understanding dawned on me; my father had mistaken me for a housemaid!

After all the difficulties and unhappiness that I had endured over the last seven months, this latest development was just too much to bear! With a gasp, I flew past him and up the stairs. As I ran, I heard Mrs. Carter starting to explain, but I kept going. Reaching my own room, I ripped off the white apron, breaking one of the strings as I did so. Then I flung myself down on my bed and beat with my fists on the pillows. How dared my father take me for one of the servants! After a while, when my anger had abated a little, I sat up. An idea was forming in my head.

No doubt everyone would expect me to stay upstairs tonight and look after Edie. That was not about to happen. Straightening my blouse and skirt and hastily smoothing my hair from my face, I marched purposefully along the corridor and through the door to the back stairs.

I re-entered the kitchen just as Drake was leaving with a large silver tray loaded with cutlery. "Drake," I said loudly, "Wait, please!"

He paused in the doorway, tray held high above his head. "I'm sorry, Miss," he began. "I'm very busy."

"I said wait!" My tone brooked no argument and Drake stood still, looking startled. "You will have to manage without Annie tonight; she will be looking after Edith," I said firmly. "I will be dining with my father."

The kitchen fell silent as I finished speaking. For a moment, I thought Drake was going to object, but then he gave a small bow. "Very good, Miss Baldwin," he said and left, the door swinging closed behind him.

I looked around for Annie. "Come along," I said. A flustered Annie looked towards Cook who flapped her hand in my direction.

"Go along," she said, sharply. "You heard Miss Ada." As I walked passed Cook, she looked down, but not before I had seen the twitch of a smile on her face.

For the first time in my life, I had given an order to our servants and seen it instantly obeyed. The feeling of power was a little unsettling.

When I reached the nursery, with Annie scurrying behind me, Edie was sitting quietly in her cot playing with her toy rabbit. She didn't object when I picked her up and handed her to Annie.

"Come on," I said, briskly. "You have to help me get dressed. I can't do this by myself."

Back in my own room, I opened my wardrobe and pulled out the blue velvet dress that Lucy had given me for my birthday. Then, moving quickly, I removed my borrowed skirt and blouse.

"Here, Miss," said Annie, putting Edie on the floor. "Let me do your hair first then we'll get you into the dress." Surprisingly, Annie proved to be remarkably adept at dressing my hair, and in no time had pinned it into a swirl of soft curls at the top of my head.

As I pulled on the skirt, I was surprised to find that it fit me well, with no need for pinning this time, and as I struggled into the bodice, I realized that I had definitely grown in the last few months.

I walked over to the mirror and looked at myself. Papa would not mistake me for one of the servants now. I reached into my drawer and pulled out Mama's necklace in its velvet box, but I knew that I could not wear it. The blue beads needed bare skin to show off their elegance, and this dress with its high neck did not suit. I wished for earrings, but did not own any.

While I was busy with my toiletries, Edie had been playing quietly at the foot of my bed. I glanced down at her, and saw that she had found my rag doll and was happily chewing on one arm. I bent to take it away from her but then I stopped and smiled to myself. Let her play with the doll; after all, Edith was her namesake.

When the bell rang for dinner, I was ready, but I did not leave immediately. Annie had already taken Edie back to the nursery and I sat for a moment at my dressing table. Then with one last glance at my reflection, I opened my door and walked slowly along the corridor.

Foolishly I had hoped that Papa would still be in the hall below, so I could sweep down the stairs to greet him, but the room was quite empty, and I made my way alone into the dining room.

They were all there, ready to say grace. Aunt Abigail, grim-faced in her black mourning gown and lace cap; Nell, her hair brushed into submission for once and tied back with a ribbon; the twins neatly turned out in tunics and shining blonde hair; and Miss Blackly looking rather wonderful in a gown of deepest plum red that I had never seen before.

Papa was standing at the head of the table. On his right, stood the man I had seen earlier.

I paused for a moment in the doorway and as I did so, my father caught sight of me. I saw his eyes widen with shock and he seemed to pale a little under his tan and I remembered then that I looked very much like my mother.

Papa left his place at the head of the table and came towards me. "Ada, my dear," he said, his voice a little unsteady. "You are quite grown up!" He did not mention his earlier error and neither did I, but as he led me to my place at the table, I smiled up at him, suddenly immeasurably glad to have him home.

Papa was obviously in a very good humour. This was not at all the grim faced man who had left us last August and happily, I prepared to enjoy an excellent meal in the company of my dear Papa.

After grace was said, Papa introduced us to his guest, Señor Juan Pablo Rodriguez. He would, Papa explained, be staying with us for a few days, before traveling on to London to begin some work he was undertaking on behalf of my father and himself. Señor Rodriguez did not speak very much during dinner and I wondered if he understood English.

As we listened to Papa and responded to his questions, I thought how very pleasant it was to be allowed to converse during a meal again. Aunt Abigail had always insisted on silence.

I was soon comfortable asking and answering questions, but the twins seemed overwhelmed and unable to answer even the simplest inquiries, so Papa gave up, turning instead to Miss Blackly for a report on their progress.

Nell chose to show off quite dreadfully, using Spanish phrases to request the salt "por favor" and telling Señor Rodriguez that we would assuredly have some rain, "mañana." Initially, both Papa and his guest seemed delighted with Nell's efforts. However, when she said something in Spanish that made Papa stop in mid mouthful and his guest sputter with suppressed laughter, Aunt Abigail suggested icily that until Nell had a better command of Spanish, she should confine herself to the English language.

As dinner ended, I glanced over to where Lucy was seated. She had answered all of Papa's questions about the twins, making us laugh with her wit and humour, and had contributed further to the conversation, asking intelligent questions and listening gravely to the answers.

I saw my father watching her with approval and, when he caught her eye, he raised his glass to her in a small toast. My heart gave a jump, and it occurred to me that Lucy would make a truly wonderful stepmother. I hoped that she hadn't yet heard from Frederick.

As I daydreamed, Papa raised his glass. "I wish to propose a toast," he said, solemnly. "This is to my kind and generous sister, Abigail, for her good care of my children while I have been away. Abigail, I can never thank you enough!" Obediently, we all raised our glasses in a toast to my aunt.

She sat, Aunt Abigail, her hands folded neatly in her lap, two bright spots of colour on her paper-white cheeks and acknowledged the toast with nothing more than a slight tilt of her head.

Then Papa put down his glass and looked solemnly around. "I now have important news to share with you," he said, "news that will affect us greatly, as a family." Lucy half rose from her seat, as if to leave, but Papa waved her back. "No, no, my dear Miss Blackly, this may even include you, if we are to count ourselves remarkably blessed."

Papa leaned forward, his hands flat on the table in a familiar gesture, and looked at each one of us in turn.

"During my time away, I came to a momentous decision," he said, "though it was not an easy one. Señor Rodriguez will attest to the fact that I have spent many hours in consideration, and my conclusion was reached after much heart searching and prayer."

While Papa was speaking, Señor Rodriguez nodded emphatically, though I was still not sure if he understood more than a few words. "I have decided," Papa continued, "to return to the Argentine at the end of the summer."

His words struck at my heart. I simply could not bear another lonely winter without him. I leaned forward, ready to plead with him to reconsider, but he held up his hand to stop me.

"Wait, Ada, let me finish." He paused again, and looked around the table. "I am taking all of you with me. Our steamship sails out of Liverpool on September tenth."

As I took in my father's words, I felt colour spread up my throat and into my face. I could scarcely believe what I was hearing. "You're ... you're taking us to Argentina, Papa?" I managed at last.

"Yes," he said. "All of you children and those servants who choose to come with us. I know that this will mean a great change for you, but it will also be a great adventure. I have already procured a house for us just outside the city of Buenos Aires." He smiled and nodded towards Señor Rodriguez, who inclined his head but didn't speak.

I looked down at my lap, at my hands twisting my table napkin, then up at my father, my eyes still wide with disbelief.

Papa smiled at me with a hint of sadness. "It was what your mother and I had planned, Ada," he said as he rose from his chair.

After the two men had left, Lucy took the excited twins upstairs, leaving Aunt Abigail, Nell and me to go into the drawing room. As we reached the door, Aunt Abigail stopped. "If you will excuse me, I have one of my headaches," she said. "It is very late so you may tell the servants that I have retired for the night."

Nell and I watched as our aunt turned and made her way stiff-backed up the stairs then I pulled my sister into the drawing room and closed the door. "Can you believe this?" I said. I was hanging onto her arm and almost in tears. I started to drag her towards the sofa, but she shook me off impatiently.

"Really, Ada, you have to be the only person in the whole house besides the twins who didn't know!" she said, scornfully.

"What do you mean?" I demanded, the words tumbling out much too fast. "How did you know? Did Papa write and tell you? I can't believe that! That is so unfair, just because you think you're so smart and learned Spanish and everything. I'm going to talk to Papa right now!" I started towards the door, but Nell pulled me back.

"Don't be so stupid, Ada!" she said sharply, pushing me onto the couch. "No, Papa didn't write and tell me anything. I figured it out ages ago. There were all kinds of clues. Remember the letter that Drake didn't want us to see, back in November?" I nodded dumbly. "There was stuff in there about the servants coming with us, that's why Cook was so upset." She paused for a moment, looking thoughtful. "You can be sure she won't be coming."

Nell was in full flood now, marching up and down the room. I tried to speak, but she stopped me. "Didn't you ever wonder what Papa was doing in Argentina for over six months? You know he's an engineer, Ada. Well, he's involved in building the new railways; it's a huge undertaking. Miss Blackly and I have been following some of the politics there. Her sister, Suzanne, sends her newspapers from London and there have been lots of articles published about riots and things." Nell seemed to have forgotten my presence and was speaking quite slowly now, absorbed in her subject. "It's actually been quite dreadful; the slave trade was very strong there up to a few years ago." As she continued talking, my sister sat down, pulled off her glasses, and began busily polishing them.

But I scarcely heard her. I jumped up from my chair and turned angrily on my sister. "Why didn't you tell me, Nell? How could you and Miss Blackly have all these secret discussions without telling me anything? Did you and Aunt Abigail have big discussions, too, on how to convert all the poor pagans, while I was busy upstairs counting sheets and changing Edie's dirty bottom?"

Nell shook her head. "There aren't any pagans," she began reasonably. Then she paused. "Look, I read the letter. I went into Drake's room and found it the day after we were up in Mrs. Carter's room. It told everything."

I stared at my sister in disbelief. "Nell, how could you do that and not tell me?"

Nell shrugged and turned away. In silence, I rose and left the drawing room. I walked slowly up to my bedroom, thinking deeply. I was very tired, and it wasn't until I had struggled out of my clothes and was about to climb into bed that I remembered Annie, sitting patiently upstairs waiting for me to continue my duties as nursemaid.

Throwing on my dressing gown, I trailed miserably up to the top floor of the house. There was a dim light coming from the schoolroom and, for a moment as I stood in the corridor, I found myself reliving that night last winter when, as Nell had reminded me, I had crept up the stairs behind Annie to hear news of my father. There had been a candle in a pot of water in the schoolroom that night, too.

As I walked in, Lucy stirred. She was sitting in one of the armchairs and the door to the nursery was closed. "Ada, there you are," she said softly. "I hope you don't mind, but I told Annie to sleep in the bedroom," she gestured with her head towards the closed door. "The poor girl was falling asleep in the chair, and it seemed the easiest thing to do. I didn't know what time you would come up. Mrs. Carter has agreed to do the early chores so Annie can be free to look after Edie until Mabel gets here." She smiled kindly up at me.

I was still very angry and feeling out of sorts, so I folded my arms across my chest and glared down at Lucy.

"Thank you so much, Miss Blackly," I snapped. "You seem to have taken care of everything. You're very talented at organizing other people's lives aren't you? I gather that you and my sister have been making plans regarding our trip to Argentina, though you saw fit not to include me in your secrets. It's a pity that you aren't as good at organizing your own life with dear Frederick, isn't it?" With that, I turned on my heel and left the schoolroom, leaving Miss Blackly alone in the dim light, sitting in her favourite chair.

I knew that my outburst was quite unwarranted and very unfair, but I was angry, and Lucy Blackly was the first person upon whom I had been able to vent my anger. Later, as I closed my eyes and tried to sleep, the events of the day kept swirling about in my head. For the second night in a row, I did not sleep well.

CHAPTER 13

The next few days were difficult for me. On Saturday, Papa spent most of the day with Señor Rodriguez. Drake was also included in the discussions, called into the study after breakfast and not emerging until well after lunch.

Mabel had arrived early. I heard the clop of horses' hooves and the crunch of cart wheels swinging round to the back entrance as I went down to breakfast, but I did not go to meet her; I had no intention of visiting the top of the house for some time. Nell and I ignored each other during breakfast, though that was not much different from any other morning. Miss Blackly brought the twins into the room just after I arrived, then left, with a murmured excuse to Aunt Abigail.

When breakfast was over, Nell took the girls up to the schoolroom without being asked and I was left alone with my aunt. She looked pale and tired; a thin purple vein throbbed at her temple and, in a rare moment of sympathy, I wished that she had allowed herself to remain in her own room until she felt better.

The morning was spent as usual, supervising household tasks. Annie was back in her role as housemaid. She ducked her head when she saw me pass by the dining room, as if she wanted to avoid me, I wondered if she had heard my outburst the night before. She was polishing the already gleaming surface of the dining table and I heard Aunt Abigail remind her not to forget to polish the chairs, as well. I went looking for Mrs. Carter then remembered that she was upstairs with Mabel. I ate a cold lunch alone in the dining room.

Restless and lonely now, I felt the need to talk to someone about the events of the previous night, so I went looking for Cook. When I entered the kitchen, I felt the atmosphere change; it reminded me of the days when Aunt Abigail first made me supervise the servants.

Cook was busy at her big baking table, hands covered in flour, and her apron bespattered with juice from a jar of preserved plums that stood open beside her on the table.

As I walked in, she dropped a small curtsey. "Good afternoon, Miss Ada." Her voice was cool.

How was it, I wondered, that the servants always knew everything? I wondered if Annie had told Cook what had happened the night before when I was so rude to Lucy. Or perhaps Nell had been here already, telling Cook how stupid I was not to know about our proposed move.

Whatever the reason, Cook was obviously upset with me. As I walked over to my favourite seat, she picked up the large jar of plums and placed them squarely on the stool.

"Is there something you'll be needing then, Miss? I'm really ever so busy," she said, not quite meeting my eyes.

I stopped in mid-step. "I was looking for Mrs. Carter," I blurted, not knowing what else to say.

"She's not 'ere, Miss, as you can plainly see. She's up with young Mabel seein' as she's the only one as can quiet Miss Edith today!" Cook glanced angrily up at me, not pausing in her work.

I felt a surge of relief. So that was why Cook was angry! I was meant to be upstairs with Mabel looking after Edie, especially now that everyone was extra busy with my father's return.

"Where's the girl?" I asked, nodding briefly in the general direction of the scullery.

"Over at Stanton's." Cook was beating angrily at the contents of her mixing bowl and didn't look up. Like many servants hired casually, our kitchen maid served several of the bigger homes and took work wherever it was offered, and Saturday was a busy day.

I watched Cook for a moment more, then turned and left the kitchen. I was not, I thought stubbornly, about to rush upstairs to the nursery. For once, I would go my own way. So I walked into the vestibule and, taking my shawl and bonnet from their hook, walked out of the front door and headed for the river.

I hadn't walked alone there for a very long time. I loved the way the river changed with the seasons. It was spring and starting towards the long, gentle days of summer. The willow trees overhung the bank, trailing their long, silver-edged leaves into the water and small blue and yellow flowers dotted the edge of the path. The mud from the day before had dried overnight, and all that was left of my unsuccessful outing with the perambulator were a few deep scores in the grass where the wide wheels had dug themselves in.

Stepping off the path, I took a few steps up the grassy slope and pulled my black bonnet impatiently from my head. Dragging the pins and combs from my hair, I let the wind lift and blow the weight of it from my neck. I took a deep breath and closed my eyes before lifting my arms above my head and turning around in giddy circles. My shawl fell from my shoulders as I revelled in the moment of freedom.

A sudden shadow falling across my face startled me, and I opened my eyes. Señor Rodriguez was standing on the path, watching me. I stopped abruptly, embarrassed at being caught in such childish behaviour.

Señor Rodriguez bowed deeply. "Señorita," he murmured, and before I realized what he was doing he stepped forward, grasped my hand, and kissed it. With a small gasp, I snatched my hand back, involuntarily wiping it on the side of my skirt.

He watched me, his dark eyes narrowing a little. Then he bowed again, stiffly. "Pardon, Señorita, if I have offended you. In my country, it is customary," he gestured to my hand that was now clutching a handful of fabric.

I stared at him wordlessly for a few moments, then, stooping, retrieved my fallen bonnet and shawl and hurried back to the house.

Once inside, I went quickly up to my room and lay for a long time on my bed. I wished that I could escape into the world of books as Nell did, but I found little joy in reading. Eventually, my eyes closed and I must have slept for a long time because when I awoke, dusk was falling and it was time to dress for dinner. I rang for Annie.

That second night, Papa entertained us as he had the previous evening with tales of life in South America, but they were no longer just interesting stories—now he was telling us about our future life. I was relieved that Señor Rodriguez remained silent throughout much of the meal and did not attempt to address me. As dinner progressed, I found myself watching Aunt Abigail. She seemed smaller, somehow diminished, since my father's return, and I wondered how soon she would return to Sussex.

On the following Tuesday morning, Ned brought the carriage to the front door and Señor Rodriguez and all his baggage left, bound for London. I was relieved to see him go.

That afternoon when Papa called me into his study, I was apprehensive. I wondered if word of my rudeness towards Lucy had reached my father's ears. To my surprise, Papa rose to his feet as I walked into the room, something he had never done before.

He smiled at me. "Sit, Ada," he said, waving me to the chair in front of his desk. Reseating himself, my father leaned back in his own chair and inspected me closely. I dropped my eyes and fidgeted nervously with my skirt.

"You've done well, Ada. I'm proud of you."

My head flew up at his words. "Thank you, Papa," I said, unable to hide my surprise. "But I've made so many mistakes." I broke off, not knowing what else to say.

My father gave a brief smile. "Yes, I am aware that you continue to be headstrong, impulsive, and sometimes given to inappropriate outbursts, Ada, but I also have reports of your kindness and willingness to take on responsibilities. And I hear that you are becoming competent at managing the household." I felt myself blush with pleasure. Then my father leaned forward, his face suddenly stern. "So why is it Ada that you were so remarkably lacking in good manners towards my guest? Your behaviour to Señor Rodriguez was quite unacceptable!"

I clasped my hands together, squeezing them tight. "Papa, I'm sorry, but he surprised me. He came upon me quite suddenly when I was alone, down by the river. And he - he kissed my hand!"

"That is no excuse. You must learn to mind your manners, young lady, and in future you are not to go walking by the river alone. Is that clear Ada?"

I nodded my head without speaking. My father gave a small sigh. "Thank you, Ada. That will be all," he said, his tone gentler. "Please ask Nell to come and see me."

As I rose and walked towards the door, he spoke again. "Ada, Señor Rodriguez has asked me if I would consider his offer for your hand in marriage."

I whirled about, staring at my father in horror. His lips twitched a little and his tone was not unkind. "Don't worry, I told him that you are much too young; and there are other considerations, as well." I waited for him to continue, but he bent his head to the papers on his desk, clearly dismissing me.

I closed the study door behind me and, taking a deep, shaking breath, returned to the drawing room to pass Papa's message to Nell and to spend a quiet afternoon with Aunt Abigail, reading and sewing. It felt oddly comforting.

The next morning the carriage was called for again and Ned carried Aunt Abigail's small black leather trunk out of the front door and strapped it to the roof of the carriage.

My aunt descended the stairs slowly, her back straight and her gloved hands holding her black reticule. We were lined up in the hall in order of age, just as Aunt Abigail preferred.

My aunt started with Edith who was squirming in the arms of Mabel, the new nursemaid. She put her hand on Edie's head for a moment and, in a surprisingly gentle gesture, stroked the little girl's curls. She did not speak.

The twins were watching her warily as she approached them. They seemed quite unable to move until Miss Blackly, who was standing behind them, gave each one a little push forward. Then they curtsied in unison and Lily presented Aunt Abigail with a small posy of spring violets, the stems bound tightly with white ribbons that fluttered a little as she handed the flowers to my aunt. Aunt Abigail gave a glimmer of a smile and murmured her thanks.

I felt Nell shuffle uncomfortably next to me as her turn approached. Before she reached us, Aunt Abigail paused and withdrew two identical bibles from her purse. Unlike the big unwieldy book from which we had read each afternoon, these little books fit neatly into the hand.

Each one was bound in black leather with gold lettering along the spine and a simple cross etched into the leather of the front cover. The pages were gilt edged. My aunt handed one of the bibles to Nell who, with a gasp, flung her arms impulsively about Aunt Abigail's thin body and hugged her fiercely.

Aunt Abigail stiffened in Nell's embrace and drew back sharply. "Goodness, Nell," her tone was forbidding, "such an outburst is most unseemly."

Then she turned to me. "Ada, go with the Lord," she said, handing me the other bible. I took it from her and, risking her further displeasure, bent and dropped a swift kiss on her paper-dry cheek. She did not scold me, however, but laid her hand on mine for a second before she turned away.

Then she was gone through the doors, past the line of hastily assembled servants, to where Drake stood stiffly holding the carriage door. My father bowed over her extended hand then handed his sister into the carriage. Aunt Abigail did not look back.

Surprised by my own emotions, I bit back tears and turned to see Miss Blackly with her arm around a weeping Nell, while the twins embraced each other, though whether it was from joy or sorrow, I was not entirely sure. I watched them for a moment before carrying my bible upstairs and placing it beside my bed.

I have it still, much worn and fingered now, with the gilt edging lost. The faded inscription on the flyleaf reads "From Abigail Ada Baldwin, 1885." Until then, I had not known that I bore my aunt's middle name.

CHAPTER 14

Spring gave way to golden summer and, as the days and weeks flew by, I found that our upcoming journey filled my mind to the exclusion of almost anything else. At first, I had imagined that all the servants would come with us, but that was not to be. Nell and I took turns to plead with both Mrs. Carter and Cook, but to no avail.

Mrs. Carter assured us that she had already made plans to go and live with her sister in Truro, and Cook shook her head stubbornly and announced very loudly to anyone who would listen that the Good Lord never meant for civilized folk to go and live with a bunch of savages. No amount of reassurance on Nell's part or downright pleading on mine made the slightest difference. Cook was not coming with us. Neither was Ned; his health problems would not allow it, and I wondered if the matter of Bessie had ever been resolved.

I had great hopes for Annie, though. Over the weeks, I had come to use her skills more and more. Although not trained to be a lady's maid, she was quick with her hands and had shown increasing skills in dressing my hair and caring for my meager wardrobe. She was also very comfortable looking after little Edie when the need arose.

Annie had no family that I knew of. Mama had taken her from an orphanage when she was a very young girl—put there, I suspect, by a family who could not cope with a child so disfigured about the mouth. I decided to speak to my father first and, with his approval, invite Annie to come with us, in part as my maid, and also as Edie's nanny. I was delighted with my plan and even more pleased when Papa readily agreed to my suggestion. All that remained was for me to tell Annie.

Lately, I had developed the habit of ringing for her at the end of each day. I liked her to help me undress and then to brush out my hair. I knew that Jennings had done this every night for my mother and I suppose, in my foolishness I thought myself to be the woman of the house and in need of such special care.

I could hardly wait to share my wonderful plan with Annie. She was brushing my hair when I told her. As usual, her head was bent to hide her face, but her hands were steady as she brushed with one hand and stroked with the other, gently teasing out the tangles of the day. At my words, she raised her head and stared at me in the mirror. All colour drained from her face, leaving her twisted mouth a crooked gash against the pallor of her skin; her eyes were huge and her hands stilled in the act of brushing. I beamed at her in the mirror, pleased with her reaction, glad that I had surprised her.

Then Annie bent her head again and continued brushing the length of my hair, slowly letting the strands fall through her fingers. I continued to watch her in the mirror, waiting for her to speak, waiting for her happy reaction. After a few moments, I saw her take a deep breath then she raised her eyes to mine in the mirror and slowly shook her head.

"No, Miss Ada," she said, softly. "I'm ever so sorry, Miss, but I can't."

I swung around, knocking the brush to the floor as I jumped to my feet. "Of course you can, Annie. Don't be so silly!" I grabbed at her hand as she bent to retrieve the brush. "What's to stop you? I've already spoken to Mr. Baldwin, and he's delighted. Oh, Annie, we'll have such fun!"

Annie pulled away from me and took a step back. "I'm to be married, Miss," she said, speaking softly, her head once more bent to hide her face.

"Married?" I blurted out. "But who would?" I stopped, horrified by what I had nearly said.

Colour flooded back into Annie's face as she raised her head deliberately and looked straight at me. "My young man would, Miss, you saw him once last Boxing Day, when you come running into the kitchen when you were so sick. You may not remember him; he was playing the fiddle."

I sank back down onto my dresser stool and thought for a moment. I had been mostly intent on screaming at Bessie that night, but now I thought about it, I did remember a young man, seated next to Annie.

I looked up at her. "Yes, I do remember. But I had no idea that he was your young man. Who is he, and is he suitable? I've no wish to see you hurt by some tinker lad who's just passing by."

Annie slammed my hairbrush onto the dresser and, turning, made for the door, anger showing in every line of her body. "If you please, Miss," she said thickly, "I think I'm done here for tonight."

I jumped to my feet and ran after her, grabbing once more at her arm. "Annie," I said. "I'm so sorry. I didn't mean to insult you. I'm just shocked and . . ." I paused, realizing the truth of what I was saying. "I'm so disappointed; I really wanted you to come with us. Please forgive me and tell me about your young man."

Annie's anger had disappeared as quickly as it had come and now she looked both contrite and a little frightened. "I'm sorry, Miss Ada, I don't mean to show disrespect, but me and Owain have been walking out for more than a year now, and he's very respectable, Miss." I pulled her back towards the dresser and gestured for her to take the stool, while I sat on the carved wooden chest at the end of the bed.

Annie perched uncomfortably on the edge of the seat, looking as if she might take flight at any moment, but I smiled encouragingly and, reaching forward, patted her hand. "Come on Annie," my tone was teasing, "tell me about your Owain."

Annie wiggled her shoulders a little and began to pleat her apron with nervous fingers. "Well, Miss," she started. "He's appenticed to the smith down the village, and used to come up here to take the horses down for shoeing and such, and we got to talking an'" her voice faded to nothing, but her fingers kept busily pleating. Her voice was stronger when she spoke again.

"He never seems to see me mouth, Miss, just like it weren't there, and he's ever so kind and gentle. He's about done his time with smithy so he'll be going off home soon. He asked me to wed him just last week."

"Oh, Annie, that's wonderful." I was genuinely pleased. "And you said yes."

Annie nodded shyly. "Yes I did, Miss, though I'm not sure how I'll fit in with his folks." She looked up suddenly. "Owain Davies, he is, Miss, from near Pontypridd in Wales."

I stared at her in alarm. "Wales! That's a long way from home, Annie. Are you sure?"

She nodded then gave a sudden unexpected gurgle of laughter. "Well, Miss, so is this here Argentina you're going to, from all accounts." I stared at Annie for a moment then I, too, started to laugh.

In the end, Drake was the only servant who accompanied us to our new life.

Lucy Blackly had kept very much to herself during the weeks following my father's arrival, although I saw her in deep discussion with him on more than one occasion. Our relationship was still strained and I had not spoken to her directly since my outburst the night of my father's return. I knew very well that I should apologize, but the opportunity did not seem to present itself and Lucy did not seek me out. It was the end of May before things came to a head.

Dinner was early, as it often was on Thursdays, for this was Cook's afternoon off and she always left us something simple that we could attend to ourselves. This particular meal had been a cold one, and only Nell and I had presented ourselves in the dining room at the sound of the dinner bell. Papa was closeted in his study and I had seen Drake take a food-laden tray into him as I walked downstairs.

By now my sister and I had formed an uneasy truce. Trying to persuade the servants to come to Argentina with us had given us a common goal, so our earlier differences were largely forgotten.

We had finished our meal and were preparing to leave when the door opened and Lucy Blackly came in. She hesitated for a moment, looking from one to the other of us, then bowed her head in a graceful gesture and turned to leave. I glanced at Nell, who was inspecting her table napkin with great interest, then rose quickly to my feet.

Miss Blackly—Lucy—please don't go. Nell and I," I paused, "we'd be pleased to keep you company for a while." Lucy Blackly looked at me steadily for a moment then inclined her head again, this time in acquiescence.

Nell, however, jumped quickly to her feet and, with a muttered excuse, scuttled out of the room as fast as she could. I was dismayed; I thought that since Nell and Miss Blackly were on good terms, she might at least have stayed to ease the tension between the two of us.

I sat at the table and waited in silence while the governess helped herself to a small amount of food from the still piled platters. As she seated herself, I looked at her properly for the first time in weeks.

She had lost weight, I noticed, and her skin had an almost translucent look. She picked up her knife and fork, but put them down again as if she was reluctant to start eating. The silence lengthened and now it was my turn to fiddle nervously with my napkin.

"Miss Blackly," I said at length. "I owe you an apology for my rudeness the night I found out about our move to Argentina." There was no response and Miss Blackly continued to look down at her plate as if I hadn't spoken.

"I was angry and upset that you'd shared so much with my sister but said nothing to me," I continued. "But I should not have said what I did."

Lucy Blackly lifted her head. "Ada," she said her voice level. "I am not a servant in this house nor am I your governess. I had thought that we could be friends, but I think now that I was wrong. Nell did not tell me anything. She said only that she wanted to learn to speak Spanish and had a great interest in Argentina, as Mr. Baldwin was staying there for such a long time." She smiled. "You also expressed interest in Buenos Aires and I hoped that by giving you my brother's dictionary, you, too, might become interested in learning to speak Spanish."

"You did not continue to visit me after your illness and I thought perhaps you did not wish to continue deceiving your aunt, and I beg your pardon for ever encouraging you to do so."

I made to interrupt, but she held up her hand to stop me. "When Nell told me that she had read Drake's letter from your father, I tried to insist that she confess this to your aunt, as well as to Drake. However, Nell was saved from that necessity by the timely return of your father and the departure of your aunt."

She looked down once again at her plate of untouched food. "As for my fiancé, Captain Atkins, so far as I know, he is still serving in India.

The postal service from there is notoriously bad and I shouldn't be so foolish as to expect letters with any frequency."

As I listened to Lucy, I was filled with a deep sense of shame. As usual, I had seen things only from my own point of view. She had not been plotting and planning with Nell, and had never shown anything but kindness to any of us. I remembered the blue dress she had given me for my birthday, the generosity with which she had helped Bessie, and the small kindness of Christmas gifts freely given. And I remembered how often I had seen her glance anxiously at the mail as it lay on the hall table, waiting for a letter from India; a letter that never came.

Impulsively, I put out my hand and reached for hers. "I'm so sorry," I whispered. "Please forgive me!"

Lucy Blackly did not take my proffered hand, but instead straightened in her chair. "Of course I do, my dear," she said, briskly. "Now why don't you go and do some of the many things that I'm sure are awaiting your attention, and leave me to eat. I have some darning to do before I go to bed. The twins seem to put holes in every pair of stockings that they own."

As I left the dining room, I felt relief that Lucy and I were on speaking terms again, but wondered if we would ever recapture our old, easy relationship.

A week later on a beautiful summer evening, our lives changed once again. The flowers in the garden were blooming in riotous abundance and their perfume mingled with the sweet smell of freshly cut grass. Nell and I were walking side by side, watching the twins who ran ahead of us, occasionally chasing each other with dandelion heads that had escaped Ned's watchful eye. We had not been speaking much. I think that our imminent departure was becoming a reality for both of us.

Earlier in the day, Nell had begged Papa to allow us to include Mama's piano with the things that were to go with us. We were taking many of our smaller possessions, and while the piano was a large piece of furniture, it was one that we both valued greatly. Papa's response to Nell had been an unequivocal refusal, and I knew that she was hurt and angry, so I walked next to her that evening, hoping that the beauty that surrounded us would help to soothe her.

We had just taken a second turn around the rose garden and I had called to the twins not to stray near the river when I saw my father and Lucy Blackly emerge from the house. Papa offered Lucy his arm, but instead of taking it, she stepped away from him and twirled around on the newly cut grass, before finally stopping and laughing breathlessly as she looked up into his face. I saw my father laugh too then he took her hand and raised it to his lips. I caught my breath. Beside me, Nell was standing quite still, her eyes also on Lucy and Papa.

My heart began to beat strongly. I was sure that this could mean only one thing. I remembered the times I had seen the two of them together. The night of Papa's return, when he had raised his glass to Lucy in a toast and she had laughed back at him, her face glowing in the candlelight. And other occasions, too, when I had seen the two of them deep in conversation, and I knew that it had been months since Lucy had heard from Frederick. I gave Nell's arm a squeeze. "Come on," I said happily. "It looks as if Lucy will be coming with us, after all."

I started towards them, with Nell two steps in front of me. As we approached, Lucy pulled something white from the pocket of her skirt and began waving it.

"Look," she called breathlessly as soon as we were close enough to hear. "I have such wonderful news! My darling Frederick is home safe. We are to be married immediately. He must return to India soon, but insists that he will take me with him this time!" Lucy's face was aglow with happiness and my father stood beside her, his own face beaming with delight. My dream of having Lucy Blackly as a dearly loved step-mother shattered in that instant, and I knew by her sudden stillness that Nell had harboured the same foolish dream.

We now had two weddings to prepare for and the days were slipping into weeks and the weeks to months and September, when we were to embark on our own great adventure, was fast approaching.

CHAPTER 15

Annie and Owain Davies were married at the end of June. It was a simple wedding, with all of the people from the local village attending, as well as the entire Baldwin household. We were, after all, Annie's only family and she was well loved.

After the service, everyone walked back to the house where there was a fine spread laid out on the back lawn: huge platters of meat and baskets of fresh-baked bread. There were jellies and trifles and pies and a wedding cake to please the grandest folk.

My father toasted the couple's good health with the finest blackberry cordial and we all raised our cups to wish them well, though I think that more than one of those cups held something a little stronger than fruit cordial.

During the festivities, I was shocked to catch sight of Bessie flaunting her great belly proudly, laughing and joking and seemingly enjoying herself immensely. I looked for Ned, but did not see him.

As darkness fell, we saw Annie and her new husband off in fine style. Owain had not come empty-handed to his marriage, for he owned a good sound workhorse purchased from the smith, once his seven years of apprenticeship were finished. It was a sturdy beast, well suited, I was told, to the hilly ground of Wales, where Owain owned a small plot of land close to a river and where he was planning to start his own smithy.

The kindly blacksmith had thrown in a stout cart, freshly painted in dark green, brushing aside the thanks of the young couple and telling everyone loudly that since he'd had no need of it for nigh on five years, he wouldn't miss a plank of it!

We had contributed, too, and Annie went off to her new life with a feather mattress and pillows, some good bed linen, and a selection of pots and pans dangling from the back of the cart.

The bride was wearing a simple green dress that I recognized as one of Lucy's, made over to fit her slight figure, but it brought out the colour of her eyes and set off her pretty brown hair. I gave Annie a soft woolen shawl of mine. It had a deep fringe around the edge and she looked wonderful in it. I knew that I would always remember her the way she looked on her wedding day.

As the young couple trotted off into the night, I wondered what lay ahead of them and, even more, what lay ahead of us. I never saw dear Annie again, but pray that she had a long and happy life in Wales with her gentle Owain.

Lucy's wedding was a much grander affair. She was married in the Anglican Church where her father presided as minister. We were all invited, but Papa would not allow us to go to the wedding ceremony.

We were, however, allowed to greet the young couple as they emerged from the church and ran laughing under an archway of swords, provided by Frederick's brother officers. Frederick himself was something of a disappointment. I had thought that he would be tall and handsome, with dark wavy hair and piercing eyes. But Frederick was a little shorter than Lucy, with receding sandy hair and a slightly plump waistline. He looked quite grand in his uniform, though, and his smile was jolly and Lucy obviously adored him.

Lucy's wedding gown was beautiful. Her sister, Suzanne, had brought it with her from London and it was very elegant. She carried a small bouquet of orchids. When I asked Nell if she had supplied the flowers, my sister just smiled and shrugged, but didn't answer me.

The wedding took place on a beautiful summer day, and the reception was held in the gardens of Lucy's home. Up to that time, I had not met Lucy's parents, though my father was well acquainted with their son-in-law, Mr. Matthew Kent. Indeed, it was through the Kent's that Lucy came to us as governess for the twins. Mrs. Blackly looked very much like her younger daughter, for they shared the same warm brown eyes and gentle manner.

The Reverend Blackly was quite different. He was a round, anxious little man who seemed incapable of staying still. He fussed from table to table, greeting everyone with great enthusiasm. But for all his fussy ways, the Reverend Blackly seemed to attract the love of children, and once the formal part of the day was over, I was much diverted by the sight of him surrounded by little ones, laughing and playing happily. The twins were part of this group, screaming and giggling along with Lucy's young cousins. In the end, Mrs. Blackly had to remonstrate with her husband and suggest quieter games.

Lucy's sister, Suzanne, and her husband, Matthew Kent, proved to be very pleasant company, though they seemed quite grand to me. Suzanne, for so she insisted I call her, was very kind and asked many questions about our upcoming journey. Before we parted, she gave me her London address and I promised to write to her when we arrived at our destination.

Now with Lucy and Annie both gone, many of the daily burdens fell onto my shoulders. We still had Mabel to take care of Edie, but she was adamant in her refusal to care for the twins, and Nell was of little help.

The need to find someone to keep my young sisters occupied ended abruptly at the end of July, when both girls came down with chickenpox. Dr. Wainwright was called and prescribed bed-rest and quiet. He supposed that one or more of the children at Lucy's wedding had been harbouring the disease and had passed it along to the twins.

He smiled encouragingly at me as he snapped his bag shut and prepared to leave. "Just make sure that you don't catch it, my dear," he said kindly as I walked down the stairs with him. "As I recall, young Nell caught chickenpox when she was just a little thing. Got it from one of the village children, but you never did." I promised that I would do my best to stay healthy, though I had little choice, for it fell to me to nurse the twins through their sickest days.

Lucy Blackly's replacement arrived at the beginning of August and I was very glad to welcome her. Miss Mavis Walsh was a small, efficient

Scottish woman who had spent the previous eight years in India acting as governess to three young boys who were now all of an age to attend school in England.

Miss Walsh made it very plain during her interview—which, surprisingly, Papa had asked me to attend—that she had a small income from an inheritance, but that she preferred to keep busy working for the betterment of children. However, her years in the tropics had thinned Miss Walsh's blood, and she could no longer endure the damp chill of her native Scotland. She seemed happy to accept the position that my father offered her, though she stated clearly that she would not be in any way responsible for Edith until my little sister was of an age to enter the schoolroom. We were very glad to have her.

The question of what would happen to our home once we had left had troubled me for some weeks. Then one afternoon, Papa returning unexpectedly from one of his trips to the city, was accompanied by a young couple. They spent a good deal of time looking at the house, ranging from room to room and even poking about in the attics. Then they retired to Papa's study where tea was served.

I was crossing the hallway when they emerged a short time later, and Papa introduced me to the people who would be renting our house. This would include much of the furniture and both of our carriages. They had a young child already and, as the husband blushingly explained, would shortly need nursery space for another. I was glad that a young family would occupy our home, but it was difficult to imagine someone else in our rooms, eating off our table, or seated at Mama's piano.

That we would all need new clothes as we set out on our great adventure had not occurred to me, and it was Suzanne Kent to whom I owed a debt of gratitude in this regard. A few days after Lucy's wedding, apparently at Mrs. Kent's urging, Papa sent for the dressmaker, who arrived, complete with tape measures, pencil, and notebook.

As had happened before, we were poked and prodded and hummed over, and a short while later, several bulky parcels arrived containing lightweight skirts and cool bodices for Nell and me, along with two more formal gowns each. There were also dresses and pinafores for the twins. I was delighted, and even Nell did not object to her more adult attire.

By now, it was well into August, and on the second Monday of the month, Papa called Nell and me into his study. The room looked strangely bare. Even the polished surface of Papa's desk was empty except for a stack of important-looking documents. My father rose from his seat and walked over to the window before addressing us.

"Things are not going as smoothly as I had hoped," he said, "and Señor Rodriguez has sent an urgent request that I join him in London."

I had quite forgotten Señor Rodriguez in all the hustle and bustle of the previous few weeks. My father turned from the window and walked slowly back to his desk, seating himself in his big leather chair.

"I am very much afraid that I will not be able to return here until very shortly before we leave," he said. "Drake will return in good time and it will be his responsibility to make the final arrangements. We sail on September twentieth and I will do my best to be with you on the nineteenth, at the very latest. I leave for London in the morning."

My heart sank; there were so many things yet to be done. I opened my mouth to protest, but realizing the futility of doing so, closed it again. As if reading my mind, Papa spoke directly to me.

"I'm sorry, Ada, but this is unavoidable if we are to leave on time. I plan to hire another maid to serve both of you girls. Mrs. Kent has kindly undertaken to look for such a person in London and she will be sent here as soon as possible. I will also endeavour to find a new nursemaid for Edith. If I am not able to do so, Mabel has agreed to stay until our last day here and then the new maid can assist you with the child.

My head swirled and I wondered how I could possibly manage this alone, but once again my father seemed to read my mind, for he smiled in my direction before turning to Nell. "Naturally, I expect you to help Ada in every way possible, Nell. Do you understand?"

My sister nodded solemnly then made a surprising request.

"Papa, Ada and I would like to go into town to purchase a few things that we need: bonnets and gloves."

"And -" she paused delicately.

My father held up a silencing hand. "Of course," he said quickly. "Ned can take you into Wimborne where you can purchase anything that you require. Have the bills sent to the house." With that, my father dismissed us with a wave of his hand.

As the study door closed behind us, I turned to my sister. "What was that about?" I asked, for Nell had never before shown the slightest interest in buying any clothes, least of all bonnets or gloves.

My sister smiled at me; it was a smile I didn't trust. "I thought you might like to say goodbye to your friend Angela," she said sweetly. "And there are a few things I'd like to buy for myself," she added over her shoulder as she walked away.

I stared after her, amazed that she even remembered my friendship with Angela. Nell was right, though, I should go to see my friend before we departed. Despite all of my good intentions, I had never written to her. As I hurried away, I thought that perhaps buying new bonnets and gloves was not such a dreadful idea, after all. Papa left very early the next morning.

It wasn't until the following Friday that I found time to order the carriage to take Nell and me into Wimborne. Nell persuaded Cook to pack a picnic for us and we stowed the basket, filled with cold chicken, fresh bread, and other tasty goodies, beneath one of the seats as we set off.

The sun was shining brightly that morning and I felt my spirits lifting. The twins were finally out and about again under the watchful eye of Miss Walsh and, as Ned turned the carriage onto the road, I saw Mabel Crossley pushing the big perambulator with Edie in it, headed towards the village. I sat back with a satisfied sigh and enjoyed feeling the breeze on my face and the warmth of the sun across my shoulders. Today was going to be fun.

When we arrived in Wimborne, I was determined to make Angela and her mother our very first call and I regretted that I had not thought to write a note to let Mrs. Seaton know of our intended visit.

As we descended from the carriage, bidding Ned to wait for us, Nell smiled at me. "Why don't you go along to see your friend?" she suggested. I have a shop that I want to visit; it's quite close by."

"What about your bonnets?" I asked sharply. I had counted on Nell's presence in the shop to ease the awkwardness of my meeting with Angela after all this time. But my sister was already on her way, waving a careless hand as she went.

"Choose whatever you like, Ada," she called as she disappeared around the corner. With a shake of my head, I straightened my shoulders and walked alone to the little shop that held so many memories.

I pushed open the door and the familiar bell announced my presence. There was a stir at the back of the shop and Mrs. Seaton appeared from behind the curtain. She stared at me for a moment, peering through the dim light that filtered through the curtained windows. Then I heard her quickly indrawn breath as she started towards me.

She stopped abruptly about three feet away from me, her outstretched hands dropping to her sides. Her voice sounded a little strained. "Oh, my dear," she said, "you are the very image of her!" She shook her head as if to clear it and smiled at me. "If I had known you were coming, Ada, I would have made certain that Angela was here, but I'm afraid she's out."

I cut her apologies short. "That's quite all right," I said. "I should have sent a note. I've come for some bonnets for my sister Nell and me. We're going away to South America to live." Even as I said the words, I knew how preposterous I must have sounded, but Mrs. Seaton just smiled and proffered the tiny chair in front of the mirror; the chair where my mother used to sit.

As I stared at my own reflection, Mrs. Seaton pulled out some plain dark bonnets and held them up for my inspection, but I shook my head.

"We'll need something lighter and a little more stylish if you have it please, Mrs. Seaton," I said. "It will be summer when we arrive in Buenos Aries." Mrs. Seaton nodded briskly then moved quickly to a stack of boxes that were piled on one of the tables close by. She pulled out a pale blue satin hat and held it out for my inspection.

An hour passed almost without my realizing it. Mrs. Seaton and I chatted easily and not once did she ask me why I had not written or called on her daughter.

When I left the little store, I was well satisfied with my purchases. Mrs. Seaton had promised to look for one or two of the more stylish hats that were being worn in London that season, and said that she would have them sent over as soon as possible.

As I emerged into the street, I looked around for Nell or the carriage, but could see neither one. With a familiar prickle of irritation, I turned on my heel and walked down the narrow street until I came to Young's Drapers and Haberdashers. I made several purchases there, including stockings for the twins and, with the help of one of the lady employees, I bought undergarments for Nell and me guessing at Nell's size and hoping that she would be pleased with my purchases. As in Mrs. Seaton's shop, my father's name was quite sufficient to allow me to be billed for all my purchases.

When I returned to the High street, I looked about once again, but though it was not very busy; there was still no sign of either Nell or the carriage.

A little anxious now, I turned and walked briskly up the street in the direction in which Nell had disappeared. Just as I was rounding the corner, I bumped sharply into someone coming the other way. My parcels were scattered in all directions and, by the time I had gathered most of them up, I was feeling quite flustered. Finally, I straightened, holding out my hand for the parcels that the other person had retrieved for me, and found myself looking straight into the eyes of Angela Seaton.

We stared at each other for a moment and I felt a smile spreading across my face. "Angela," I said happily, reaching with my free hand to catch her arm. Angela stared at me for a moment, then with a quick movement, she dipped a curtsey, handed me my packages and hurried on her way without a word.

"Angela!" I called after her again. "It's me, Ada!"

Angela stopped in her tracks and spun around. "Yes, Miss Baldwin," she said bitterly. "I know exactly who you are, and I have nothing to say to you. I wish you a good day." With that, she turned again and disappeared into her mother's shop without a backward glance. I stayed where I was, tears welling in my eyes, wanting to run after my friend but knowing that it would do no good. Angela had not forgiven me for my rudeness in ignoring her for so long, and I could scarcely blame her.

As I stood blinking away my tears, I heard someone call my name. I looked up to see Nell dancing along the street, for all-the world like a small child. "I got what I wanted," she called gleefully. Swinging from her hands were four large square parcels tied with string; they appeared to be very heavy.

My sister looked at me sharply as she reached me. "Why are you crying?" she demanded, peering into my face. Then, not waiting for an answer, she grabbed hold of me with one already laden hand and started to drag me along, chattering all the while.

I let Nell talk as she led the way towards the square in the middle of town. "I told Ned to meet us outside the inn," she said gaily. "He looked so bored sitting waiting for us."

"And then I thought we could all go to the minster and have our lunch in the graveyard. It's so pretty there and I love to look at the old gravestones. Cook gave us loads of food, so there'll be lots for Ned to share."

I was too miserable to do anything more than nod, though usually I would have argued with almost everything that Nell was saying. She had no right to send Ned off to the inn, I did not want to eat a picnic lunch amongst the dead, and I felt it very improper to share a meal with our handyman in such a public place.

Ned was leaning against the open carriage as we crossed the square. He was talking to several young men of about his own age who eyed us boldly as we approached.

"Come along, Ned," I said, in what I hoped was my most adult voice. "We must be going."

"Right you are, Miss Ada," he replied with a cheeky grin. "Reckon it's time for us to go and have some grub then." The other youths sniggered, pushing at each other and gawking.

As Ned handed us into the carriage and swung himself easily onto the driver's seat I was angrily certain that his friends were laughing at us, in a most vulgar and improper way.

It was a short drive to the church of Wimborne Minster. Then, with Nell leading the way and Ned bringing up the rear with the picnic basket and a blanket, we set off across the old cemetery where Nell selected a spot under an ancient tree.

"Here, this is perfect," she said. Ned put down the basket and prepared to spread the blanket but, as he did so, there was a rumble of thunder. I looked up at the sky in surprise. I had been too preoccupied with my own emotions to notice the weather. Clouds had covered the sun and the wind was starting to rise, blowing in gusts across the graveyard. There was a sudden flash of lightening not too far away, and almost immediately another crash of thunder. Ned stopped what he was doing and looked enquiringly us.

"It's nothing," my sister said, airily. "It'll soon blow over." But within seconds, she was proved wrong. The rain blew in almost at once, cold and stinging and battering at our faces. The wind picked up and caught at the tree branches as we turned and fled back the way we had come. We stumbled along, tripping over some of the old graves and slipping on the moss-covered stones of others, long since sunk into the grass, while all around us the storm increased.

At last, we reached the gate and, hastening out onto the road, headed towards the carriage. Ned struggled to raise the hood, but it did little good for we were already soaking wet. As we lurched towards home, with Ned whipping at the poor horses, Nell insisted on trying to cover her parcels with the wet blanket, pushing them anxiously under the seat, as the rain continued to fall.

Finally, I could stand it no longer. "For goodness' sake, Nell," I snapped. "Everything's wet. Be grateful for the hatboxes, at least our new bonnets will be safe. Anyway, what do you have there that is so important?"

Nell stopped what she was doing for a moment and looked at me blankly. Then as my words registered, she grabbed the biggest hatbox and pulled off the lid. Without a second's hesitation, she removed the pale blue hat that I had so recently selected, and cast it onto the wet seat. I cried out and tried to stop her, but she had already taken one of her parcels and was desperately tugging at the wet brown paper before tumbling the contents into the box and slamming the lid shut.

I stared at my sister in disbelief. "Books!" I shouted over the noise of the rain. "You bought books? Does Papa know about this?" My sister didn't answer, she was too busy removing the contents from the picnic basket and throwing the food carelessly onto the floor. Two more packages of books were pushed hastily inside the wicker basket and then the basket itself was pushed under the seat. It was only when she was sure that all her books were safe that Nell allowed herself to sit up and look at me. I stared back at my sister in amazement. Her face was red, her hair was tumbling down beneath her soaked bonnet, and her glasses were misted with rain, but she was beaming triumphantly.

"There," she said. "I think I've saved them all."

"How many books did you buy, Nell?" I asked again, pushing a strand of wet hair back under my own soaking bonnet. "I bought all the works of Miss Jane Austen," she said reverently, "and a book by George Eliot, though Lucy told me that he is really a woman; and some poetry and two of Mr. Charles Dickens' books." She paused, peering anxiously into my face. "Ada, you have to understand, I have no idea if I can even buy a book in South America. I have to have books with me or I'll go crazy. I'm sure Papa will understand." Suddenly, she grinned mischievously at me and wiped the rain from her dripping nose. "Even if he doesn't, it'll be far too late by the time he finds out now, won't it?"

The storm had almost abated by the time we arrived home and the sun was struggling out from behind the clouds. Cook started out of her chair in consternation as Nell and I straggled into the kitchen, dripping water everywhere. I had retrieved my own parcels, including the ruined blue hat, but had left Nell to struggle with hers.

My sister was behind me, dragging the picnic basket and hat boxes into the kitchen and dumping them all onto the tiled floor before sitting down next to them and anxiously inspecting her purchases. Cook clucked around us like a startled hen for a few moments before hurrying to set the kettle to boil. Ignoring my sister, I swept towards the door that led to the rest of the house. "I'm soaking wet, and I'm going to change my clothes. I'll ring for tea when I'm ready," I said grandly. Cook stared after me, her hands on her hips and her mouth open in silent protest. As I pushed open the swing door, I came face to face with Mrs. Carter.

"Miss Ada," she said, ignoring my bedraggled state, "before you go anywhere, you should know that there's a person waiting to see you in the drawing room. She insisted on waiting in there, though what she wants I can't think. She's not a person of quality, that's for certain. She took her portmanteau with her and absolutely refused to give me her name. I would have turned her away at the door but she was most particular that she speaks to you."

I stared at Mrs. Carter, my mind racing. Then I had it! Angela, I thought happily. She must have felt badly about her earlier behaviour and come here to see me. She had probably even brought the extra hats that Mrs. Seaton had promised me. I gave the startled Mrs. Carter a quick hug and, forgetting my wet clothes, ran across the hall, pulling my bonnet from my head as I did so. The drawing room door was slightly ajar and I pushed it wide open, a glad smile on my face.

The person sitting uneasily on the sofa nearest to the window was a complete stranger. She half rose when I entered, but subsided as she took in my disheveled appearance.

"I'm here to see Miss Ada Baldwin and Miss Nelly Baldwin," she said in a stilted accent, "and I won't be put off!" She pronounced "off" as "orf."

Surprise robbed me of speech for a moment, but then I recovered myself. "I'm Miss Baldwin," I said stiffly. "What do you want?"

"I wants to see the both of you, Miss Nelly, too," her tone was a little uncertain now.

"It's Nell, not Nelly," I said absently, as I became aware of my own bedraggled appearance.

The woman continued to stare at me in silence for a few seconds then she dropped her eyes. "I'm sent from London, by Mrs. Kent, as lady's maid," she said sullenly.

"I see." My tone was cold. "Perhaps then you would care to wait in the kitchen until my sister and I are ready to receive you. We do not conduct interviews with maidservants in our drawing room." I walked over and rang the bell.

When an approving Mrs. Carter had removed the woman, I made my way upstairs, wondering what kind of a person Suzanne Kent had sent us. Certainly not one well versed in the behaviour of upstairs servants. As I turned to go into my own room I heard Nell clatter up the stairs behind me. I paused in the doorway and told her briefly about the woman waiting below.

My sister shrugged. "I don't mind seeing her in the drawing room. It's warm and comfortable in there. Besides, I want some tea. We missed eating lunch," she added, disappearing into her own room, "and I'm cold and starving."

By the time I arrived back downstairs, Nell had already met our new maid and, true to her word had taken her into the drawing room. There was a tea tray set with freshly buttered scones and slices of Cook's best fruitcake before them on the small table in front of the fireplace.

"You've already met my sister Ada," Nell waved an airy hand, speaking through a mouthful of buttered scone.

I stood in the doorway looking pointedly at the woman who was once again seated, this time in an upright chair that she had drawn close to the table. She met my eyes boldly, but then rose to her feet and, ducking an awkward curtsey, extended her hand. I ignored it, and seated myself in the chair opposite Nell. I poured a cup of tea, then leaned back and regarded our visitor.

"You told me that Mrs. Kent sent you, but you omitted to tell me your name." My tone was still cool.

The woman's thin cheeks coloured, and she pulled her shawl around her shoulders and fussed with the small cloth purse that hung by a chain from her wrist. "Beggin' your pardon, Miss, I'm Lizzie Weeks, and I was sent particular by Mrs. Suzanne Kent. I was maid to old Mrs. Kent, God rest her soul, Miss."

"Can I have your letter of recommendation, Lizzie?" Nell spoke from the depths of her chair. Her tone was much warmer than mine, but she held out her hand as if the woman had already offered the letter to her.

Lizzie Weeks turned and spoke quickly to my sister. "Oh, Miss, it was all such a rush, I come away without it. But it was Mrs. Kent as told me to come, and paid me ticket and all. I'm to go to Argenteeny land with you as I understand it, Miss." She gazed anxiously from one to the other of us as if waiting for us to contradict her statement.

I looked across at Nell. She gave her usual shrug and continued eating her scone, licking her buttery fingers and ignoring my unspoken questions. I sipped my tea slowly, trying to think what I should do.

Lizzie Weeks had appeared out of nowhere, purporting to be the maid Papa had promised us, but she had no letter of recommendation. She obviously knew that we had need of a maid and it did seem reasonable that Papa had agreed to hire her. And upon reflection, I remembered that Suzanne Kent had spoken of her mother-in-law's poor health when we had met at Lucy's wedding reception.

So why did I feel so uncomfortable? Why was I sure that there was something not quite right about Lizzie Weeks? I couldn't decide what to do, but I knew that Papa would be angry if he returned to find that I had sent the woman packing, when he had been quite satisfied with her. Suddenly, I felt very tired.

"Do you know that you will also be required to take care of our baby sister Edith from time to time?" I asked, wearily.

Lizzie had remained standing all this time and now she bobbed a curtsey. "Oh, yes, Miss, and that's no trouble. I do love little ones, Miss," she added, earnestly.

I nodded. "Very well, go along to the kitchen and take your luggage with you." I gestured towards the shabby portmanteau that was resting on the floor beside the sofa. "Mrs. Carter will take care of you and she'll see that you get a proper uniform. You will not be required to help us dress for dinner tonight, but we will ring if we have need of you."

As Lizzie gathered up her bag and started towards the door, I leaned back in my chair once more and eyed my sister with disapproval.

CHAPTER 16

Our last two weeks in England flew by and I had no time to wonder if my father's choice of a maid had been a wise one. My days were taken up with packing, organizing the household for the new tenants, and reassuring the twins, who were still fractious and a little unwell from their recent illness. Even finding a few moments to prepare my own clothes and possessions for the journey was proving difficult.

Lizzie appeared to settle in well enough under the circumstances, and on the odd occasions that I asked her to help me with some personal task, she seemed willing enough, if a little clumsy.

A week after Papa and Drake had left Bert Baker arrived from the station his cart piled high with large empty steamer trunks. My father sent a brief note informing us that we were each to retain one small trunk for ourselves during the voyage; the rest, along with all our other possessions, would go on ahead of us.

Before she left us, Annie had packed up many of my clothes, folding them lovingly and tucking small bags of lavender between the folds of soft paper that enfolded each garment. I tried to do the same, picking the long-stemmed lavender from the beds that grew profusely around the edge of the kitchen garden.

I kept back very few items for my use on the voyage: two or three serviceable skirts and bodices, a warm cloak, two plain hats, and a change of boots. I did not see the need to keep any of my good gowns out. We were, after all, only to be on board a ship.

As the days went by, I waited anxiously for the return of my father, but he did not come. Then, two days before we were due to leave, I heard the clatter of wheels on the driveway. With a quick prayer of thanks, I ran swiftly downstairs to where the front door stood open. My joy quickly turned to dismay, however, at the sight of Drake descending alone from the station coach.

"Where is Mr. Baldwin?" I cried, not even bothering to greet poor Drake.

The little man looked tired and flustered. "There's been delays, Miss, and all sorts of difficulties in London. Debtors is debtors in my mind, though it was not Mr. Rodriguez's fault, I suppose, for how was he to know they'd changed the prison laws? He's not even English, Miss, now, is he?"

I looked after him in bewilderment as he hurried away. "When is my father going to be here?" I called after him.

Drake looked back over his shoulder. "He'll likely be here, Miss, don't you fret. And if not, we're to catch the train the day after tomorrow just as planned."

I had to be content with that, for Drake then became a positive dervish, flying about my father's rooms, emptying drawers and packing clothes, all the while refusing to answer any further questions. Cook was already in a fine state of hysterics as the date of our departure drew nearer, but Mrs. Carter remained calm, perhaps because she, too, was departing and I knew she was looking forward to living a quieter life with her sister.

After many loud protests of despair, Cook had ended up throwing her apron over her head one morning and admitting in muffled tones that she would stay on with Ned to serve the new people. No one was surprised, and I was sure that it would not take them long to settle into her ways.

The next afternoon with most of my tasks completed, I felt a great desire to be outside in the fresh air, so I pushed quickly past the baggage that crowded the hallway, catching a glimpse of the shrouded drawing room furniture as I passed by, and headed for the open front door. Once outside, I looked about me. It was a perfect September day, filled with the soft golden light of early autumn as I made my way across the garden, and headed towards the river. I wanted to stand at its edge and remember my childhood.

The shadows were starting to lengthen across the grass as I reached the riverbank. The river itself was running low, for even with the August thunderstorms, it had been a mostly hot and dry summer, so I turned instead and made my way to the orchard.

Most of the fruit had already been picked, but there remained a few late apples. I reached for one of the firm green-and-red globes and bit into it, tasting the sweetness of the summer in its crisp, white flesh. I looked for the stone bench where I used to sit, but it had been overturned, one end broken and its jagged pieces already overgrown with moss.

Filled with melancholy, I turned back towards the house and my mother's rose garden. Most of the standard roses were long since dead, and the garden looked oddly deserted. As I looked about, something caught my eye and, turning, I saw the bushes of white roses. They were growing beside the path, the heavy blooms reaching almost to the ground. These were her September roses; my mother could have told me that they did not bloom in June. I knew then what I needed to do before I left this house. Hurrying back indoors, I found the flat basket and sharp knife that were still on the shelf in the vestibule.

I cut only the most perfect blooms: five roses that were just starting to emerge from their buds, their full beauty not yet visible, but their perfume delicate in the late afternoon air. There was a rose for each of my mother's five daughters. I arranged them as best I could in the bottom of the basket and, pausing only long enough to retrieve my bonnet and cloak, I set off for my mother's grave.

The sun was starting to sink over the hill as I walked up the steep path to the graveyard. It was very quiet, for the evening breeze had paused in its play among the topmost branches of the trees and even the birds had ceased their chatter. The only sound was the swish of my skirts and the gentle tap of the basket of roses hitting against my boot as I walked.

I found my mother's grave easily enough, it wasn't hard to do, for my sister Nell was standing at its foot. Her head was bowed and her cloak flapped forlornly against her thin body. The grave was completely covered, smothered, drowned in flowers. As I drew nearer, I saw that they were orchids, their leaves and petals already wilting and the dark stain of their torn roots scattered like black blood amidst the glorious colours. Nell did not move as I came and stood beside her, holding my own small offering. Carefully, I set the roses on the granite edge of Mama's grave and bent my head.

We walked back home in silence and it wasn't until we were turning into the driveway that I asked my sister the question that had been troubling me.

"Why did you uproot the orchids, Nell? You've killed them all."

Nell didn't look at me, she just nodded her head. "They were Mama's orchids," she said after a moment. "I kept them for her; they shouldn't belong to anyone else."

"We might come back here some day and Ned would have taken care of them for us," I protested. But my words sounded hollow, even to me.

My sister stopped as we reached the junction of the path that led to the side of the house and looked directly at me, her glasses catching the dying rays of the sun. "I'll never be here again," she said flatly. Then she turned and headed towards the kitchen garden and the back entrance. I shivered in spite of the warmth that still lingered in the air and made my own way to the front door.

My father did not come. On the appointed day, Drake bundled us into the carriage that took us to the station where we boarded a train headed north. Mrs. Carter waved goodbye, but of Cook there was no sign.

Once we were on our way, all was confusion for me. The journey was long and I scarcely remember the trains. I remember, only that there were people everywhere, and baggage waiting in great piles. Once we arrived at the docks in Liverpool, I looked for Papa's tall figure in the crowd, but did not see him. Everywhere, people hurried to and fro. The side of the ship loomed hugely above us as Drake deposited us beside a gangplank where sailors and passengers ascended and descended in bewildering numbers. My head had begun to ache and I felt a little dizzy with people swirling all around me.

After we had been waiting a few minutes, Drake turned to me. "Miss Baldwin," he said, worry written deep in the lines on his face, "I have to go and seek out the Master. I'm sure he is about somewhere. Please stay here. I'll return soon." And with that, he hurried away.

Nell sidled up to me as we watched Drake's diminutive figure disappear into the crowd. "What'll we do if he never comes back, Ada?" she asked.

Edie had been difficult and fretful on the long journey, but was, at the moment asleep in my arms. As I hitched her weight a little higher onto my shoulder, I glared at my sister and glanced over to where the twins and Miss Walsh were standing. Lily and Iris had obviously overheard Nell's question and were now watching me and waiting for my answer.

"Don't be silly," I said, trying to make my voice firm. "Drake will be here with Papa very shortly, isn't that so, Miss Walsh?"

The older woman looked at me coldly. "I'm sure I don't know, Miss. I've never in all my life had to deal with this sort of thing. Why, when I was in India, we had servants who looked after us every step of the way." But I had ceased to listen, for Nell had grabbed my arm and was pointing excitedly. The crowd was thinning now and I caught a glimpse of Drake running towards us.

When he arrived, he was panting with exertion. "Mr. Baldwin is coming momentarily," he gasped, nodding over his shoulder before hurrying up the gangplank to supervise the disposal of our luggage.

My headache had worsened, and my arms were aching quite dreadfully with the weight of carrying Edie. I turned wearily and saw Lizzie standing idly by.

In two steps, I was beside her and, bundling Edie into her reluctant arms, I snapped "Here, take care of Miss Edith, the Master is coming." As I turned away, Edie awoke and started to cry, but I ignored her and looked again to where Drake had indicated. Nell was standing on tiptoe, the better to see. Then she grabbed my arm again and pointed.

"There they are, way down there," she said. "But I can't work out what's going on."

The dock was almost empty now, apart from a few people waiting to wave their last farewells to those already on board. Far down the length of the ship, I spied a large vehicle that looked like an enormous black box on wheels. As I watched, two doors at the back swung open and a line of men, who appeared to be roped together, descended slowly from the vehicle and made their way towards the nearest gangplank. Then a man in a light-coloured suit, jumped down from the front.

"That's Señor Rodriguez!" Nell exclaimed. Peering ahead, I saw that Nell was right and then, with a flood of relief, I saw the tall figure of my father hastening towards us. As I watched his approach, I saw him slow his pace for a moment as he looked back over his shoulder to where a small figure, dressed strangely in loose blue trousers and a matching blue tunic, was running, in an effort to keep pace with him. Then all at once, he was upon us and swept us up the gangplank and onto the ship.

Once we were safely aboard, my father looked around and nodded. "That was very close" he said, "but we're all here, are we not?" His eyes swept over our small party, pausing for a moment when he reached Lizzie, who was still holding Edie, and then continuing on to the twins, who were standing next to Miss Walsh. Finally, he turned to Nell and me. "I'm sorry that was so rushed," he said, "but we encountered some unforeseen delays in London."

While he was speaking, the small, oddly dressed person who had accompanied my father approached Lizzie and silently removed the child from her all-too-willing arms. I took an instinctive step forward, but my father placed a restraining hand on my arm.

"This is Mrs. Chen," he said, with a slight bow in her direction. "She is from China and she is your sister's new nursemaid."

I stared at the woman standing before us. She was unlike anyone I had ever seen. She was very tiny, coming scarcely to my shoulder. Her face, under an oddly shaped straw hat, was tinged with yellow, and her dark eyes were narrow slits. She did not smile, but looked coolly back at me, inclining her head slightly. As she moved to shift Edie expertly on to one hip, she used her other foot to right the small wicker basket that she had been carrying. I looked down at it, wondering if this was the only luggage that she had. It was then that I noticed her feet. They were the tiniest feet I had ever seen on an adult; they were not much bigger than Edie's.

Surprisingly, my little sister stopped crying as soon as Mrs. Chen took hold of her and, truthfully, I rarely heard Edie cry in all the time that Mrs. Chen was with us. It was only later that the weeping was so loud.

CHAPTER 17

I was very ill on our journey to Argentina. My father had secured four cabins and a stateroom for us, and I remember my dismay when Papa instructed Nell and me to dress for dinner that first night, as we would be sitting at the captain's table. I had nothing in my trunk but three serviceable skirts and some plain bodices, and I recall that I excused myself, pleading indisposition, and that Papa was not pleased. After that, I remember little.

It was awhile later that I learned that I had awakened during that first night with a high fever and that my skin had soon blossomed into the distinctive marks of chickenpox. I have dim memories of waking, of faces leaning over me, and of a bitter drink being forced down my throat. I remember that my whole body was aflame with pain and itching.

I awakened once to discover that my fingers were bandaged. I tried to call out then, but darkness overcame me again and I knew no more until I awoke one morning to a small shaft of sunlight shining on my face. This time, my head did not hurt so much and the itching seemed to have abated. I tried to lift my head from the pillow, but the effort was too great, so I turned my face slowly to one side.

Above the opposite bed, was a small round window filled with the sunlight that had awakened me, and I was comforted to see a book lying face down on the neatly folded blankets of the bed; Nell could not be far away. Once again overcome with fatigue, I closed my eyes and drifted back to sleep.

There followed an incident that, to this day, haunts me. I awoke suddenly and it was nighttime. A single lantern cast a yellow glow around the room. The bed opposite was empty, but there was someone in the room with me, though I was certain that it was not Nell.

I tried to raise my head to see who it was, but a hand on my forehead stopped me. As I strained my eyes upward, I caught a glimpse of a pale blue sleeve with a thin yellow wrist and hand protruding from it. The hand held several long golden needles and it was approaching my head. I struggled to get away, but to no avail.

Then I remembered. The person in the room was Mrs. Chen, the strange Chinese woman who was meant to look after Edie, but who was now trying to kill me by pushing needles into my head. I opened my mouth to scream, but all that emerged was a feeble croak. I tried to wriggle down in the bed to get away from her, but my feet encountered hard wood and I could not escape.

I was sobbing in earnest now but I was too weak to fight. With a low moan, I turned my head to the cabin wall and closed my eyes. Then through my sobs, I heard an odd sound; Mrs. Chen was chanting quietly, and her hand began to stroke my head. I felt a sensation that was not even as sharp as a prick from a sewing needle and I knew that she had inserted one of her needles into my scalp. There was no point in struggling; I lay quietly waiting to die, too tired even to pray.

When I awoke it was daylight and Nell was sitting cross-legged on the other bunk, reading. I must have made a noise, for she looked up and, seeing that my eyes were open, sprang to her feet and came over to me.

"Can you hear me? Are you awake?" she demanded anxiously as she leaned over and raised her hand to the top of my head as if to stroke my hair. I nodded in answer to her question and licked my dry lips.

Immediately, Nell grabbed at a cup that was lying close by and held it to my mouth. I tried to drink, but couldn't raise my head sufficiently. My sister bent to help me, and as she did so, a strange expression crossed her face and, to my surprise, her eyes filled with tears. Her hand slid to the back of my neck and she raised me so that I could drink. I remember the feel of her fingers on my neck as I gulped greedily at the cool water.

Nell took the cup away after I had taken a few gulps. "Not too much at first, you've been very ill. I'm going to tell Mrs. Chen that you're awake." My sister gave me a lopsided smile as she walked to the cabin door, but I was sure that she was still crying.

"Wait," I croaked. "Don't tell her. She came here and tried to kill me. She poked needles in my head." I lay back, exhausted with the effort of speaking.

Nell stopped in the doorway and smiled. "No, silly," she said. "It's just Chinese medicine. We thought you were going to die before she used the needles. Don't worry. I'll be back in a minute."

I lay back on the pillow feeling weak and foolish. Tears trickled from my eyes and down the sides of my face. I moved my hand to brush them away and, as I did so, I felt a space, a strange emptiness, the feel of the cotton pillowcase where my hair should have been. I raised both my hands to my head then I opened my mouth and screamed. I continued to scream my poor mewling little screams, until Nell returned with Mrs. Chen, but by then I knew what she had done. That evil woman had pulled out my hair with her golden needles and left me completely bald.

Afterwards, I discovered the truth. My head had been shaved to help bring down my fever, and it was not Mrs. Chen, but Miss Walsh who had recommended this drastic move. But for all that, I did not trust the Chinese woman.

Slowly, I began to mend. The bandages were removed from my fingers and, when the doctor came to see me, he was pleased that I had very little scarring. I didn't tell him that I still had some scabs on my body and took great pleasure in scratching at them vigorously when I was alone.

I still suffered from frequent headaches, and my stomach rebelled at the slightest movement of the ship. During one of these episodes, Mrs. Chen came and stood in the doorway of the cabin looking at me. Then abruptly she disappeared, returning a few moments later with a silk-wrapped bundle in her hand. She placed the bundle on my bed and untied it, and once again I saw the golden needles, each one tipped in white ivory. I tried to scream and wriggle away from her, but this time, she leaned forward and slapped me sharply across the face.

I was too shocked to move. I had rarely been smacked as a child, and certainly never by a servant.

Mrs. Chen leaned close to me. "Shut up, stupid girl," she hissed. "Needles help you. Leave needles in, no more vomiting. No more headaches. Now I do this, you stay still."

Terrified, I lay back and let Mrs. Chen put her needles in my poor bare head, and even into my neck. She put some into my arms and the back of my hands, as well, all the time crooning to herself. As she inserted each needle, she flicked the tiny ivory tip with her finger so that it vibrated for a few moments. I did not feel any pain when she did this, and I have to confess that her strange treatment did help me.

As the days passed, the air grew noticeably warmer. At first, this was pleasant, but as the heat increased, I became uncomfortable and longed for a cool breeze to blow across my face. However, I had no inclination to rise from my bunk, and instead spent hours gazing miserably at nothing. One day, Nell lost patience with me and forced me to sit for a while on the single chair that was close to my bunk. I was amazed at how weak I felt at first, and although I continued to sit out for a while each day, I stubbornly refused to venture outside the confines of our cabin.

By this time, my hair had begun to grow again, but the process was unbearably slow and my scalp seemed to be covered only with a thin layer of bristles. One day, unable to resist the temptation, I managed to creep over to where my trunk was stored. With great difficulty, I fumbled with the buckles that kept the stout leather straps fastened. I had to stop several times, but finally I lifted the lid and rummaged through the layer of gloves and stockings at the top of the trunk until my hand closed upon my precious mirror. It was not very big, but it was silver-backed and heavy. It had belonged to my father's mother, and was one of the very few mementos I had of Grandmother Baldwin.

I let the lid of the trunk drop with a sharp thud and made my slow way back to the safety of the chair. Then, with hands that shook, I raised the mirror and looked at myself.

The face that peered back at me was shocking. Even in the dim light of the cabin, I could see how sunken my cheeks had become. My eyes stared back at me, their orbs huge in my ravaged face. I had scabs that were half healed, and other small scars, pink and shiny on my face. Slowly, I tilted the mirror so that I could see my scalp. Here, the scabs had mostly healed, but it made little difference to me, for all that I saw, was my head, covered in tiny prickles of hair, no more than a quarter of an inch long and sticking out in every direction.

I lowered the mirror as the tears began to fall—slowly at first, then faster until I was quite unable to stop.

I had seen a monkey once long ago when I had been shopping in Wimborne with Mama and Nell. It was sitting on the side of an organ grinder's barrel, begging for coins. I looked exactly like that poor, sad monkey. I let the mirror drop to the floor and it was Nell who found me some time later and helped me back to my bunk.

For several days after this, I refused to do anything. I would not stir from my bed and no amount of persuasion from Nell made any difference. I was quite determined to die. I sent my food away untouched and barely allowed myself a sip of water when my mouth became unbearably dry.

Then one evening when the family was at dinner, I had a visitor. Once again, Mrs. Chen glided silently into the cabin. I watched her enter with no interest, and turned my head away as she approached me. She wasn't carrying her usual bundle of needles; instead, she had a small bowl in her hands. As she set it down beside my bunk, I could feel her watching me.

Resolutely, I closed my eyes and, in a flash, she was on me, dragging me to a sitting position with surprising strength. My eyes flew open with shock and I opened my mouth to protest. As I did so, Mrs. Chen grabbed hold of the bowl and forced some steaming liquid into my mouth.

Spluttering and choking, I tried to fight, but I was no match for her, and she forced more of the liquid down me. After I had taken one or two gulps, she slammed the bowl onto the floor, slopping some of the contents in the process and glared at me. "Stupid English girl. Why you try to kill self? I work hard to make you well. Mister Bal'win he cry when he think you die. Stop this! Hair grow back. Now eat!" She gestured fiercely at the bowl of soup.

Meekly, I took it from her and, with shaking hands, tried to lift it to my lips. Mrs. Chen didn't help me; she just waited, arms folded, until

I had finished most of the liquid. It tasted of fish and some herbs that I couldn't identify. Then, taking the bowl from my hands, she gave a small bow and left without saying another word.

From then on, Mrs. Chen appeared at my door three times a day. She always brought with her some kind of soup or stew. I managed to eat most of it, but the day I lifted a bowl to my lips and found myself staring at the head of a fish, whose glazed eyes stared back at me, I decided that I was strong enough to eat food from the ship's galley.

One afternoon when the air was unbearably hot and stale in the cabin, Nell bounced through the door. "Come on, Ada," she said, cheerfully. "You're going up on deck. I even have a chair ready for you. It's tucked into a corner and no one will notice you there." I shook my head in protest, but Nell ignored me and hurried over to open my trunk.

"What are you going to wear?" she asked, dropping random pieces of clothing onto the floor and scattering stalks of lavender all over herself. She sniffed appreciatively. "That smells good—better than this place. Honestly, it smells awful in here! Come on, let's get you dressed." Protesting feebly, I allowed Nell to help me into my clothes. They hung on me like rags, for I had lost much weight during my illness.

Nell wrapped a shawl around my shoulders and bent to pick up the hat that she had selected for me to wear. She put it on my head and it slipped down over my hairless scalp and fell about my ears.

I snatched it off and burst into tears. "I can't possibly do this," I sobbed.

Nell looked at me somberly for a few moments then nodded decisively. "I have an idea," she said, as she hurried out of the cabin. She returned a few minutes later holding an old-fashioned bonnet that was closed at the back and had long black ribbons to tie under the chin.

"It belongs to Miss Walsh," she said, with a smile. "Not very fashionable, but it'll do nicely." I allowed Nell to place the bonnet on my head and tie the ribbons under my chin. Then, with slow and stumbling steps and aided by my sister, I made my way out of the cabin that had been my prison for so long, and into the fresh air.

From that day on, my health improved. I still took all my meals in my cabin, but at night when sleep eluded me, I took great comfort from Nell's presence, and her frequent mumblings as a dream disturbed her sleep.

One morning as Nell was struggling to fasten her bodice, I asked why Lizzie was not here to help us. My sister gave me an odd, sidelong glance before shrugging her shoulders and turning away to pick up her hairbrush.

"She got scared when you were ill," she offered, brushing vigorously at her thick tresses. "She stayed in her own quarters and refused to have anything to do with any of us. Can't blame her, really, I suppose. Half the passengers thought it was smallpox!"

I watched Nell as she bundled her hair into an unruly bunch at the back of her neck, tying it carelessly with a crumpled ribbon. "You were right about her," she said, as she perched herself on the edge of her bunk and pulled on her boots. "Papa didn't hire her; he didn't even meet her. He hired someone called Dolly who was old Mrs. Kent's maid. But according to Lizzie, Dolly got scared about leaving England and so Lizzie, who worked in the kitchen, kindly offered to take her place."

Nell rolled her eyes as she straightened up and reached for her hat. "Heaven knows what Papa is going to do with her when we get to Buenos Aires. I think we should just keep her and train her up; I mean we did that with Annie, so why not?" I opened my mouth to protest, but Nell was gone in a swirl of skirts and a clatter of boots.

The next day, I awoke to the sounds of great activity on the ship and knew that we were approaching the harbour of Buenos Aires and that I must start to ready myself to leave the ship. I closed my eyes for a moment and thanked the Lord most fervently that this part of our journey was over.

PART II

Argentina

Buenos Aires

CHAPTER 18

We came into the Buenos Aires harbour at dusk, with just one more night on board before disembarking.

It was a warm, clear evening as I made my way up on deck and watched from my favourite chair as the ship sailed slowly into the harbour. In the distance, I was surprised to see big buildings outlined against the setting sun. They were very beautiful. Nell had told me that this was a thriving city, but I had obstinately continued to think of it as some great wilderness where we must learn to live.

After a while, I spied my father leaning over the ship's rail with Nell beside him; they were talking animatedly. Moving slowly so as not to make myself dizzy, I joined them and listened as Papa pointed out some of the landmarks, and told us of his first voyage here, when he and all the other passengers had to be carried ashore in huge carts with high wheels because the docks had not yet been built.

During the voyage, I had seen little of my younger sisters, but that evening as we waited to disembark, I saw Lily and Iris properly for the first time since we had left Liverpool. They were standing dutifully by the ship's rail with Miss Walsh, and I was surprised at how much they seemed to have grown during the journey. Mrs. Chen was there, too, holding Edie in her arms. I could see that my baby sister was clinging tightly to Mrs. Chen and showed no inclination to be put down. We stayed at the ship's rail watching until it was too dark to see clearly then I retired to our cabin and slept deeply.

The next morning I awoke late. My body, glad to be rid of the constant movement of the ship, had begun to settle into its normal rhythms. As I dressed, I wondered idly who had tidied the cabin while I slept. I had sent for Lizzie on more than one occasion, but she had never come.

Now everything was packed into my trunk, with my clothes for the day folded neatly on top. I supposed that this was Nell's doing.

Once up on deck, I leaned against the rail and looked at the busy scene below me. After a while, I spied Drake fussily supervising the unloading of our luggage. As my gaze drifted further along the dock, I saw a string of men being hurried down a gangplank. These were the same men that I had seen boarding the ship as we waited to embark upon our journey, so I was not surprised to see Señor Rodriguez, distinct in his white suit, standing at the bottom of the gangplank supervising the unloading of this human cargo.

I looked around for Papa but could not see him; however, I spied Nell leaning precariously over the ship's rail, calling down to somebody already on the dock. After a few minutes, I managed to catch her eye and she came dancing over to me. The sunlight glinted on her glasses and she was beaming happily. Nell, I realized, had enjoyed every moment of this voyage.

As she came closer, I asked if she knew anything about the men who had just disembarked. Nell chewed at an end of dark hair that had, as usual, escaped from its ribbon, and peered in the direction that I indicated.

"Those men?" she said, as if they were of no importance. "They're our workers. Señor Rodriguez obtained them for Papa while he was in London. They were all in prison, but they're not real criminals. Debtors' prisons were closed last year and there was nowhere else to put them, so Papa undertook to pay off their debts and they're to work for him for five years without pay. I think it's a splendid idea, don't you? It was Señor Rodriguez who thought of it!" She rolled her eyes as if surprised that my father's friend could think of such a thing. Then, losing interest in the conversation, she waved frantically at someone over my shoulder.

"I have to go," she said, hastily. "The Hunters are leaving and I must say goodbye."

Shaking my head at my sister's impulsive nature, I turned back to the scene below. As I watched, the ragged line of men shuffled forward, each one climbing slowly onto a big wooden cart harnessed to two large horses.

All at once, there was a clatter of hooves and the sound of shouting directly below me. I looked down to see several men on horseback, milling around a large, very smart carriage that had just arrived at the dockside in a flourish of dust and flashing wheels. I shaded my eyes against the bright sun and watched as a figure detached itself from a group of men who had been standing below the ship, deep in conversation. With a start, I realized that the man was my father.

He strode over to the carriage, raising his arm in greeting. Seconds later, he was surrounded by the newcomers, who all seemed to be talking to him at once. My father said something, and they all roared with laughter. I continued to stare down at them. This was a side of my father that I did not know.

It was early afternoon before Papa came to get us. I had soon grown tired of watching the activity on the dock and returned to my cabin to rest. A while later, Nell came to find me to tell me that we were about to disembark. As I came up on deck, I saw my father striding towards me. With a quick smile, he swept me up in his arms and carried me swiftly down the gangplank, depositing me somewhat unceremoniously into the carriage that I had admired earlier in the day.

As I settled into my seat, gasping a little from the sudden rush of movement, Nell, the twins, and Miss Walsh hurried down the gangplank, followed closely by Mrs. Chen carrying a sleeping Edie. Of Lizzie there was no sign.

When everyone was seated in the carriage, I asked about our missing maid. Mrs. Chen looked at me, her dark eyes gleaming. "She leave ship last night. She not work for you. She come here to be with her man. He on board with other prisoners Mr. Bal'win have. She trick you."

Nell and I were staring at the Chinese woman. "Did you know that all along, Mrs. Chen?" asked Nell.

Mrs. Chen gave a small shrug. "Too late when she already on ship," she answered, enigmatically.

It was obvious that Lizzie had taken matters into her own hands and hadn't waited for my father to deal with her deceit.

When we were all settled, the driver of the carriage called to the horses; my father and the other men mounted and we were soon on our way.

As we set out, I looked about me, confused by the noise and turbulence all around. I had never seen so many people. Some looked much like us, but many looked very different, with skins that ranged from beige to brown and some were even black in colour. I stared at them in amazement.

We continued on our way through the city and I gazed in awe at the beautiful new buildings that lined the wide streets, some of them still under construction. But alongside these buildings, we glimpsed mean little laneways with squalid houses, crying children, and women standing, arms crossed, gazing sullenly after the carriage as we clattered by.

The journey to our new home took almost an hour, over roads that were sometimes rough and dusty. But as the carriage turned at length into an avenue lined with trees, I glimpsed for the first time the house that was to be our home. As we approached along the curved driveway and the house came fully into view, all my misery of the past weeks was quite forgotten.

The house was magnificent. Its white walls were washed softly in the golden light of the afternoon sun, a huge porch wrapped itself around the whole of the ground floor, and the upper level gleamed with many windows. Great vines clung to the pillars that supported the porch and a graceful set of steps led up to the front door.

Our welcome, however, was not what I had anticipated. There were no servants to greet us; only Drake tumbling out of the front door, looking flustered. He and my father conferred briefly then Papa strode up the steps and disappeared into the house.

Drake hastened to open the carriage door for us, apologizing profusely for the lack of welcome, shaking his head and muttering to himself about foreigners. As Drake handed me down, I heard my father's voice raised in anger from inside the house. Moments later, two figures emerged onto the porch. One was an enormously fat man with long black hair tied carelessly at the back of his head with a leather thong. He was in his shirtsleeves and his feet were bare. Accompanying him was a thin-faced woman dressed completely in black. She followed the man reluctantly down the steps and watched as he started to unbuckle our hand luggage. Finally, she turned to where we were standing and gave the barest sketch of a curtsey. At this point, Drake stepped forward and ushered us quickly up the steps and into the house.

Miss Walsh, who had followed closely behind us, looked disdainfully about. "My previous family would never have permitted this!" she said loudly, her prim Scottish accent very noticeable. "We always had servants to look after our every need. Why, in India, the servants didn't even dare to look us in the face."

Nell turned to the governess. "This isn't India, though, is it?" she snapped. "So why don't you just wait and see what happens. I'm sure that eventually someone will direct you to your quarters." I was shocked at Nell's rudeness and raised a questioning eyebrow at her.

"Honestly, Ada," she whispered. "If she doesn't stop with her 'when I was in India,' I think I shall go crazy."

At that moment, my father reappeared, still looking a little annoyed. He apologized briefly and explained that we had arrived in the middle of "siesta," which he said was the time of day when everyone slept to escape the heat.

Then he turned to the serving woman who was standing with her back to the door and spoke to her in rapid Spanish. She curtseyed and, with a sullen face, beckoned to Nell and me to follow her. As we ascended the staircase, I heard my father directing Drake to show Miss Walsh, the twins, and Mrs. Chen to their quarters, which I later learned were somewhat separate from the rest of the house.

At the top of the stairs, the serving woman turned left and with a small gesture, indicated two doors. She nodded curtly." For you" she said briefly, then turned on her heel and left us.

I looked enquiringly at Nell. "I think these are our bedrooms," she said, looking thoughtfully after the woman's disappearing back. "Apparently, she doesn't like to have her afternoon nap interrupted. Never mind, Ada. Let's see what our sleeping arrangements are like and I think you should rest. I'll try to find some food, if you like, and something to drink. My throat is parched from all that dust."

But I wasn't listening. I had opened the first bedroom door and stepped inside. It was a very beautiful room. The ceiling was high and ornate and the windows were draped in a soft blue fabric that let in enough light to show me an enormous bed, set in the centre of the room. At each corner of the bed was a beautifully carved wooden post, intricately decorated with flowers and leaves, and draped about the bed was a fine muslin curtain that hung from a hook in the ceiling and fell gracefully to the floor.

I walked over to the bed and pulled one of the curtains back. It moved like gossamer under my hand and I sat myself wearily down on the silk quilt that covered the bed. I was suddenly tremendously tired.

"Don't worry about food, Nell," I said, sleepily. "I think I'll just lie down for a few minutes and have a little nap and then I'll come to find you." I pulled off my bonnet and, without even bothering to remove my boots, lay down and was instantly asleep. I slept until morning.

When I awoke, I had no idea where I was. My mouth was dry, and I was hot and uncomfortable. I was still wearing my travelling clothes, but while I slept, someone had removed my boots and draped the mosquito netting around my bed, enclosing me in a soft tent. As memory returned, I reached out a hand and pulled back the draperies. Then, climbing off the bed, I looked about until I found the bell pull. I rang it vigorously, hoping for a maid to appear with hot water so that I could wash.

While I waited, I examined my room more carefully. It was at least twice the size of my bedroom at home, but the windows looked out onto green lawns and flowering borders that were not so very different from the ones I remembered. The view made me suddenly homesick. Turning from the window, I rang the bell again, but there was still no answer.

Eventually, tired of waiting for someone to appear, I opened my door and listened. I could hear sounds of movement in the house—a woman's laughter, the slamming of a door in the distance, and quick footsteps crossing the wide hall below—but still nobody mounted the stairs in answer to my summons. So I closed the door and walked over to my luggage that had been placed against one wall.

Struggling out of my traveling clothes, I dressed quickly in a crumpled skirt and blouse and pulled on some stockings. As I fumbled into my summer shoes, I caught sight of myself in the large oval mirror that hung above the heavy dressing table. I stared at my image for a moment with a sinking heart.

Since that one awful glimpse of myself on board ship, I had carefully avoided any encounters with mirrors. The face that stared back at me now was not quite as dreadful as it had been. Most of my scars had faded, but my skin still held the pallor of recent illness and I had a scar just above my right eyebrow that looked raw and angry.

But it was my hair, not my face that caused me so much distress. It had grown in the past few weeks, but it was still ugly. It was no more than two inches long and clung in greasy strands about my head. Desperately, I rummaged in my portmanteau until I found my hairbrush and began to pull it through the short ends of hair. I continued brushing until my scalp was sore, but my looks were not improved.

I could not think what to do until I spied the long silk scarf that I had been wearing around my neck the day before. It was lying beside the bed where it had fallen. Picking it up, I wound it experimentally around my head. The effect was not particularly pleasing, but at least it covered my dreadful lack of hair.

As I descended the stairs and crossed the hall, I could smell food cooking and my stomach gave a great gurgle of hunger. A glance through an open door into what was obviously the breakfast room revealed no signs of a table being laid. I stopped for a moment to catch my breath then followed the sounds I had heard earlier. I pushed open the baize doors at the end of the hall and found myself in a short corridor that led to another set of double doors. Behind them, I could hear voices raised in animated conversation amidst the clatter of china, so I walked forward and flung open the doors. Immediately, the room fell quiet and all heads turned in my direction.

I was in a kitchen with an open range against one wall. At least ten people were seated around a big table in the middle of the room. As I looked about, I recognized one of the riders from the day before, as well as the fat man who had taken our luggage from the carriage. He was sprawled at one end of the table with his chair tilted back and one large bare foot balanced on the table edge. The thin woman in black was there, too, standing by the range. She had a pan in her hands that contained some kind of fried grain. It smelled delicious.

For a moment, no one moved as I stood in the doorway, my eyes sweeping the room. Then the man I recognized from the day before rose to his feet, followed with obvious reluctance by everyone else seated at the table.

I spoke slowly and clearly, trying to keep my tone pleasant. "I rang several times, why did nobody come?" There was no response.

Most of the people around the table looked blankly back at me, apparently not understanding. My eyes swung towards a row of bells that were hanging along one wall. They were all clearly labeled and looked to be in good working order. I walked over to them. Pointing to myself and then to the bells, I said, "Which bell is mine?" I jangled one of the bells experimentally and pointed again to myself.

A young woman who had been standing in the shadows came forward. She gave a small curtsey and said in heavily accented English, "Señorita, we do not answer. That bell is for," she turned questioningly to the man who had risen from the table first and spoke to him in rapid Spanish. He thought for a moment then shrugged and responded briefly.

The girl turned again to me, and smiled. "Señorita, it is for your own servant woman. And," she looked around expressively, spreading her hands in front of her, "she is not here."

I stared at her. The fact that she spoke the truth did little to allay my frustration. I turned and addressed myself to the man who had already spoken. I searched desperately in my mind for one of the few phrases that Nell had taught me during our afternoons sitting in the shade on board ship, but my mind was completely blank. At last, "Where is my father?" I asked slowly.

The man grinned engagingly, showing a row of remarkably white teeth. "Ah, Señorita, Señor Baldwin gone. He come mañana."

"Tomorrow!" Even I understood that word, but I could scarcely believe that my father would desert us in this strange house so soon after our arrival and without even telling us.

I looked around the room, but nobody would meet my eyes, so, not knowing what else to do, I turned and walked swiftly back the way I had come. As the door swung behind me, I heard a chorus of voices raised and, amid the babble of Spanish, there were spurts of laughter.

Lifting my skirts, I crossed the hall and remounted the stairs, and without bothering to knock, I burst into Nell's bedroom. Gasping for breath, I leaned heavily against the door. As I did so, Nell sat up, sleepily reaching for her glasses.

She listened silently as I sobbed out my story, and when I was finished, she waved me to a chair by the window. Then stretching widely, she fumbled her way out of bed.

"Papa got called away last night while you were sleeping, Ada. He and Drake will be back tomorrow sometime," she said, yawning hugely. "I told him that we would be perfectly fine until he gets back. Why do you always fuss so much?" she added, peering at me crossly.

Wearily, I sat back in Nell's chair. My outburst had left me feeling drained. Nell was right: I was probably fussing too much, but I was still unwashed, cross, and extremely hungry.

While Nell was dressing, I looked about her room. It was much the same as mine, but I was surprised to see that all her clothes were hanging neatly in her wardrobe, and her trunk had been pushed to one corner of the room as if it were empty.

Nell glanced over to where I was looking. "I did that last night; I wanted to get it out of the way. Today I want to see if all my books are safe. Miguel has the other trunks out in the back, so I'm going to get the rest of my stuff after breakfast."

I shook my head. "You shouldn't be unpacking your own clothes, Nell. That's why we have servants. And who is Miguel?"

Nell grinned, pulling on one wrinkled stocking. "You know which one," she said, and held her hands wide apart. "He's the big one. He's quite nice, but I don't much care for his wife."

"I suppose you know her name, too," I said sourly.

"Mmm, it's Carmelita," she mumbled through a mouthful of hairpins.

As I watched, my sister twisted her hair into an untidy bun at the top of her head, and pinned it securely in place. "Nell!" I said sharply. "Why are you putting your hair up?"

"Because I turned sixteen on board ship, sister, dear," she answered, pulling a small face at me in the mirror. "Most of the time, I can't be bothered, but it sounds as if you have upset the entire household, so I will have to try to look very mature, and use my best Spanish if we are to get anything at all to eat today." Then, taking me by the hand, my sister pulled me to my feet, and together we went downstairs.

We made our way tolerably well through that first day—thanks, I must admit, to Nell, who worked her particular brand of charm on most of the servants. She determinedly tried all kinds of words and phrases in Spanish, rolling her eyes and throwing up her hands in a wonderful parody of Drake, when she was not understood. It was fortunate that Drake himself was safely out of the way in Buenos Aires. I found myself laughing aloud at the absurdity of her clowning. Nell had always been able to make people laugh when the need arose.

On our second morning, I was awakened by a gentle tap at the door. "Who is it?" I called sleepily.

"Señorita, I am Anna." For a single, foolish moment, I imagined that it really was Annie, behind the door, somehow magically restored to me. Then the young woman who had spoken to me the day before opened the door and slipped into the room.

"Pardon, Señorita, I have water for washing." She held out a large jug.

I sat up and, nodding gratefully, waved her towards the big ornate washstand. As I watched her cross the room, an idea occurred to me. "Anna, do you work in the kitchen?" I asked.

She looked at me over her shoulder as she set the steaming jug down. "Si, Señorita."

I looked at her carefully. Her hair was clean and her clothes looked fresh. Her hands and feet were small and her smile was open and kind. As I flung back the covers, Anna moved forward, picking up my dressing gown and held it out towards me. That small gesture decided me.

"Anna, would you like to be my personal maid?" I asked impulsively.

She looked at me as if she did not quite understand me, so I ran over to the bell-pull and mimed pulling it and then pointed to her.

Understanding dawned on her face. "Si, Señorita! I like very much! But first I must ask my Mama!" Although I did not understand why she must ask permission, I had heard her say yes and that was enough. I smiled happily. "Good, now go while I wash. I will ring for you later."

Once again, I mimed the actions and she nodded and left. I finished my ablutions quickly then went to wake Nell to tell her the good news.

My sister was already awake, sitting in a chair by the window, reading. As I blurted out what I had just done, she looked at me thoughtfully. "You know, you should have asked Papa first, Ada, but I don't suppose he'll really mind, provided, of course, Anna's mother lets her."

I sat on the edge of Nell's bed. "Why wouldn't she? It's an honour, she should be delighted!"

Nell removed her glasses and polished them absently on her nightgown. "Yes, but I don't think Carmelita likes you very much." She broke off as she saw my face, a delighted grin spreading across her own countenance. "You didn't know, did you? Anna is Carmelita and Miguel's daughter! In fact, I think everybody in the house is related in some way.

Perhaps Anna didn't tell her mother at once. Or maybe Carmelita overcame her misgivings, because when I rang for her a little later, Anna came quickly and we chattered happily in a mixture of English and Spanish as she helped me to dress.

My father returned late that afternoon when we were all enjoying a siesta. The practice of having an afternoon nap was one change in our lives that I found much to my liking.

That night, we ate dinner very late. Señor Rodriguez had returned with my father and he appeared at the table looking very confident and pleased with himself. In England, my father's friend had seemed so out of place, his white suits, odd hats, and strong accent marking him as a foreigner. Here, he was totally at ease, the crumpled white suits replaced by impeccable cream linen. Gold rings gleamed on several fingers and, as he smiled, I saw that one of his teeth also gleamed gold. I also noticed that he was once again eyeing me with keen interest.

While Anna was helping me to dress for dinner that night, she had touched my short hair with one hand and looked at me questioningly in the mirror. Instinctively, I put my hands to either side of my head as if to hide the ugliness. I had taken the time to wash my hair earlier in the day, but there was no hiding how short it was. Anna pulled my hands away with gentle fingers then, taking a brush, she set to work until l I was left with a mop of small, shining curls.

Earlier in the day, she had unpacked my trunks, hanging each garment carefully and exclaiming to herself at the pretty clothes that emerged. Now she opened a drawer in my dressing table and pulled out a pink silk scarf that Lucy Blackly had given me. I had not thought to wear it, as pink was not a shade that I had ever favoured. I had kept it more as a memento of my friend.

Skillfully, Anna parted my hair in the centre then wrapped the scarf around my head, catching the short ends into the silk but leaving a good deal of my hair still showing in the front.

She tied the scarf in a soft knot at the nape of my neck. The effect was pleasing, and the soft bloom of colour framing my face was almost becoming. Then she hung the blue necklace that had belonged to my mother around my neck and stood back to admire her work. "Ah! Bella Señorita!" She smiled at me in the mirror and when I smiled back, I almost believed her.

During dinner, Señor Rodriguez set himself to entertain us, almost, I thought, sourly, as if he were the host and we the guests at our own table. His English, in spite of his heavy accent, was very good indeed.

After the main course had been cleared, he raised his napkin politely to his lips. "Perhaps, my dear Robert," he said, inclining his head towards my father, "you will allow me to share the history of this house with your most enchanting daughters?"

Nell leaned forward eagerly. "Yes please, Papa," she begged. "The house is so English. I had expected a hacienda." she paused, turning her head to look first at Señor Rodriguez and then at my father.

Señor Rodriguez smiled at her. "Señorita, you have noticed. Yes, this is a very English-style house and, if I am allowed, I will tell you why."

My father smiled easily at our guest. "Certainly, Juan Pablo I'm sure the story will interest them greatly."

Señor Rodriguez leaned back deliberately in his chair and spoke directly to Nell and me. "Your father is correct—it is an interesting story. This house was built some forty years ago and the gentleman who built it was an Englishman who, when he left his native shores, was penniless, and had few hopes of betterment." He paused for a moment as if to contemplate the sorry state of the gentleman in question.

"He came here to Argentina forty-five years ago at a time of great political unrest and soon realized that there was great profit to be made in a particular area of, shall we say, 'imports?'

"He began by trading in a small way, but in three years, he already owned four ships that were sailing regularly out of Cape Town. His cargo fetched good prices and he was doing very well when he met and fell in love with a beautiful woman. She returned his affections and they were happy, except for one thing." Señor Rodriguez paused and looked slowly around the table.

Nell, who had been listening wide-eyed to the story, interrupted. "I know," she said breathlessly. "She was an English duchess, and he had to build the house so her parents would allow them to marry!"

Señor Rodriguez glanced across at her with an indulgent smile. "Alas, my dear young lady, it was not quite so. He did indeed build this lovely English home for his bride, but it was in the hope that she would someday come to be accepted by the local community, especially by the English immigrants. You see, the woman he loved was part of his 'cargo.' He was a trader bringing slaves into this country, and she was one of them. She was a black woman."

I sat in shocked silence, but Nell leaned forward, her eyes blazing and her cheeks flushed. "Are you telling us that this house was built from the profits of slave trading? That's terrible!" She turned quickly to my father. "Papa, I cannot live in a house that was built on the blood of poor, unfortunate slaves! Please, can we find somewhere else to live immediately?"

My father frowned and when he spoke his tone was forbidding. "Kindly control your emotions, Nell! I have absolutely no intention of moving. This is your new home. The sale is complete and, as of yesterday, this house belongs to me."

There was a moment of absolute silence then Nell pushed back her chair and, not waiting for permission, turned and fled from the room. A few moments later, I heard the sharp slam of her bedroom door and guessed that she had flung herself, weeping, onto her bed.

Señor Rodriguez had not moved while this little scene had unfolded, but now he placed his napkin on the table. "Excuse me, Robert I seem to have upset at least one of your daughters." He spread his hands in a small, deprecating gesture. "I meant only to enlighten them."

Then he turned to me. "The end of my story is really quite happy; would you care to hear it?" I nodded silently, aware of my father's eyes upon me.

"The gentleman did marry his lady," Señor Rodriguez continued, "and they were very happy. Eventually, as more people of different races married, they were accepted socially in many quarters, though I regret to say, never quite as equals in the English society of this city. They had two children, a boy and a girl. The girl was the oldest, her name is Maria and she is my sister. My late father was Mr. John Paul Rogers—I was called after him. My mother lives now with my sister and her family and we no longer have need of this house. I am pleased that your father has purchased my childhood home and I trust that you will all be very happy here."

I bowed my head, unsure of what to say. Finally, with a word of thanks, I excused myself, pleading fatigue. As I walked up the stairs, I saw my father and his guest disappear into the study, and I found myself wondering what thoughts had run through John Paul Rogers' head as he was entertained in the house that must have been full of his own childhood memories.

The next morning, I rose early, determined to speak to my father about the servants. I paused for only a moment to listen as I got to the bottom of the stairs. I could hear voices issuing from behind the closed door of the study. Next to the study, the door to the breakfast room was partly open and I caught a glimpse of an impeccably dressed Señor Rodriguez sipping coffee and reading a newspaper.

Moving silently, I approached my father's door and knocked. Hardly waiting for Papa's response, I opened the door and walked in. I had not been in this room before and I was surprised at how luxurious it was. Two of the walls were lined with leather-bound books and the third wall framed large windows that overlooked the wide porch.

Papa's desk was of a rich dark wood, topped with leather. There were heavy drapes on either side of the windows, and several chairs were dotted about the room.

I thought of my father's small study in England, with its comfortable clutter, and was ridiculously glad to see the familiar inkwell and penholder already in place on this new desk.

As my eyes came back to the two men in the room, I saw that the person with my father was not Drake, as I had thought, but a tall, thin man I had never seen before. As I moved away from the door, he rose from the wooden chair where he had been sitting and moved swiftly to stand behind it.

"Ada," said my father pleasantly, "I was just about to send for you. I would like you to meet Horatio Gilbert."

As my father spoke, the man behind the chair bowed very slightly in my direction. I moved forward, ready to curtsey to Papa's guest, but he stopped me with a small movement of his hand. "I'm Gilbert, Miss Baldwin, just Gilbert," he said, and I realized that I was looking at a well-trained servant.

"Gilbert will be joining us immediately, Ada," my father continued. It is our good fortune that his previous family is leaving to return to England immediately, and he has no wish to return with them." Papa looked across at Gilbert as if for confirmation. "He has also undertaken to attend to the hiring of the other servants that we require." Gilbert nodded his head in silent assent. I opened my mouth to speak, but no sound came out.

When I entered the room, I had come armed with a list of requests: I wanted English-speaking servants, a cook who could prepare plain English food, and to make sure that Anna would become my maid. But now I looked from Papa to Gilbert before sinking into the nearest chair completely at a loss for words.

"If I may, Sir, I would suggest keeping the present kitchen staff but hiring an English cook and housekeeper, as well as at least two housemaids, and" said Gilbert smoothly, "I understand that the young ladies," he turned towards me with a bow, "are presently without maids. I would be happy to amend that, Sir. I have two sensible young women in mind."

I leaned forward, finding my voice at last. "I have a maid," I said, a little too loudly. Both men turned to look at me in surprise. "Her name is Anna, and she speaks some English and she's Carmelita's daughter," I ended in a rush. Gilbert looked down the considerable length of his nose and said nothing.

My father leaned back in his chair. "Ada," he said his tone firm. "You are not the best person to decide this. Please leave such matters to Gilbert." I felt the colour rise in my cheeks, but remained silent—I was not about to argue in front of our new butler.

There was an uncomfortable silence then Gilbert gave a small cough. "Excuse me, Sir, but there is one other matter that I wish to discuss."

Frustrated with this turn of events, I started to rise, but Gilbert turned towards me. "Miss Baldwin, I would like you to stay if you would be so kind," he said. Then he turned back to my father. "It's a matter of a dog, Sir. I have a small dog. One of the children of my previous employer was not fond of animals and mistreated the poor creature, who now resides with me. I wondered if this would be a problem." Gilbert waited.

I was aware that both my father and I were staring at him. Servants simply did not have pets, and from first impressions, a less likely candidate than Gilbert to break this rule was hard to imagine.

Papa looked thoughtful but then shook his head regretfully. "That might pose some considerable difficulties, Gilbert," he began, when to my own surprise I interrupted him.

"Papa, I think that a dog is a good idea," I found myself saying. "I should enjoy it and I'm sure that the twins would benefit from having a small animal about the place."

My father looked surprised, but then he smiled. "Gilbert, it seems that your pet has a champion. Very well, you may keep the dog, as long as it does not cause difficulties in the household."

Throughout this exchange, Gilbert's face had remained blank, but now he looked down at me. "Thank you, Miss Baldwin," he said, before adding, "I will interview Anna for you, Miss. Perhaps she can be trained up, given a little time." As I looked into his faded blue eyes, I had the oddest feeling that I had just made a friend. The thought pleased me very much, for I had few enough friends in those days. In the end, Duchess—for that was the little dog's name—became a great favourite with the entire household, for she had a sweet and gentle disposition.

As I closed the study door behind me and walked swiftly past the now empty breakfast room, I paused. The large double doors leading to a room across the hall were open a little, and I could hear music coming from within. This was another room that I had so far not ventured into and I was suddenly curious. I crossed the hallway and pushed open the double doors. I found myself in a beautiful drawing room. There were several deep sofas and occasional chairs scattered about the large space, and at the end of the room, backed by a full-length window, was an enormous baby grand piano. Its polished lid was raised and the sounds issuing from it were familiar and much beloved.

Nell was seated on the piano bench, her head bent in concentration, her fingers wandering lovingly over the keys. The piece she played—falteringly at first and then with more certainty—was a simple little piece from our childhood. Almost without realizing it, I drifted into the room.

As I approached, Nell looked up, her voice husky with emotion. "It's a Steinway, Ada. It's the most beautiful thing I have ever seen."

I looked curiously at the piano. I had no idea what a Steinway was, but this certainly was an elegant pianoforte. The wood gleamed in the morning light and, as I leaned closer, I could see that the keys were rich cream and soft ebony. No wonder Papa had refused Nell's request to bring Mama's small piano.

My sister flinched as she played a chord. "It needs tuning," she said regretfully, "but it has a beautiful tone."

"I'm sure that your father would be happy to employ the services of the man who has always tuned this piano," said a voice behind us. Startled, I whirled around to see Señor Rodriguez rising from a high-backed armchair where he had been sitting, unseen by either of us.

"Excuse me, Señoritas," he said with a bow. "I did not mean to startle you. I was enjoying the music, and the moment." Then he bowed again before turning and leaving the room.

Nell looked after him with pure hatred in her eyes. "Why doesn't he just go away!" she said bitterly.

I put a placating hand on my sister's arm, but she shook it off. "I know who he is," she said, angrily. "Papa called me down last night after you had gone to bed and made me apologize, and then that horrible man told me the rest of the story. Wonderful, isn't it! Papa's business partner, the child of a slave trafficker! No wonder he didn't have any problem bringing those poor convicts here from England."

I decided that this was not the time to remind my sister that a few days ago she had thought this to be a very good idea.

"Señor Rodriguez' mother was a slave herself," I pointed out, "and you can't blame him for what his father did."

Nell looked at me pityingly. "I'm glad you feel that way, Ada, because he still wants to marry you. Then he can have his house back and eventually own everything of ours into the bargain. Drake told me so, and then he said that if you refuse, he'll ask for me."

I gazed at Nell in horror. I certainly did not want to marry Señor Rodriguez, but neither did I expect him to consider asking for my sister's hand if I refused. Really, the man was quite incorrigible.

Nell was looking at me contemptuously. "Don't worry, Ada, he's all yours," she said. I'd kill myself before I married the likes of him!" Then she slammed down the lid of the piano and almost ran from the room. I followed her slowly, more deeply troubled by this piece of news than I cared to admit.

True to his word, by the end of the week, Gilbert had found the staff we needed and our lives became easier. Our new housekeeper, Mrs. Johnson, was a sensible woman, whom I thought was related to Gilbert, for she certainly looked very like him. Cook was a large English-woman of few words who quickly took over the kitchen, returning the other servants to their previous stations. We had two new parlour maids and an upstairs maid called Bella, who also looked after Nell. At first, I wondered if Gilbert would allow Anna to be trained as my maid, but she showed herself very willing to learn and Gilbert was soon pleased with her.

We had arrived in Argentina in late November and Christmas was fast approaching. I found that first festive season very confusing. It was high summer and hot, with such a heavy dampness in the air that sometimes I could scarcely breathe.

Papa was busy and his work called him away often. I was lonely and very homesick for England, and to make matters worse, there seemed to be no social opportunities for us to meet new people. This was partly my fault for I had made no effort to have us attend the local Methodist chapel though I knew that it was a scant ten-minute drive away.

Early in December, things changed. I arrived downstairs one morning to find three finely engraved visiting cards lying on the hall table. The names on the cards were those of Mrs. Beulah Hamilton and her daughters, Sonia and Sophie. Unsure of how to proceed, I went in search of Gilbert.

"Well, Miss," he said, clearing his throat and gazing into the middle distance, "cards have been left, so now you must return the courtesy. At which time, the three ladies in question will be pleased to visit with you."

"But, Gilbert," I said anxiously, "we don't have any visiting cards."

Gilbert looked down at me. "At your father's suggestion, Miss, I took the liberty of having cards made up for you and Miss Nell. They should arrive today or tomorrow. I could certainly have them sent out then, if you wish."

I drew a breath of relief. "Yes, please do, Gilbert," I said, gratefully. And so in due course, the Hamilton's were invited to afternoon tea.

The days leading up to the impending visit were nerve-racking for me and I consulted Gilbert on every detail until he finally rolled his eyes and suggested that I address any further questions to Mrs. Johnson, the housekeeper.

It was eventually agreed that Nell and I would entertain the Hamilton's, and Miss Walsh and the twins were to be ready to be presented if called upon. I didn't include Edie and Mrs. Chen in my plans.

Predictably, on hearing of these arrangements, Nell objected strongly, and in the end, I had to threaten to report her behaviour to Papa before she would agree to help me in our first social engagement.

For the first time in many months, I missed Mama. Distance and time had done their work, and I could scarcely even recall my mother's face when I tried to. More than that, I had difficulty remembering any of the social graces that she had taught us.

I thought perhaps I should ask Nell to play for us. The piano had been tuned a few days previously and I had vague memories of Nell playing Mama's little piano at home and of myself singing, but in my memory, the room was candlelit, so perhaps that was an evening entertainment and would not be appropriate for afternoon tea.

When the day finally came, I put on one of my new gowns and had Anna dress my hair low on my forehead, with my pink silk scarf wrapped about my head. By the time she had finished pinning and pleating with her clever fingers, I had an acceptable hairstyle that did not shame me.

I pleaded with Nell until she agreed to wear a dress of soft cream cotton that showed her dark hair to great advantage, and even seemed to diminish the steel frames of her spectacles. By the time that I noticed her footwear, however, it was too late—the ladies had already arrived and Nell greeted our first visitors wearing stout walking boots.

It quickly became obvious that Mrs. Hamilton and her daughters were pillars of the local Methodist church, and that Mrs. Hamilton was delighted to add another family to the congregation.

"The Reverend Dr. Cyril Fisher has ministered to us for quite ten years," Mrs. Hamilton told us. "But Mrs. Fisher is quite unable to help him, poor dear Violet is very delicate." Mrs. Hamilton settled herself comfortably in a chair, and accepted one of our best teacups. "So I take many of these duties upon myself." She gave a self-deprecating smile. "We have been in this country for more than fifteen years, and I do know the congregation, though of course my dear young ladies, we were originally from Essex."

Mrs. Hamilton smoothed the black satin folds of her ample skirt with her free hand. "I wear black in memory of my dear Harold," she continued, cheerfully. "Dead these seven years, but black has always suited me, so I've no mind to change now." Then she paused and viewed Nell and me searchingly. "Which one of you has been so ill?" she demanded, then, not waiting for an answer pounced on me. "You, my dear, undoubtedly, for there are the pock marks clear above your eye, and I see they cut off your hair." Her eyes lingered doubtfully for a moment on my carefully arranged coiffure. "Well, no doubt it will grow back soon enough, and I shall have to take you in hand, and find you a tonic that will put the roses back in your cheeks."

She turned then to Nell, "Now you, dear child, spend too much time with your nose in a book I shouldn't wonder. I know that look." Then Mrs. Hamilton took a sip of tea and looked curiously about her.

All this time, Sonia and Sophie Hamilton, who had seated them-selves close together, had taken no part in the conversation. Instead, they had spent their time looking about the room as if they were not-ing each piece of furniture.

I was disappointed. I had hoped that they would be of an age with Nell and me, and that we might become friends. But they were much older—in their twenties at least—and did not seem particularly friendly. In appearance, Sonia and Sophie were startlingly alike, with pale brown hair and equally pale eyes, though I thought that Sonia was a few years older than her sister.

When they spoke, however, their voices were completely different. Sophie had a deep, husky voice that was surprising in one who looked so delicate. Sonia, on the other hand, spoke in the voice of a young girl, lisping her words earnestly.

Eventually, as I knew it would, the conversation turned to our motherless state. Mrs. Hamilton was sympathetic but brisk. "The Lord gives and the Lord takes away," she said, practically. "Your Papa is a brave man to bring his family here, but no doubt the Lord has a purpose."

Then Sonia Hamilton leaned forward, interrupting her mother in mid-sentence. "Your Papa, where is he?" she lisped.

I heard a snort from Nell and nudged her sharply with my foot. "He is away at present," I replied. "He –"

But once again Sonia interrupted. "Where are the other children? We should like to see them."

"Yes, do bring them here, we are anxious to meet all of you," added Sophie. "We know that your mother did not survive the birth of the last baby, but we would like to see the child. I opened my mouth to answer but before I could say anything, Nell spoke up.

"Unfortunately, Lily and Iris are ill at the moment and Papa does not allow the baby to be seen in public," she said in her most ear-nest voice.

I stared at my sister in surprise. As far as I knew, the twins were in fine health and Edie was one of the prettiest children ever to grace the earth.

I started to protest, but Nell held up her hand. "No, Ada," she said, keeping her eyes on the elder Miss Hamilton. "We must be honest and truthful." She removed her glasses and blinked several times, as if holding back tears.

Then my sister clasped her hands in front of her. "The truth," she said sorrowfully, "is that Papa brought us here to escape the tragedies that plagued our family in England. We are all of a very delicate disposition. Poor Ada almost died during the journey here, and the twins are very sickly and, as I said, the baby is not yet seen in public. I am the strongest of all, but even I am subject to terrible headaches that make me quite lose my senses."

Nell replaced her glasses and turned her gaze to Mrs. Hamilton. "As for dear Papa . . . when our mother lay dying, she begged him with her last breath never to marry again, and he vowed that it would be so." Nell allowed her voice to trail off into a small sound that might have been a sob. There was absolute silence in the room.

I had been gazing at my sister with growing horror during this outburst and now turned my head to look at our guests. Sonia and Sophie were watching Nell with deep interest, but Mrs. Hamilton was staring over Nell's shoulder with an odd expression on her face. Glancing back at my sister, she pursed her lips and, returning her teacup to its saucer with a sharp click, heaved herself to her feet.

"Come along, girls," she said briskly. "It is obvious that these young ladies have many tasks to keep them busy, not least of which is that of nursing their sick family."

I rose quickly to my own feet, and as I turned towards the window, I saw, as Mrs. Hamilton had, my twin sisters run shrieking across the flower-bordered lawn that spread green and inviting at the front of the house. I wondered where Miss Walsh could be.

Mrs. Hamilton turned to me with a frosty smile. "I trust your ill health will not prevent you from attending chapel on the Sabbath," she said.

I felt my colour rise as I babbled my assurances and rang for Gilbert. He appeared immediately, almost as if he had been waiting outside the closed doors. As he ushered the three women to their carriage, I noticed that the tip of his nose was white. In time, I came to know that Gilbert's nose was an excellent barometer. Red often suggested suppressed laughter but white was usually the sign of anger.

As the door closed behind our visitors, I turned to my sister. "Why did you say those things, Nell?" I demanded. "Mrs. Hamilton saw the twins running around outside. She knew you were lying, and that stuff about Edie was just silly. And as for the things you said about Papa," I broke off, shaking my head in exasperation.

Nell looked at me scornfully. "This wasn't just a social visit! Mrs. Hamilton was husband hunting for those two awful daughters of hers, and Papa is a rich widower with a ready-made family and a lovely home. Didn't you see how they were looking over the place?" Nell stopped for breath and I sat down sharply in the chair recently vacated by Mrs. Hamilton.

"Maybe they were just here to welcome us to the community," I said. "We can't cut ourselves off from all society just because you think someone wants to marry Papa. You must write a note of apology at once, Nell. You'll just have to say that you were overwrought or something. Really, you are impossible sometimes." But even as I spoke, I knew that Nell would never write that note. I shook my head, but my lips started to twitch.

Nell glanced at me quickly. "Did you see the way Sonia's mouth was hanging open? She looked exactly like a goldfish," she said with a mischievous smile. "And Sophie practically swallowed her teeth when I said that Edie couldn't be seen in public."

Suddenly we were both giggling helplessly. "Nell, where did you get the idea that Papa had vowed never to remarry?" I gasped through my laughter.

"From one of the really bad romance books that Miss Walsh reads all the time."

I mopped the tears from my eyes and looked askance at Nell. "How do you know she reads those things?" I asked.

"I heard her reading aloud to herself one night on board ship. It was so romantic, and so very, very sad!" Nell rolled her eyes theatrically, and we were off laughing again, until one of the maids came in to clear away the tea things and we had to stifle our giggles.

Eventually, Nell got up and wandered over to the piano. She let her fingers drift over the keys then started to play one of the songs that I had loved to sing when I was younger. Tentatively at first and then with growing confidence, I joined in, singing the familiar words that brought comfort to my soul. So we whiled away the hot afternoon until the rays of sun slanting onto the polished wood of the piano told us that we should snatch a few minutes' rest before we had to dress for dinner.

CHAPTER 19

I was pleased when, on the following Saturday, my father returned home alone. Señor Rodriguez must have had business elsewhere. Papa did not speak much during dinner and I thought that he was tired or preoccupied with some problem concerning his work. I was beginning to understand that things did not always go well for him; helping to build a railway was no doubt a difficult undertaking. I hoped that he could stay with us for a few days this time, but he looked so forbidding that I hesitated to ask.

The meal was almost over when Papa put down the small fruit knife that he had been using to dissect an orange into neat pieces, and looked from Nell to me.

"Is there anything you girls would like to tell me regarding the visit by Mrs. Hamilton and her daughters?" he asked. I drew in my breath sharply. How could he know about that? I certainly hadn't mentioned it and I was sure that Nell hadn't, either. I glanced across at my sister, but her head was down and she was paying a great deal of attention to the remaining food on her plate.

I smiled cautiously, aware that a guilty flush coloured my cheeks. My father waited in silence. "Mrs. Hamilton and her two daughters visited us on Wednesday afternoon for tea. They seem very pleasant," I volunteered uncertainly.

Nell put down her spoon with a sharp bang. "Papa, they were perfectly awful," she said. "At least the daughters were. They practically made lists of everything in the room, and then they wanted us to parade the rest of the family in front of them, like horses or something!"

My father continued to look from one to the other of us, his face set in forbidding lines. "Enough!" he said coldly. "I am ashamed of the way you behaved to guests in this house. This is our new home, and these are people who share our faith and our language. Mrs. Hamilton is an old and trusted friend of mine. It was in their home that I resided on both of my previous visits. You will apologize to them for your ridiculous lies and your ill manners. You can expect to see them at chapel tomorrow.

"No!" he held up his hand as Nell made as if to speak. "I will not hear another word from either of you. I do, however, expect you to return the courtesy of a visit, in the unlikely event that Mrs. Hamilton is gracious enough to invite you."

Then my father rose, pushing his chair back abruptly from the table and looking directly at me. "I am very disappointed in you," he said, as he left the room. Lily and Iris, who had joined us for dinner that evening, were left staring after Papa, open-mouthed. Miss Walsh looked primly down at her plate.

I understood the reason for Papa's anger, but I wondered who had told him the details of that visit. Could it have been Gilbert? He had entered the room very quickly when I rang for him, so perhaps he had been listening outside the door. I felt a ridiculous sense of betrayal. I had thought that Gilbert was my friend.

Then as I pushed my own chair away from the table and started to leave the dining room, I glanced back. Miss Walsh was now leaning back in her chair and on her face was a small, tight smile of absolute satisfaction. Like a cat, I thought—a cat that has caught two small mice. Then I remembered the twins running unheeded across the lawn in front of the drawing room window, as Mrs. Hamilton watched, and I knew that it was Miss Walsh who had told Papa of our silly behaviour. I guessed that Gilbert had caught her listening at the door. That would certainly explain his hasty entrance and his air of suppressed anger.

The door of Papa's study shut with a sharp click as I turned and crossed the wide hall and walked quickly through the breakfast room.

I was seeking solace, as I sometimes did, at the far end of the enclosed porch where I had discovered two old wicker chairs tucked into the corner. The space was shaded with broad-leafed vines and sweet hanging wisteria.

I sat in the half-light breathing in the perfumed air then lifted my face to the cool breeze that crept through the trellis and lifted the damp tendrils of hair from my forehead. I was annoyed with Miss Walsh for her betrayal, but exasperated with Nell, too, for once again putting me in my father's bad books. It was a long time before I left my refuge and made my weary way to bed.

The next morning, we were up early and, when the carriage was brought round, all of us with the exception of Mrs. Chen and Edie set off to our new place of worship. When I was growing up, I never questioned my family's right to be seated in the reserved pew in the front row of our little chapel, but this first Sabbath in our new country served as a rude awakening for me.

The Methodist chapel was a simple building, somewhat bigger than we were accustomed to, with tall windows and a very fine steeple. Its whitewashed walls sparkled in the morning sun, and when we arrived, there were already several carriages drawn to one side of the wide path that led to the door.

As Drake handed me down from the carriage I saw that the chapel was situated on a rise in the ground and the wind swept hot and damp over the brow of the hill, blowing small pieces of grit into my eyes and tugging at my skirt, making me hurry into the shelter of the porch.

When we were all assembled, Papa led us inside. Although it was not yet time for the service to begin, the pews were already filled almost to capacity. As we waited to be ushered to our places, I told myself that I should smile and incline my head graciously to those people who showed us welcome as we approached the front of the chapel. But to my dismay, we were shown unceremoniously into a pew three rows from the back, without even enough hymn books for each of us. I didn't dare to question Papa about this, for he was still angry and had given us no more than a cursory nod of greeting that morning.

As the service began and I looked about me, I saw to my horror that Gilbert the butler and Mrs. Johnson our housekeeper were several rows in front of us. This was intolerable! Angrily, I peered towards the front of the chapel and caught sight of Mrs. Hamilton in the very front row. Of her two daughters there was no sign.

The service was long and the chapel quickly became unbearably hot. Most of the women were carrying fans which they put to good use, while many of the men used their hats to the same good purpose. I did not carry a fan, and Papa kept his hat resting firmly on his knees. The twins wriggled and fidgeted on the hard wooden benches and I glared at Miss Walsh in the hope that she would discipline them, but she ignored them and seemed lost in prayer.

Finally, running out of patience, I leaned across Nell and slapped Iris sharply on her wrist. Immediately, her eyes brimmed over with tears, but both she and Lily quieted down. I was sure that I heard a disapproving murmur from the pew behind me, but I set my face firmly forward and looked around to see if any other children were behaving badly. After searching each row as far as I could see, I realized that Lily and Iris were the only children in the congregation. I was horrified; what Godless people were these that they didn't teach their children to pray?

The Reverend Dr. Fisher droned on, but I could barely hear a word over the buzzing of some large flies that had drifted through the open door and were circling noisily around.

Sweat ran in small rivulets down each side of my face and I was filled with a sudden fierce longing for the peaceful gloom of our own little chapel in England and the cool rain on my face on the walk home.

Towards the end of the service, a side door close to the altar opened and Sonia and Sophie Hamilton emerged, shepherding a line of children, the youngest not more than three, the oldest a gangling boy of about twelve. The children sat at the feet of Dr. Fisher and he spoke quietly to them while the rest of the congregation shuffled a little in their seats and murmured together. I felt a surge of relief; obviously, the children worshipped separately. I saw the wisdom in this arrangement and decided to do my best to have Lily and Iris included in this group in the future.

As the service progressed, the heat in the building continued to rise, and by the time we struggled to our feet for the final hymn, I felt sure that I should faint at any moment. I was even secretly glad that, close to the back as we were, I would be able to escape quickly into the fresh air.

In that assumption, however, I was wrong. There had been many times in the past when my family had done just what Mrs. Hamilton and her daughters were doing. As Dr. Fisher walked swiftly down the length of the aisle, the people from the front pews followed him at their leisure, while the rest of us waited for our turn to leave. Mrs. Hamilton came first, flanked on either side by her daughters, nodding and smiling as they approached. They paused from time to time in order to exchange greetings with various acquaintances and friends. Finally, the little group reached the pew where we were waiting. Mrs. Hamilton smiled warmly at my father then her eyes passed over Nell and me without a flicker of recognition as she continued towards the door. I felt my face flame and bent my head in shame as people filed past us. I came to myself with Nell pushing me sharply in the back.

"Come on, Ada," she muttered. "Hurry up before we all faint from the heat."

As we reached the door of the chapel, I stepped to one side and paused for a moment to let the others pass me by; then, straightening my shoulders, I lifted my chin and moved forward. I knew what I had to do.

Outside, the air had become even more humid and the wind that earlier had blustered and gusted about the building had died away. I looked about until I found Mrs. Hamilton and her daughters. They were standing close by, deep in conversation with Miss Walsh. While they were talking, the twins were pursuing a small, fat boy who was waving Lily's hat above his head and whooping with delight as he ran away. Nell was standing idly by, watching with apparent amusement.

I moved quickly to where my sister was standing and grasped her firmly by the elbow. "Come on, let's get this apology over with before Papa makes us do it in public," I muttered. To my surprise, Nell did not object, but allowed me to lead her to where the Mrs. Hamilton was standing. I was thankful that Miss Walsh chose that moment to move away to take charge of the errant twins.

Mrs. Hamilton watched us as we approached. Her grey eyes were cold and her lips had thinned into a grim line as she waited for us to speak. Beside her, Sonia and Sophie were also silent. I felt myself blushing as I fumbled for words.

Then beside me Nell spoke. "Mrs. Hamilton, Miss Hamilton, Miss Sophie, we do beg your pardon for our foolishness the other day. It was very rude and silly. I don't know why I spoke as I did. Perhaps it was because we are so new here and are so far from home with no mother to guide us." Nell's voice trailed off. I glanced quickly at my sister. She was peering up at Mrs. Hamilton, her glasses a little smudged, her dark hair curling in tendrils around her face in the heat. In that moment, Nell looked like a small, lost child.

Mrs. Hamilton's face softened. "Very well, child, your apology is accepted, but I believe that lies should never go unpunished. Don't you agree, Robert?"

I looked around in surprise. My father had approached while Nell was speaking, his footsteps silent in the coarse grass. Papa and Mrs. Hamilton smiled easily at each other, but when my father turned to us, his face was stern. "Yes, indeed," he said. "And it is to be hoped that praying for forgiveness on your knees before the altar of the Lord will make you realize the error of your ways." He gestured towards the chapel. "Go and consider your foolish actions and I will send for you presently."

Nell and I turned back and re-entered the chapel, for neither one of us would have dared to disobey.

Inside, it was unbearably hot, and the smell of stale bodies was heavy in the air. Putting my hand to my mouth, I walked up the aisle and knelt dutifully on one of the faded kneelers before the altar. Nell thumped down beside me.

"This is ridiculous," she whispered fiercely. "How long are we expected to stay here?"

"How should I know? This is your fault," I snapped. "You shouldn't have made up those silly stories. Now just be quiet and pray!"

I should have taken my own advice, but prayer did not come easily. As I knelt before the altar, I felt none of the peace that prayer usually brought, and instead spent my time wondering how I could continue to live in this new country that I hated so much.

I don't know how long we knelt in the heat of the church, but I was becoming increasingly aware of my own discomfort. My dress clung damply to my back and my knees hurt from kneeling on the hard cushion. Sweat trickled slowly down my neck, and under my tightly fastened bonnet, my hair stuck in sticky wisps to my head.

Nell had been very still beside me, but now she leaned towards me. "That's it," she whispered. "I've counted to 3,000. I'll give it another 100 and then I'm leaving. Are you coming with me?" I turned to stare at my sister. Nell had not even tried to pray! I shook my head fiercely. Nell shrugged and started to rise, but subsided quickly at the sound of light footsteps hurrying up the aisle towards us.

In a moment, I felt a firm hand on my shoulder and Sophie Hamilton leaned down and peered anxiously into our faces. "Honestly," she said in her odd rough voice, "I'm surprised that you haven't both fainted! Mama and Mr. Baldwin have finally finished their conversation and sent me to fetch you."

Nell rose instantly to her feet and rubbed her knees. "Thank heavens," she said loudly. "Come on, Ada, let's go!"

I stayed where I was. "I wish to finish praying," I said coldly. "I'll join you shortly." I don't know why I chose to be so obstinate at that moment, and have often wondered since, if things might have turned out differently if I had simply walked out of chapel with Sophie and Nell on that hot Sunday. As it was, I stayed stubbornly on my knees for as long as it took me to say the Lord's Prayer, then, rising stiffly to my feet and putting a hand to my aching back, I spoke aloud. "Lord, please, take me away from this dreadful country, for I truly hate every part of it."

"Actually, it really isn't that bad once you get used to it," said a voice behind me. I spun around and found myself looking at a young man who was reclining gracefully against one of the supporting pillars. He smiled engagingly as he straightened up and came towards me. He was tall, with straight blonde hair that fell a little over his eyes, and even in the dim light that filtered through the high windows of the chapel, I could see that his face was tanned and his eyes were a disconcerting shade of blue. I was uncomfortably aware of my own disheveled state as he stepped in front of me and gave a small bow.

"Who are you?" I stammered foolishly. "We haven't been introduced."

He looked at me for a moment, the smile still lurking about his lips. "I'm Arthur Mitchell," he said. "I came to collect Aunt Bee and I was curious to see the latest additions to our little community. I'm a sort of honorary nephew to Mrs. Hamilton, and you, I believe, are Miss Ada Baldwin."

I nodded. "Yes, I am, but how do you know my name?" I spoke in what I hoped was a tone of indifference.

Arthur Mitchell gave a boyish grin as he turned and offered me his arm. "Dear Sophie filled me in while we were waiting for you to repent," he said with a small wink..

After a moment, I took the proffered arm, for it would have been churlish not to do so, and together we walked out of the chapel into the sunshine that seemed, all at once, very pleasant.

As we emerged, I noticed that Nell and Sophie Hamilton were standing close together, having what appeared to be a very serious discussion. The twins and Miss Walsh were already waiting in our carriage and my father was handing Mrs. Hamilton into hers. Another young man was waiting to join them and Mr. Mitchell nodded towards him. "That's my friend Edmund Nichols," he said. "He's here for the holidays as his folks are back in the Old Country. The 'varsity has long holidays at Christmas. We're at Cordoba."

I nodded silently, not sure how to respond to his easy conversation. By now we had reached our carriage. "Do you girls ride?" he asked as he handed me in. "Everyone here does, you know." Not waiting for my answer, he added casually, "I'll speak to Aunt Bee about it and we'll have you mounted up in no time."

"Mr. Mitchell, there's no need," I started to protest, but he had already turned away.

Then he paused and looked back at me. "Call me Arthur, won't you?" And with that, he was gone, striding long-legged to where the other carriage and its occupants already waited.

Arthur Mitchell swung himself easily into the driver's seat and, with Edmund Nichols alongside, gave a crack of the whip that sent the carriage sweeping in a sharp curve, jolting onto the grass before it bumped down again onto the dusty path. I heard squeals of laughter as the carriage and its occupants disappeared around a bend in the road.

We were very quiet on the journey home; even the twins were subdued. Nell gazed out at the passing scenery and Papa kept his own counsel. As for me, my mind was whirling. It had been a very strange morning, indeed, beginning with the unfamiliar prayer service and ending with my encounter with Arthur Mitchell. I felt my face flush a little as I wondered if I would see him again. Silently, I berated Nell for her stupid prank. I was quite sure that Mrs. Hamilton would not extend an invitation for us to spend time with her or her holiday visitors.

A few days later, when we were all seated at breakfast, Papa put down his fork and cleared his throat. "I have been speaking to Mrs. Hamilton," he said, "and on her advice, I have arranged riding lessons for all of you. Two of the ponies already in the stables are quite suitable for you girls." Papa smiled at the twins, who immediately squealed with delight and had to be hushed by Miss Walsh, who looked grimly pleased. I had overheard her talking to Mrs. Johnson shortly after the housekeeper had arrived. She was bemoaning the lack of riding facilities here, and explaining that in India, she had ridden daily.

"You may continue to ride the horse you have already borrowed from the stables, Miss Walsh," Papa continued smoothly, and I had the satisfaction of seeing the governess flush with embarrassment as she realized that my father already knew of her stolen morning rides.

Then my father turned to Nell and me. I have arranged for two suitable mounts to be purchased for you girls. Except for the Sabbath, you will be receiving lessons daily, and I expect all of you girls to make good progress."

As he rose to leave, my father looked across to where Nell and I were seated side by side. "I will see you two girls on another matter in my study immediately."

My heart sank; I was certain that we were in further trouble, though this time I had no idea what it might be. I glanced uneasily at Nell, but she was busy spreading marmalade on a final piece of toast before popping it into her mouth and rising to follow Papa.

My father seated himself behind his desk and motioned us to the chairs. I perched uneasily on a wooden chair next to the desk, but Nell flung herself into a big leather armchair close to the window. Papa looked steadily at each of us for a few moments before picking up his pen and fiddling with it. I felt a surge of relief. My father did not appear to be angry; on the contrary, he seemed a little uneasy.

At last, he spoke. "I think I owe both of you girls an apology," he said. "Since we arrived in this country, I confess that I am guilty of failing to see the changes in you. But as Mrs. Hamilton has pointed out to me, you are fast becoming young ladies."

He paused, and I saw him glance over to the small oval portrait of Mama that once again graced the corner of his desk. It had been painted when they were first married and showed my mother laughing with happiness, and surrounded with a sort of joyous light. It had always been on my father's desk at home, though I had not seen it since Mama had died and wondered if perhaps he had carried it with him all this time.

My father was speaking again. "When your mother died, I made the very difficult decision to continue with the plans that we had made together, to bring all of you here to live in Argentina. Now I think that I may not have made the wisest decision."

There was silence in the room as my father stopped speaking and I held my breath. All at once, I remembered my prayer in chapel, when I had begged the Lord to let me return to England.

Papa continued. "I confess that I had not considered the social needs of you two girls; Lily and Iris are young yet, and are well looked after by Miss Walsh, and Edith is just a baby. However, it has become clear that both of you girls are in need of some guidance. Mrs. Hamilton has most kindly undertaken to act as your chaperone, especially during the upcoming social season. Ada, you will 'come out' this year and Nell perhaps the following year." Papa sounded triumphant, as if he had just handed us a gift, but Nell and I looked back at him a trifle blankly.

Nell was the first to speak. "Thank you, Papa," she said in a voice that was remarkably subdued for her. "But just who is Mrs. Hamilton; I mean, how do you know her?" I could hear the slight edge in Nell's voice and could guess at some of her fears. Perhaps it was

Mrs. Hamilton, and not her daughters, that we should be concerned about when it came to seeing Papa as a good matrimonial catch! I was amazed at my sister's temerity and waited to see how my father would react.

Papa gave a slight smile and leaned back in his chair. "Don't worry, Nell," he said, placing his fingertips together in a familiar gesture. "I have known Beulah Hamilton since I was a very young man. I worked for her husband when I was a junior engineer. We built bridges in those days, but Harold Hamilton had a vision that he shared with me. He dreamed of building railroads that one day would cross and re-cross this country.

"About fifteen years ago, he and his family came here to follow that dream. They made me welcome when I visited them and I was deeply saddened by his untimely death. He saw, long before many others, that trains could bring great wealth and economic growth to this country. Argentina is very large with much potential, but great poverty. Up until quite recently, much of its wealth lay in slavery, and all its industrial goods, both imported and exported, were moved by pack animals or human labour."

While my father was speaking, Nell had risen and was now leaning on Papa's desk, listening eagerly to his words, but I allowed my mind to drift. I half heard my sister's questions and my father's answers as he, in turn, leaned forward and pulling a sheet of paper close he began to draw the railway lines that had already been developed. I wondered dreamily if we should have to go and live with the Hamilton's for a while. My heart gave a jump as I thought of living under the same roof as Arthur Mitchell. Then almost immediately, I remembered that he and his friend would soon be returning to Cordoba University.

No, it would be much better if we stayed in our own home. I took pleasure in managing the household, discussing daily menus with Cook or the need to purchase new bed linens with Mrs. Johnson. I liked that, for the most part, the staff were beginning to accept me as mistress of the house. The prospect of spending several months as a houseguest with the Hamilton's did not appeal.

Nell and Papa were still discussing the merits of the new railway line that would eventually run far beyond Rosario to Cordoba. I stifled a yawn; the temperature was rising again and I found it difficult to accept that Christmas was less than a month away. I allowed my mind to drift into a very pleasant dream in which I was the mistress of a beautiful home, and a young man, with blonde hair and the deepest blue eyes, was master of the household.

I was brought back to reality by the sound of Nell calling my name. "Honestly, Ada, you weren't listening to a word," she complained.

My father shook his head with a smile. "Ada is like your mother, Nell. She's a dreamer. Now you, my dear, if only you had been a boy! You have a fine mind, child." Nell made as if to interrupt, but my father held up a protesting hand. "That's enough for now I have more work to do. Mrs. Hamilton will be taking care of your social life from now on. You will no doubt be hearing from her in the next little while."

We had both risen to our feet as Papa was speaking, but as my sister reached the door, my father called after her. "Nell," he said gravely, "you may rest assured that I do not intend to remarry in the foreseeable future, so you have no further need to make up stories." Then he bent his head to the pile of papers on his desk, but not before I saw what looked suspiciously like a smile, quickly suppressed.

Late one morning two weeks before Christmas when I was tending a patch of lavender that I had discovered growing in a shaded corner at the front of the house, Miguel appeared silently beside me.

"Come, Señorita," he said softly. "The horses are here, come." So I pulled the earth-stained gloves from my hands, smoothed my apron, and followed him to the back of the house.

Here was a sort of stone courtyard flanked on three sides by buildings. The kitchens and nurseries were attached to the house on one side, with a long, low, whitewashed building that was the servants' living quarters adjacent to it. Next to that were the stables.

As I approached, I heard raised voices interspersed with shouts of laughter, and in amongst the babble, I could make out my sister's voice shrieking words that I could not understand. I quickened my pace as I rounded the corner and entered the courtyard where I came to an abrupt halt.

As usual when anything of interest was happening, the entire kitchen staff had abandoned work, and now everyone was crowding into the courtyard, laughing and shouting words of encouragement.

But it was the sight of Nell that brought me to a halt. She was attempting to ride a large dappled grey horse, the reins of which were being held firmly by a stable lad who was beaming up at Nell in obvious delight.

My sister's hair was down around her shoulders in complete disarray, but worse than that, she had hitched up her skirts and was sitting astride the horse like some hoyden. Her legs were quite visible, revealing the painful fact that she had omitted stockings while dressing that morning. Nell's face was flushed as she laughed down at the gathered crowd.

Raising my voice above the hubbub, I called out to my sister. "Nell, get down from there at once," I demanded angrily. "This is no way to behave! Get down at once or I shall tell Papa."

My sister glanced over at me, still laughing. "I'm learning to ride a horse, Ada, and this horse is mine, so I'll do as I like." With that, she attempted to wheel the animal around and ride away, but the stable lad still held firmly onto the reins, with the result that Nell, with a sharp squeal, tumbled off the beast and ended sitting in the dust displaying a great deal of petticoat and bare legs. There was a great hoot of laughter from the onlookers.

Careless of my own safety and humiliated by my sister's behaviour, I ran around the now prancing horse to help her up. Scarlet with shame and anger, I hauled my sister to her feet, realizing as I did so that the servants had suddenly fallen silent. I looked up to see Gilbert standing in the kitchen doorway. I did not hear him speak, but within moments, everyone had returned to work.

Then Gilbert walked stiffly across the courtyard to where Nell was angrily nursing a bruised hand and I was standing next to her, still breathing heavily.

He bowed slightly. "Riding lessons begin tomorrow morning at six o'clock sharp," he said, his face betraying nothing. "Miss Nell, I will send your maid to assist you in cleaning up," he added, as he turned away.

Once again, I faced my sister. "This is too much, Nell," I began, but she interrupted me furiously.

"Mind your own business, Ada, and for goodness' sake, stop trying to be Mama. You're not her and you never will be!" And with those hurtful words ringing in my ears, I watched as my sister stamped out of the courtyard and around to the front of the house.

The next day, just as Gilbert had promised, our riding lessons began. Promptly at six o'clock, a small man wearing a large sombrero, worn boots, and riding leathers arrived in the yard. He introduced himself to us as Jose. He was to be our teacher.

Jose was a man of few words and when Nell attempted to question him, he just smiled and gestured for us to mount. I was terrified. The horse that had been chosen for me was a roan mare. At any other time I would have admired such a beautiful beast, but now she represented yet another challenge in my life.

Up to now, we had not ridden at all, unless you count occasional trips into the village on our old cob, Dobbin. He'd plodded down the lane to the smithy and back again, unconcerned by the small human burdens on his back. I knew that my mother and her sister, Jessica, had ridden as children, but Papa had not seen the necessity for such extravagance in our small community at home.

The more I looked at the horse, the more afraid I became. It was a gentle beast, and well suited to my needs, but even so, I found myself taking an involuntary step back as the horse turned and sniffed the air in my direction.

Jose watched me for a moment. Then, taking me by the arm, he led me to the horse's nose, murmuring to the beast all the while. He insisted that I stroke the long velvet nose and pat the strong neck before helping me to mount.

I rode sidesaddle, but Nell, showing no fear whatsoever, demanded that she learn to ride astride. Jose shrugged and disappeared into the stable, returning a few moments later with a different saddle that he placed on the back of Nell's horse.

In a few minutes, Nell was riding triumphantly astride, her skirts once again raised almost to her knees, but I saw with relief, that she was wearing high boots that covered her bare legs this time. I wondered where she had found them.

Our new teacher gave us an easy lesson that first day, but I was more than ready to stop when Jose led us back to the stable yard and helped me to dismount. Nell was already on the ground and she handed the reins to Jose with a brief "Gracias."

Jose handed them back to her. "Señorita," he said, "your horse has carried you; now you must care for him." And he led us into the cool gloom of the stable and showed us the first steps in how to groom a horse.

As the days passed, I became more comfortable in the saddle and even began to look forward to the feel of the horse moving smoothly under me, as we rode out each day. I enjoyed the freshness of the early morning air and the sound of birds calling high and clear in the blue sky above us.

I called my horse Blaze, for the white streak that ran over her left ear and down to the tip of her nose. After a while, she seemed to know me, and I was pleased one morning when she came cantering over to the fence when I called her name. She and several other horses, including Nell's, were allowed to run free in a small paddock that stretched behind the servants' quarters, though once the sun was up they spent most of their time in the shade of a group of trees at the far end of the field.

I gave Blaze the small treat that I had picked up on my way through the kitchen. I held my hand quite flat as Jose had taught me, and thrilled at the feel of her soft lips on my skin. For the first time, I experienced the thrill of ownership.

CHAPTER 20

Christmas came and went almost unnoticed by the Baldwin household. We went to chapel on Christmas morning and ate a simple dinner late in the evening, as usual. There were no guests at our table that night and Papa had given most of the servants the day off.

Gilbert and Mrs. Johnson served us that night, moving quietly around the table with the ease that comes with long years of service. At the end of the meal, Papa signaled to Gilbert, who disappeared for a moment, before reappearing with several identical flat packages, each wrapped in fine paper. He distributed a package to each of us, including Miss Walsh.

I looked down at the present in front of me and was filled with dismay. I had not given a thought to the making or exchanging of Christmas gifts this year, for each day had been filled with new experiences, and it was high summer and seemed very far from the cold days of Decembers past.

As I gazed at the slender package before me, I remembered those other times, making gifts with Mama, or one year sitting cozily with Cook and Mrs. Carter as the afternoon light failed and the kettle hissed gently on the hob as I knitted woolen mittens, my own small tokens of love and appreciation. My eyes filled with tears as I looked up at my father.

He was watching me, but as I opened my mouth to speak, he shook his head slightly and I was sure that he could read my mind, and wished me to keep silent. The twins, Miss Walsh, and Nell were eagerly opening their gifts, so I bent to undo mine, but my fingers fumbled clumsily with the ribbon and I pulled it into a knot. By the time I had untied the parcel, the others were all exclaiming happily over their gifts.

Gently, I pulled back the folds of paper to reveal a pair of riding gloves fashioned in the softest of leathers. Each glove was cuffed and on each cuff was embroidered in exquisite stitching my initials, "A.B.," surrounded by a wreath of flowers. Perfect in each last detail, every tiny petal a reminder of what I thought I had successfully forgotten. Roses— each bloom a small reminder of my mother's death. I choked back a sob before taking a deep breath to steady myself.

Nell had risen from her seat beside me and was kneeling at my father's side, holding his hand to her face. "Papa," she said, looking up at him. "How did you know I would want orchids?"

My father looked down at her fondly. "Nell," he replied with a smile, "I am not completely blind. I know quite well that it was you who kept the orchids growing in the greenhouses until we left." He patted her cheek. "I'm glad you like them, child."

As Nell returned to her place, Papa looked down the table to where Lily and Iris were seated. "You two were easy," he said, with a twinkle. "I had your gloves each embroidered with your very own namesake flower. Then he turned to Miss Walsh. "I trust, Miss Walsh, that you find your gloves also to your liking?"

Miss Walsh had two bright spots of colour on her cheeks and sounded a little flustered as she replied with a quick affirmative. Glancing over, I saw that she had also received gloves. They were not as fine as those that Papa had given to us, but they were nevertheless a handsome gift. I could see that they were embroidered with a large "W," surrounded with thistles, the emblem of Scotland, but also remarkably appropriate to Miss Walsh's own disposition. Finally, Papa looked at me. "What about you, Ada?" he asked. "Do you like your roses?"

I swallowed the lump in my throat. "Thank you, Papa. They are beautiful," I managed to whisper. But even to my own ears, my voice sounded a little bleak.

The Sabbath found us once more in chapel. I prayed very hard that day and took some comfort from the familiar prayers and hymns. For the first time in many months, I found myself praying for those we had left behind and sent a heartfelt prayer winging across the seas to all those I held dear. Then as I bent my head in prayer, I thought I felt, just for a moment, a gentle touch on my head; a loving hand passing swiftly by. I shivered in spite of the heat, wondering briefly whose hand had touched me.

By this time, we were no longer seated at the back of the chapel. Within a month of our arrival, Papa had procured a pew for us three rows from the front, almost opposite the Hamilton's. Nell had been anxious to know how this had come about, but my father's answer to her questions had been brief and had brooked no discussion. "I pay my tithes, Nell," he said shortly. "If others do not, they must pay the price of losing their place."

Nell had taken a breath, ready to ask more questions, but I laid a restraining hand on her arm. "Let it be, Nell, or Papa will make you do penance again," I whispered.

My sister had glared at me then, before turning on her heel and walking away. As she did so, Sophie Hamilton hailed her and the two of them were soon deep in conversation. As I watched them together, I wondered what it was that Nell talked about so often with the younger of the two Hamilton girls.

New Year's Day, 1886, dawned bright and clear, though I knew the heat would soon become oppressive. But in those first waking moments, I rejoiced in the small breeze that floated through the open window, making the mosquito nets around my bed stir, as I stretched lazily.

Tonight, Nell and I were going to our very first social event. Mrs. Hamilton, or Aunt Bee, as she now insisted we call her, had invited us to a New Year's supper, with music to follow, and I allowed myself a moment of excitement at the thought of seeing Arthur Mitchell again. Papa would not accompany us as he had returned to his worksite two days after Christmas and we did not expect to see him again for several weeks.

There would be no riding out for us today as there was a mare in foal and Jose was not willing to leave her, and I wasn't ready to venture out without him, but I knew that Nell was anxious to ride again. She and Papa had gone out on several occasions without me over Christmas, and I was a little surprised that he had not objected to Nell's tomboy insistence on riding astride. In spite of what he had said earlier, I think my father still thought of Nell as a child. She was not very tall and, with her untidy hair, ready smile, and perpetually smudged glasses, it was easy to think of her as a precocious twelve-year-old rather than a young woman.

The day dragged heavy on my hands. Nell was about her own business and Mrs. Johnson made it obvious that she had no immediate need of me. I stopped briefly in the schoolroom during the morning, but the sound of Iris and Lily bickering over their lesson made me hurry away before they caught sight of me. Finally, I wandered out into the courtyard behind the house, with the half-formed idea that I might check on Blaze, when my eyes alighted on the long white building that housed both servants' quarters and the nursery.

I felt a stab of guilt that I had not seen Edie for such a long time, though this was not entirely my fault. Mrs. Chen kept much to herself, hurrying past with my sister bundled in her arms whenever our paths crossed. Now I headed purposefully to the heavy door that led from the yard into a small vestibule and, from there, into the rooms that formed the nursery.

There was a long corridor at the back of the building that led directly from the nursery to the kitchen and, from there, into the house proper. This was the usual approach, and few people entered the nursery from the outside as I was doing. I had to push the door hard to make it open. I found myself in a small, whitewashed room that was entirely without furnishings. The floor was covered in tiles that were a rich shade of brownish red, much like the terra cotta tiles that had covered our kitchen floor at home. Wooden shutters were closed against the heat of the day and sunlight shone in thin bars across the floor.

As my eyes became accustomed to the gloom, I saw a half-open door to my right. I walked towards it, taking care to move quietly, for

I did not want to disturb my sister if she was sleeping. The nursery was a sparsely furnished room with a small, low chair to one side that was draped with a single blanket. Edie's cot was on the other side of the room and, between the two, pushed back against the wall, was a waist-high table. Edie was perched on this table, long skirts trailing over the edge. Her arms were stretched out in front of her and each chubby hand had familiar ivory-topped needles sticking out of it.

I gave an involuntary cry at the sight and stepped through the door. Mrs. Chen had been standing behind it, folding long strips of cloth into neat bundles. She spun around as I entered and darted towards Edie, grabbing the startled child and holding her protectively against her thin body.

"Mrs. Chen, what are you doing to Edie?" I demanded accusingly. The sight of the needles that had been such a disturbing part of my own illness was very upsetting. I took a step forward, but Mrs. Chen clutched Edie even tighter in her arms. My sister gave a startled yelp, and began to cry.

"Why are you using those needles on my sister?" I demanded again. "Is she sick?"

Mrs. Chen stroked the soft brown curls beneath her fingers, her face expressionless. Then holding firmly onto the still sobbing child, she bowed slightly. "No, Miss, she not sick; is just mouth sore from teeth coming." She turned away dismissively, fussing slightly over Edie's left hand, where a needle had fallen and now hung quivering in a fold of her trailing skirts.

I stayed where I was for a moment, unsure of what to do next and feeling a little foolish at my outburst. "I just came by to wish you and Edie a happy New Year," I said at last. Mrs. Chen stared blankly at me. Uncomfortably, I turned towards the door then paused for a moment. "Do you have everything you want here, Mrs. Chen?" I asked. "The room seems very bare; there is plenty of furniture in the house and I can arrange for you to get whatever you need—a dresser, perhaps, or a wardrobe for Edie's clothes." I stopped uncertainly, but Mrs. Chen ignored me. Feeling thoroughly uncomfortable now, I retreated back the way I had come. "Just let me know," I called as the outside door closed heavily behind me.

I stood for a few moments in the bright sunshine, wondering why Mrs. Chen had made me feel so unwelcome. As I walked slowly to the paddock to look for Blaze, I shook my head at my own foolishness. Edie was my sister and I had every right to be in that room, so why should I feel that I was intruding? I decided to talk to Nell about it at the earliest possible opportunity. I hoped that perhaps she had a better relationship with Mrs. Chen and my little sister.

I had not given much thought to what I should wear to the Hamilton's party, but in the end I settled on the lilac dress that I had worn for Lucy Blackwell's wedding. Anna had trimmed the neckline for me, using white silk flowers fashioned from an old scarf that I no longer used, and although the skirt was perhaps an inch shorter than I would have liked, I thought it would do very well for a simple evening out at a friend's house.

My hair had still not yet grown to my shoulders, but Anna spent extra time dressing it that night, wrapping a wide band of lilac silk around my head and pulling the short ends into high curls to give the illusion of length. I was pleased with the overall effect.

When I was ready, I went to find Nell. As usual, she had hardly bothered with her appearance and I had to insist that she allow Anna to dress her hair in a more becoming style. When she was ready, I was startled by the transformation and had to admit, if it were not for her glasses, without which my sister was virtually blind, Nell was quite pretty.

Until that day, I had not known the exact location of the Hamilton's house, and was surprised to discover that they were in fact our nearest neighbours. I knew that beyond our own house and gardens stretched several acres of undeveloped brush and grassland, for this was where Nell and I had ridden in recent weeks, but now I realized that the narrow wire fence that had been our turning point on several occasions was the dividing line between the Hamilton property and our own.

When we arrived, the house was already filling with people and to my dismay it quickly became obvious that Beulah Hamilton's New Year celebration was not a quiet evening at home with a few special friends.

The house itself was magnificent. It stood surrounded by tall trees and sweeping lawns, much wider and deeper than our own and was built in the Spanish hacienda style, long and low, with rooms that fanned out from a central courtyard that featured a beautiful fountain that splashed water into a huge white marble bowl. Around its edge, plants and flowers bloomed, just as if they were in their natural state.

Aunt Bee, resplendent in black satin and lace, welcomed us warmly before passing us quickly along to Sonia and Sophie who were, as usual dressed in almost identical and very unflattering gowns.

Sophie stepped forward at once and pulling Nell's arm through her own, drew her away, all the while speaking in low urgent tones. I was left with Sonia who walked me quickly towards a pair of double glass doors that swung open easily under her touch to reveal a drawing room of breathtaking proportions. There were at least four or five large couches scattered about the room, together with an assortment of armchairs and small tables. The focal point in the room was an enormous piano that even I could see was far superior to our own, and in front of this were arranged twenty or thirty small, elegant chairs.

I remembered with embarrassment how Nell and I had been sure that the Hamilton's were scheming to acquire our simple property and was very glad that our prideful error had not been discovered.

Sonia tugged insistently at my arm and led me over to two young women of about my own age. "My dears," she lisped at them, "you simply must meet Ada Baldwin. She is quite new here, and is so very, very sweet. She and her sisters are our neighbours and they have been left motherless, so dear Mama has taken them under her wing." Sonia rolled her eyes expressively, and giggled girlishly into her fan.

The two girls surveyed me as Sonia was speaking, and I became increasingly aware of my faded mauve dress with its homemade flowers, and of my embarrassingly short hair. I felt my colour rising and had an almost overwhelming urge to turn and flee. The two girls glanced at one another before the taller of them extended a languid hand. "Marianne Forrester," she said, "and this is Dora, Dora Phillips."

I glanced quickly at the girl who had not spoken. She was the most exquisite creature I had ever seen. She was small, with a perfect, heart-shaped face, a rosebud mouth, and large green eyes. Her hair was a mass of tiny golden curls and her diminutive figure was encased in a dress of pink lace, cut, I was absolutely sure, in the very latest London style.

As I opened my mouth to speak, she raised a small, gloved hand to her mouth, barely hiding a yawn. Turning to her friend, she spoke for the first time, cutting across my greeting.

"For goodness sake, Marianne," she said petulantly. "This is so boring. Where are the boys? I told them not to be late!" She gave a stamp with one small pink satin-clad foot and turned away, ignoring me completely. Sonia had slipped away during this exchange and when I looked around for her, she was nowhere to be seen.

I caught a glimpse of twinkling lights and heard the sounds of voices raised in laughter from outside. Feeling very out of place, I drifted to one of the small chairs and sat down, fidgeting uncomfortably with my fan. Papa had promised me that this should be my year to "come out," but I hoped most sincerely that I should not have to attend any more parties such as this.

I looked down at my hands, miserably wishing myself back at home, when a familiar voice spoke beside me.

"Miss Baldwin! How delightful to see you . . .!" My heart leapt as I looked up to see Arthur Mitchell smiling down at me. His blue eyes twinkled as he swept his blonde hair back with a careless hand. "You look rather forlorn sitting there by yourself. Why don't you come outside with the others? Aunt Bee is just getting the food organized."

I felt colour flood into my face and wished that I could think of something bright and clever to say, but Arthur didn't seem to notice. Taking my hand in his, he raised it to his lips, and drew me to my feet.

"This is a beautiful house," I blurted out. "It's bigger than ours."

Arthur raised a quizzical eyebrow. "Yes, I suppose it is," he agreed, "but I've spent most of my life here, so I really don't notice."

There was a silence as I tried again to think of something to say. Arthur was still watching me intently. "Are you girls riding yet?" he asked at last, with a smile.

I took a shaky breath, glad to have something to talk about.

"Yes, we are. I have a wonderful horse called Blaze. I call her that because . . ." But I was cut off abruptly by a loud shriek, and Dora Phillips was suddenly beside us. Ignoring me completely, she addressed my companion.

"Arthur, you naughty, naughty boy," she said, pouting charmingly. "Where have you been? I've been looking everywhere for you! Come on, you absolutely have to come outside, it is so much more fun out there!" And attaching herself firmly to Arthur's arm, she dragged him towards the open French doors.

I stood looking after them, my face burning. Arthur's head was bent towards Dora, and he did not look back.

"I see Dora is up to her usual games," said a quiet voice at my side. I turned and found myself looking almost directly into a pair of kind brown eyes. The young man beside me gave a small bow. "Forgive me," he said. "We haven't been introduced, but I know who you are. It's hard not to know everyone around here, and Arthur pointed you out to me. He has an eye for a pretty girl."

He stretched out his hand and grinned engagingly, showing teeth that were a little crooked. "I'm Edmund Nichols, Arthur's friend. We're at university in Cordoba together. My folks are back in England now, but Aunt Bee always makes me welcome here. She's very kind." Still smiling, he offered his arm.

"Miss Baldwin," he said gallantly, "may I escort you outside to see what all the fuss is about?" I took his arm, glad of his kindness, and found myself chatting easily as he asked about our recent journey. I even told him of our early difficulties with the servants. He listened attentively and made me laugh by recounting some of his own mishaps as a young boy in a foreign country. But when we emerged from the house, I found my eyes drawn once more to Arthur Mitchell. He was standing close by, with his back to me, and next to him were Dora and Marianne. Dora turned her head as she caught sight of us. She stared for a moment, then reaching up she whispered something laughingly into Arthur Mitchell's ear.

My hand tightened on Edmund's arm and I hoped very much that he would escort me to supper, but no sooner had the thought entered my head than I heard Aunt Bee call Edmund's name and he excused himself hastily and hurried away.

I stood uncertainly, feeling very alone, and looked about hoping to see my sister, or even one of the Hamilton girls. Eventually, I caught sight of Nell on the other side of the lawn. She was surrounded by a crowd of young women; she seemed to have had no problem making new friends. Sophie was with her and, as I watched, she leaned into the circle and said something. I couldn't hear her words, but the group broke into a cheer, laughing and waving their hands in the air.

With an inward sigh, I looked about the garden. It was delightful. Huge banks of flowers surrounded the lawns and at one end was a grove of tall trees. Small tables and chairs were scattered on the velvety grass and long tables had been set up and were piled high with the most amazing array of food I had ever seen. Central to each was an enormous piece of roast beef, and standing behind each table were servants, ready to spring into action to serve the guests.

At that moment, Aunt Bee bustled into the middle of the lawn, her face flushed with heat and pleasure. In one hand, she carried a silver bell that she now rang with great gusto.

"Come along, everyone," she called. "Dinner is ready".

There was a flurry as people moved about, and I heard small gusts of laughter and exclamations of delight as people found their seats and discovered who their dining companions were to be.

I tentatively approached a table, looking for my name. As I did so, I heard Dora Phillips' high tones carry clearly across the lawn. "Arthur, not her, she is an absolute bore, you can tell; besides, I would rather have Edmund at our table." I looked over in time to see Dora's friend Marianne move a card from the place beside her and put it swiftly on a nearby table where several elderly people were already seated. I had no need to check to know that the name on the card was mine.

As daylight faded, hanging lamps were lit and excellent food was served. As the meal progressed, I noticed that each table was hosted by a member of the Hamilton family—or, as in our case, by one of the elders of our Methodist congregation.

This pleased me, for I was concerned about Nell and her companions. I asked the gentleman if he knew who these ladies were; however, he was hard of hearing, and I was forced to repeat myself several times. Finally, his wife, a tall, thin woman, looked up from her plate, pausing for a moment as she mopped up the pink juices left from her meat.

Swallowing audibly, she said loudly, "they are militants." She looked across to where Sophie along with Nell and perhaps ten other young women, had pushed two tables together and were involved in a very animated discussion, punctuated with shrieks of laughter and occasional cheers. I was about to ask further questions when our hostess once again rang her silver bell, announcing that the musical part of our evening was about to begin.

At that, chairs were hastily pushed away from tables and the whole group trooped back into the house. Replete with good food, people soon settled into their seats in anticipation of the musical evening ahead.

I had a small, persistent headache and wondered if I could persuade Nell to leave a little early. I glanced around for her, but she was nowhere in sight. Aunt Bee was hastening towards the piano and, once again making use of her bell, she gained our attention. As she stood, face flushed and beaming, I felt a surge of affection for Beulah Hamilton. She was obviously at her happiest tonight. My warm feelings were short-lived, however, as I realized what she was saying.

"For our first presentation this evening," she said with a smile, "I wish to introduce the very newest members of our little community. The Misses Ada and Nell Baldwin will now sing and play a short selection of traditional melodies to remind us all of our beloved England."

There was a polite spattering of applause as I turned my startled face to look for Nell. She was approaching confidently from the back of the room, with several pieces of sheet music in her hand. She looked for me and changed direction as soon as she saw me. As she approached, I half rose from my chair, shaking my head in silent protest, but Nell took me by the arm and almost dragged me to the piano.

"What do you think you're doing?" I whispered fiercely, as she seated herself on the wide piano stool.

Nell looked up from arranging the sheets of music. "For goodness' sake, stop fussing, Ada. I was here all afternoon practicing." She nodded at the sheet music. "You know all the words—just sing them." And with that, she struck an introductory chord. At that moment, I could happily have strangled my younger sister.

The room had quieted at the sound of the piano and, in the silence I heard a quickly stifled giggle. Even from a distance, I was quite sure that it came from the rose-petal lips of Dora Phillips. Taking a deep breath, I turned around, rested one hand on the polished surface of the piano, and looked out at the audience. Nell was right, I did recognize the music. I raised my chin and began to sing "Where Sheep May Safely Graze." It had been one of Mama's favourite songs.

We performed five songs in all, and at the end of our performance, I hurried back to my seat, colour still high, but pleased that I had not disgraced myself. I was still furious with Nell for arranging this without me, though a small knowing voice in my head told me that I would never have agreed to sing in public if my sister had not forced me into it.

As I caught my breath, an old gentleman next to me patted my hand kindly. "Wonderful, my dear! Brings back old memories don't y'know. . . . "

It was when I turned to thank him that I heard Dora's voice behind me. "I thought it very quaint!" she said, raising her voice a little to include the people sitting around her. "And I do actually know some of the songs. One of our kitchen maids used to sing them before Mama turned her off for stealing." I bent my head, and waited miserably for the remainder of the evening to be over.

At the end of the musical recitals, everyone applauded and I was thankful that surely we would be able to leave very soon. But once again, the older folk broke into small groups chatting easily together, and drifting towards the more comfortable chairs. My head still hurt and I was sure that the hour was late, so I went looking for Nell, determined to persuade her that it would be quite proper for us to leave.

I approached Aunt Bee first, ready to make our apologies, but on seeing me, she smiled brightly and said, "Ada, dear, go and join the young people outside. I want you to make friends. Remember that you are 'coming out' this year!" and she shooed me determinedly towards the French doors.

I stepped outside and halted uncertainly. The terrace and lawns were still flooded with light from the lit torches, but the garden appeared quite deserted. I stood listening for a few moments and gradually became aware of voices and laughter in the distance.

I trod lightly over the grass following the sounds; I hoped that I could find Nell and persuade her to leave with me after all.

The sound of music and laughter became louder, and as I turned the corner, I stopped and felt my eyes grow round in astonishment. In front of me was a courtyard, not unlike our own, but it was brightly lit and the walls of the buildings were garlanded with flowers and greenery.

The space was crowded with young people, some of whom I had seen earlier. But there were other faces there, too, faces that seemed dark and lean and menacing. In one corner of the courtyard, there was a small gathering of musicians, enthusiastically playing instruments, most of which I did not recognize.

I hesitated on the edge of the crowd, looking for Nell. I caught sight of her at last, on the other side of the courtyard talking animatedly to three of the women she had been with earlier. As I strained to see her, I suddenly heard my name. Turning, I was surprised to see Marianne and Dora standing close by.

"Aren't you very hot in that frock?" asked Dora with a thin smile. "You should have something to cool you. She gestured towards a long table that carried an assortment of jugs and bottles, together with glasses and cups of various sizes.

I shook my head. "No," I replied. "I was looking for my sister. I think we should leave now."

As I was speaking, Marianne had turned to the table and poured something into a tall glass which she held out to me. "It would be a shame to leave now when things are just getting started. Do try this, Miss Baldwin. I think you'll like it. "Yes," added Dora with a tiny smile. "Stay for a few minutes and enjoy yourself. You do know how to enjoy yourself, don't you?" Her voice was mocking.

I felt anger rising in me and took the cup from Marianne. "Thank you," I said coolly. "Perhaps we will stay for a little while longer."

I took a deep gulp of the drink and choked. The liquid burned down my throat like fire, but as it reached my stomach, it warmed me with a sudden glow. I stared down at the glass in my hand then turned to ask Marianne what she had given me to drink. But the two of them had gone, disappearing into the crowd that all at once began to move and swirl to the insistent beat of the music. Cautiously, I took another sip from my glass. This time, it didn't seem to burn my throat so much, and the warm glow in my stomach increased. I listened to the music and it was like nothing I had heard before. There was the beat of a drum, and a fiddle that played notes that were high and wild and sweet. Hastily, I put the glass back on the table and tried to make my way across the open space that had separated me from my sister, but unknown hands grabbed me and pulled me into the dance.

Catching my breath, I tried to free myself, but people all around me were laughing and calling and the music filled my ears. Then Arthur was there; he took me in his arms, and laughed down at me. We whirled together, around and around, faster and faster then he grabbed a cup from a passerby and pressed my lips to its edge. Gratefully, I gulped at the cool liquid. It tasted quite different from the drink that Marianne had given me, and I coughed and gasped and Arthur held me close and held the cup to my lips again and again.

I looked up into his eyes as I drank deeply and thought that I was in heaven. He smiled at me and lowered his mouth to mine. I clung to him for a moment, giddy with shock. Then he put his head back and laughed and he was gone, whirling through the mad crowd as I was passed on to other eager, waiting arms.

After that I didn't struggle, but let the music take me higher and higher, as the tempo of the dance rose faster and faster. I remember eager lips and outstretched hands and I remember laughing and twirling until I was too dizzy to stand. Then I was sitting on the damp grass with my head down as someone, I think it was Nell, urgently called my name. But all the while, the beat of the music called to me, and all I wanted to do was dance with Arthur's arms around me, drowning in the wonderful magic of the night.

I remember vaguely stumbling back to the house with strong arms about my shoulders. I remember mumbled good nights, and the sudden cool breeze on my face as the carriage started towards home. And then I do not remember anything at all.

I was very unwell the next day and kept to my bed. I told Anna that I had eaten something that had disagreed with me at the party, and I was glad that Nell seemed too busy to inquire after my well-being.

CHAPTER 21

January drifted into February and we were quiet at home. Arthur and Edmund had returned to Cordoba University in the New Year, but they had come visiting one afternoon a few days before they departed, riding up through the pasture and hitching their horses familiarly down by the stables.

I was checking the contents of our small stillroom when they arrived. One of the kitchen girls had scalded her hand badly the day before, and I had been forced to look on helplessly while Mrs. Johnson had ministered to her injury. I was troubled by my lack of knowledge in caring for such minor mishaps. If I truly wanted to be considered mistress in this household, I needed to learn as much as possible about simple remedies and cures.

The stillroom door was open to catch even the slightest breeze and I was sniffing at a jar of sticky brown ointment when I heard cheerful male voices outside. Thinking that Papa had returned early, I hastily replaced the jar on the shelf and ran quickly down the corridor and through the swinging doors that led to the main hall. I stopped abruptly at the sight of Arthur and Edmund. I was thoroughly flustered by their unexpected visit, and embarrassed by my own appearance. Since the weather was so hot, I had simply tied a kerchief around my head, leaving my hair loose beneath it, and I could feel the ends of it sticking to my neck. I was wearing my oldest skirt with an apron over the top, and on my feet I wore a pair of old shoes, but no stockings against the heat.

I felt my colour rise as I stammered a welcome, but Arthur strode quickly to where I was standing and smiled warmly down at me. "Please forgive us for arriving unannounced," he said apologetically, "but we're leaving for Cordoba in a couple of days and I wanted to be sure that you had quite recovered from the party. I understand that Nell didn't warn you that you were to perform." I nodded silently, glad of his sympathetic gaze. "We both felt," he continued, nodding to where Edmund stood silently by, "that your performance was," he paused, "quite remarkable." His blue eyes looked deep into mine, and a tiny smile lingered on his lips. Once again, colour flooded my cheeks. I felt sure that Arthur was not only referring to my singing, and I remembered the feel of his arms around me as he lowered his lips to mine.

Later, after Gilbert had shown Arthur and Edmund into the drawing room and I had changed into more becoming attire, I ordered tea, and attempted to make conversation. Arthur seemed very restless, though, and after a few minutes, he rose from his chair and stood by the empty fireplace, tapping his fingers nervously on the mantle. Edmund continued to sit quietly in one of the deep armchairs, not saying anything, but watching his friend closely.

At last, Arthur spoke. "Ada, do you know when Mr. Baldwin is returning?" he asked abruptly.

I shook my head. "No, I don't. I think not for another week, but he sometimes returns a few days early. We never quite know." Suddenly, my heart was pounding in my chest. I wondered why Arthur was so anxious to speak to Papa. I clasped my hands together to still them, while my mind whirled back once again to that moment when Arthur had lowered his face to mine and kissed me full on my lips. Could this mean that he was about to speak for me? With an effort, I stilled my breathing.

Arthur continued to move restlessly about the room, finally coming to a stop beside the piano. "Do you know if your father is looking for engineers right now?" he asked abruptly. I stared at him blankly.

"We'll be graduating at the end of this year," he continued, "and it would be a great advantage to have employment already set." I glanced across at Edmund, but he was gazing out of the window, clearly uncomfortable.

Arthur's eyes followed my gaze. "Oh come on, Edmund, old boy," he said with an easy laugh. "There's no harm in asking. And, besides, she doesn't mind putting in a good word for us, do you, Ada?"

Arthur turned to me, his smile dazzling, but I could not admit to him that I would move heaven and earth to persuade Papa to give him employment. I lowered my eyes, and sighed with relief when Gilbert entered the room pushing the tea trolley.

I didn't tell Nell that Arthur and Edmund had visited. In fact, I didn't tell anyone. I kept it as my own small secret, but I was determined to find out if Papa would consider hiring at least one new engineer in the near future.

It was the last week in March when I was awakened from my siesta to the sounds of a carriage in the driveway, and the excited chatter of the servants below my open window. Intrigued, I swung my feet off the bed and walked over to the window. Peering out from behind the curtains, I saw a hired carriage on the driveway, and emerging from it was a familiar figure. Drake was back.

Since we had been in Argentina, Drake had played little part in our lives. With Gilbert ably carrying out the duties of butler, Drake had reverted to his role of manservant to my father and, a month or so after our arrival, Papa had sent him back to London on some urgent business. Drake was only just now returning. Papa himself had returned from Rosario two weeks after Arthur and Edmund's visit, but as far as I knew, Arthur had not been in contact with him.

Stepping back from the window, I rang for Anna to help me dress, but by the time I arrived downstairs, Drake had disappeared into my father's study. I doubted that they would emerge before dinner. Frustrated, I wandered across the hall. News from England was scarce enough and I was hoping very much that Drake might have brought letters. To my disappointment, there was nothing on the hall table, but as I turned to retrace my steps, I saw Gilbert emerging from the drawing room. His face was grave.

"Miss Baldwin," he said, "Perhaps you would join your sister. She has news she needs to share with you." I glanced sharply at Gilbert, but as usual, his face gave nothing away.

Nell was sitting on one of the sofas with a letter lying open on her lap. It was edged with black. In a few quick steps, I was at my sister's side and taking the single sheet of creamy vellum from her hands, I read:

London, England
December, 1885

My Dearest Ada and Nell:
It is with great sorrow that I must tell you of the death of my beloved sister, Lucy. As you know, she sailed for India with her new husband immediately following her wedding last summer. We had word from dear Frederick a week ago. It is my understanding that Lucy had become very ill with spots and a fever while she was on board ship (I took a sharp breath, so Lucy had contracted chickenpox too!). *She recovered, but was much weakened from the rigours of the journey. Despite Frederick's wishes that she remain in Bombay, Lucy insisted on accompanying him to join his regiment. On the journey, she took sick with a fever, and died two days later.*

She is buried in a small Christian cemetery. Frederick did not name the place of her burial. I understand that Lucy was in a delicate condition at the time of her death. The child would have been born in July.
Yours most affectionately and with great sadness,
Suzanne Kent

I placed the letter on the cushion next to Nell and sat down beside her. After a while, she sighed. "Do you suppose that the baby helped to kill her?" she asked in a small voice. She sounded very young.

I shook my head. "I don't know, Nell," I answered. "It just says that she died from a fever." My own voice broke and I turned to my sister with a helpless gesture. Nell had removed her glasses and tears were streaming silently down her face. She made no effort to stop them. She just let them fall, splashing onto the front of her dress, soaking the blue fabric until it darkened into a deep indigo. I held out my arms, but Nell shook her head and, standing abruptly, left the room.

I was left staring with unseeing eyes at the black-edged paper and remembering the kindhearted, smiling woman who had surely deserved a happier destiny. It was hard to think of her lying in a foreign grave so far from all those she loved. Then with a start, I remembered the feel of a soft hand brushing my head while I was praying in church on the Sabbath after Christmas. I remember that I had turned quickly to see who was touching me, but finding no one there, had shrugged it off as a passing fancy. Now I wondered if it had been Lucy's departing spirit that had paused to say goodbye.

CHAPTER 22

My "coming out party" was held on the last Saturday in May. True to his word, Papa had left all the details to Aunt Bee. It was to be held in our own home and would certainly not be as grand as the New Year gathering at the Hamilton's. Nevertheless, we expected thirty or so people to accept our invitation.

Aunt Bee had spent several mornings at the house before the big day, deep in conversations with Gilbert, Mrs. Johnson, and Cook, and the whole place was thrown into a great flurry of cleaning and polishing. Early on, Nell and I had been whisked off to the dressmaker who had served the Hamilton's for the previous ten years.

Aunt Bee had made a fruitless attempt to persuade us into matching gowns of bright buttercup yellow with bows and lace at elbows and neck, but the dressmaker, Senora de Sousa, after taking one look at my sister, turned to a shelf behind her and selected a fabric striped in broad bands of rich burgundy and black. She held it up to Nell's face. The colours gave my sister's pale complexion a soft glow, and though Aunt Bee shook her head doubtfully and Nell shrugged in apparent indifference, I knew that my sister was secretly pleased with the selection.

Senora de Sousa chose a soft turquoise for me, trimmed with creamy lace and narrow ribbons just one shade darker than the dress. I too, was very pleased, and thought with sympathy of the fashion disasters that consistently haunted the Hamilton girls.

The Senora assured us that our dresses would be ready in plenty of time, but before we left, she insisted that we should both be fitted for corsets. This was the first time that either of us had ever worn a full corset, and I quite thought I should faint as the laces were pulled tighter and tighter.

At first, Nell objected and refused to be laced in but Aunt Bee insisted, and once she was corseted and able to admire her new shape, artfully draped in her chosen fabric, even Nell agreed that at least for this occasion she would attend to fashion's dictates.

In spite of my earlier misgivings, I found myself looking forward to this special evening in my honour, not least because both Arthur Mitchell and Edmund Nichols would be attending; they were home for the half-term break on the weekend of my party.

Dora Phillips and Marianne Forester were both invited. Those invitations had been sent grudgingly on my part, but I had no choice; their families were part of our social circle and Aunt Bee would have questioned me closely if I had not included them on my list.

When the day came, Anna helped me into my new corset and dress. As she finished lacing me in, I reached for Mama's beautiful necklace and held it up for her to place it around my neck. When it was done, she stepped back admiringly, clasping her hands in delight. "Ah, Senorita," she said happily. "Tonight, you are beautiful!"

Knowing that I looked my best helped me to find the courage to face my guests. I had little need to worry though, for since the dinner was in my honour, I had no chance to be nervous and little time to myself. I had no opportunity to speak to Arthur alone, though he was very attentive to me during dinner, leaning close and addressing remarks to me on several occasions.

After dinner, Nell and I were to perform again, and this time I was willing, for we had spent time practicing, and had chosen quite new songs. I was pleased with our performance and, at its conclusion Arthur jumped to his feet and offered an arm to both Nell and me, gallantly escorting us back to our seats amidst laughter and much applause.

There was no dancing, as Papa would not allow it. I was a little surprised that he had allowed us to sing, but Aunt Bee had prevailed upon him to do so, and we were not alone, for there were several other performers.

Among them to my considerable dismay was Miss Dora Phillips. On this occasion, she was exquisitely dressed in pale green silk with a tiny hat made entirely of feathers perched on her golden curls.

"She 'came out' last year in Paris, my dear," I heard Aunt Bee whisper to her neighbour, "and is such a catch."

Dora sang three songs in French. Her voice was high and clear, but had little depth. Like small pieces of glass, I thought unkindly, shining in the light, but sharp enough that it would cut you if you tried to hold it. I was very jealous.

Shortly after that, Arthur and Edmund excused themselves and left the party. It was very dull afterward.

Up to that time, I had not had any opportunity to speak to Papa on Arthur's behalf, and I could not think of a way that I could do so without Papa questioning my motives. The day after my party, however, it was very natural for me to invite dear Aunt Bee and her family to take tea with us. I had Gilbert send an invitation that included Arthur and Edmund, and I made sure that they knew that Papa would also be in attendance.

My ruse worked, for while we took tea in the drawing room, I heard Arthur ask Papa if he might speak with him in private, and shortly afterward, they retired to the study. Edmund had not accompanied the Hamilton's, and I was sorry that he would not have the opportunity to present his own credentials.

When the men returned, they were chatting easily, and when Arthur left shortly afterwards, he bowed to me and raised his hat to my father. "I'll look forward to seeing you in September then, Sir," he said lightly, before driving off.

I waited until the carriage had disappeared from sight. "Will Mr. Mitchell be working for you, Papa?" I asked as casually as I knew how.

My father looked down at me sharply. "Yes, in a manner of speaking Ada. I told him that he can spend time out at the work site and can help me with some clerical work but that is all. I really have no need of an untried lad under my feet."

Then he smiled at me. "Come, my dear," he said, tucking my hand through his arm. "Now that you are a young lady, let us take a turn around the gardens and I'll tell you about some plans that I have regarding alterations to the house next summer.

One grey winter morning a few weeks later, there was an incident that began a series of troubling events. We were sitting at breakfast when my sister, who had been toying with a piece of toast, looked over to where my father was sitting. "Papa," she said abruptly, "I want to attend the university."

My father stopped in the act of folding his newspaper and looked across at Nell. "Don't be foolish," he said. "Girls don't do such things." He shook his head dismissively and rising from the table, headed towards the door.

Instantly, Nell jumped to her feet and ran after him, blocking his way. "Papa," she cried. "I'm perfectly serious! I want to do something with my life. I'm clever, you've always said that, and I know that I could do it." She hesitated for just a moment, sucking air into her lungs as if she couldn't quite breathe. "I want to be a doctor. Women in other parts of the world are doing it and I could go to the university in Cordoba." Her voice trailed off, but she continued to stand stubbornly in the doorway.

My father looked down at her for a moment before pushing past her. "Do not be foolish Nell," he said shortly. "I'll hear no more of this nonsense."

Nell watched him leave then she spun around and threw the piece of toast she was holding as hard as she could at the wall, and flung herself out of the room.

She didn't speak to anyone for days after that, and when, a week later, Papa set out once again for an extended period, Nell also began to disappear for long periods of time.

At first, I hardly noticed. But after a while, I became aware that my sister was leaving early in the morning and not returning until late afternoon. I tried to speak to her about it, but she always pushed past me scornfully and refused to answer.

Then one afternoon, with rain lashing outside the windows, things came to a head. There had been no sign of Nell over lunch and I was alone in the drawing room when there was a tap on the door and

Gilbert entered. His normally pale face was flushed and he was hold-ing my rain cape in his hands.

"Miss Baldwin," he said quickly, "you must come at once, for I think Miss Nell may be in grave danger."

I sprang to my feet in alarm. "Why? What's happened?" I demanded. But Gilbert just hustled me from the room, placing my cape over my shoulders as we went. "I have the carriage waiting, Miss," he said grimly.

Moments later, I clambered up onto the seat beside Gilbert, bend-ing my head against the stinging rain and clutching at the bench seat. It would have been more comfortable and dry inside the carriage, but I needed to know why we were rushing off in the middle of a rain storm to rescue my sister.

Gilbert flicked the reins and the carriage pulled forward, around the curved driveway that led to the road. I looked across at him hop-ing that he would tell me what was happening, but he had his head down, peering out from under an amazing top hat that was crammed down about his ears. At any other time, I would have laughed at the sight of our dignified butler so strangely attired, but now I tugged anxiously at his sleeve.

"Where are we going?" I shouted, raising my voice over the pound-ing of the horses' hooves and the sound of the wheels swishing along the rain-soaked road.

Gilbert shook his head, but then a moment later he cupped his hand around his mouth so that the gusting wind wouldn't carry the words away. "It's the women," he shouted. "They're marching. There's a rally in the Plaza de Mayo today. They're all there, and there's going to be trouble."

I stared blankly at Gilbert, but then a sort of understanding dawned. The whispered conversations between my sister and Sophie Hamilton after chapel on Sundays and the many times my sister had mysteriously disappeared for the day, only to return in time for din-ner, and refusing to say where she had been.

I cast my mind back to the New Year's party at the Hamilton's, when Nell had been sitting with that group of women who obviously shared some common cause. I upbraided myself then for not paying more attention to what Nell had been doing and I knew that my sister must be involved with these women in some way, but I did not understand how. Gilbert obviously knew more than I did, but when I tried to question him further, he pursed his lips and jerked on the reins, indicating the need for greater haste.

The rain had eased a little as we reached the outskirts of the city, and Gilbert was forced to slow his pace to make way for other traffic. At one point, he turned the carriage down a narrow laneway, urging the horses past ugly little houses with the rain dripping off broken gutters, and piles of rubbish lying in sodden heaps at the edge of the narrow street. We splashed through deep puddles and felt the carriage wheels lurch in the slippery mud. Soaked through and chilled to the bone, I huddled inside my cape and desperately willed this nightmare to be over.

After a while, Gilbert swung the carriage around a corner and we found ourselves once more on a main thoroughfare, surrounded by carts and carriages and people hurrying to get out of the rain. Muttering under his breath, Gilbert eased the carriage along, ignoring the occasional curses and threatening fists that were raised against us.

Gradually, we edged forward until, finally, over the heads of the hurrying crowds, I glimpsed an open plaza and a large building that I remembered from the day we had arrived in Buenos Aires, for it was a most distinctive shade of pink. As we entered the plaza, I glimpsed a group of perhaps twenty women standing in front of the building. They were huddled close together on some kind of low platform, with rain-soaked banners flapping sluggishly above them. I couldn't see her, but I knew with certainty that Nell was one of these women: defiant, jubilant, and no doubt filled with zealous fervor.

Above the noise of the milling crowd, I caught the sound of singing, broken and disjointed, small words gusting on the wind, brave syllables, demanding to be heard. Next to me, Gilbert gave a startled exclamation and I looked over to where he was pointing. Across the plaza, a line of horsemen was advancing. They looked as if they were militia and they were obviously armed.

Gilbert urged our carriage forward, but we made little headway. Then as the horsemen advanced, some of the watching crowd melted silently away, fearful of what might happen next. As the crowd thinned, I caught sight of Nell. She was standing at the very edge of the platform. Rain-spattered spectacles gleaming, hands waving high in the air, she was directing her attention to a particular group of four or five women who were standing directly below her, hollowed eyes watchful, shawls wrapped close around their thin bodies.

As I watched in growing horror, the militia advanced towards the group of women. Then, without thinking, I flung myself down from the carriage and ran towards my sister. I pushed through the crowd, ignoring angry shouts and grabbing hands. I scrambled past the group of women that Nell had been addressing and stumbled towards her.

Careless of what was happening around me, I grabbed hold of Nell's wet skirts and dragged her forcibly off the low platform. If I hadn't taken her by surprise, I know that I could not have persuaded my sister to come with me.

As it was, she stumbled and fell, her glasses dislodging from her face and tumbling somewhere under the feet of the onlookers. Ignoring her angry protests, I pushed and shoved her in front of me until, with a sob of relief, I felt Gilbert beside me and together we tumbled my furiously struggling sister inside the carriage, and made off with what speed we could.

The return journey was painful. Nell screamed and raged all the way, scratching at my face with her nails and pulling angrily at my hair. But I held onto her with all my strength, and eventually she slumped to the floor of the carriage, sobbing furiously, and I gasped for breath as I lay back on the seat and closed my eyes.

When we arrived home, Gilbert helped us out of the carriage. But when I tried to thank him, the face he turned towards me was courteously blank, as he once more assumed the role of butler.

Without her spectacles, Nell was virtually helpless, but she stumbled up the porch steps into the house, shaking off my outstretched hand with an angry slap. Dropping her outer garments onto the hall floor, she fumbled her way upstairs, stomping each booted foot noisily as she went. Moments later, I heard the sharp slam of her bedroom door. Wearily, I removed my own cape and bonnet and wondered how we might procure another pair of spectacles for my sister.

Sometime later, I went looking for Gilbert but there was no sign of him. He was not in the hall, nor was he in the butler's pantry, so I headed for the kitchen. As I did so, I saw Mrs. Johnson approaching. She was carrying Gilbert's little dog, Duchess, and she looked angry and upset.

"Gilbert has gone back to the city, Miss," she said abruptly when I enquired as to Gilbert's whereabouts. "He's gone looking for Miss Nell's spectacles, though I cannot imagine that he would ever find them in this weather!" Then she swept past me, still clutching the squirming Duchess.

My thoughts were on Gilbert as I walked slowly across the hall. I thought of him out in the chill afternoon, perhaps putting himself in danger, all for the sake of a pair of spectacles. I opened the front door and peered out. The rain had almost stopped, but the wind still tossed at the trees that lined the driveway. With a shiver, I closed the heavy door and went slowly up the stairs. It was siesta time.

Wearily, I lay down on my bed and was asleep in an instant. When Anna came to help me dress for dinner, I asked her if Gilbert had returned from the city and felt a flood of relief when she told me that he had returned an hour earlier.

When Papa was away, Miss Walsh and the twins often joined us for dinner and I was usually glad of their company, especially since Nell and I had not been speaking much lately. That evening, however, I was impatient for them to leave, and was pleased when Miss Walsh excused herself and her charges. Nell had not come down to eat with us.

Gilbert was standing in his usual place beside the dining room door, and the moment he closed it behind Miss Walsh and the twins, I jumped to my feet.

"What happened, Gilbert?" I demanded. "Did you find Nell's spectacles?"

Gilbert addressed the air just above my head. He was as impeccably dressed as ever, though I noticed that he limped a little as he moved away from the door. "Unfortunately, Miss, I did not, though I searched very thoroughly. There were few people around by the time I got back, but I understand that several of the ladies who resisted the militia were arrested and will be spending the night in prison." I gasped in horror at the thought of Sophie Hamilton and her friends in the depths of some filthy prison. Seeing my expression, Gilbert hurried on. "Rest assured, Miss, Miss Sophie and a few others managed to get away, though I have no idea by what means."

"Thank you, Gilbert," I said. "I can't bear to think what would have happened if you hadn't intervened; but how did you know about it?"

Gilbert lowered his gaze and looked directly at me for a moment. "One has one's sources, Miss Baldwin," he said. Then, with a dignified bow, he turned and rang the bell to summon the maids to clear the table.

The next morning, I woke early and, slipping into my dressing gown, padded down the corridor and knocked briefly on my sister's bedroom door before walking in.

As I entered, Nell rolled onto her side and pretended to be asleep, but I marched over to her bed and sat down heavily.

"I know you're not sleeping, Nell," I said, "So you'd better tell me what this is all about, before I tell Papa."

This had the desired effect, and my sister rolled onto her back and peered up at me, shortsightedly. "Ada, please don't tell him, he'll kill me!"

"I doubt that he will do that, Nell, but you will certainly be punished. You almost brought disgrace on the family and put yourself in great danger into the bargain. If Gilbert and I hadn't rescued you . . ." I left the sentence unfinished.

Nell struggled up, her hand reaching instinctively to the empty spot where she always put her spectacles, then with a small gesture of annoyance, she rubbed her eyes. "For goodness' sake, Ada, stop being so dramatic," she snapped. "I didn't need rescuing! We were doing it for the cause."

I spread my hands in despair. "What cause, Nell? What are you talking about?"

"Women's rights, stupid! I was there because I wanted to be there. I want to fight for the rights of women; the right to do and be anything we want."

She was sitting up now, her dark eyes peering at me, a gleam of fanaticism lighting her face. "We'll keep on fighting, and one day men will have to listen to us, Ada, you mark my words!"

I looked pityingly at my sister. "Don't be silly, Nell. That's not what we're supposed to do. Girls are supposed to get married and raise families and . . ."

Nell interrupted me with a shriek of fury. "Get out! Just go! You're too stupid to even begin to understand." She flung herself around then and, burying her face in her pillows, put her hands over her ears. After a few seconds, I left. There was no reasoning with Nell when she was like this.

Later that morning, Mrs. Johnson came to find me. "There's a person here says she wants to see you, Miss Baldwin," she said abruptly, ignoring my greeting.

I was surprised at the way Mrs. Johnson spoke and wondered anxiously if it was one of Nell's new militant friends come to upbraid her for leaving yesterday's rally.

"I'll receive her in the drawing room," I said, starting to remove the large apron that I wore when I was doing household tasks.

Mrs. Johnson shook her head. "No, Miss. she's not the sort you should see in the drawing room. I tried to send her off, but she wouldn't leave. Please come to the kitchen, Miss. I've put her in the back scullery."

Thoroughly mystified, I hurried after Mrs. Johnson. After the escapade of the day before, I was beginning to feel that nothing would surprise me, and I hoped fervently that this did not involve my sister Nell.

It did involve her, though. As I stepped into the heat of the kitchen, I saw the figure of a woman standing in the doorway of the scullery. Her back was halfway turned as she peered suspiciously behind her. She was wrapped in a filthy shawl that had slipped a little, revealing equally dirty hair. As she turned to face me, I saw that she was far along in pregnancy.

She moved forward as I approached and peered at me. "Yeah, it's you, I thought so," she said. "I got sumfink of yours if you make

it worth me while." She smiled, showing a mouth full of dirty, yel-
lowed teeth.

I stared at her; I had no idea who she was. She looked at my blank
face and gave a snort of laughter. Then she pushed her tangled hair
back from her face and spoke in a prim little voice. "Good morning,
Miss Baldwin. Is there anything you might be wanting, Miss?"

"Lizzie!" I stared at her in shock, for I had never thought to see
our runaway maid again. "Whatever are you doing here?" I demanded.
"Mrs. Chen said you'd run away."

"That nasty piece of goods?" she replied with a toss of her head. "I
'ope she's not still around. She's trouble, you mark my words. She was
right, though, I did jump ship. I only come with you so I could follow
my old man." She narrowed her eyes. "Never even guessed, did you?
Those fellas, the ones your Pa and 'is foreign friend paid for, like they
was slaves or summat, well, some of them 'ad families. Never thought
of that though, did they? Oh, no! Just sprung them out of jail and
promised them the bloody moon.

"Well I wasn't goin' to be left be'ind. Not me. So I got meself hired
by you lot so I could follow 'im, see? Followed 'im right to the railway
camp, I did. Oh, and everso glad to see me 'e was. I stayed with 'im
long enough to get this." She pointed contemptuously at her swollen stomach. "Then that fancy Mister Rodreegs finds me out and 'alf
a dozen like me, and puts us on a train back 'ere, quick as you like.
So what am I s'pposed to do now, I asks you? What now? I ain't got
nuffink. No man, no 'ome, no money, and a babe due soon enough!"

I had listened to this tirade with growing dismay. Lizzie was right.
My father had paid the debts of the men we had brought with us, and
some of them must have had families. It was hard to believe that my
father would abandon those people, but I was not so sure about Señor
Rodriguez. I remembered with a shudder that his own father had been
a slave trader in his time. Perhaps the son was not so different!

While Lizzie was speaking, everyone in the kitchen had stopped
working and was listening with great interest, if not complete understanding. Turning my head, I spoke sharply. "Everyone get back to
work at once," I snapped, and rather to my surprise, they obeyed,
thanks in part to Cook, who, suddenly mindful of her duties, started
giving brisk orders. Lizzie and I were left staring at each other. She

twitched her shawl up over her shoulder and I caught the smell of her. It rose in nauseating waves, a mixture of sweat and dirt and rotting teeth. I put my hand over my mouth to prevent myself from gagging.

Her sharp eyes caught the movement and she sneered. "Bit ripe for you, am I then, Missy? You always was a bit squeamish as I remember!" She grinned and wiped a hand across her nose.

"What do you want?" I asked, edging past her and opening the outer door of the scullery so that a gust of blessedly clean air wafted in.

Lizzie shivered. "Like I said, I've got sumfink' you might want, or at least that sister of yours might be glad of." She fumbled inside her tattered shawl and brought out a small, dirty package. "Dropped these yesterday, didn't she? Valuable, I should think. So what'll you give me for them? Them and the price of me keeping me mouth shut about what she was up to yesterday?" I looked down at the package in Lizzie's outstretched hand and knew that she held Nell's spectacles.

I reached for them, but Lizzie jerked her hand away. "What do you want?" I said again. "I don't have any money and Mr. Baldwin's not here."

She looked at me slyly for a few seconds. "I needs a place to stay and a bite to eat for a bit. Like I said, the babe'll be 'ere soon enough.

During this exchange I had edged outside, but Lizzie was still in the doorway. Suddenly, a large pair of hands grasped her from behind and, with a grunt, Miguel attempted to pick her up bodily and throw her into the yard. But he had reckoned without Lizzie's native skills. She had no doubt grown up in the slums of London and, quick as lightning, she pushed a sharp elbow into Miguel's stomach and wriggled free. Then she started running, shoving me roughly out of her way as she went.

Before I had regained my balance, she was across the yard, running fast in spite of her bulk, with Miguel and several other servants in pursuit. As she stumbled along, in her haste, she dropped the small bundle that held Nell's spectacles. I flew to it scooping the package off the ground before turning and running inside, not stopping until I reached the safety of the front hall. I didn't care what was happening to Lizzie; I was just glad to have Nell's precious spectacles back in my possession. Sinking onto a chair, I undid the filthy wrapping with hands that shook. The spectacles were twisted and dirty, but they were not broken.

As I raised grateful eyes to heaven, I saw Gilbert approaching. He held out his hand. "Could I take those from you, Miss Baldwin?" he asked pleasantly, "I will see that they are returned to Miss Nell as soon as possible." Wordlessly, I handed the spectacles to him and hurried upstairs to my own room.

Still shaken by recent events, I sat by the window for a long time. It was the end of June, the winter season here, and I longed to be back in England. I wondered suddenly if today was little Edie's second birthday, but I had no way to find out.

Lunchtime came and went, but I didn't stir. I felt very tired. I was tired of trying to adjust to our new life, and all the burdens that I carried. I thought of Nell's passionate speech about freedom for women. Freedom, I thought bitterly. I am not even married yet, but already I'm choked under the burdens of caring for a whole household. I have no time to fight for the right to take on even more responsibilities!

Nell came to find me in the afternoon. She knocked, and poked her head around my door. Her spectacles were in place and looked none the worse for wear. I turned my head but didn't speak as she slipped into the room, closing the door behind her.

Crossing to where I sat, she knelt down beside my chair. "Ada, I'm sorry," she said. "I was stupid to get so caught up in things. When I'm at the Hamilton's with Sophie and the other women, I feel so alive, so able to make changes in my life." She touched my hand. "You saved me from getting into real trouble and I'm grateful."

I looked down at my sister and shifted my hand away from hers. "If you think that saying sorry means that I'm not going to tell Papa about this, you're wrong," I said, trying to still the quiver in my voice.

Nell looked up at me, her eyes suddenly dark with anger. "No, that isn't why I came," she said, rising to her feet. "I'm going to tell Papa myself. If I don't, I'm sure that you or Miss Walsh or somebody else will gladly tell him for me. I really did come to say sorry, but I won't make that mistake again." And with that, she turned and left the room. I should have gone after her, but I didn't. Instead, I continued to sit by the window and the rift between us became even deeper.

My father returned early the following week and, true to her word, Nell confessed her misdeeds to him. They were in the study for a long time, and when Nell emerged, her eyes were swollen from crying. I was sewing in the drawing room when Papa sent for me. As I entered the study, my father waved me to a chair, but did not speak. I thought that he looked drawn and tired.

"Ada," he said at last, "I am truly disappointed in you. I had thought that by asking Mrs. Hamilton to be your chaperone, and by allowing you to come out into society this year, you would have learned some maturity. However, I now discover that your sister has been embroiled in activist politics which you have done nothing to prevent. Nor did you make any effort to communicate any concerns about this to me. You must have been aware of what was happening." He steepled his fingers and looked over them at me. "What do you have to say?"

Bright colour suffused my face, but I could not find words to protest my own ignorance

As the silence lengthened, my father gave an irritable sigh. "I have told Nell that she is not to visit the Hamilton's home again," he said tersely. "She is also to return to the schoolroom under the tutelage of Miss Walsh until I am satisfied that she can be trusted. You will let me know if she does not comply with my orders. Do you understand me?" I nodded my head. My father then turned to the pile of paper on his desk, summarily dismissing me.

As I walked away, I was angry at the injustice of what Papa had said, and wondered if he even knew of the role I had played in Nell's rescue.

Winter drifted on with everyone angry and out of sorts, and there was little to lighten our days. One morning in August, I went down to the paddock looking for Blaze. Since my sister's relegation to the schoolroom, she and I had not gone riding together. Over time, Nell had become a proficient horsewoman, but I was never really at home on horseback.

I found Blaze cropping grass contentedly in the pasture behind the stables with the other horses, and I stood leaning on the gate, enjoying the moment of peace. Several servants were cutting down weeds that grew along the edge of the fence. As I watched idly, I saw that one of them was a woman and, intrigued, moved closer.

Lizzie peered at me from under a bonnet that was too big for her. She grinned broadly and ducked her head for a moment before returning to her task.

I looked further along the fence and caught sight of a large basket lying tucked in a corner, well protected from the cold wind. As I watched, a small foot lifted into the air, then disappeared. I drew a breath of amazement. The last time I had seen Lizzie she was running away, with Miguel in full pursuit. Now she was working on our land and seemed content enough to let me see both her and her child.

Forgetting about Blaze, I made my way back to the house. I was anxious to find out what had happened to Lizzie, so I went to find Gilbert.

He was polishing silver in his pantry and, when I told him what I had seen, he smiled. "Yes, Miss, that has worked out very well. She's a strong girl and we can always use another pair of hands around the place". I stared at him in puzzlement. Seeing the confusion on my face, Gilbert put down his polishing cloth and leaned on the high counter that ran along one side of the narrow room.

"I had a choice that day, Miss," he said. "I could have let Miguel run the poor soul off the property and the good Lord knows where she and the child would have ended up. Dead in a ditch like as not. I chose instead to keep her on here, with your father's permission, of course.

"She's a good worker and when her babe grows up, he'll likely be a loyal servant, too." With that, Gilbert picked up his polishing cloth and resumed cleaning a large serving spoon.

As I listened, I felt ashamed that I had not given a thought to poor Lizzie since the day she had returned Nell's spectacles. I stretched out my hand, and laid it for a moment on Gilbert's sleeve. "You're a good man, Gilbert," I said. He didn't answer, but continued to rub fiercely at the already gleaming spoon.

"She has a fine boy, Miss," he said, as I turned to go. "She called him Robert after your father, but Mr. Baldwin is unaware of that."

CHAPTER 23

Eventually, the winter passed and spring came, and for a few blessed weeks, the weather was bearable, but as the December sun rose higher in the sky and the days lengthened, the heat of summer was with us again. I was sick at Christmas, plagued this time with a fever and headaches that left me nauseous and spent. Nell offered to send Mrs. Chen to me, but I refused, starting up from my pillow and holding fiercely to Nell's hand.

"No! I don't want her near me, I don't like her," I said fretfully, and in the end my fever broke of its own accord and I began to recover.

We did not expect, nor did we receive, an invitation to the Hamilton's New Year party. My memories of the last celebration still troubled me from time to time.

Towards the end of January when I was feeling stronger, I ventured downstairs one morning to find Arthur Mitchell in the house. The previous September, true to his word, Papa had allowed Arthur to accompany him to his work site and they continued to journey back and forth every few weeks. Arthur seemed to fit well into my father's plans, but this was the first time that I had seen him in the house when my father was away.

Arthur was emerging from Papa's study with a bundle of papers under his arm, just as I was making my way into the breakfast room. Seeing me, he stopped. "Good morning, Ada," he said pleasantly. "Are you feeling better? Nell told me that you've been ill."

I nodded and heard the wobble in my voice as I answered him. "Yes, thank you, I'm much better." My voice trailed away and, as usual when I was with Arthur, I could think of nothing else to say.

He smiled easily at me. "Well, I'm glad to see you're up and about again." Then with a small grimace he indicated the papers under his arm. "Mr. Baldwin sent me on ahead to do some paperwork. I'll be finished with these today, so why don't you ride out with me in the morning? There's something I'd like to show you." He grinned engagingly down at me. "Riding isn't as tiring as walking, and it's cool first thing. I'll be waiting at six o'clock."

I opened my mouth to protest, but he gave a cheery wave and was gone. I looked after him, half laughing and half exasperated. I had no intention of riding with Arthur Mitchell, none at all.

Just the same, early the next morning, I was up, dressed in my riding habit, and descending the stairs just as the clock in the hall finished striking the quarter hour after six.

He was waiting at the stables, blonde hair shining in the morning sun. At the sight of him, my heart started thumping so loudly that I thought he must surely hear it.

As I approached, he turned with a welcoming smile. "Come on," he said briskly. "You're late. Blaze is already saddled, and I have given her a run—I thought she would be too frisky for you to handle. You haven't ridden her in a while, have you?"

"There was really no need," I said, attempting to sound confident. But I spoke with more bravado than I felt, for it was true, I had not been in the saddle for some considerable time.

Arthur regarded me steadily for a moment then gestured casually to where my horse was waiting next to the mounting block. "I hope I didn't tire her out for you," he said dryly as he swung easily into his own saddle and waited. Under his amused gaze, I struggled fruitlessly to mount Blaze. In spite of the earlier exercise, she was still frisky, sidestepping and tossing her head as I tried to control her.

All at once, Arthur was there, holding Blaze's head and gentling her with murmured words until she calmed. Then he put his hands around my waist and lifted me effortlessly into the saddle. My heart was still pounding as we turned out of the gate that led through the paddock and headed towards the open fields.

We let our mounts walk slowly at first, one behind the other, until Arthur dropped back and we rode quietly side by side. From time to time, Arthur would point out something of interest. We watched as a family of rabbits fed voraciously on some fresh green shoots, and once Arthur held his hand out to stop our progress and we saw a small deer standing motionless in a patch of shade. Its head was turned away from us, its yellowish grey fur ruffling in the early morning breeze. Then the wind changed and it caught our scent and bounded away in small, graceful arcs.

As the sun rose higher in the sky, I became anxious; I hadn't thought to tell anyone that I was going out. Reluctantly, I reined in my horse. "Arthur, I should go back or I'll be missed," I said.

Arthur grinned boyishly at me. "I already told Gilbert you were riding with me, and it's only a bit further, I promise. There's something I want to show you."

Not waiting for an answer, he spurred his horse forward, and I followed. I would have followed him anywhere on that morning.

The land had been rising slowly as we rode, and at last we came to the crest of a hill and drew rein. Below us, the ground fell sharply away. At the bottom of the steep incline was what at first appeared to be a jumble of rocks. Then as I looked more closely, I could see the remains of a chimney and a half-fallen wall. To one side, there was part of an outbuilding, the roof caved in, a rotting fence lurching drunkenly against it, and there were creepers everywhere, the tendrils grasping at the ruins as if to suffocate them.

Beyond this lay what must once have been sweeping lawns, for the ground there was level and the grass grew shorter. There was a belt of trees planted close by, perhaps as a windbreak, and beyond that again, stretched acres of rough grass, rippling and waving in the early morning sun.

Arthur was watching me with a half-smile on his face. "Welcome to the Mitchell estate," he said, dryly.

I glanced quickly back at the ruins then turned in my saddle to face Arthur. "The Mitchell estate - What do you mean?"

He gave a short laugh. "You really don't know, Ada? I thought everyone knew."

I shook my head without speaking, and Arthur shifted a little in his saddle. When he spoke, his voice was soft.

"This was my family home. My father built it, and then he brought my mother here. She didn't like it, so she burnt it to the ground. I was three years old. She died in the fire."

Horrified, I gazed up at Arthur's handsome profile. He was looking straight ahead. "I told you I was a poor orphan boy, didn't I?" he said mockingly. "My father was shot a couple of years later. Some quarrel over money, and eventually the Hamilton's took me in."

He stopped speaking and made as if to move on, but impulsively, I leaned across and touched his hand. "Arthur," I said. "I didn't know any of this." I paused uneasily. "Who owns the land now?" Arthur looked down, absently stroking his horse's ears, but remained silent. I caught my breath. "Señor Rodriguez?" I whispered.

He didn't respond immediately then he nodded and said quietly: "It's my dream to get it back one day, and I'll build another house even more splendid than the first." Then taking up the reins in earnest, he clicked his tongue softly at his horse.

Once again I stopped him, and laid my hand on his bare arm. A small frisson of pleasure ran through me at the feel of his warm skin beneath my hand. "Arthur, will you tell me the whole story?" I pleaded.

He looked out across the valley and I thought he was going to agree, but he shook his head. "Perhaps another day Ada." Then he drew his horse close to mine, and smiled down into my eyes. I lifted my face to his, knowing quite certainly that Arthur Mitchell would kiss me, so I closed my eyes as I raised my willing lips to his.

Abruptly, I felt him stiffen beside me and heard his sharply indrawn breath. Opening my eyes, I turned my head and followed Arthur's gaze. Together we watched as a small figure on a large horse plunged wildly over the edge of the steep incline to the right of us, and went floundering down into the heart of the ruins below. The rider was a young boy, and the horse he was riding was obviously out of control. With a smothered exclamation, Arthur gathered his reins and started in pursuit of the fleeing pair.

Helplessly, I watched as he set his horse fearlessly down the steep hillside. The poor animal slithered and scrabbled frantically as the ground gave way beneath a hail of small stones and earth, and I was sure that both horse and rider would fall and be injured, but Arthur clung to the beast's back and spurred him ahead. Then they gained firmer ground and were quickly out of sight among the ruins.

My heart was still pounding with excitement and I looked about for a safe way to follow. Then a little way to my left, I saw that the land fell away in a gentler slope. Grasping the reins, I coaxed Blaze down the grassy embankment, determined to discover if Arthur had managed to catch the runaways. There was no sign of him or the other rider now, but I turned my horse's head in the direction in which they had disappeared.

I came upon them suddenly, for a portion of creeper-covered wall hid them from my view, until I was almost upon them.

They had dismounted and the horses stood panting and blowing beside them. Arthur had both sets of reins grasped in one hand, and he and the runaway rider were standing very close, facing each other. As I approached, I saw Arthur take hold of the slight figure and give a fierce shake. A cloud of dark hair descended around the rider's shoulders and only then did I realize that this was no boy—it was my sister Nell.

Arthur was undoubtedly very angry, but so was she. She shook him off fiercely. "Don't touch me!" she screamed. "Leave me alone! I can ride a damned horse as well as you. For God's sake, just get out of my life!"

They glared at each other in silent fury for a moment more, then Arthur swung away, deliberately dropping the reins of Nell's horse as he turned. She caught them deftly and as she did so she turned her head and saw me.

"What are you doing down here, Ada?" she demanded angrily. She glanced across at Arthur and I saw her face tighten as she turned back to me and gave a small shrug. "Come on. I suppose I'll have to damn well take you home now."

I was too shocked to speak. I hated to hear such blasphemous words coming from my sister's mouth, and I didn't understand why she was so angry with Arthur. Nell glared across at me, then without another word, swung herself onto her horse's back and urged him into a trot, back the way I had come.

Arthur didn't speak. He just stood beside his horse and watched us go. I turned to look back at him once, but he had already mounted up and was heading away from us. Nell and I did not speak on the way home.

As I followed my sister's small, straight-backed figure, I found myself wondering why Nell was riding out here alone. Was this just further proof of her recklessness? I knew that spending time in the schoolroom with Miss Walsh and the twins must have been difficult for her, and I had planned to beg Papa to release her from this when he returned home. Now I would have to let him know about this incident. I did not intend to hide anything from my father again.

When I neared the house, I saw men milling about on horseback. It looked as if Papa had returned home a day early. Nell had ridden on ahead of me as soon as we were in familiar territory and there was no sign of her now.

As I reached the paddock gate, one of the stable lads ran towards me, grabbing Blaze's reins. "Please go to the house very quick, Señorita," he said anxiously, helping me to dismount.

I didn't understand the need for haste, but picking up my skirts I walked swiftly round the side of the house towards the front door.

As I neared the porch, I saw two horses standing by the entrance. Between them was slung a sort of makeshift hammock. A man I didn't know was standing at the head of one of the horses talking to Miguel in rapid Spanish, waving his arms, and gesticulating wildly.

Ignoring them, I hurried up the steps that led into the house. As I walked towards the front door, I caught the overwhelming smell of the roses that climbed and bloomed in great fragrant clusters along the front of the porch, and I was filled with a sudden sense of foreboding.

Gilbert was standing at the bottom of the stairs and he turned towards me as I entered. "Miss Baldwin," he said his tone kind. "There has been an accident." I froze, waiting for him to continue.

The butler took a step towards me. "It's the Master, Miss Ada. There was a bad landfall out at the site, and he was injured, so they brought him home. The doctor is with him now and Miss Nell just went up. You should go, too."

I nodded silently, then turning, ran up the stairs, my heart pounding in my chest. When I got to the top, I had to stop for a moment. Fighting off dizziness, I clung to the newel post, then steadied myself and walked to the big double doors that led to my father's bedroom. Turning the handle, I went in.

The doctor had his back to me. He was leaning over a basin. As he turned, towel in hand, I saw that he was wearing a blue-and-white striped shirt and there was blood on one of the sleeves.

Memory flooded my mind. Instantly, I was back in England standing at Mama's bedroom door. I remembered it so clearly: my mother lying on the bed, the smell of blood, the heat, the perfume from the rose petals, and the doctor with blood on his striped shirt.

All at once, the room began to tilt, and when I came to myself, Nell was kneeling beside me and the doctor was holding something that smelled very unpleasant under my nose.

Feeling ashamed, I tried to sit up, but Nell held me down, her eyes wide with fright. "It's fine," she said over and over. "It's going to be fine." I didn't know if Nell was saying this just to comfort me, or to reassure herself, but it had the desired effect and, after a few moments, I was able, with Nell's assistance, to scramble to my feet and sink into a nearby chair.

My father was lying on the bed. His eyes were closed and his face was deathly pale. As I watched, he moved slightly, turning his head and groaning. The doctor gave a grunt of approval and bent over Papa once more, his fingers probing along the hairline until, with a satisfied puff of breath, he found the source of blood that had trickled down the side of my father's face.

Then the doctor glanced up and spoke to someone who was standing silently on the far side of the bed. For the first time, I realized that Drake was in the room. Silent as a ghost, he waited in the shadows.

"When did you say this happened?" the doctor asked.

"Three days ago, Dr. Hawthorne, Sir." Drake's voice was pitched high with tension. "Mr. Baldwin went down to inspect a stretch of track that had a problem. Then some of the rock above him collapsed while he was standing there. The fellow with him was killed." Drake made this last statement very matter-of-factly.

"Oh?" The doctor looked questioningly at the little man standing opposite him.

Drake waved a deprecatory hand. "No one of importance Sir, a man called Weeks I believe, one of our English crew. They dug Mr. Baldwin out from under the rocks and we got him and back home as fast as we could."

"Three days," repeated the doctor, all the while gently feeling the contours of my father's head. He shook his own head. "That's a lot of traveling for a man in his condition," he said grimly before turning to us.

"I need to examine Mr. Baldwin more fully; if you ladies would please wait downstairs, I will come down as soon as I have finished here."

Nell and I left the room and made our way downstairs. Miss Walsh was waiting in the drawing room with the twins sitting solemnly, one on either side of her. Mrs. Chen had also joined us, carrying a sleeping Edie.

No one spoke as we waited; even the twins were silent, frightened, I think, by whatever Miss Walsh had told them. I tried to pray, but no words came, and I couldn't even rouse myself enough to send for my bible. The house itself seemed to be holding its breath.

Eventually, I heard a door open and close, and the sound of footsteps descending the stairs. Nobody moved. Dr. Hawthorne entered the room and, sitting down heavily in one of the armchairs, looked around at our little family.

"Mr. Baldwin is still with us," he said, "though how he survived such an arduous journey I do not know." Then he attempted a thin smile before turning to me. "It is, of course, difficult to say exactly what damage your husband has sustained, Mrs. Baldwin."

I held up my hand in horror. "He's not my husband!" I gasped. The doctor's eyes slid away for a moment to the peacefully sleeping Edie, then back to me.

"Oh," he said, uncomfortably, "forgive me. I didn't realize . . ."

Nell straightened up beside me, fixing the doctor with a steely eye. "Our mother died in England giving birth to the baby," she said coldly, indicating Edie with a nod of her head. In other circumstances,

I might have smiled, for in that moment, my sister sounded exactly like Aunt Abigail.

The doctor looked around at all of us. "So you girls are out here by yourselves, without a mother? How extraordinary . . .!"

"We are well cared for, thank you, doctor," Nell responded tartly. "As you can see, we have a nursemaid, an efficient governess," Miss Walsh gave a satisfied nod at this comment, "and a household of loyal servants. In addition, we have Mrs. Beulah Hamilton, who is our mentor and chaperone." Nell sounded very sure of herself.

"I do beg your pardon." The doctor cleared his throat. "Mrs. Hamilton is well known to me. After a moment, he smiled and nodded at both of us. "Of course, I remember now. Mrs. Hamilton has spoken of you. You must be Ada." I nodded. "Well, my dear young ladies, your father is going to need a great deal of care in the future. With the right treatment, he may recover somewhat, but you should know that in my opinion, Mr. Baldwin will never walk again."

The weeks that followed were difficult. At first, Papa lay in bed, scarcely able to speak, and when he did, it was not of people or things we knew. At other times, he would lie completely still and I would fear that he had left us.

The doctor came almost daily, and the faithful Drake never left Papa's side. A small trundle bed was put in the room so that Drake might sleep there at night, and only occasionally could I persuade him to go and take some time for proper rest in his own room. It was on one such afternoon, as I sat at Papa's bedside sewing, that my father stirred. I looked up from my stitching and saw him watching me. He moved his hand towards me and I rose quickly, bending over him. "Ellie!" he said softly, eyes alight with love. "I have missed you so. Where've you been?" I straightened up. Ellie was the name he used to call my mother.

"I'm not Mama, Father. I'm Ada," I said abruptly. He stared at me for a second and the light faded from his eyes, and he closed them again and turned his face away. Perhaps I shouldn't have minded so much. I knew that I looked a little like my mother, but I was young then, and wanted to be loved for myself. I buried my face in the soft fabric of my sewing and wept softly so that my father would not hear me.

After a month or so, Papa was able to sit up. At first, he had difficulty remembering even the simplest things, but in time, he improved. His legs, however, continued to be paralyzed and his moods were very unpredictable. Of the accident, mercifully, he had no memory at all.

Once again, I was exasperated with Nell. Since Papa's accident, she had spent little time with him and she was back to her old tricks of disappearing for long periods of time. I knew that she wasn't going to the Hamilton's, for that had been expressly forbidden. We saw both Mrs. Hamilton and Sonia at church on Sundays, but of Sophie, there was no sign.

Mrs. Hamilton visited Papa several times during those early days arriving with baskets filled with fruit and baked goodies. Since the incident with Nell during the previous winter, I had felt cool towards Mrs. Hamilton, but we were civil enough, and after her second visit to Papa, we took tea together in the drawing room.

She asked after Nell and the twins, and commented on how beautiful little Edie had become. I answered as truthfully as I could, but then an uncomfortable silence fell. Finally, Mrs. Hamilton replaced her cup purposefully in its saucer and looked directly at me.

"Ada," she said, "I know that you hold me somewhat to blame for that dreadful business with the girls last winter, but I would like to assure you, as I did your dear father, that I had no idea that things had gone so far. It started out as innocent, girlish fun. Sadly, it turned into something far more serious." Leaning forward she continued, "Sophie is away visiting relatives in England and will not be back for several months, and Sonia was never involved in any of this. The dear girl stays close, and is a great comfort to me."

Mrs. Hamilton shifted uneasily in her chair, pushing out her bottom lip for a moment and puffing softly, causing the small wisps of hair that had escaped from under her hat to blow upwards like feathers around her head. All at once, I felt sorry for her; after all, this had not been any of her doing. Impulsively, I leaned forward and kissed her soft, damp cheek. "Don't worry, Aunt Bee," I said, once again using the name she liked best. "I'm just glad that all this silliness over women's rights is over."

Aunt Bee looked startled for a moment, and her hand flew to her cheek. Then she smiled at me and, in turn, leaned over and patted my hand. "Dear child, you are such a comfort," she said.

After Aunt Bee left, I went to find Nell to ask her how she was spending her days. I searched everywhere for her. She was not in her room, nor in the stables, which were deserted at this time of day. So I went down to the paddock, but it was empty except for the horses standing slack-hipped under the big oak tree.

Almost ready to give up, I wandered to the front of the house. Then, remembering the little hidden room at the back of the greenhouse at home, I wondered if Nell had found herself a new hiding place. There was no need of a greenhouse here—the flowers and trees grew in great abundance at any season.

I shook my head in frustration as I mounted the steps to the porch that wrapped itself so gracefully around the outside of the house. Then as I reached the top step I stopped. I knew just where to find my sister! Turning to my right, I walked around the curve of the porch, past the window of my father's study and the wide French doors that led into the breakfast room.

At the very end of the porch was that small, sheltered space that I remembered. I had not taken refuge there for a long time. It was still there, though, lush with flowers and creeping plants. Wisteria hung in perfumed bunches from the roof and a screen of broad leaves enclosed the space, keeping out both sun and prying eyes. Someone had replaced the old furniture, and now a small round table and two white rattan chairs were set at a comfortable angle deep within its shelter.

Sitting in one of the chairs almost hidden from view was my sister. She was not, as I had expected, reading. Instead she was sitting with one hand to her face as if she was thinking deeply. She had removed her spectacles and placed them on the table and her feet were propped on the other chair. The sight of Nell sitting so comfortably in the spot that I had once called my own was too much for me.

Angrily, I marched towards her. "So there you are!" I snapped. "For heaven's sake, Nell, can't you ever think of anyone but yourself? You never spend time with Papa. I know it isn't much fun, but at least you could make some effort!"

My sister didn't answer. She just watched me, and I couldn't read the expression on her face, though I was standing very close to her.

Finally, Nell gave a small shrug. In a second, I reached down and pulled her feet roughly from the chair where they were resting. She had not expected this, and her slippers made a sharp slapping noise as they hit the wooden floor of the porch.

My sister reached out one hand and held the edge of the table to stop from falling, then without haste she reached for her glasses and replaced them on her face.

She looked at me coldly as she stood up. "Ada, why don't you just leave me alone?" she said softly, and pushing past me, disappeared quickly into the house through the French doors.

I didn't follow her but stood for a moment trying to catch my breath. It was very quiet here; a small breeze had sprung up from somewhere and was whispering through the leaves, and I knew that there would be thunder in the night.

At last, I turned and retraced my steps to the front door, all anger drained from me. I couldn't force Nell to be any different, but not for the first time, I wished for the old days when the two of us had shared our troubles, and laughed at silly things the way sisters ought to do.

CHAPTER 24

As time went on, my father showed even more signs of improvement and now when I visited him in his room, he was often propped in an armchair that Drake had pulled close to the bed. Papa had always been tall and slim, but these days he seemed positively gaunt, with sunken cheeks and deep lines that ran down on either side of his mouth, giving him a grim and forbidding look. A blanket always covered his lower limbs, but his knees cut sharply across the fabric and his slipper clad feet looked as if they had been placed there without his knowledge.

Although he seemed pleased to see me, Papa often became fractious and irritable during my visits, demanding that I fetch this, or see to that. They were always small, unimportant things, and I wondered how poor Drake managed to stay with him day after day.

One morning as I was coming down from Papa's room, shaking my head in exasperation, Gilbert met me in the hall. Since my father's accident he and Drake had become unexpected allies. I saw them sometimes, late at night when Drake knew that Papa was getting his best sleep, walking up and down the lawns, side by side, like two solemn old birds of prey.

"What is it, Gilbert?" I asked, glad of any distraction. Gilbert bowed gravely. "If I may have a word, Miss?" he said opening the drawing room door for me and ushering me into the room.

"What is it?" I asked again, afraid now that he had bad news of some kind.

He waited until I was seated before beginning. "As you are aware, Miss, your father has suffered greatly as a result of his accident." I nodded impatiently, wondering where this might be leading. "Miss Baldwin," he continued, "I have the opportunity of procuring a conveyance that would make life easier for Mr. Baldwin." He held up his hand as if to stop me interrupting him, though in fact I had no such intention. "The problem being that Drake feels Mr. Baldwin will not accept that he is unable to walk, and might be unwilling to even discuss the matter."

Curious, I leaned forward. "What sort of a conveyance, Gilbert?" I asked, for I couldn't imagine what he meant.

"A bath-chair, Miss," he answered, promptly. I stared at him blankly. I had never heard of such a thing.

Gilbert beamed happily and hurried on. "It's a chair, a sort of comfortable chair with wheels that can be pushed by someone else—or if one is able, one may turn the wheels oneself."

I gazed at him wide-eyed. "A chair with wheels?" I tried to imagine what Gilbert meant.

"If I might, Miss?" Gilbert pulled from his pocket a small picture, torn from a newspaper. It showed what appeared to be an upright chair with large wheels on either side of it.

I looked down at the picture for a moment then back up at Gilbert. "You can get one of these for my father?" I asked incredulously.

"Certainly, Miss, and although Drake has his doubts, I think that we should pursue the matter. With your permission, I could have it here by week's end and then all we have to do is to help Mr. Baldwin see that these wheels can be his new legs."

I leaned back in my seat. "Yes, Gilbert," I said. "I think it's a wonderful idea." Then I smiled at him. "What would we do without you?" Gilbert gave a small bow, but I could tell that he was pleased, for the tip of his nose was quite pink.

To everyone's surprise, my father did not object at all. At first, he had the chair in his room, wheeling himself about, banging into furniture and generally driving poor Drake to distraction. As time went on and Papa started to regain his strength, he had Drake bring some of his business papers upstairs, and he would sit by the window working, the papers propped on a large wooden tray in front of him.

Then one dreary morning in May, my father sent for Miguel. The wheelchair, for so it is now called, was carried down the stairs with care, and Miguel returned for my father, picking him up as easily as if he had been a child, and depositing him safely in his wheelchair at the bottom of the stairs.

Drake fussed about, tucking in the blanket like a mother hen with its chick. Papa caught my eye, for I had been watching the whole process with baited breath. He raised his own eyes to heaven as if in exasperation, but I knew that this was an important day for him. Finally, he waved Drake away and pushed his laborious way towards the study door. Leaning forward, he turned the handle and triumphantly entered his study. I looked across at Drake—there were tears of joy in his eyes and I blinked back my own tears of relief.

With Papa starting once more to take care of his business affairs, the household returned to a more normal life. Initially, Papa had a small daybed put in his study so he could nap without needing Miguel to carry him back upstairs. But in time, even this became burdensome, so Papa had a permanent bed placed in the enormous bay window so that this room became both study and bedroom.

Then the first wheelchair was replaced by another. A very fine model, indeed, it was made out of bamboo with a wicker seat. It was light to push and my father became very adept at moving swiftly from one room to another, though I noticed that on more formal occasions, he preferred to have Drake push him.

During all this time, I had not seen Arthur Mitchell. Then one day he returned, heading towards Papa's study with papers under his arm, just as if four whole months had not passed since we last met.

As he saw me, he stopped and bowed. "Miss Baldwin," he said formally. "How pleasant to see you again. As usual, I felt the colour rise in my cheeks as I dropped a curtsey. "Have you been riding lately?" he asked, eyeing me with his usual air of amusement.

I shook my head. "No, with Papa so sick I haven't had the opportunity," I managed, breathlessly.

Arthur nodded briefly. "I'm glad to see Mr. Baldwin so much recovered. I have these for him to look at," he indicated the bundle under his arm. "I went to the site immediately after the accident, trying to help keep things going there." He smiled. "I'm back for a while now though."

I raised my eyes to his, hoping fiercely that he would ask me to go riding with him again, but he just bowed and, moving quickly to the study door, knocked and entered.

It was at about this time that I became determined to build a better relationship with my younger siblings. I had given up trying to remain close to Nell, for whenever I approached her she turned from me, or railed at me with bitter sarcasm.

I started with the twins. In spite of Miss Walsh's sharp tongue, she had certainly made improvements in the twins' behavior; though of course she could never measure up to dear Lucy Blackly, whom I still mourned deeply.

In time, the twins came to enjoy their hours with me and I was equally pleased that I was beginning to know them better. They still clung to each other—Lily always the leader, Iris following blindly, no matter what mischief Lily proposed. Sometimes, I spoke to them of our life in England, for they seemed to have almost no memory of those years. This saddened me. My own memories were still so vivid.

While my relationship with the twins was improving, getting to know my baby sister proved to be more difficult. Mrs. Chen was fiercely protective of Edie, carrying the child everywhere in her arms. Edie never seemed to mind—indeed, she clung to Mrs. Chen, burying her head in the Chinese woman's neck if anyone spoke to her.

This disturbed me, for I was sure that by now Edie should be running about and playing with her toys, but Mrs. Chen kept her in the long trailing dresses of babyhood and I had never even seen the child stand upright.

An opportunity to visit Edie on my own came quite unexpectedly one afternoon, when Miss Walsh came to tell me that the twins were unwell. A slight fever, nothing more, but she had decided to keep them in bed. Iris in particular was quite delicate.

With an hour or so stretching before me, I had little desire to work productively, so I thought I might stroll outside for a while for, the day was pleasant. As I was crossing the hall, I saw Mrs. Chen disappearing into Papa's study, her bag of golden needles in her hand. Papa had suffered from severe headaches since the accident, especially on days when the weather was humid or particularly changeable.

On sudden impulse, I turned and headed towards the kitchen. With Mrs. Chen safely out of the way, this was a good opportunity to visit my little sister.

Slipping through the baize doors that led to this part of the house, I ran lightly down the corridor and into the deserted kitchen. Walking over to the larder, I stepped inside. Immediately, I spied a plate of small, fruit-filled pastries, and wrapped three of them in a clean napkin which I slipped into my pocket before heading to the nursery. I felt sure that Edie would be sleeping, but I planned to wake her and, with the help of the pastries, persuade her to play with me.

I walked down the inside corridor and opened the door that led to the nursery. All was quiet as I pushed open the door to Edie's room. She was not asleep. She was sitting in her crib sucking her thumb, with her faithful rabbit beside her. I smiled at the sight. Poor rabbit! His ears were in great need of repair. In one corner, a charcoal brazier was burning, making the room almost unbearably hot. Edie's hair curled damply about her head and tiny beads of perspiration covered her forehead.

She watched me solemnly as I came into the room. Then, as I approached, her eyes became very big and she removed her thumb ready, I was sure, to emit a piercing shriek. In all probability, Anna or one of the other girls had been told to listen out for Edie and I did not want them to come running.

Quickly, I reached into my pocket and withdrew the napkin. Leaning towards her, I opened it and held out one of the pastries. "For Edie," I said, coaxingly. Immediately, Edie smiled, and reached her chubby fingers eagerly towards the sticky treat. I gave her the pastry and watched as she pushed it hungrily into her mouth, almost choking in her haste to eat it. Swallowing most of it, she stretched out her hand again and said something that I could not understand. I waited.

She watched me for a moment, then her small face became flushed and her bottom lip trembled ominously. Hastily, I pushed the second pastry towards her.

She leaned forward to reach for it, but in so doing, she tipped over. My little sister let out an angry roar as I picked her up out of her cot, quickly pushing the goody into her hand. Once again, she gulped it down greedily and reached for the third pastry.

When I did not give it to her, her eyes filled with tears and she began to whimper. Bending down, I stood her on the floor, tucking her long skirts up around her waist and backed away, holding the pastry invitingly in my hand.

Edie took a tottering step towards me and fell flat on her face. Swiftly, I reached down to pick her up. She was screaming in earnest now, but I didn't really notice. I was staring in horror, for as Edie had attempted to take a step forward, I had seen the tiny bandaged stump that was her foot.

Blood gushed down my sister's chin where she had pushed a tooth through her tender lip, and I mopped at it ineffectively before lifting her once more in my arms and placing her gently in her crib. I wiped the blood from her face with the sheet then with fingers that shook, I started to unwrap the yards of white cotton bandage that bound one tiny foot. As I did so, I was aware of running footsteps that stopped at the door. I didn't look round.

"There's nothing to worry about," I heard myself say calmly. "Miss Edie is just a little upset and I'm tending to her." After a moment, the footsteps retreated and I continued alone, unwrapping layer after layer of bandage.

As the pressure on her foot was released, Edie screamed, tossing and turning on the mattress in an effort to escape the pain. The smell of urine was sharp in my nostrils, but I continued my task. Sweat ran down my face and I dashed it angrily away as I worked feverishly to reach the end of the bandages.

I did not hear any sound; there was just a slight frisson in the air. A stirring, a shifting, and I knew that Mrs. Chen was behind me.

She spoke softly, her voice hissing in my ear. "What you doing, stupid girl? Leave this child alone. I make her beautiful for man to love, not like you great pink pigs. Leave her!"

So venomous was her tone that, for a fleeting moment my hands froze, and I almost stopped what I was doing. Then the last of the bandages slipped away and I could see my sister's bare foot. Each tiny toe was twisted back. The top of her foot had been bent back in an arc, and the flesh was white and wrinkled from the tight bindings. Edie's screams had gradually subsided to gulping sobs, and now she lay with her head turned away from me, her small arms shielding her face. Mrs. Chen was standing close to me and, as I turned to look down at her, her dark eyes stared up into mine, fearless and filled with fury.

Black rage of my own swept over me. "Get out," I said, softly. "Get out now, before I kill you." I truly think that the Chinese woman saw murder in my eyes, for she took a hasty step back and then turned and disappeared into her own room, closing the door behind her.

I bent back to my sister, gently unwrapping the other foot. Once again, Edie screamed as the bandages were released, but I continued with my task until the last wrapping fell away and I stared down at the ruin of my sister's feet. Tears filled my eyes and I stroked her damp head. "My poor, poor little one," I whispered. "Don't worry, I'm here now. Ada will look after you. No one will ever hurt you again."

I looked around and saw a pile of folded cloths on the table beside the crib. Marveling a little that I still remembered how to do this, I changed Edie's wet bottom, talking softly to her all the while. Her lip had stopped bleeding and I licked my own handkerchief and wiped her face clean.

Obviously my father must be told of this at once, but I knew he would be sleeping. Drake always gave him a sedative after Mrs. Chen had poked her needles into him. I hesitated for a moment before picking Edie up and turned, ready to do battle with Mrs. Chen. I looked across to where she had disappeared into the other room, but the door was wide open now and the room was quite empty.

Edie was heavy in my arms, so I hitched her onto my hip as we made our way along the corridor, but I must have banged her foot for she gasped with pain and started to cry again. I paused for a moment, and pushed her thumb into her mouth. "Hush now, pet," I soothed. "Let's go and see Papa."

I was glad that the kitchen was still empty, and decided that I would keep Edie with me until my father awoke and I could explain the horror of what had happened to her.

Holding my sister tightly in both arms now, I backed through the baize doors leading into the hall. As I did so, I felt a hand on my back. Startled, I turned my head; it was Gilbert. At a glance, he took in my disheveled appearance and the still whimpering child in my arms.

"Is the little one hurt?" he asked softly. I nodded wordlessly and held Edie closer to me.

"Come," he said calmly, and not waiting to see if I was following, he walked swiftly through his pantry, and opened the door that led to his private quarters. There, sitting at ease as usual at this time of day, with her feet propped on a cushion, was Mrs. Johnson.

She looked from my tear-stained face, to the child in my arms. Then she held out her own hands for Edie. "There, there little one," she crooned, patting Edie's tangled curls as I gladly relinquished my little sister to the comforting arms of the housekeeper.

"What ails her?" Gilbert looked questioningly over his shoulder at me. I was crying again. With shaking hands, I lifted Edie's long dress and revealed her crippled feet.

Gilbert saw them first and I heard his sharp intake of breath. Following Gilbert's eyes, Mrs. Johnson looked for herself. There was a long silence, broken only by Edie's occasional hiccupping sobs.

At last, Gilbert spoke. "Goddam little heathen," he said softly beneath his breath. He slammed a clenched fist into his other hand then he turned abruptly to me. "Did you know about this, Miss?" he demanded.

"No!" I felt my face flame. "No, of course I didn't. Mrs. Chen," I almost choked on her name, "she wouldn't let us touch Edie."

I pulled at Gilbert's sleeve. "We have to tell my father, but he's sleeping and I don't know what to do." My knees buckled and I sat down abruptly on a chair.

Mrs. Johnson reached out a comforting hand to me before turning to Gilbert. "Put the kettle on, Horatio, and we'll have a nice cup of tea and talk it over."

The housekeeper's words were familiar, and for a moment, I felt that I was back in the kitchen at home with Cook and Mrs. Carter solving smaller, more familiar problems.

In the end, Mrs. Johnson soothed Edie to sleep and Gilbert escorted me up to my room with a firm promise that he would have Anna wake me as soon as my father stirred. I fell upon my bed and sobbed myself to sleep and the next thing I knew I was being shaken rudely awake.

CHAPTER 25

I opened my eyes to see Nell glaring down at me.

"Hurry up, Papa is waiting," she said tersely before turning and striding angrily to the window. "Ada, did you know about this thing with Edie?" she asked, keeping her head turned away.

Then, not waiting for an answer, she hurried on. "No, of course you didn't, but I might have guessed." She paused for a moment then turned around to look at me. "Do you know why she was doing it?"

I swung my feet over the edge of the bed and reached for my shoes. "No! Why would anyone try to cripple a child's feet?" I looked down at my own foot, lying straight and slender on the floor and felt a little sick.

Nell had turned back, and was gazing reflectively out of the window again. Her voice was flat as she answered me. "It's a custom in some parts of China. They bind the feet of female children so that they can give pleasure to men when they are grown." Then she added reflectively. "They don't usually do so until the child is older. But perhaps Mrs. Chen believed that doing so earlier, would make it easier to accomplish."

I stared at my sister. "What do you mean? How can feet give pleasure to men?"

Nell looked at me, her face grim. "You should read more, Ada," she said. "You need to know what still happens to women in today's wonderful, modern world."

I looked up at Nell helplessly. I had no idea what she was trying to tell me. Then my younger sister came close to where I was sitting.

Leaning down, she spoke in a carefully pleasant voice. "Men in China like to see women with tiny feet that look like hooves. So for two years little girls of high birth have the bones in their feet broken and bandaged, until they are set into this shape, but their feet must remain bound for the rest of their lives. Of course they cannot walk properly and by the time these girls are grown into young women their hips have also become so misshapen that they can only hobble along, swaying as they walk which looks most seductive to Chinese men, and excites them to thoughts of extreme lust!" Is that explanation enough for you, dear sister?" With that, she swung on her heel and left the room, slamming the door behind her.

I sat without moving for several moments then I got up and splashed cold water on my face. I wasn't ready to believe Nell, for what she had said, made little sense to me at that time. I confess my knowledge of men's needs was limited at best, and of his baser urges, I knew nothing.

As I entered Papa's study, I saw that my father was seated as usual behind his desk with Drake hovering in the background. Papa's face was pale and strained. Nell was sitting in one of the big leather armchairs, and Mrs. Johnson was standing next to her, holding Edie. My little sister was clutching happily at the housekeeper's lace collar, seemingly intent on poking small chubby fingers into the delicate fabric and ruining it. Mrs. Johnson didn't seem to mind. Gilbert closed the door behind me and remained standing against it, almost as if he was guarding the entrance.

When I was seated, my father looked at each of us in turn. "Mrs. Chen has gone," he said, at last, in a voice that betrayed no emotion. "However, I feel I must tell you that what she did was for love of Edie." There was silence in the room. "In China" my father continued, "the custom of binding the feet of small girls is not uncommon. Tiny feet are considered a mark of beauty and good breeding. I cannot discuss further the particular practice that Mrs. Chen adhered to. It is enough to say that she was gravely mistaken. She has been sent away and will not return." My father paused for breath then continued.

"I do not want news of this event to be spread among the servants, nor do I want it to reach the ears of our friends and neighbours." Papa paused and looked from Nell to me. "Not to anyone," he added, with sudden emphasis. I glanced over at Nell in time to see her look away with a small shrug of her shoulders.

"I mean what I say, Nell!" My father's voice was stern and forbidding. "You will keep this information to yourself. Do you understand me?" Nell mumbled an assent. The sharp slap of Papa's hand on his desk made me jump. "Eleanor, I require your word now," he snapped. My own gasp was lost in that of my sister's. Papa never called Nell by her full name.

"Yes, I understand, Papa," she said in a small voice, shaken for once out of her usual self-confidence. "I promise, I shall tell no one."

Satisfied, my father turned to Gilbert. "Do any of the other servants know what Mrs. Chen was doing?"

Before Gilbert could reply, Mrs. Johnson took a step forward. "I'll make some enquiries, Sir. Young Anna must know something. Her little one sometimes plays with Miss Edith, and that woman had Anna mind Edie from time to time, Sir."

My father tapped his fingers restlessly on the desk. "Yes, make sure you speak to Anna at once, Mrs. Johnson."

I found myself staring at our housekeeper. Whatever did she mean when she said 'Anna's little one?' Did Anna have a child? And, if so, why had she never told me?

My thoughts were interrupted by Papa giving instructions for Edie to be brought to the study in the morning, the moment Dr. Hawthorne arrived for his weekly visit. In the meantime, her feet were to remain uncovered and Mrs. Johnson was to take care of her overnight.

As soon as Papa dismissed us, I looked for Nell. I wanted to talk to her about Anna's child, but by the time I left Papa's study, she had disappeared. I waited uncertainly outside the study door. My father was still talking to Mrs. Johnson, and I could see Drake busily straightening chairs.

A quiet cough behind me made me turn. Gilbert was standing close by. "Is there something that I may assist you with, Miss?" he asked.

"Yes, Gilbert, there is. Can you tell me why no one has said anything to me about Anna having a child out of wedlock?" I demanded.

Gilbert looked thoughtfully down his nose. "Well, Miss, to the best of my knowledge, Anna's child was born well within the sanctity of her marriage. She has been wed for some four years, I believe. Her husband, Jose, gave you riding lessons, did he not, Miss? He's very reliable and a good worker. I have always thought them a fine match, if I may say so." Then Gilbert looked directly at me. "Things are very different in this country, Miss. It is not uncommon for the servants to marry and to continue working in one household. It makes for very loyal servants for the future. Little Tomas will likely consider himself bound to this family forever. He's scarce three years old yet, though, Miss, so he's a might young to go into service." With that, Gilbert bowed gravely and departed, leaving me standing with my mouth slightly open in a manner most unbecoming in a young lady.

Later, when I asked Anna about her little boy and why she never spoke of him, she seemed genuinely surprised. "When I am here, I care only for you Señorita," she said with a smile. I felt better after that.

So once again our family settled itself into a new routine as we shared in the care of little Edie. In time, my baby sister did learn to walk in a stumbling and unsteady way, helped by many willing hands, but most of all by the little pushcart that Gilbert made for her, with its sturdy handle and four low wheels. Often she was to be found in the kitchen, or playing with Gilbert's little dog Duchess, regardless of how dirty she had become.

Edie was a happy child much loved by everyone, but what pleased me most, was that every afternoon, waking from his siesta, my father would demand that Edie be brought to him, and the two of them would sit close, Edie often pulling herself up on the side of Papa's wheelchair, and he, helped by the ever-faithful Drake, drawing her onto his knee, where she would sit and chat with him in an odd mix of English and nonsense talk. I have never seen Papa look happier. But, truthfully, no matter how hard we, or Dr. Hawthorne tried, there was no way to undo the dreadful damage that Mrs. Chen had inflicted on little Edie.

As time went on, I was sometimes made uneasy by visits from Señor Rodriguez. I would catch his eyes upon me, and thought that he looked at me in a very calculating manner, and I could not help but remember that he had once asked for my hand in marriage. I hoped that he did not intend to repeat the request. Papa could scarcely put him off with my youth, for I was becoming quite an old maid.

Then all at once, things improved. Arthur Mitchell became a regular visitor at the house, for Papa now relied on him to journey back and forth to the worksite. At this time, Arthur became most attentive and charming towards me, sometimes even taking a turn about the gardens in the evening when the heat of the day had abated and before the mosquitoes came to plague us.

He and I were never alone on these occasions; Nell was always there, and sometimes the twins were allowed to join us. But it was to me that Arthur offered his arm so that he might walk beside me. He was most entertaining and spoke to us of his journeys to and from the worksites, and occasionally told us amusing and even slightly mischievous tales of his student days with Mr. Edmund Nichols.

I was sorry that Mr. Nichols no longer called on us, for I thought then that he might have made a very good match for Nell. However, Arthur told us that Edmund had recently returned to England with little expectation of coming back to Argentina in the near future.

Arthur and I never spoke of that morning ride when he had shown me the ruins of his family home, and I found that he turned the conversation and spoke of other things whenever I tried to broach the subject. Nor did he invite me to go riding with him again, but I consoled myself with the thought that my father kept him very busy. Sometimes though, I wondered when Arthur would declare himself, for surely he had feelings for me, as I had for him.

CHAPTER 26

One day when the summer heat was almost unbearable, my father joined us for lunch. This was unusual, for as a rule, he took his meals in his room, and only appeared at dinner if he was feeling very well. On this particular day, the twins and Miss Walsh were also with us.

Over the past weeks, the care of my small sister had fallen almost entirely upon Anna and me. We had worked out a schedule that allowed Anna to continue to assist me when I needed her, but the rest of her time was now spent with Edie. I took it upon myself to put the little one to bed each night, and it gave me great joy to see her stretching her arms out to me as she lay in her crib after her bath. I had thought perhaps Nell would join me in caring for Edie, but when I broached the subject with her, she shook her head.

"Sorry, Ada, it's just not something I do," she said. "I'm not the mothering sort."

Although I was annoyed with Nell for shirking her duties, in my heart I was glad that I would not have to compete for Edie's affection.

Now as Drake deftly maneuvered my father's wheelchair into place at the head of the table, Papa let his glance linger on each of us in turn. I was pleased to see that for once he looked a little less stressed. Of late, the lines around his mouth had deepened and his hair, once a rich, dark brown, now showed broad streaks of grey.

After lunch was over and the dishes had been cleared, Papa dismissed the maids, leaving only Gilbert and Drake in the room with us. Then, leaning forward, he placed his hands flat on the table in a familiar gesture.

"My dear girls and Miss Walsh," he said, solemnly. "I have grave news. As you may know, over the past months, I have consulted with several doctors, and they all agree that my accident has left me permanently paralyzed. This has forced me to make considerable changes to our lives."

"When I bought this house, I had every hope of living here for many years. Alas, such a thing is not to be. I must sell the place as soon as I can and we will all be moving to Rosario, where I am already changing the nature of my business so that we may continue to live in a reasonably comfortable manner. Our circumstances, however, will be much reduced."

There was not a sound in the room. I'm not even sure that Lily and Iris understood what Papa had said. I darted a sidelong glance at Nell, but she had put her hand to her face and I couldn't see her expression.

My own thoughts whirled. I had come to love this house with its gracious rooms, sprawling kitchen and yard, the paddock where Blaze was no doubt at this moment dozing in the shade. And, most of all, I loved the great porch that wrapped around the outside of the house, keeping us close and safe.

Fearfully, I looked across to where Gilbert was standing, his face impassive. I wondered if he and Mrs. Johnson would accompany us to Rosario. The thought of losing them and starting all over again was almost too much to bear. In spite of myself a sob escaped my lips. The small sound seemed to break the spell of silence, and my father looked inquiringly at me.

"Do we really have to leave, Papa?" I asked tremulously. "We're settled here now and have social obligations." My father looked at me quizzically for a moment and I was glad when he did not ask what those obligations were, for apart from my small place in the chapel choir, I could not think of a single one.

Instead, he sighed. "Ada, this was not an easy decision, but it is made and is final." Then he turned to Nell, who was sitting silent beside me. "What about you, Nell?" he asked. "I thought that you might be pleased. This will be a whole new city for you to explore." Nell remained silent, not looking at Papa, and after a few moments, my father sighed impatiently and signaled to Drake, who stepped forward with practiced ease and wheeled him out of the dining room.

We remained seated at the table for a few moments, then Miss Walsh excused herself and the twins, and Nell and I were left alone. I looked across at my sister and saw, to my surprise that she was crying. Tears were running silently down her face and she made no move to wipe them away. I stretched out a hand to her, but with an impatient gesture, she waved me away. Then, pushing back her chair, she rose hurriedly and left the room.

At first nothing changed following my father's remarkable announcement. Nell refused to discuss the matter, and I did not find an opportunity to speak privately with Gilbert. After a while, I allowed myself to think that this need not concern us immediately. Papa had said that he must sell the house first, and that might take a long time.

My hopes were dashed, however, when scarcely a month later Mrs. Johnson announced that we were expecting guests for dinner. I was taken aback, for I had not been given any indication that we were to expect company.

"I'm sorry, Miss," she said, seeing the shock on my face. "Mr. Baldwin told me not five minutes ago. There's a Mr. and Mrs. McKinley coming—it seems they hope to buy the house. So they're to be here for dinner, along with Señor Rodriguez." She turned to go then paused for a moment. "Young Mr. Mitchell is to join us, too. Most particular the Master was about that." I stood looking thoughtfully after her; it seemed that things were already in motion.

I wasn't surprised that Señor Rodriguez was invited. He and my father still shared business interests and Papa relied on him for many things. I did wonder, however, why Arthur Mitchell had been invited.

I asked Anna to take especial care dressing my hair that evening, and took a long time deciding what gown to wear. I wanted something that would be particularly flattering. It had been a long time since Arthur had joined us socially.

Later, when we were all seated at dinner, I noticed that the seating arrangements were unusual. My father had insisted that Mr. McKinley be seated on his right hand and Señor Rodriguez on his left. Arthur was next to Mr. McKinley, with Mrs. McKinley seated opposite him. Nell and I were relegated to the lower end of the table with the twins, while Miss Walsh was seated at the end of the table, in the place that was rightfully mine.

Throughout dinner, Papa discussed matters of business with the gentlemen at the top of the table. They used hushed tones throughout, for clearly Papa did not intend to include the women in his conversation, and we were reduced to chatting politely with Mrs. McKinley.

The McKinley's were recent immigrants from Scotland, and were delighted with the opportunity to purchase such an elegant home so quickly. Mrs. McKinley asked many questions about the country and our way of life. She noted the various flower arrangements in the room, clasping her plump hands together in rhapsodies of delight. I confess that I was impatient with the conversation.

I longed to hear what my father was discussing so earnestly, and I found my glance straying to where Arthur was sitting. As I watched, I saw him lean forward and speak very earnestly to Papa, but my father shook his head and turned again to Mr. McKinley. I strained my ears, but try as I might, could not catch any of what was being said over Mrs. McKinley's round Scottish vowels. I vowed that I would not look at Arthur again, but it was difficult to keep my eyes from straying towards his handsome profile.

Mrs. McKinley had moved on from floral arrangements to fashion, and was loudly extolling the very latest style in bustles and throwing up her hands in outraged delight at our obvious ignorance of the new fashion in bonnets.

Then she turned her attention to Lily and Iris who had, for the most part, been sitting quietly, overwhelmed by the occasion, for they were not usually allowed to dine with us when we had company.

From praising the twins, it was but a single artless step for Mrs. McKinley to launch into her favourite subject: the charms and delights of young Master Willie McKinley, presently at school in Scotland, but scheduled to join his doting parents at the end of the school year.

It was during this interminable meal that Miss Walsh became remarkably animated. Delighted to find herself in the company of fellow Scots, she became quite effusive, and spoke out far more than I felt appropriate. Nell was no help; she remained very quiet throughout dinner, seemingly much preoccupied with her own thoughts, though from time to time, she did ask Mrs. McKinley a polite question.

At the end of the meal, Papa pushed his wheelchair back from the table and signaled Drake to take him to the study, where he and the other gentlemen could continue their discussion over a little brandy. Since his accident Papa had allowed himself the occasional solace of spirits, as he found it eased his pain, especially at night.

As the gentlemen rose from the table, I felt a prickle of irritation. Could Papa not remember, just this once that the women should withdraw first? Nell and I were no longer children and it was most discourteous to Mrs. McKinley, though she seemed quite oblivious of this, for she continued to chatter brightly as the men left, praising the joys of her native Glasgow. Silently mutinous, I remained in my seat, watching as the men rose and followed my father.

In spite of my earlier resolution not to do so, I found myself watching Arthur as he stood for a moment by his chair. He looked very tall and handsome in his dinner jacket and snowy linen. His eyes sparkled blue in his tanned face as he smiled. Placing a hand on his heart, he gave a small bow that included all of those who remained seated, though I thought that his eyes lingered on mine for just a moment.

Then Arthur turned, and instead of taking the most direct route to the door, walked swiftly around the top of the table, down behind Señor Rodriguez's empty chair, past Nell and then me. It was very naturally done and I would not have noticed had I not been watching him so intently. As he came level with me, he paused for a moment and, bending quickly, retrieved a table napkin that must have fallen to the floor. As he straightened up, I heard his urgent whisper.

"The porch, at midnight, we need to talk." Then he was gone.

Scarcely daring to breathe, I cast a quick glance at Nell sitting next to me. Thankfully, she must not have heard Arthur's hurried message, for she was leaning forward a little, listening with polite interest to Mrs. McKinley's latest foolish tale of young Master Willie.

My cheeks burned and I bent my head, in case either Lily or Iris noticed and asked me why I was blushing. I was filled with happiness. At last, Arthur was ready to declare himself. I took a deep, steadying breath and allowed myself to smile as I turned towards Mrs. McKinley and invited her to join us in the drawing room.

The remainder of the evening seemed endless. Miss Walsh was much inclined to linger and discuss the joys of Glasgow with our guest, until I had to tell her quite sharply that it was long past the twins' bedtime and she should be attending to them.

After they had left, I excused myself for a short while, explaining to our guest that I needed to check on Edith. Nell glared angrily at me as I left the room. I was sure that she was not pleased at being left to play hostess, but after tonight, perhaps my dear sister would be forced to take up some of the duties that I had performed for so long.

As I crossed the hall, I heard male voices coming from behind the study door. I hoped fervently that Arthur would present himself well to my father when he asked for my hand a little later.

I thought that we should live in Rosario for a while, so that Arthur could continue to help Papa make the necessary changes to his business. But in the end, I vowed we would return here and rebuild the Mitchell house and make it even more beautiful than it was before the fire. As I continued walking towards the nursery, I wondered if we would marry immediately; there seemed little reason to delay. I could scarcely bear to wait until midnight when I would meet my beloved Arthur on the porch.

Edie was sleeping peacefully, arms out-flung, with one chubby hand clutching her precious rabbit. Her feet were still bandaged and Dr. Hawthorne checked on them regularly as the slow painful process of straightening the tiny bones continued. We prayed that one day Edie would be able to walk, but when I asked the doctor if her feet would ever be completely straight, he pursed his lips and shook his head. "I have no idea, Miss Baldwin," he said. "We can but hope."

As a rule, I visited Edie just before I retired for the night, to be sure that she was well settled, and afterward, Anna would follow me upstairs to help me out of my gown and brush my hair. Tonight though, I did not want my maid's assistance, and I wondered what I should tell her. As I leaned over Edie's cot, Anna came into the room carrying a basket of clothes. Keeping my eyes on the sleeping child, I spoke coolly. "No need to come up tonight, Anna, Miss Nell will help me to undress." I straightened up and turned around.

Anna was watching me, her dark eyes puzzled. "Very well, Señorita," she said, putting her head a little to one side. "You are sure?" She hesitated. "Miss Nell does not usually help you." Her voice trailed off into silence.

"I'm quite sure," I said curtly, making for the door as Anna looked curiously after me. I did not take the corridor back to the house, but left instead by the outside door that led to the yard and stables.

"Buenos noches, señorita," Anna called softly after me as I closed the outside door.

I stood for a moment breathing in the warm night air. My face felt flushed and my knees were a little wobbly. I took a deep, steadying breath, then forced myself to walk calmly back to the house.

CHAPTER 27

It was late when Gilbert finally closed the front door behind the McKinley's and Nell drifted up the stairs ahead of me. There was no sign of Arthur. I looked at the grandfather clock that stood at the bottom of the stairs. Quarter past eleven. I hurried to my room and closed the door.

Frantically, I peered at myself in the mirror. The dark green dress that I had chosen for dinner was becoming enough, but I unpinned my hair and brushed it fiercely. It was long and glossy now, and I coiled its length into a soft, low bun at the nape of my neck. This was a becoming look for me, and I was glad of that.

Restlessly, I paced the room, my mind filled with jumbled thoughts. I wondered how Arthur would propose. Would he take me in his arms, or kneel humbly at my feet? I wondered if he was speaking to Papa at this very moment. I worried about who would look after Edie when we moved away. Finally, I shook my head to clear it, and wondered for a moment if I had imagined the whole thing. Then I smiled to myself. I could still hear Arthur's urgent voice in my ear. "Meet me at midnight!"

Impatiently, I crossed the room and opened the window. I leaned out then just as suddenly withdrew my head. I did not want Arthur to see me peering out like an anxious scullery maid waiting for her beau.

As I drew my head back into the room, I heard the sound of a door shutting nearby and, for a moment, I froze. Then I took a shaky breath of relief as I realized that it was only Bella, Nell's maid, finished for the night. Once again, I paced the floor. I had almost persuaded myself that I should not go down at all when I heard the clock strike midnight.

With trembling hands, I patted my hair and, with a final glance in the mirror, walked to the door, turned the handle, and slipped out. I walked soft-footed along the corridor and down the stairs, and felt that my feet hardly touched the ground, so sure was I, now that I was going to see my beloved.

I stopped by the open door of the breakfast room. All was dark and still as I slipped into the room and made my way past the table that was already laid for breakfast, silverware gleaming dully against the white linen tablecloth.

I reached the French doors that opened onto the porch and was surprised to find them already unlocked. They swung open at my touch and I smiled a secret smile; of course Arthur would have seen to that.

As I stepped through the open doors, the air was filled with night sounds: the high chirruping of tree frogs, the insistent call of crickets. A dark shadow swooped across the moon and I wondered what small creature would become supper for a hungry bird tonight. I leaned for a second against the doorframe, willing myself to remember this moment forever.

Straightening up, I looked cautiously around. I could not see Arthur anywhere. Papa's bay windows were closed tight against the night air and I knew that Arthur would not linger there. I thought for a moment then, nodding to myself, turned to my left; I knew where he would be waiting.

As I rounded the curve of the porch, I stopped. I could smell the smoke from Arthur's cigar, and ahead of me, I could just distinguish the small table and two chairs in the arbour at the very end of the porch.

Just as I had guessed, Arthur was there, sitting sprawled in one of the chairs. I could see the gleam of his white shirt against the darkness of the leaves and I watched for a moment as his hand moved in a familiar gesture to brush his hair away from his eyes. I stepped forward, his name on my lips, but as I took a breath to speak, I realized that he was not alone.

I watched in frozen silence as Arthur rose abruptly to his feet with a small, impatient gesture and waited as his companion rose to stand with him. The moonlight gleamed softly through the rustling leaves as she reached up and wound her slim arms around his neck, for she was not very tall. Arthur bent his bright head to hers and, in a moment, they were locked in a passionate embrace.

Inexperienced though I was, even I could see that this was not a first, tentative kiss. They clung together, the two of them, as if they would never part. Then Arthur, taking her face in his hands, kissed her eyelids, her forehead, and the hollow of her throat. She pulled her head away from his a little, and gave a small moan as he ran his fingers hungrily through the dark hair that had tumbled down with the familiar pull of a single ribbon.

This was an embrace that spoke of other meetings, of stolen afternoons and early-morning rides, and of a love that was already burning with a white-hot passion. I watched as Arthur pulled at her robe and she, in turn, raised her leg, winding it around him, pulling him ever closer and gave herself to that embrace, her bare flesh pale in the moonlight. I did not need to see the gleam of my sister's spectacles on the table to know that it was Nell, not me, to whom Arthur Mitchell had whispered his urgent message after dinner.

I watched for a moment more then turning, I walked slowly back the way I had come. As I rounded the curve of the porch, a small breeze caught at my hair and with it came the overwhelming smell of roses.

I slipped silently through the French doors and then, in a single decisive movement, turned and locked them behind me. With a sharp tug, I removed the key and laid it with care on the table where it lay, gleaming dark against the white damask tablecloth. Only the grandfather clock watched as I climbed the stairs back to my room. I lay, dry-eyed, on the bed until the first grey light of dawn came creeping in my window, and although I listened carefully, I did not hear the sound of Nell returning.

I suppose I must have slept a little, for Anna woke me at the usual time, crying out when she saw that I was still fully dressed. I let her fuss over me and allowed her to scold me for not calling her when, just as she had predicted, my sister had not helped me.

I went down to breakfast, but sat alone at the table, my food untouched. It was amazing to me that the world continued as usual. The birds still sang, I could hear the glad cry of a child coming from the direction of the nursery, and the sound of Gilbert and Drake talking quietly in the hall as they went about their daily business. It was as if my world was not lying in shattered splinters outside my sister's door.

I did not see Nell for the rest of that day. She must have sent down to say that she was feeling unwell because I saw Mrs. Johnson carrying a tray up to her room. It came down again untouched.

I moved through the next hours like someone in a dark dream. I suppose I carried out my usual duties, for no one commented. I sat with the twins in the afternoon and read from the bible, but I do not recall what passages I selected. I took dinner in my room, pleading a headache.

During my solitary breakfast on the second day, I overheard Gilbert tell Mrs. Johnson that an agent was already looking for a suitable home for us in Rosario and that we should expect to leave as soon as a house was found.

Later that day, as I crossed the hall deep in my own misery, I heard the name of Arthur Mitchell spoken. I stopped abruptly; Drake and Gilbert were deep in conversation, but as I approached on silent feet, Gilbert became aware of my presence and straightening quickly turned towards me.

"Is there something, Miss?" he inquired smoothly. I shook my head and continued on my way up the stairs. I stopped as I reached the door of my bedroom, then straightened my back and walked resolutely to my sister's door and knocked. It was time that Nell and I had a talk.

There was no answer to my knock, but I turned the handle and walked into the room. I closed the door behind me and leaned against it. Nell was lying on her bed fully dressed, her face turned away from me. She did not turn to greet me, but I saw the balled-up handkerchief in her hand and knew that she had been crying.

I stayed where I was, waiting until at last Nell turned her head towards me. I was shocked by her appearance. Her hair lay in dark tangles on the pillow and her eyes were swollen to slits with weeping. Her glasses lay close by, but she did not put them on.

"What do you want?" she asked wearily.

In three quick steps I was beside her bed looking down at her. "I saw you," I hissed. "I saw you and Arthur Mitchell. I saw what you were doing. How dare you, Nell? Arthur was mine. It was me he wanted to marry. He showed me his old home, and you . . . you saw that, didn't you? You followed us that day when we went riding. You ran over that cliff on purpose, I know you did. "Well, you can't have him, he's mine! He doesn't want a dull bookworm like you, he wants a wife who can look after him and give him children and make him happy and . . ." My voice trailed away. Nell had not moved; she just lay on the bed staring up at me. I had not meant to spill out all my secret dreams and hurts like that.

Slowly, Nell raised herself onto one elbow then she swung her feet over the side of the bed and shook her head, wincing a little as if it hurt to move.

"Don't be a fool Ada," she said. "Arthur and I have been lovers for nearly a year. We have spent every possible moment together; I thought you knew. The day that Arthur took you to his old home he was just getting back at me." She gave a thin smile. "We'd had a dreadful quarrel and he wanted to hurt me." She put her head in her hand and winced again. "Didn't you see how fiercely we were fighting that day? Why do you think that was?"

I sat down abruptly next to her. Thinking back to that morning, I remembered how close together the two of them had been standing and how angry they were, and the contemptuous way that Nell had spoken to Arthur. Of course I should have known.

Then I remembered the evenings when Arthur had joined us in the garden. True, he always gave me his arm, but it was Nell he watched as she walked ahead of us. And so often, when he regaled us with amusing tales of his student days, it was Nell who laughed up at him and begged for more stories.

"I feel so stupid, Nell," I said at last. "I just wanted him to care for me. He was always so nice to me. And I am the oldest," I added, a little petulantly.

Nell regarded me steadily for a moment then blew her nose into her already soggy handkerchief.

"Actually, Ada," she said, through the folds of cloth, "I'm the fool." She raised her head and smiled bleakly at me. "I thought he loved me. We planned to run away and be married. But he left. Just like that. He's gone!"

I stared at my sister in disbelief. "What do you mean, gone? He was here the other night, I saw you. I saw you together, out on the porch."

"Yes." Nell's voice was barely above a whisper. "Papa told him after dinner that he would no longer need his services now we're going to Rosario. We're ruined financially, Ada, you must know that. Now that Papa is crippled, he cannot continue to work as an engineer. He can't visit the railway sites. He's going to change what he does and he doesn't need Arthur anymore." Her voice broke and she bent her head again, her tangled hair falling forward to cover her face.

I sat staring at her for a moment, then moved closer and put a tentative arm around her shoulders. I felt her stiffen, but she didn't push me away.

"Nell," I said softly, forgetting my own misery for a moment. "He can still marry you if that's what you both want. He can get employment anywhere as an engineer."

Nell shook her head. "He isn't an engineer. He dropped out of university because he was failing. That's why Papa wouldn't employ him permanently. He kept saying he would go back to take his exams again, but I know he won't. Papa invited him to dinner with the McKinley's to suggest that Arthur might find a position in Mr. McKinley's business."

"The man's a butcher, Ada. He's a little Scottish butcher who wants to own some cattle so he can send meat back to his 'wee shops in Glasgee!'" Nell spoke in a bitter parody of Mr. McKinley's broad Scottish accent. "Can you imagine Arthur doing that? He was furious with Papa, and so he's left and he told me that he's not coming back."

She was twisting the damp handkerchief in her fingers, still hiding her face with her hair and I could barely hear her next words. "I think I'm carrying Arthur's child."

"What?" I demanded, catching desperately at her hand, but she twisted away, then turned and faced me defiantly.

"I told you I love him. You wouldn't understand. We planned to get married."

I rose to my feet. My hands were cold as ice. In my mind's eye, I saw again two figures lying in the straw of a stable. Bessie, her legs spread wide, Ned between her thighs, heaving and grunting like one of the barnyard animals.

"Oh, but I do understand." My voice was filled with loathing. "I understand that what you have done is so disgusting that I can scarcely believe you." I turned quickly away from her.

Now it was Nell's turn to reach for my hand, but I pulled away angrily and walked to the window. I leaned my head on the glass, my breath coming in small gasps.

Behind me, I could hear Nell's soft voice, pleading. "Ada, listen to me! It's . . . it's wonderful and magical, and so beautiful when you love someone, you have no idea. Please, you have to believe me."

I turned to face my sister. "I do know what it's like, Nell. I once saw two of the servants rutting like pigs in the straw just like you did with Arthur." My lip curled with disgust as I spoke. Pushing past her, I walked to the door. "Of course Papa will have to be told," I said, coldly.

In an instant, Nell was beside me, her strong arms closing round me, preventing me from leaving. "Ada, please don't tell! I'm not even sure yet. I thought we were going to be married. Please, Ada, please, Oh God!" She was on her knees now, dragging at my skirts, tears pouring down her face. I looked down at my sister, but I felt no pity. I think there was a part of me that was terribly jealous of Nell, who had loved a man so much that she had given herself to him and risked ruin in this world and eternal damnation in the next.

In the end, I did not go to Papa. I went instead to my room. I sat by the window for a long time, thinking. I thought of all the things that had happened to us since that terrible day when my mother's dying screams had destroyed the life I knew.

I thought of Edie growing up without a mother, her small feet twisted and broken. I thought of the twins, living through each day at the mercy of whoever was hired to look after them.

I thought of Nell, first hiding her misery in the little room at the back of the greenhouse, and secretly growing orchids for my mother's grave, and now facing the ruin of her own life.

Finally, I thought about myself. Stupid Ada, thinking myself in love with a man who scarcely knew that I existed, and who saw me only as a way to spend time with my vibrant, funny, clever younger sister. At last, I put my head down and sobbed.

CHAPTER 28

It was almost dark when I knocked again at my sister's door. Nell was standing by the window, but she turned as I entered. She had changed her clothes and braided her hair and pinned it into a thick coil at the back of her head. Her face was no longer swollen with tears and she looked pale and strained.

I closed the door behind me and took a shaky breath. "Nell, I'm sorry. It was just such a shock. I truly had no idea until I saw you together the other night."

Nell gave a half-smile. "So it was you who locked the French doors," she said. I didn't need to answer for my face gave me away. Nell looked at me steadily for a moment. "Gilbert caught me; I couldn't get back into the house, so I had to pretend that I had fallen asleep outside. I don't think he believed me, but he's very kind; I know he won't say anything but can you imagine if it had been Drake?" For just a moment, I was looking at the old Nell, her dark eyes gleaming with suppressed laughter, then the light died, and she was once again the pale young woman that I scarcely recognized.

She turned back to the window then, and her voice sounded a little muffled. "Have you told Papa? He hasn't sent for me yet."

"No, I can't do that, Nell. It's something you have to do."

She nodded in agreement. "I would prefer not to tell him for another week or so, just to be quite sure, if that's agreeable to you?" My sister's voice was low-pitched, but I heard every word she said. There was no sign of pleading now; just the polite voice of a stranger asking for a small favor.

"Of course," I mumbled, and turning, fled.

I spent a long time with Edie that night. I sent Anna away and played with my little sister. She didn't seem to notice the tears that made her soft curls damp, and I hugged her firm little body to mine and rocked her softly in my arms until she wriggled and squirmed and demanded a story about rabbit. Eventually, she slept relaxed in my arms, breathing softly, but it was a long time before I found sleep that night.

Nell was right about Gilbert. He must not have told my father about finding her on the porch, for nothing was said, and for the next few days, I was kept busy counting linen and silverware once again as we started to make ready for our move into a house that we had never seen, in a city we did not know.

The day after Nell's confession to me, she appeared downstairs again, but she remained very quiet. She ate little, and spent much of her time in the drawing room, reading.

One afternoon, I heard the sound of the piano being played, and hurried in, sure that my sister had recovered and that all talk of unwanted babies was now unnecessary. But it was Señor Rodriguez, not Nell, who was seated at the piano. I stopped abruptly in the hope that he had not heard me enter, but he turned his head immediately and stopped playing.

Rising from his seat, he bowed. "Pardon, Señorita, I did not mean to disturb you," he said pleasantly. "I am just passing a little time before I speak with your father. He is sleeping at the moment."

I attempted a smile. "You did not disturb me, Señor. I thought it was my sister playing, I'm sorry. Please don't let me stop you."

He smiled and bowed again. "Alas, my dear Miss Baldwin, I do not play as beautifully as your sister, but I would be most honoured if you would join me. It would be a pleasure to hear you sing again. Your voice is like a nightingale."

I shook my head vehemently. "No! I'm looking for my sister, please excuse me!" And, turning, I hurried away. As I made my way across the hall, I realized that Señor Rodriguez had been smiling at me with his dark eyes. They were warmer than I remembered. I shivered suddenly. Whatever was I thinking? I despised the man!

A week later, Papa called a meeting in his study. I was nervous; Nell had promised to speak to him about her circumstances, but I had been afraid to ask her if she had done so.

I wrinkled my nose a little as I entered the room. Now that Papa lived here every day, it had taken on a stale, sweetish smell. It was the smell of sweat and sickness, and had about it the feel of restless sleep and barely tolerated pain. The curtains were drawn against the sun and the air hung still and heavy.

Papa was sitting behind his desk as I sought my usual chair. Nell slipped into the room behind me and sat quietly to one side. Drake was standing in the shadows behind my father, and Gilbert was beside the door. I breathed a sigh of relief.

This was not a meeting about Nell, for if it had been, the servants would not have been included.

Papa placed his thin, pale hands face down in front of him and cleared his throat. "As you know, we will be moving shortly and there will be more changes in our lives."

He paused for a moment, and I could see the sweat break out on his brow. Drake saw it, too, and leaned forward with a small white towel in his hand, but Papa waved him impatiently away before continuing. "Our household will be greatly reduced, and we will not be taking most of the servants with us. However, Gilbert and Mrs. Johnson have both agreed to stay with us." He flashed a smile at Gilbert, who inclined his head silently. "I will entrust them to take care of hiring new servants in Rosario. I'm sorry, Nell, but Bella will not be coming with us. I hope that we may hire someone to look after both of you girls."

I wondered about Anna. I could not imagine that she would leave her family to come with us. I had not thought to mind so much, but Anna was a dear soul and was wonderful with Edie.

I looked up to see my father watching me. "No need to look so glum, Ada," he said with a hint of a twinkle in his eyes. "Jose and Anna have also agreed to come with us. Anna will become nursemaid to Edie, and Jose will take care of the outside work. It will not be so different from the old days back home. Our household will be smaller, but we'll manage well enough."

Nell's voice from the depths of the armchair startled me. "What about Miss Walsh and the twins?" she asked.

My father turned to her. "Nell, you have hit upon my biggest problem. Miss Walsh has decided to stay here, as companion and governess. She and Mrs. McKinley have formed a bond of friendship, and when young William McKinley arrives, Miss Walsh will take on the task of tutoring the lad."

My father had picked up a pen from the holder on his desk and was twirling it in his fingers. He kept his eyes on the pen, as he continued speaking. "I have decided that Lily and Iris could have no better teachers than their own two sisters, so I will not be hiring a governess. Instead, you girls will continue to educate them. It shouldn't be too difficult, Nell, you will tutor them in reading, Spanish, and French, and I will expect you to begin music lessons with them."

My father then turned to me. "Ada, you will teach them household skills, to which you will add simple addition and subtraction and some knowledge of accounting. I will also charge you with the task of teaching them the bible."

There was complete silence in the room as we absorbed my father's words. My mind was reeling. That Nell and I should become teachers to our younger siblings had never occurred to me, but then I felt a stirring of excitement. Both Lily and Iris had shown a willingness to learn in the last few months, so I did not think that the task would be too difficult.

I leaned forward, ready to speak, when Nell cut across me. "No! I cannot do that, Papa," she said brusquely. "I just cannot! Please don't ask me to!" For one dreadful moment, I thought that my sister was going to blurt out her terrible secret, but she rose quickly from her seat and, with a mumbled apology and a quick curtsey, left the room.

There was an uncomfortable silence. My father was frowning deeply as he looked across at me. "And you, Ada? Do you also have difficulty seeing yourself as a teacher to your younger sisters?" he asked grimly

I shook my head. "No, Papa, I don't mind at all." Then I hesitated before hurrying on. "I should also like to continue to help with Edie.

I know that Anna is to be her nursemaid, but I think that Edie needs me in her life, as well."

My father thought for a moment, then nodded his head. "Thank you, Ada, I think that would be satisfactory," he said.

Then abruptly he raised a tired hand in dismissal, and this time when Drake stepped forward, he did not protest, but allowed the sweat to be wiped from his forehead and accepted the glass of dark liquid that Drake gave to him.

CHAPTER 29

In the days that followed, I found myself too busy to take heed of anything except my own tasks. While it was true that we had purchased this house together with its furnishings, many of our personal possessions had been integrated into each room. There was my mother's sewing machine, and a small writing desk, as well as some Turkish rugs that my father had brought with us. All the china and silver belonged to us, as well as linens, ornaments, pillows, and the like. I wanted to be sure that we did not leave anything behind.

I worried, too, about the horses. I wanted to take Blaze with me, but doubted that this would be possible. Gilbert told me that the great carriage was to be sold, but that we should keep the two smaller ones. My father needed the larger of the two to accommodate his wheelchair on the rare occasions that he left the house.

Finally, the news came that a house had been found for us, just outside Rosario. It was a hacienda-style house, with all the rooms on one level, which was of great importance to my father. While the new house was not large, we were assured that it would suit our needs admirably. I was not surprised when I discovered that it was Señor Rodriguez who had found it for us. He had returned one morning after an absence of several days, and after consulting with my father, he joined us for lunch.

The twins were excited at the thought of moving and exclaimed delightedly when they heard about their new home, which, Señor Rodriguez assured them, was an elegant house with a central courtyard and spacious rooms. He did not mention that the kitchen was only one room, with a tiny scullery leading off it, and that there was nowhere at all to do the laundry or store articles not presently in use.

Not long after this, on an afternoon when I was too restless to settle, I slipped through the breakfast room and opened the French doors that led onto the porch. As I walked around the curve of the house, I stopped abruptly, realizing where I was going. Then I saw that someone was already sitting in one of the white rattan chairs at the end of the porch.

Nell turned her head as she heard my footsteps. She gazed at me for a moment as I took a step towards her, thinking that perhaps now would be a good time for us to talk. But my sister turned her head away and folded her arms against me. Whoever she was waiting for, it wasn't me.

I turned and walked the other way until I reached the front steps. I looked around before starting across the soft sweep of the front lawn towards a glade of trees that offered some shade. As I did so, I saw a movement out of the corner of my eye.

Lizzie, head down, shawl wrapped closely about her body, was heading towards the house. I couldn't think of any reason why Nell would want to speak to our ex-maid, but I knew quite certainly that she was the person Nell had been waiting for.

Lizzie was still in our employ, working on the land, so perhaps Nell thought that she could get news of Arthur Mitchell's whereabouts from someone that Lizzie knew. I watched her for a moment more then, with a shrug, continued on my way towards the trees. If Nell chose not to share these things with me, I certainly could not force her to do so.

A week later, Papa told me with a smile that Nell and I might keep our horses, as he saw no reason why we would not require them in our new home. Delighted beyond measure, I thanked Papa warmly and hurried upstairs to Nell's room to break the good news to her.

Apart from brief appearances at meals, I hadn't seen anything of my sister since that day on the porch, though I knew that she still rode out in the early-morning hours, for I had seen her returning.

I had tried to talk to her once, but she scarcely even glanced at me before turning away with an impatient shake of her head. I didn't pursue her—I think I was still frightened of what Nell had done and I didn't want to face the truth of it. But now I had good news to share and I was smiling as I knocked and opened her bedroom door.

The room was empty. I looked around; it was as usual, very tidy, for although Nell was careless of her own appearance, she had always kept her things very neat. But this was different. It was as if no one lived here. I glanced around nervously. Her silver-backed brushes lay neatly beside the hand mirror on her dresser and a tiny cut-glass vase held a small bouquet of dried flowers, tied with a narrow ribbon. Nothing stirred. I looked around the room again, wondering at my own unease.

The day was grey and overcast and the light from the window scarcely filtered through the drapes. Then I saw the note. It was propped against the pillows on Nell's bed. The bold scrawl of her hand clear against the parchment read "ADA." Moving swiftly, I picked up the folded paper and opened it. The contents were brief.

"Please don't try to find me. I am doing what I have to do. I may not come back. I'm sorry. Nell."

My father heard me out in grim silence. I faltered when I told him of Nell's entanglement with Arthur Mitchell and felt my face flood crimson as I attempted to let him know of Nell's condition. He let me stumble my way through the whole story before he stopped me. "Why didn't you tell me of this before?" he rasped, his eyes boring into mine. "Did you not think it your duty to inform me of your sister's disgraceful behaviour?" He swung his wheelchair away from me, his face contorted with anger. "Get out! Get out of my sight." Trembling, I started forward.

"But what about Nell - what should we do?" I begged. My father gestured with his hand. "Go!"

I fled from the study and stumbled miserably towards the drawing room. Once there, I rang for Gilbert. He would know what to do. He had helped me save Nell before, and would assuredly do so again.

Gilbert was a long time coming and, when he did arrive, his face was grim. I started to blurt out my story, but he stayed me with a raised hand.

"If you please, Miss Ada, I should like Mrs. Johnson to join us—she may be able to throw some light on these events," he said quietly.

Mrs. Johnson came quickly into the room, and looked anxiously from her brother to me. I had scarcely started my story again when she interrupted. "Pardon me, Miss Ada, my dear, but we know some of this already. Servants do gossip and Bella told me a fortnight since that Miss Nell has missed her courses for a while now. I told her to mind her business, but I was starting to wonder myself, what with all that has gone on between Miss Nell and Mr. Mitchell."

How silly of me, I thought. Servants know everything. Of course they knew of my sister's love affair with Arthur Mitchell.

Mrs. Johnson looked over to where Gilbert was standing. "Have you told Miss Ada the rest of it?" she asked.

He shook his head. "No, I thought it best that you were here, Daisy." Then Gilbert turned to me. "We don't know if there's a connection, Miss, but Lizzie Weeks has gone missing. She disappeared this morning and left her babe behind. Miss Nell's horse is missing, too, so now we're wondering."

"Yes!" I almost shouted. "I saw Lizzie looking for Nell about a week ago!" And I told them about the day I had found Nell sitting at the end of the porch. "She was waiting to meet Lizzie, I'm sure of it."

Gilbert and Mrs. Johnson exchanged glances. "I reckon Miss Nell's gone with Lizzie to get rid of her trouble then," said Mrs. Johnson, with a sidelong glance at me.

"But where is she?" I demanded. "If Nell is in trouble, she needs to be safe here with us. My tears threatened to start up again. "And what do you mean, get rid of her trouble?" How could she do that? I don't understand."

Ignoring me, Gilbert glanced across at his sister. "I'd best go get the carriage, while you let Miss Ada here know what's what," he said briskly before slipping out of the room.

I turned to Mrs. Johnson. "Please tell me what you meant," I said. Without asking permission, Mrs. Johnson sat down next to me and, in a few terse sentences explained, just how a baby might be "got rid of." She didn't spare me the details.

By the time Gilbert returned, I was sitting shakily sipping from a small glass that Mrs. Johnson had filled from a bottle taken from the locked cupboard next to the fireplace. The liquid tasted very bad, but it warmed my stomach as it went down and I thought that I might not, after all, disgrace myself by being sick.

Gilbert nodded briefly. "We're all set then, Daisy. Let's get going. I've an idea where they might have gone, but we'd best hurry—they've had a few hours start."

I clung to Mrs. Johnson's sleeve. "Where are you going?" I demanded.

"You just stay here, Miss Ada," she said. "We'll be back as soon as we can." She spoke firmly, but I wasn't listening.

"I'm coming with you," I said determinedly. "Gilbert, you and I rescued Nell before and we can do it again. I tell you, I'm coming."

Gilbert started to shake his head, but Mrs. Johnson glanced at me sharply. "Just a second now, Horatio," she said. "Maybe that's not such a foolish notion. If we have Miss Ada with us, who's to know that we aren't looking for a bit of help, too, as you might say?"

Gilbert regarded us both doubtfully for a moment then seemed to make up his mind. "Very well, Miss Ada, but be quick. Get your oldest cloak and bonnet and meet us by the stables as soon as you can. We won't wait on you, Miss, so hurry."

I flew up the stairs as fast as my feet would carry me. Rummaging in my wardrobe, I found an old cloak, and the bonnet I had worn when my hair was so short. Gathering both articles, I slipped from the house as quickly as I could, thankful that no one noticed my going.

Gilbert and Mrs. Johnson were waiting for me; Gilbert nodding his approval when he saw my clothes. He helped me up into the carriage and, once we were out on the road, he whipped the horses to a greater speed.

My mind was whirling. I tried to think where my sister would go in her extremity, and I thought of the Hamilton's. Nell had been very close to Sophie when they were involved in the women's rights movement, and I knew that Sophie had recently returned from England, for I had caught sight of her at chapel. I had no idea if she and Nell had been speaking to each other. Now that I was in the choir, I was always one of the last people to leave. It was entirely possible that she and Nell had resumed their old friendship without my knowing it.

I leaned towards Mrs. Johnson, who was lurching and bouncing uncomfortably in the carriage beside me. "I think she's gone to the Hamilton's," I said. "Please, let's go there first. She knows them very well." Gradually, the dreadful things that Mrs. Johnson had told me earlier were sinking in, but I could not believe that my sister would put herself in such danger and clung to the hope that she would turn to old friends in her time of need

The housekeeper leaned precariously out of the carriage and relayed my message to Gilbert. I saw him shake his head dubiously, but I insisted, and as we approached the long driveway that led to the Hamilton's home, Gilbert turned the horses and slowed them to a gentle trot.

I didn't wait for Gilbert to hand me out, but as the carriage drew to a halt, I jumped quickly to the ground and ran swiftly up the steps that led to the Hamilton's front door and pulled at the bell. As I waited impatiently, I heard the sound of horses' hooves behind me. I turned quickly, hoping against hope that it was my sister. But it was a young man who dismounted. As he came closer, I saw that it was Edmund Nichols. I thought him still in England. As he ran lightly up the steps and bowed courteously, I saw him take in my disheveled state, my faded cloak, and unfashionable bonnet.

"Miss Baldwin," he said kindly. "May I be of assistance?" He looked towards the carriage where Mrs. Johnson and Gilbert waited for me.

I tried to hide my distress. "I'm looking for my sister Nell," I said. "There is some urgency. I have to find her at once and I thought she might be here."

At that moment, the door swung open and the Hamilton's butler stood in the open doorway. "Mr. Nichols," he said, with a respectful bow. "Mrs. Hamilton and Miss Sonia are away from home, Sir." Then he turned his disapproving gaze on me.

Edmund walked confidently past him. "We're here to see Miss Sophie, thank you, Walters," he said cheerfully. "No need to announce us." And Edmund swept me along with him.

We entered the elegant drawing room that I remembered so well. Sophie was seated at the piano. Her appearance had changed considerably since her return from England. Gone were the frills and pale colours that she had once favoured. She wore a simple, high-necked gown in a warm shade of brown. Her hair was elegantly dressed high on her head and amber earrings hung from her ears.

She gave a low cry of pleasure at the sight of Edmund, but froze when she saw me. Edmund strode towards her and to my surprise, took her in his arms and embraced her. Sophie cast a cool look over her shoulder at me and, with a tight smile, disengaged herself.

"Dearest Sophie," Edmund began earnestly, "I fear that Miss Baldwin is most distressed. She is seeking her sister Nell with some urgency."

Sophie Hamilton looked at me and an expression of disdain crossed her face.

"My dearest Edmund," she said, laying a hand along his arm so that I could clearly see the large emerald and diamond ring that now decorated her finger. "I'm afraid that Nell Baldwin is not welcome here. I do not forgive people who espouse a cause and then run from it and abandon their friends."

Although she was addressing her fiancé, her eyes never left mine while she was speaking, and I knew that Nell had not come here for help. I made my stumbling apologies and left the Hamilton's house as fast as I could. Gilbert and Mrs. Johnson were waiting impatiently for me.

As we drove away, Mrs. Johnson explained in short staccato sentences—for nothing else was possible in the swaying carriage—that Sophie Hamilton and Edmund Nichols had met again in London and a romance had grown between them and, to the delight of all, Mr. Nichols had been persuaded to return to Argentina. I listened distractedly to what Mrs. Johnson had to say, but matters of much greater urgency filled my mind.

CHAPTER 30

It was late afternoon when we reached the outskirts of the city. The streets were almost deserted, for Buenos Aires did not come to life until the evening was well advanced. Gilbert seemed to know where he was heading, and we soon left the wide, tree-lined avenues and turned into smaller streets that in turn became mean little laneways, roughly cobbled, or, in many cases, just hard-packed dirt that rose in small swirling circles around the carriage wheels.

Gilbert had slowed our pace by now and both he and Mrs. Johnson seemed to be looking out for something in particular. At last, Mrs. Johnson called out sharply and Gilbert brought the carriage to an abrupt halt. He glanced questioningly back at his sister who nodded briefly in the direction of a small group of men who lounged around the door of a dingy building to our right. They were roughly dressed and very dirty. Gilbert climbed down from his seat and approached the group of men. I heard him raise his voice in question. The men took their time in answering, one or two of them glancing over at the carriage. Then one of the men said something, and they all laughed. The laughter had a cruel, jeering note to it that made the hair on the back of my neck rise up.

I glanced across at Mrs. Johnson as she laid a hand on my arm as if to stop me from speaking. She had no need to do so. I was too frightened to make a sound. Then one of the men spat casually and waved in the direction from which we had come. Gilbert tipped the brim of his hat and returned to the carriage.

He didn't climb up onto the driver's seat, but walked the horses in a slow turn while Mrs. Johnson and I sat silent inside the carriage. I did not look at the men again, but as we drove away, the sound of their laughter followed us down the narrow street.

We made our way past perhaps three narrow laneways before anyone spoke. "Well, Horatio, what did they say?" Mrs. Johnson leaned forward and tugged impatiently at Gilbert's jacket.

"You were right, my dear," answered Gilbert, with a backward glance over his shoulder. "We're in the right part of town, but it seems we've come too far. Our friends back there reckon we should look for Carniceros Carril and ask again." "That's Butcher's Lane, that don't sound so good to me," Mrs. Johnson muttered to herself.

I listened to this exchange in puzzlement. Finally, I turned to Mrs. Johnson. "Why are we in this dreadful place?" I asked. "I thought we were going to see a doctor of some kind!" The housekeeper looked at me pityingly then shook her head. "Oh, Missy, dear," she said softly. "It's not a doctor we'll be seeing. It's more like a woman with a rusty spike, like I already told you." My hand flew to my mouth and unable to help myself, I broke into sobs.

"There, there, Miss," said Mrs. Johnson. "Don't you fret, Horatio and me, we've been through worse than this. We'll find Miss Nell, but you'll have to listen to me and do just as I say. Don't say a word, mind, just do it." She patted my hand kindly and I felt the carriage make a sharp turn into what proved to be another narrow laneway.

Several women stood or squatted next to dark doorways and, in the dull afternoon light, I could see children playing in the dirt. They watched us with suspicious eyes as we passed slowly by. Gilbert seemed to be looking for a particular building, but was unable to find it. After a while, he stopped the carriage and turned to look at his sister.

"Right you are, Daisy, your turn now."

With a brief nod, Mrs. Johnson climbed heavily out of the carriage and walked over to the nearest group of women. Hands on hips, she made her demand. I couldn't hear what she said, but her tone was very different from the one that Gilbert had used and I saw her reach into the deep pocket of her cloak and heard the clink of coins changing hands. In a moment, she was back.

"Three doors down on the right," she said. Then she looked at me. "Mind now, Miss Ada, you do just as I say, and not one word." I nodded mutely.

Gilbert brought the carriage up to the door of the building that Mrs. Johnson indicated. The house was tall and narrow and stood a little back from the other row houses. As Gilbert climbed down from the driver's seat, Mrs. Johnson leaned forward and, with great care, wrapped my cloak about me.

"Try to look poorly, dear, and don't let them see your face. Some folks can tell just by looking," she whispered urgently. I had no difficulty with this, for my legs were shaking beneath me as I put my feet to the ground.

We approached the faded blue door and Mrs. Johnson rapped firmly with her knuckles on its cracked surface. There was an alley that ran down one side of the narrow building and Gilbert nodded towards it.

"Likely the horse is around the back," he said. "I'll go and see. Be careful now, Daisy—this could be unpleasant."

With a brief nod, Mrs. Johnson turned back to the door and knocked again, harder this time, and I thought I heard a movement from within.

After a moment, the door was cracked open a few inches and an ancient female face peered out at us. Mrs. Johnson planted one stoutly booted foot in the opening and smiled pleasantly at the old woman.

I didn't understand much of what was said, for they both spoke in rapid Spanish, Mrs. Johnson placing a hand protectively on my arm.

The old woman peered suspiciously at both of us for a moment then turning, gazed directly at me. She looked me carefully up and down before wiping a grimy hand across her mouth and giving me a toothless smile. I kept my head down as Mrs. Johnson had directed me, but listened intently. As the old woman started to speak again, Mrs. Johnson interrupted her with another stream of Spanish, and I heard the words "Ingles" and "problema."

I opened my mouth to explain that I was not the person in trouble, but Mrs. Johnson gave my arm a sharp warning squeeze.

As she continued to speak, Daisy Johnson dropped a hand into her pocket, and once again I heard the unmistakable chink of money.

The old woman continued to peer at me for a moment more before opening the door wider to let us pass. As she did so, she continued to speak, her voice taking on a whining and protesting tone, but Mrs. Johnson pushed purposefully ahead.

As the old woman closed the door behind us, I looked around, fearful of what I should find, but the place seemed reasonably clean. The hall was bare of furniture, and directly in front of us, a steep staircase led to the upper floor. To our right, a doorway opened into what was obviously a parlour. There was a heavy table in the centre of the room, covered with a faded chenille cloth, and two worn armchairs were set one on either side of the mantle. The drapes were closed across the small front window, and an oil lamp cast its yellow shadow against the wall.

The woman waved us in the direction of the parlour. "Espere aqui por favor! (Wait here) She said. Then, turning to Mrs. Johnson again, her head bent a little to one side as if she were hard of hearing, she asked another question.

Once again, Mrs. Johnson's voice was confident as she responded, and with a small shock, I heard the name of Lizzie Weeks. At the sound of Lizzie's name, the old woman's face changed. Even through the grime and wrinkles I saw that the colour had drained from her face. She backed away and glanced quickly over her shoulder. "Usted debe esparar aqui!"(You must wait here!) she said anxiously, before creaking her way up the steep staircase that led to the dimly lit landing above.

Mrs. Johnson watched her go then gave me a little push towards the parlour. "Something's not right here," she muttered as she indicated that I should sit in one of the chairs.

As I turned to do as so, I noticed a small desk tucked into the corner beside the chair, and on the desk was something I recognized. Reaching forward, I picked up the red velvet bag that was lying on its cluttered surface. I knew this bag very well, for it had once held jewelry that belonged to my mother. And for the last while, it had contained the carved silver bracelet that Nell had inherited on our last Christmas in England.

I clutched the little bag tightly to me, and turned to Mrs. Johnson. "She's here," I whispered. "This is Nell's."

Mrs. Johnson nodded absently but did not hear me; she was listening for something else. Then she nodded grimly. As I strained my ears I thought I heard distant voices from upstairs, but I couldn't be sure. A fly buzzed against the window, fat and green and glistening. I shuddered; I hated flies.

Then I heard what Mrs. Johnson had been listening for. It was a sound that I knew, but did not expect to hear in this place.

It was the sound of liquid dripping: a slow, heavy drip. It was the sound that blood made when it was dripping from a slaughtered calf or sheep hanging from a hook in the cooling shed at the back of our kitchen at home. I looked across at Mrs. Johnson and knew that my eyes were filled with terror.

"Stay here Miss, I'll take a look in the back," she said grimly, and walked towards the dark doorway that led into a back room. I hesitated for a second then hurried after her. I did not want to be left alone in this place, even for a moment.

Mrs. Johnson was standing motionless in the tiny scullery that might once have been used to cook meals. Now it was empty save for a narrow table. Lying on the table was a body. A rough sheet had been thrown over it, and the slow metallic drip of blood hitting the floor was loud in the heavy silence. The air was thick with the smell of it, and I could hear flies buzzing as they circled the widening pool on the floor at the foot of the table.

I let out a small, gasping cry and ran forward. Mrs. Johnson tried to stop me, tried to shield me from the figure lying on the table, but with a quick movement, I pushed past her and pulled back the cloth that covered the still form.

CHAPTER 31

It was Lizzie's waxen face that stared back at me, serene in death, as it had never been in life. I dropped the sheet from nerveless fingers and whirling around, ran as quickly as my long skirts allowed through the empty parlour, into the hall and up the narrow staircase. I could hear Mrs. Johnson's booted feet behind me.

At the top of the stair, I stopped to catch my breath. A blank wall was ahead of me, but to the right, a narrow passage ran along the length of the house. At the far end, I could see a gleam of light under a closed door. The sound of voices raised in argument came from behind the door and, impulsively, I started towards the sound.

Mrs. Johnson had reached the landing behind me and she pulled me back sharply and pointed to the darkened doorway of another room closer to the stairs. This door was partly open and, as I peered inside, I thought I could see a small, shadowy figure huddled on a narrow bed.

Still, I hesitated, and looked again towards the shaft of light shining from under the far door. I was desperate to find my sister before it was too late. Then I heard a small whimper coming from the darkened room and knew that we had found Nell.

We reached her in an instant. Mrs. Johnson didn't hesitate. She had taken off her cloak at some point and now wrapped it firmly around Nell's thin body. Dragging her from the bed, we bundled my sister down the stairs, half carrying, half dragging her between us until we reached the front door. As we did so, Nell reached out her hand, clutching desperately at the rotting wood of the doorpost.

"Lizzie," she sobbed. "I can't leave her."

Glancing up, I saw the old woman's startled face peering at us from the top of the stairs. Grasping Nell's fingers, I twisted hard and pushed her roughly into Mrs. Johnson's arms and out into the street. I struggled to close the door behind me, but it stuck fast and I had to leave it. I could hear angry voices getting louder, and the sound of footsteps pounding down the stairs.

Desperately, I looked around for Gilbert. Then I saw him waiting by the side of the carriage. Even as I started forward, Gilbert was grabbing hold of Nell and lifting her to safety. A few seconds later, Mrs. Johnson and I had joined her, bundling ourselves quickly into the carriage, as Gilbert urged the horses forward. I could hear the sound of Nell's horse trotting behind us and knew that he was safely tethered to our back rail.

Gilbert did not attempt to race the carriage over the rough terrain, but kept a steady pace until we were safely away. I heard angry shouts behind us, and someone hurled a rock, but it glanced harmlessly off the side of the carriage.

As we left the slums behind, I chanced a look at my sister. Nell was deathly pale and had not moved or spoken since we had rescued her.

I could feel her body shaking as she sat close to me in the carriage. At last, she turned and looked at me.

"Lizzie's dead, isn't she?" she asked softly. "She screamed and screamed and then she just stopped. They took her downstairs, I saw them."

I nodded soberly. "Yes, she's dead. I saw her, too, but I don't understand why they killed her. She was only helping you."

Nell gave a ghost of a smile. "Ada, we were helping each other. She was pregnant again and had no money to rid herself of the child, so I paid for both of us with my bracelet and the horse."

My sister paused for a moment to take a small, quivering breath before she continued. "Lizzie knew those people and I didn't know what else to do." She broke off, tears rolling unheeded down her cheeks.

I leaned closer and took hold of one of my sister's hands. "What about you, Nell. Did they?" My voice trailed off—I didn't know how to ask the question.

Nell glanced at me once before lowering her head. I had to strain to hear her over the creak of the carriage wheels. "It was all so terrible," she whispered. Then my sister turned her face away from me and would not be comforted. She didn't speak again, not even when we were home and she was lying safely in her own bed.

I wasn't there when Gilbert told my father about the events of that dreadful day, and I did not ask what was said. Mrs. Johnson had tucked me into my own bed as soon as Nell was safely settled, and gave me a drink to make me sleep and I didn't wake until the following day.

After that, Nell kept to her room. She ate little and would see no one. Each time I went to her door, she sent me away, or lay with her head turned from me, even when I eventually ignored her protests and ventured in to sit with her.

In spite of all that had happened, there was still much work to be done, preparatory to our leaving. Most of the servants who were not coming with us showed little willingness to help with the task of packing, and so it fell to me to do much of the work myself, helped, of course, by Mrs. Johnson and Gilbert.

One morning at the beginning of the second week after we had rescued Nell, I was crossing the hall with a box of ornaments in my hands when I heard footsteps approaching the front door. Gilbert was nowhere to be seen, so setting the box on a table, I opened the door myself.

Arthur Mitchell was leaner and more tanned than the last time I had seen him. He was dressed in worn riding gear and in his hand was a hat that looked well used. He had a great bruise on his forehead and one hand was roughly bandaged. Behind him, I caught sight of three men standing by their horses, watching him.

I stared at Arthur for a moment, unable to move or speak. He was equally surprised to be confronted by me, but he recovered himself quickly, and bowing, wished me a good morning.

I didn't answer him immediately because I was consumed with anger so great that I shocked even myself, and my voice when it came, sounded strange to my own ears.

"What are you doing here?" I asked, my voice barely above a whisper. Then, not waiting for an answer, I continued. "How dare you show your face in this house, with my sister lying upstairs, half dead from ridding herself of your bastard child? Get out and don't ever come back!" I had not raised my voice or moved as I glared at the man who had ruined my sister and brought shame on our family. Then, with a sudden quick movement, I grabbed hold of the door, ready to slam it in his face. As I did so, a hand came over my shoulder and prevented me.

Gilbert stood behind me. "Excuse me, Miss Baldwin," he said formally. "The gentleman is expected."

He turned to Arthur Mitchell. "I will see if Mr. Baldwin will receive you now, Mr. Mitchell. Please wait." And turning on his heel, Gilbert made his unhurried way to my father's study door.

Arthur Mitchell had paled under his tan as he listened to my furious outburst, and now he glanced nervously at me as he stepped through the doorway, smoothing the brim of his hat between his hands. Behind him, I saw the three horsemen mount up and ride leisurely away.

I stood for a moment looking at the man I had once dreamed of marrying, then very deliberately, I turned my back and walked away.

I was still shaking half an hour later when I ventured back downstairs to find Gilbert. He had been watching out for me, for he met me at the bottom of the stairs and ushered me into the drawing room, and stood stiffly by the closed door until I was seated.

"Miss Ada," he said. "After I had told Mr. Baldwin of all that had happened to Miss Nell, we set about finding Mr. Mitchell; it was not too difficult. He has assured your father that he had already decided to return here and ask for Miss Nell's hand in marriage. A wise decision in the circumstances, don't you agree, Miss?"

Gilbert asked the question smoothly, but as I nodded mutely, I remembered Arthur Mitchell's bruised head and bandaged hand, and I recalled the three men watching as he presented himself at the door. I gave a nod of satisfaction. Undoubtedly, Mr. Mitchell had been given some help in his decision to return.

CHAPTER 32

The wedding was very quiet with only the family in attendance. I thought Mrs. Hamilton would be there to see her "dear boy" wed but she declined, claiming a previous engagement. The twins were allowed to come, accompanied by Mrs. Johnson. Miss Walsh was not invited.

Drake wheeled my father's chair to the front of the church, but Nell walked alone down the aisle, for my father would not allow anyone to accompany her.

She had become very thin since her ordeal, and she wore a simple dark gown with no adornments. Her face was pale and still as she stood at Arthur Mitchell's side waiting for the ceremony to begin.

In all the time that the arrangements were being made, Nell had shown no sign of interest. She didn't speak to anyone, and seemed to have gone into a world where no one could reach her.

The short ceremony began with the minister sternly admonishing the young couple to remember the sanctity of their vows. Then there was Arthur's voice, sounding a little unsteady, and Nell's surprisingly clear tones. The rain wept down from heavy clouds that had suddenly obscured the sun and the wind swirled and gusted through the open chapel door as they completed their vows.

Gilbert drove them to Buenos Aires in the small carriage, immediately after the wedding. Nell had almost no luggage—just a few clothes, but none of her other personal possessions.

I had given her back the red velvet bag that had once held the silver bracelet and that was the only time I saw my sister cry.

They were to take a ship to England the next day, and we did not see them again.

Papa had signaled Drake to push him out of the church the moment the register was signed, and Gilbert and Drake had together lifted him into the great carriage before Drake drove him back to the house.

My father had not spoken to either bride or groom since the day that Arthur Mitchell returned, but earlier that morning he had informed me that my sister was dead to him and to all of us, and that her name was never to be spoken in the family again.

Mrs. Johnson and the twins were waiting for me to join them for the ride home, but the skies had begun to clear and I felt an aching need to be alone. I paused, with one hand on the carriage door.

"Mrs. Johnson, could you please take the twins home?" I asked. "I should like to walk. It really isn't far, and the rain has stopped."

Mrs. Johnson looked at me keenly. "If you're sure, Miss?" she asked. I nodded and stood watching for a long time until they, too, had disappeared into the distance.

So I made my slow way home, relieved to be by myself. I was glad that we were leaving this place. Perhaps we would have a chance to start anew in Rosario, for my father was planning to set up an import-export business there, tied to the railway that he had helped to build. I just did not know how I would learn to live without Nell. She was so much a part of me, part of the life we had known. My sister! My friend! My most beloved enemy! I stood desolate for a moment as the emptiness spread within me, small at first, then blossoming into a void that threatened to engulf me.

As I walked unheeding along the road that led to home, I was unaware that I had company until a voice behind me called, "Whoa." I looked up, startled to see a smart new carriage draw up beside me. Señor Rodriguez looked down at me.

"My dear Miss Baldwin," he said with a smile. "What a pleasant surprise. May we assist you by taking you to your destination?"

I gazed up at him for a moment. The sun was shining in my eyes and I couldn't see him clearly, nor could I see his companion. "Thank you, Señor, but no," I answered. "I have chosen to walk. I find it clears my head."

A tinkling laugh broke across Señor Rodriguez's polite response. "Darling," said a familiar voice, "we really mustn't linger. We have to be at Aunt Bee's very shortly. Everyone is waiting and we simply cannot be late when the party is for us."

I shaded my eyes and found myself looking into the smugly smiling face of Miss Dora Phillips. She was wearing an outfit of palest lavender. A small matching hat was perched on her carefully arranged golden curls, and she had removed one long lavender glove, the better that I should see the diamond that sparkled brightly on her left hand.

"Imagine," she added with a breathless little laugh, "first Edmund and Sophie, and now my dearest Señor Rodriguez and little me." She fluttered her eyelashes coquettishly at her foolishly beaming companion.

"Congratulations," I said through frozen lips.

Dora leaned forward, one small hand flying to her lightly rouged lips. "Oh my dear Ada, of course, I had quite forgotten why you aren't able to attend. And how is your poor sister?" Her voice trailed away into nothing as she smiled artlessly down at me.

"My sister is wed and she and Mr. Mitchell are on their way to England," I said, a little too loudly. "Please don't let me keep you from your celebration."

For just a second, the smile above me faltered and the guileless blue eyes turned cold. Then, with a toss of her curls, Dora Phillips turned again to the man by her side and laid a possessive hand on his arm. Señor Rodriguez smiled at me once more, then raised his hat courteously and flicked at the reins. Sunlight danced off the carriage as it disappeared over the rise in the road and I heard Dora's malicious, sparkling laugh carried on the wind.

It took me longer than I had thought to walk the rest of the way home, but I came at last to the paddock where the horses were running free. Nell's horse came nudging over to me and snuffled hopefully at my hand, but I had nothing for him.

As I approached the back of the house, I could hear the sound of children laughing. Anna was sitting in the doorway that led to the nursery, mending a small garment. My little Edie was seated in a wagon that Anna's husband, Jose, had made for their son.

Four-year-old Tomas, red in the face and puffing with exertion, was pulling the laden wagon while Edie screamed his name delightedly. Unable to say Tomas, she called him "Toe-Toe," and was now giving him orders in an imperious mixture of Spanish and English. I watched from the shadows for a few moments then turned and walked to the front of the house.

Through the open door, I heard the grandfather clock strike eleven. We would be taking the old clock with us, for Mr. McKinley had a great dislike of clocks and had presented it to me as a parting gift.

As I walked up the porch steps, the wind caught at the bushes and white rose petals scattered like snowflakes at my feet.

THE END

ABOUT THE AUTHOR

Author Margaret Worth took great pleasure from the exercise of telling this story. It is, after all, her own to tell. Baby Edie Baldwin was Margaret's grandmother, and she learned the details of Edie's and her older sisters' lives from her own earliest days.

Born and raised in the south of England, Margaret now makes her home in Canada. She has five children, ten grandchildren, and to date, two great-grandchildren. She also has a somewhat overweight cat named Millie who serves as her writing muse. Margaret is currently at work on a sequel to Most Beloved Enemy that continues the story of young Edie's life, where this book left off.